MW00475362

Erotically charged and intellectu... ...ces with its layers, its characters, a... ...ics, and desire. The story circles ar... ...of) Pacifica and sent to live in the U... ...eks out a stranger for domination/... ...nd herself is she trying to uncover, a... ...how are they linked to Ernst, her nonbinary lover? How does her story—and that of her father, her mother, her daughter and grandsons—reflect and change the history of her homeland? The novel is structured like indigenous myth, where past, present and future do not exist, and where everything is present at once and connected to each other: fairy tales, the struggle against a dictator, poetics, colonialism, motherhood, gender identity, sexual passion, romantic love, and even a recipe for *adobo*. Eileen R. Tabios uses her pen like Elena uses her whip, provoking tenderness through intense sensation as well as illumination through sensuality and a passionate, hungry mind.

— Reine Arcache Melvin, recipient of two Philippine National Book Awards for her short story collection *A Normal Life and Other Stories* and her novel *The Betrayed*, which also received the Palanca Award for Best Novel

Meet Elena Theeland, poet, rapscallion, nimble art gourmand, and colorful sleuth. Her reason for being in time is Ernst Blazer, a painter, lord of hues and ripples, and a container of the fragrance of memory. Not since the meeting of the poet Rainier Maria Rilke and the artist Auguste Rodin (while Rilke wrote *The Notebooks of Malte Laurids Brigge*, an autofiction like *DoveLion*) has there been a melding of true artistic minds. As well, philosophers will be entranced by this book that hearkens Martin Heidegger's magnum opus, *Sein* und *Zeit* (*Being and Time*). Eileen R. Tabios has achieved a Gabriel García Márquez with the emotion and aplomb of Laura Esquivel. Recommend for all fine libraries and personal collections.

— Nick Carbó, author of the poetry collections *Andalusian Dawn*, *Secret Asian Man* (winner of an Asian American Writers Workshop's Readers' Choice Award), and *El Grupo McDonald's*.

DoveLion: A Fairy Tale for Our Times is Eileen R. Tabios' mythic imagination enlivened! History marks bodies and cultures, making up stories deemed worthy and purposeful by the powerful until the Storyteller/Poet reveals the secrets and shadows lurking beneath power's machinations. The figure of an indigenous community and spiritual leader known as "Baybay"— inspired by the Philippine Babaylan—emerges as the Medicine that calms the heart's longings and reweaves the fragments of diasporic displacements. Eileen R. Tabios welcomes us into the world of "Kapwa-time" where the past, present, and future comingle and entangle with our own capacity to believe in the potency of myth-telling. Kapwa-time and mythic imagination form a descent into the underworld, or a psychic and archeological exploration into the subconscious; it's notable that the indigenous Filipino concept of 'Loob' has internal and external dimensions. If this descent is done well and blessed by the deities, it becomes manifest in the Beauty of the novel's form—such is Eileen R. Tabios' accomplishment with *DoveLion*. As a reader going deep into Kapwa-time, I find my inner compass and this compass floods my life like the light of a thousand suns.

— Leny Mendoza Strobel, Founder of the Center for Babaylan Studies, Author of *Coming Full Circle: The Process of Decolonization Among Post-1965 Filipino Americans* and Editor of *Babaylan: Filipinos and the Call of the Indigenous*

DoveLion

A Fairy Tale For Our Times

Eileen R. Tabios

978-1-939901-19-4

Published by AC Books, an imprint of AC Institute
www.acbooks.org // www.acinstitute.org
Cover and Interior design by R. Hazell
Illustration by R. Hazell

Printed by Maple Press in Pennsylvania
Distributed by Small Press Distribution

Contents

For (All) Poets: *Dios ti agngina*

I. THERE ~~WAS~~ IS

Chapter 1

31 DECEMBER:
Once upon a time, I thought Poetry is a fairy tale. From that delusion, I came to stand in front of a grey building. Inside, a stranger waited for me.

I raised my finger to push the dirty-white button next to their apartment number: 3J. Before my flesh touched the button's chill, I heard faint music. I turned my face towards the sound and saw children playing in a park across the street. In their bright, colorful outfits, they were wildflowers chasing each other in circles. Nearby, a nanny's boombox sent forth innocent tunes befitting innocent creatures.

But is anyone really innocent? I returned my attention to the grey building.

1 FEBRUARY
Once upon a time, I heard children laughing but turned my back. I was bored with innocence.

I stood in front of an anonymous grey building. I searched the intercom panel for their apartment number: 3J. Its resident was a stranger to me, but my searching finger was eager. Decades later, I would hear an adolescent proclaim to the furrowed brow on his cautious grandmother:

"Tomorrow *is* present!"

Exactly.

My finger found the right button and pushed.

The world did not end.

27 AUGUST

Once upon a time, a young poet and an experienced artist looked at each other across an abyss. They each formed their own worlds and the abyss between them could be measured only in light years.

But the abyss, too, can be a page or a canvas. The empty page longs perpetually for its lover: the writer who would, upon it, write. The blank canvas longs similarly for its artist who would, upon it, interrogate space.

Aesthetics was not the most important layer to their engagement. But it mattered. The young poet wanted to learn. The experienced artist began with no preconceptions, just curiosity. In the beginning, curiosity sufficed.

Curiosity is a form of desire.

6 NOVEMBER

Once upon a time, I looked at my reflection on the steel plate of an intercom to a grey building. My hair was fluttering in the slight breeze. A lock stumbled over my right eye, blocking its view. Within that instant, my left eye grasped something I had not discerned with both eyes: an eyelash dangling from another lash, a gust away from falling. When a narrowed focus reveals a previously-unknown fragility, one's nature is revealed by whether one aborts vision or not.

I did not close my eyes. I shook my head and both eyes watched as the lash lost its grip and began to fall.

As well, I watched myself watching the sunder, the flailing, the fall.

20 SEPTEMBER

Once upon a time...

18 JUNE

Once upon a time, I willingly fell into a stranger's arms. Such testifies to the reach of a dictator's cruel reign—how a dictatorship can continue long past its demise through the tight clench of *Aftermath*.

When I stood in front of the stranger's building, the sunlight that began that day felt like a dream. It was sunny, then suddenly it was not. Years later, I comprehend that the dreamlike phenomenon is not a symbol whose significance one concocts. It was just a condition precedent to revamping my vocabulary, including the definition of light. Darkness, for one, provides its own illumination.

No new world is possible without a new vocabulary.

But like everything else in this world, during all of human history, the new must come with fresh sources of pain. Once, a businessman heard me share the story of my beginnings and reacted by calling me "Aftermath."

"Just kidding!" he insisted as I twisted myself out of his embrace, a protest at his careless nickname. Any study of history reveals patterns, and a consistent behavior among the privileged is unintentional cruelty—for carelessness to wound.

But was he only joking? Years later, after visiting a grey building numerous times, I know to question: did not this businessman and his Wall Street firm make billions from doing business with dictatorships?

Still, no new world is possible without a new vocabulary—this will always be true even though, decades later, I understand that those who want to create a new world never arrive in that world. A new world is not for staying *in* but holds borders one must always push at in order to expand that world into new possibilities. It's exhausting. Yet that exhaustion is the least of its tolls.

4 AUGUST

Once upon a time, I left the dimness of the subway system to break out into daylight. In the five-block walk required to reach a grey building for an appointment with a stranger, the sunlight evaporated. By the time I was standing in front of an intercom panel, searching for the apartment number "3J," it might as well have been a wintry day in London.

Once, they took me to London. The stranger's pronouns: they, their, them, themself. *They*—it seemed apt for the stranger's gender fluidity to translate to non-singular pronouns. I'd long thought their paintings of deliberately-failed monochromes hint at multiple layers impossible to contain with a single category. The single surface colors of their paintings do not translate to single dimensions.

The stranger, too, mirrored their paintings—though perhaps it was the other way around since they and their art melded into a circle where no separation between the two can be observed. Tall and muscular, the stranger usually dressed in black jeans and black t-shirts or shirts. Their wavy black hair, sun-darkened complexion, and dark brown eyes contributed to presenting the sense of a single color whose darkness in paintings has been compared to a void. The stranger presented themself as one who can't be judged through mere appearance. As with their monochrome paintings, the significance of what the viewer sees arises through engagement—months later when I was more comfortable with them, I often found myself saying certain things just to spark a light in their eyes from an interested or humored response. Such light interrupted darkness—sometimes the light slanted to give inexplicably the impression of green, as from a verdant

3

rainforest or sunlit ocean. Or I would find myself touching them as if to confirm they really were there, standing there close enough to exchange air. I memorized the slant of their cheekbones and the solidity of their shoulders widened from years of lifting large canvases. Thankfully, when we were more comfortable with each other, they reciprocated—they reveled in touching me, especially when they realized that their touch made my skin increase their warmth, made my skin blush.

So easily did I memorize their scent: a mix of coffee, mint, vanilla, citrus, and determination. Fanciful perhaps, but I saw the same determination in the consistent jut in their jaw and straightened back even when they were supposed to be relaxed; it's as if their body had memorized certain stances until they became the default positions.

They took me to London. But we traveled on separate planes so that, they said, we both "could more fully relish anticipating our London adventure." Anticipation provides its own pleasure, they taught... even as that lesson showed that, before their presence, my life rarely offered reasons for anticipation.

While in London, we debated a play that attempted a contemporary version of Shakespeare's *King Lear*. The 30-year-old playwright thought to recreate the story in the jungle context of the Tasadays, once thought to be a Stone Age tribe in the Philippines but which later was discovered to be a fraud; a crony of dictator Ferdinand Marcos set up the deceit to acquire millions of dollars of international donations for preserving the tribe's indigenous lifestyle before diverting the funds into his Cayman Islands bank account.

One of us called the scam an "obscenity."

One of us replied, "Love is always haggled."

Love is always haggled.

In London, I learned to anticipate tears.

Through the stranger, I learned to anticipate the lucidity of pain.

2 MAY

Once upon a time, I stood in front of a building dimmed by a sun in hiding. It became a moment frozen in amber, stilling time—a mental object I fetishized as I struggled to understand how I became a creature willing to meet a stranger for the first time in the privacy of their residence.

There is a significance to a lack of witness: only participants can articulate what happened, which is to say, the story may never be revealed. Participation makes objectivity impossible.

Or, the story can be revealed only if the participant-turned-documenter is willing to undergo the suffering that truth-telling requires. Once, a poet observed, "The deepest meditation must require the self-infliction of unrelenting anguish."

14 OCTOBER
Once upon a time, I...

16 MARCH
Once, I found myself in a hospital waiting room. I was four decades younger than the average age—65—of those undergoing cataract surgery; but I wanted to improve my vision. As I waited, I wrote up and emailed a dream to myself:

> Subject: Once upon a time
>
> An angel fell to land behind me. The fallen angel pushed me towards a grey building. I visited the building often but always left wanting more. As soon as I exited the building after a visit, I began wishing to return. It was like the type of poem we both favored: an open-ended poem, a poem that concluded with a widening, a poem that concluded with possibilities, a poem that ended with a beginning.
>
> I wondered where the angel lurked until I felt its push toward the grey building. Perhaps it lurked between the feathers of a bird's wing, perhaps within the fur of a nearby squirrel, perhaps behind the blinding screen of a sunbeam, waiting for the next opportunity to bring me welcome havoc. It was not a time for timidity. It was a time for—

The email ceased prematurely when nurses arrived to bring me into the surgical room. A cheerful nurse announced, "Time to better your sight!"

Yes, I agreed. It was time for the scalpel. It was time to enhance lucidity.

29 NOVEMBER
Once upon a time, I was lonely. The bleakness of the grey building facing me did not instill foreboding. It did not spark fear. It was a nondescript building and yet I wasn't scared even though I was aware that anonymity can mask frightening elements. Such is one of loneliness' more unstable effects—bypassing reason simply to make things happen.

I was lonely. Thus, did I choose to conclude: the grey building didn't frighten because it mirrored that with which I was profoundly intimate: loneliness.

Curiosity, yes. But loneliness also raised my finger with its freshly-manicured and painted tip to push on the buzzer to Apartment 3J.

I had painted my fingernails with my favorite color: the blue of an ocean by which shores the stranger and I never strolled. Though those shores could have been part of something labeled "Paradise," the stranger taught me to avoid escapism, like running away to Tahiti or similar venues. As another Type-A personality once observed about Bora-Bora, "Boredom-Boredom."

24 JANUARY

Once upon a time, I stood in front of a building I'd never seen before, readying myself to meet a stranger. But while they were a stranger, I did know some things about them: their paintings. When viewed in the chronological order of their making, the paintings are not just different from each other but each provides no foretelling of what the next painting might look like. They are monochromes but each color is singular—a red painting might be followed by a yellow painting rather than a color created by mixing red with another color. Ernst said the progression reflects something they learned from a brief foray into photoshop—"Pixels have no memory. Pixels don't need to generate meaning from proximity." (At the time of their explanation, I hadn't yet understood the anguish embedded in their memories.) As well, cracks only discernible when eyes were an inch close to the canvas revealed motion, sensed images, or other colors not obvious when the paintings were viewed farther away.

They laughed when, once, I asked them if their art is exhausting.

"Doesn't something happen to the brain—and body—if one is ever searching for the new? Perhaps it's unhealthy..."

"That's irrelevant," they said. "That's just how one chooses to live, or not. That's just life."

I understood their comment on January 11, 2016 when I learned David Bowie died after an 18-month struggle with cancer. I posted on Facebook:

> I didn't become a poet because of David Bowie. But I want each of my books to be different from each other because of David Bowie and artists like him—My take? They *feel* physics: the world is an infinite series of parallel universes where overlaps can occur due to curvature and weave. Thus, the artist's work will be multiple and varied and ... prolific. I didn't become a poet because of him, but if I stay one it will also be because of his inspiration. R.I.P.

If aesthetic achievement can be defined as David Bowie's *expansive* life and art, then standing in front of a grey building to meet a stranger was not a price. It was simply what one did.

I never asked, but I assumed the stranger shared my admiration of David Bowie. For the stranger, too, never revealed a barrier between life and art—even when life's multiplicities translated to multiple sources of pain.

9 APRIL

Once upon a time, I emerged from darkness to place my first step in a neighborhood containing a grey building. As I walked away from the subway stop, I noticed debris some storekeeper had bunched together from sweeping the sidewalk. While the trash awaited the storekeeper's return, some fragments had fluttered away from the small mound. My steps faltered as I noticed the residue scattered by a stray breeze. Some of the random bits looked like black sand. In turn, they evoked black pepper...

...like the pepper once rubbed harshly against lips and genitalia in an attempt by soldiers to elicit information. They called the method "pepper torture" and it was one of many tools used by a dictator to prop up his regime. Of course, knowledge of that particular experience, like many, still haunted.

It haunted me.

It haunted them.

Torture contains a long resonance.

27 FEBRUARY

Once upon a time, I entered a certain building and realized the world outside was grey when the sun accompanied me inside. The outside world curtsied into greyness to emphasize the radiance of life inside Apartment 3J.

Their embrace was heat in gradations, their thick hair coiling into damp ropes, their flesh reddening to lava. Warm. Warmth. Warming up. Heat. A boiling. Once, a sage whispered, "Poetry must burn!"

30 NOVEMBER

Once upon a time, I left the darkness of the underground subway to find myself on the street that led to your grey building.

My cheeks were damp.

19 DECEMBER

Once upon a time, long before I first approached a grey building, I discovered romance as a practice of deceit. My first love affair was with a married man. I realized years later how I'd enabled his adultery because his wealth gave him power and I'd fooled myself into thinking I could siphon off some of his strength for mine.

Nonetheless, for love, I learned to hide—that seems apt now, given what I've learned about the manner of my entry into this world.

It was certainly convenient that his Wall Street earnings allowed for a second home that required a "house sitter."

Thus, even my first romance contributed to my willingness to meet a stranger inside a building which should have looked foreboding with its greyness and anonymity.

Anonymity as asset—what a risky path. And risk, as ever—what a lonely path. Especially if one hides so long that one loses one's self.

My affair with Wall Street ended with a revelation. He said, "This isn't unusual. Many of my colleagues have mistresses as well as wives."

Then he added—and I still don't know whether he realized the fullness of his cruelty—"What we have here is a cliché."

Most poets know to avoid clichés, but sometimes you just stumble into them unknowingly. Especially if you're afflicted with youth. How to be a good poet? Most if not all good poets will instruct you: *Wide reading. Wide experiences.*

3 OCTOBER

Once upon a time, I walked towards a building in a neighborhood I did not know. I walked towards a stranger. The moment was one fated by the violence of my entry into the country we came to share. I was a refugee from a dictator.

I was a refugee. From a dictator. Each characteristic deserves its own sentence, even if ungrammatical, as each are individual—they need not have collided with each other. That they did collide resulted in me standing before a building I had never seen before to press a fingertip upon a white enamel button that proclaimed their apartment number: 3J.

The door unlatched with a buzzing sound. To its buzz, I pushed open the door. I entered a hallway bathed in light; only later would I realize the "light" was sparked by the garish yellow painted upon the walls. *Garish*—normally an unattractive feature. But there are so many ways for illumination to occur.

Such as their hands. When they pressed my face to their chest to still my nerves, I also would hear the rapid beating of their heart. Which is to say, despite the impassivity of their face, they were not unmoved by what we were experiencing together—a realization that consoled. From such consolation,

I obtained fresh impetus to continue despite the exhaustion that already had dampened the veined marble under our bare feet.

They wanted me to break them. But, sometimes, I was the one who broke. Once, my face against the floor allowed me to see the marble's veins at close range. In that context, it was easy to misconstrue what I was seeing. Those fragmented lines could have been viewed, not as veins naturally embedded in stone but as cracks sundering something that was supposed to be solid or strong.

Years later, I am solid. I am strong. But only as Japanese *kintsukuroi*: a self strengthened because it had been broken, then repaired. A self more lovely for revealing cracks repaired with gold. As I write this, I am ensconced in a lovely limestone hotel. But while the hotel looks like it's constructed of oversized limestone bricks, the slab effect is fake. The limestone first was pulverized into dust. The dust, then, was mixed with aggregate and mortar to result in a material stronger than the original limestone—the same material once used to construct the Pantheon in Rome which bears the world's largest unreinforced dome. The material was slathered together to form walls. Once they dried, workmen etched lines across the walls to offer the impression of slabs or bricks raised atop each other. Artifice, yes. But as strong as the truth of a poem for which a poet first lived in order to create it. For some great poems, a poet first had to break or, yes, in some cases even be pulverized.

But all this is years, decades, after I first stood in front of a grey building where a stranger waited for me. I had been broken but I was also healed. They had been broken but professed to be healed. The traditional trope of a teacher-student relationship is imperfectly conceived: sometimes, the student reflects the teacher's gaze back upon the teacher.

1 DECEMBER

Once upon a time, I heard the intercom buzzing that signaled the unlatching of the front door into a grey building. Inside, a stranger waited. I pushed open the door and walked into a hallway awash in light. I moved forward: I walked through light.

I had been so focused on the stranger I would have chosen the metaphor of walking through a dim tunnel where they waited as the light of destination. Instead, I walked through light and to reach them was to reach the onset of darkness.

Darkness. And what a contrast they were against the suns inhabiting their paintings. There is so much light in their paintings. Large paintings. To stand in front of one could be to stand on a sun-drenched white granite balcony overlooking a sunlit sapphire Aegean Sea. I confessed this private metaphor to Ernst after several meetings enabled me to consider them by their name instead of as a stranger. Later that week, we were sipping d'Yquem in Rhodes.

"This wine is known as 'nectar of the gods'," Ernst said as they filled my goblet with an orange-gold liquid bearing the viscosity of honey. "A gift from an oenophile and art collector who wanted to match wine to one of my monochrome paintings."

The following morning, we woke to my metaphor-turned-reality.

"If your metaphors lack reality, you don't have to drop them," they said, blowing sand off of my cheek as their hand touched me elsewhere under a towel as turquoise as the sea. "You can test metaphors by making them real and see if they collapse from such reality."

I relished the roughness of their skin—their arms could never be smoothened from the calluses and scars of their labor or the tiny but ever-present flecks of paint. Trying to be cool, I said, "Your paintings show you've visited Greece before."

Their hand paused, then became more gentle, prolonging pleasure.

"You have a good eye, Elena," they said at the peak of my pleasure.

So quickly did the Grecian sun turn hot, turn blinding-bright. They gave me Greece—an experience whose pull lingers after decades, past even the changing of a century from the 20th to the 21st (as monitored by those favoring linearity for its convenience). Greece lingered so that, once, long after I ceased visiting them in a grey building, I even lived with huge German Shepherds named Achilles, Athena, Ajax, Neoptolemus, Nova...

12 FEBRUARY

Once upon a time, I pushed open a steel door and entered a building I had never visited before. I would visit it often for two years. The first time I visited, I wore thick-soled walking shoes clad in gold leather. New York City, the city we shared, is made for walking and I wanted comfort. Gold was sufficient, I supposed, for spicing up my footwear.

They accepted the gold. But they called comfort "irrelevant." Not too long afterwards, I could run to them in stiletto heels, black with soles of red.

With each step toward—and then, *with*—them, I dared falling, breaking, hurting.

But when I didn't fall, I soared. Such as when we visited an exhibit of an artist who was one of their former students.

"Look," they whispered as they positioned us in front of the smallest painting in the show by Angelina Merk. Most of the paintings were large, at least six feet tall. But this one was a foot tall and no wider. Scale was not the only difference. The other paintings presented riotous color combinations of vivid if truncated brushstrokes, the artist's own take on fauvism (the artist clearly didn't care about sales). The small painting was realistic and featured subdued tones. Against a beige background, the artist had painted a wooden, brown frame that contained nothing. Thus, attention was drawn only to the frame. And the frame was broken, lying askew on its side.

"What do you see?"

I looked at the painting, then looked at them, then turned away to look at the larger paintings in the one-room exhibition space.

"I see what you want to do to me," I whispered.

I could feel them pause, as if they were mentally shifting assumptions.

"Why do you say that?" they asked in a tone indicating genuine curiosity.

"Look at her large paintings—they are all successful."

"Successful," they slowly repeated as I looked back at them.

"Yes," I said, suddenly impatient as I felt they knew—or should know—what I was fumbling to say. "Successful in manifesting her intent, thus, beautiful."

They didn't react. No doubt to push them for a response, I continued.

"But Beauty costs, right? For whatever reason, you had to break her—whether literally or metaphorically—or break her away from something, perhaps the preconceptions she brought to your studio—for her to achieve these paintings."

They nodded.

Or perhaps they didn't—it was a small, brief gesture whose agreement I could have imagined, especially given their next words:

"Elena, I have zero interest in leaving you broken."

25 MAY

Once upon a time, I opened the door of a grey building to walk down a hallway suffused with sunlight.

Because of the light, they first would appear as a dark profile. Such darkness! Yet only as an aestheticized contrast to light. It was my darkness that complied with their guiding me to bend over cold porcelain.

... my warm breasts swiftly chilling against cold porcelain ...

But, once, I made them doubt themself.

They were standing over me but with a bowed head and slumped back. Beneath the fall of their hair, their eyes were obsidian from grief. They were pleading, "Elena, please forgive me."

21 JANUARY

Once upon a time, the sun hit steel and blinded me. I blinked several times to shoo off the effect of the errant sunray flaring against the metal intercom. Later, when I considered the significance of fighting off temporary blindness, I was reminded blindness is not something to desire.

When I could see again, I saw that the intercom panel wasn't particularly clean, but retained enough sheen so that I could discern my reflection.

My finger paused when my eyes caught their mirrored image. I was unsurprised by my searching gaze and its intensity. But I had not anticipated the anguish looking back at me.

But I did recognize the particular nature of its sadness: the plea of someone begging the entire universe, "Please. Don't let me end on my death bed wondering, *What if?* Please."

I stared at my plea for a minute, or an hour, whatever. I stared at my hunger, and hunger looked back at me.

12 JULY

Once upon a time, after we'd already begun meeting in a grey building, the stranger and I saw each other in one of New York City's many museums. But we only looked at each other across the wide gallery before returning to the paintings that caught our attention. I noticed we shared a predilection for the same artist who painted abstract canvases sized as four-foot squares. The paintings presented pale monochromatic tones of scarlet, orange, and yellow—vivid colors whose vigor was diluted into wash-like approximations. But each canvas also presented the same color as vibrant, thin edges. When I looked at the center of a painting, I saw a timid stillness and my eyes were easily drawn to the edges where color joyously dazzled. I overheard two women discussing the works as they stood in front of the painting next to the one I was perusing.

"You see how the artist privileges the margins?" one said enthusiastically.

"Yes! I love that! It could symbolize so many things!"

"Like questioning privilege…"

"Like questioning the arrogance of vanity…"

"Like questioning standards by which people judge…"

"Yes, that! Questioning how certain things or people become anointed as important as if subjectivity is not a factor…"

Ernst raised the exhibition at our next meeting.

"It wouldn't be a good way to end—solitary, ever looking at the world, including looking at how others look at the world."

"You mean to end up alone, alone, alone?" I said.

"No need to be histrionic," they said. "The single word suffices."

"Alone," I whispered, though I heard the loneliness resonating, repeating itself, in my poor, fraught mind.

Alone, though I had even, once upon a time, entered a neighborhood alien to me to stand in front of a building I had never visited before. Inside the building, in its Apartment 3J, a stranger waited for me.

Once, the stranger advised for staving off loneliness, "Write your reality!"

I could feel my eyes widen in surprise.

"Poets shouldn't just write about what they know. Write your desired reality, then enact it!"

That glint then in their eyes was not of mockery. For here is a *Truth* feared by the prescient few artists: in the "studio," there are no ethics. Not even for someone like me, a bit of *both* flotsam and jetsam tossed into the diaspora precisely because to be a dictator is to be unethical.

So, what happens when, for a poet, there is no difference between "studio" and "world"?

21 SEPTEMBER

Once upon a time, someone who thought she suffered from prosopagnosia stood in front of a grey building formed around a stranger awaiting her. From Wikipedia, the 21st century's definition of knowledge—a standing that makes Wikipedia my secret Beloved because dictators fear the educated—

> **Prosopagnosia** (/ˌproʊsoʊpæɡˈnoʊziə/)
>
> (Greek: "prosopon" = "face", "agnosia" = "not knowing"),
> also called **face blindness,** is a cognitive disorder of face
> perception where the ability to recognize familiar faces,
> including one's own face (self-recognition), is impaired, while
> other aspects of visual processing (e.g., object discrimination)
> and intellectual functioning (e.g., decision making)
> remain intact.

There was so much confusion—I had tricked myself into believing I was afflicted with this disease. Once, I actually thought the objects that would define my context, or offer parameters within which my self defined itself, was a list that began with scarlet silk and ended with a puddle of blue chiffon. In the middle of the list, a whip. No need to offer the actual list—the objects between beginning and end. Why dabble in others' clichés?

There was so much confusion—I tried so many ways to cope with the past until I finally determined to attempt lucidity. To see instead of being willfully blind.

Thus, Ernst.

I thought the stranger knew what they were doing. Many times, they did. But sometimes they were confused. Other times, they welcomed not knowing.

All fine and good. Except when a wave requires a stolid shore: one to be roiled by external elements before crashing, the other to remain unscathed.

Once, they whispered, "I am not as strong as you think me to be."

Did I want to hear *that* when they hovered over me, and I was a wet, naked heap darkening their foyer's already-dark, antique mahogany floor?

7 NOVEMBER

Once upon a time, I opened the door into a grey building where a stranger waited for me. They would tell me that as they'd looked at their bathroom mirror that morning, they'd asked their reflection whether my visit was a "good idea." The problem, they said with a laugh, was that they never turned away from anything that made them uncertain.

"Occupational hazard," they explained.

Artists are human. Consequently, I was not surprised when I began to learn Ernst was not only an artist but someone with hidden agendas. But as an artist, they began our engagement with no preconceptions, just the openness of curiosity. In the beginning, curiosity held sway.

The paintings that first brought them to the world's attention came from a series of dense abstractions, deceptively intense through color. They aren't monochromes but Ernst said they learned much from them about making monochromes. Much of these early paintings' surfaces are covered by white, grays and pale blues. But the paintings pulsate despite the cool palette for their surfaces covered layers of more vivid colors. My favorites among them display slight cracks through which can be discerned colors so loud they seem radioactive. The bottom colors seemingly struggle to break through the surface—that the paintings' surfaces retain their cool tones suggests an impassivity that manifests how control is possible.

Occupational hazard—it seems they always must leave themself to the possibility of being overcome by elements not under their control. But their goal, nonetheless, is to retain control. Once, they said about the pioneering abstract artist and founder of Suprematism, "As your darling Wikipedia notes, Malevich wanted to invent a new world of shapes and forms. When Stalin forced him to abandon what Stalin decried as 'modern art,' Malevich had to paint again in representational style. From there, he logically became afflicted with cancer which eventually killed him."

Control, until that, too, became predictable. I met them as they began looking for a different art practice, which is to say, a different way of life.

They didn't know that day as I stood in front of their building what my role in their search would become, or if I had any role. They were just doing their job, they said.

They said, "I was open. I was open for anything..."

21 DECEMBER

Once upon a time, I approached a building in a neighborhood I had never before visited. It was the beginning of a new vocabulary. Some decades into the future, a college student in a library will open a dictionary of words invented by poets to reflect the anthropocene. She will read her poet-ancestor's entries, two words wonderingly caressed by her fingers against a page browning to amber:

> **Cloudygenous:** the results of lifestyles and practices resulting from living in the internet so that internet becomes the "place" generating its own indigenous peoples and/or practices. This could be positive, e.g. when the internet facilitates engagement with the universe beyond one's physical borders. This could be negative, e.g. when the *e-magination* replaces physical reality and engagement with such reality. It's not an adjective that's inherently negative or positive; it's more complicated, in the way a cloud can obscure but also generate life-supporting rain.

> **E-magination:** see "Cloudygenus"

The student's grandmother will explain that my "experiment" with the stranger in a grey building e-maginatively began in the cloud.

So often did it rain for me and the stranger. More often than gentle and succoring, our rains were thunderstorms. So swiftly did we realize the path we were on—and refused to leave—was turbulent.

Storms were also convenient for camouflaging tears when one insists on keeping one's face looking up, as in when neither of us would bow.

5 AUGUST

Once upon a time, time...

15 OCTOBER

Once upon a time, I walked towards a grey building to the faint music of laughing children. I noted the laughter. I didn't laugh much as a child. As I grew into adulthood, I laughed even less.

Nor did my experiences with the stranger in the grey building change my glee trajectory. I continued to laugh less frequently as time continued unrelentingly to unfold.

When I considered what made us laugh together during our first year together, I usually recalled a city I've never visited: Berlin.

Ernst was describing a painter—Gerhard. They met in Prague when they exhibited together there in a group show. Gerhard painted mono-chrome paintings; apparently, they glowed in a way that erased the walls supporting them.

"They seemed like large melted jewels floating in air."

Impressed, Ernst struck up a conversation with Gerhard who later invited them to visit his studio in Berlin.

"An interesting space," they said. "Gerhard divided the area into two sections. The first was a white-walled, well-lit room—a typical studio. But the second area had walls painted a dark purple.

"Gerhard would work in the white space for most of his process. Then he'd finish the paintings in the dark studio. He said the darkness allowed him to test, or enhance, the luminosity of the painting's surface. Each painting seemingly presents a single color but that color was actually laid on the canvas through a tight grid. Between its lines were layers of different colors.

"I observed how his grid must be laid tightly to create the seamless effect across the surface."

In response, Ernst said, Gerhard beckoned them to get closer to one of the paintings, to peer at it closely, nose nearly touching the canvas surface.

"It was intriguing—such a tight grid. I told Gerhard that he'd made it really difficult for colors to escape, to 'taint' the single surface color. But, close-up, some colors do seep through the grids' cracks. At a distance, each painting presents a single color. But when seen up close, another color or colors can be observed."

"What made one color surface and another not?" I said.

"I'd asked Gerhard the same question. He laughed. At first he laughed. Then he said it depends on the relationship among colors—the surface color versus underlying colors—which color was more headstrong than another based on color contrast. 'Headstrong' was the word he used..."

I looked at Ernst. Their eyes were still seeing their memories of Gerhard. To bring them back to me but also because I was curious, I asked, "Why did he laugh?"

Ernst shook their head briefly. "He thought it was perversely funny that colors had to fight each other—that some colors had to clash. Gerhard said, even things that need not engage in battle often end up in war."

Ernst coughed, then continued, "I guess Gerhard was painting reality, or his reality. He didn't have an easy life."

"Or," I said, "Gerhard was painting faith despite reality? After all, he persevered? He kept painting?"

Ernst didn't say anything. They just looked at me. I began to be nervous they would chastise me again, perhaps for idealism, or failing to acknowledge the dismal sides of life. But they remained silent.

Trying to lighten the moment, I asked, "And what color do you think I am?"

They looked at me as if they were trying to decide whether to answer. They said, "We're still working on the underlying colors."

"The ones I'll never reveal to the world?" I quipped.

That's when we shared a laugh.

But it was a brief moment, a short laugh. We moved on to another matter. As with other times before, I'd end up wishing the ending was...softer.

That time, though, they ended that day's engagement by whispering against the damp nape of my neck, "That was a lovely violet, just like your eyes—you glowing to defeat darkness."

It was not a soft landing, but their lips against my skin were soft enough. Soft enough to bring me to a dreamless sleep. I remember my last thought before my eyes shut to total darkness: *Someday, we shall laugh robustly together, laugh long, laugh hard...*

28 AUGUST

Once upon a time, I entered a grey building and became overwrought over the yellow-painted hallway. I felt as if I was walking into sunlight—I became barefoot walking in a sunlit meadow...

... as if there was a warm breeze lifting my hair instead of the faint scent of bleach still discernible from a space not much aired from the last time someone mopped the floors.

As if at any moment, invisible indigo hornbills or yellow-breasted fruit doves would crack beaks into song.

As if the buzzing sound emanated from bees surrounding blooming vipers bugloss, columbines, red campions, ragged robins, white clover, yarrow, daisies, Welsh poppies, and maiden pinks instead of a television behind a closed door.

As if I was dressed in a sarong enjoying a stroll through the natural world instead of clad in boots, a wool coat, and a long scarf trying to dilute the chill foretelling a snowy onslaught.

I walked down a sunlit hallway until I reached the elevator doors. Because the doors were metal, I could see my reflection. But because the sun entered the building with me, the glare against the metal prevented me from recognizing my features. All I could see was the blurred outline of my body.

The blurriness did not prevent me from noticing the tenseness of my stance. I looked poised for something unknown to happen. My pose was one of somebody who could not prepare, psychologically, for something unforeseeable.

I was not prepared. But what I wanted, the stranger later whispered against my hair, was not something for which I could prepare. In response, I breathed in their familiar *coffee, mint, vanilla, citrus, and determination...*

The sun hit metal. Its gesture did not blind. It only highlighted my blurriness, the murk from which I was slogging out to go meet them. I raised my hand. I saw a blurry finger extend to call for the steel box that would bring me to them.

Of course, I wrote poems all the while I engaged with them. About six months into visiting the stranger, I wrote one about poetics, the theory—or *my* theory—of poetry:

Poetics (#1)

What we wanted
to do
to be

was what we were *helpless*
against doing
against being

17 MARCH

Once upon a time, a building's elevator opened in front of me. Its interior was as grey as the building's outdoor facade. But I was awash in sunlight which flowed swiftly through the open door to brighten its space. When I stepped inside the sun continued to accompany me.

I looked up and saw myself looking up. It was clear the ceiling mirror had not been cleaned for some time. But it did its job: I saw my uplifted face.

I saw myself and I saw hope.

I saw myself raise a hand to smoothen my hair. I saw my gesture and saw fortitude.

I saw my hand and it did not tremble. I saw my discipline.

I saw my eyes and its unblinking gaze as they looked back at me. I saw my desire.

I looked up and saw my ambition.

Because of what I saw, I felt joy blossom as I lowered my eyes towards the elevator panel of floor numbers. Joyfully, I looked for Apartment 3J.

19 JUNE

Once upon a time, the sun entered a grey building. I thought it was following me but of course I wasn't leading the light. Light led me.

Light led me to a grey building I'd not seen before, into a neighborhood new to me, and where I rejected the sound of children's laughter because I wanted to reject innocence.

If I was doing something foolish, call me "Fool"! What an easy challenge to fling out at the universe: there are so many more dangerous things to distrust—or fear—than foolishness. One example: passion. Another example: poetry. Last example: *duende*.

Once upon a different time, a long-haired woman beat her shoes against a wooden stage. Her shoes featured strong wooden heels, nails on the bottom of the toes and heels, steel shanks, and steel toes. The *bailaora* wanted to dance the metaphor of machine guns shooting at an ancestor, shooting long after the ancestor had fallen to, and stopped twitching on, the indifferent ground. Several times, she left the stage to venture among the café patrons, feet still beating history and fingers weaving air as if it was solid, as if it was physical. *Duende*—to live life no differently from dreaming. *Duende*—the stage lacking a proscenium's edge.

13 FEBRUARY

Once upon a time, there was a building that looked like a grey egg. I cracked it open.

In its elevator, I rose to another type of sun. Like the building and its neighborhood, I'd not previously seen this sun.

First, the sun would take the shape of them.

A political poet once insisted, *Never dismiss the power of eros.*

The stranger and I did not yet know the creatures we would become when mixed together and baked in what most assuredly will be heat. *Poetry must burn!* I heard the echo echoing.

The elevator ascended. Then its doors opened onto the third floor. When the doors opened, the first thing I saw was a mirror in a gold frame. *Of course,* I whispered to my reflection as I left the elevator and walked towards it. *Of course you would be waiting for me.*

I was waiting for me.

Chapter 2

15 MARCH

Once upon a time she entered a grey building, a hall of sunlight, a steel box, and a hallway whose ridiculous paisley carpeting she at first didn't see for the hallway mirror reflecting the wonder on her face.

Perhaps some interior decorator wanted to imbue cheer within the grey building's long dim hallways. But the ill-conceived decision made walking down the halls a slightly dizzying experience. Pale green curlicues atop orange reflects nothing more than the ad nauseum aesthetic.

But perhaps, she would think years later, the dizzying effect had little to do with the carpeting and more to do with the nervous anticipation she felt whenever she approached the door to Apartment 3J.

Sometimes, she felt as if she was wading across a sea floor as she walked across the carpet. The algae of memories. The coral of possibilities, sharply-edged in places. The sea water of "Kapwa," an indigenous trait of interconnection that bonds everyone and everything with everyone and everything across all of time. All of these emanated from a sensed logic—as they would observe to her many times during their ~~engagement~~ enrapturement with each other, "Color is a narrative." *Color as narrative. Even the colors of an over-eager decorator, cheap for being as inexperienced as I was*, she thought.

Water, too, as narrative, along with the salt and grit it contains.

She met the stranger as a 25-year-old infant. She met them as someone struggling to form identity. She met them as someone who'd clutch at color as a rationale—she was a shape-shifter looking for a center, a core.

I was fragile when I met them. How could it have been otherwise? Their father killed mine.

23 JANUARY

Once upon a time, she became I and I became she, then we switched again as she walked towards a grey building and I opened the steel door into it. For the next two years I occasionally left my body to look more intently at what she was doing as she engaged with the stranger. And vice versa. When psychologists study our switching inclinations, all consistently cite a past trauma at its root source—I certainly won't disagree. No doubt my struggle was observable by the stranger. But on this matter the stranger was irrelevant. Identity, while often contaminated by the observer, remains the battle stage of the I.

Sometimes, when I became she, the switch occurred to allow me to lick her wounds. Or a switch occurred for her to lick my wounds. From the stranger, prolonged and arduous effort was required before they could guide she and I to meld.

Meanwhile, I remained present for her, and she for me: the author of one's life cannot be dead.

10 APRIL

Once upon a time, a woman entered a grey building to meet a stranger for a second time. She entered the building accompanied by doubt. She had considered not returning. But after their first meeting, they had emailed:

> From: Blazer
> To: ElenaTheeland
> Re: mtg.
>
> I'm glad you're interested in art, my art. Because, actually, I've been looking for you. I hope you visit again—our family histories overlapped in Pacifica.
>
> It may seem risky, but ask yourself: Are you not in pain? Don't you finally want to know the forces that structured your life against your will? And not just know but...transcend?

The stranger was Ernst Blazer, a prominent artist. They'd come to her attention because she was a fan of their paintings. But she hadn't expected that her fan letter would begin a series of email correspondence that would lead to their invitation to meet. She hadn't known that they were aware of her name, of her existence.

She wondered, *Who will I become, Ernst, because I chose to meet you?*

That's when I told her the obvious: *For now, just meet. Let's not pretend we have a choice not to meet them.*

3 JANUARY

Once upon a time, she raised a hand towards the intercom panel on a grey building and noticed its knuckle. Scarred. Chewed. Pitted from many unconscious but obsessive scratchings.

"Dear you," she whispered at her knuckle. "You, too, deserve a new life."

Then she pushed a finger at the button denoting Apartment 3J. A stranger waited in the apartment for her. As a stranger, they will be new.

And as her finger pushed, she noticed how the gesture's aftermath made the knuckle...*relax.*

3 MAY

Once upon a time, she paused before a grey building and asked it, "Did you know Mars' largest moon, Phobos, will be torn apart by gravitational forces leading to the creation of a ring that could last up to 100 million years?"

"Destruction," she belabored the point at the grey building whose stillness she chose to interpret as a listening stance, "can still create something lovely and more lasting."

When I raised her hand to push at the intercom button marked Apartment 3J, she considered her ready finger. *Are you about to destroy yourself by pushing a button?*

My finger pushed.

29 AUGUST

Once upon a time, a soccer ball came flying out of stage left and hit the door to a grey building. The ball bounced back towards her.

Hello Innocence, she thought as she caught it, then turned towards the children calling out for the ball.

Throwing the ball back towards the children, she thought, *Goodbye Innocence.*

Then she continued approaching the grey building. Because she refused to shiver, the sun appeared.

Because she refused to shiver, the sun accompanied her to the grey building, then entered along with her. Outside, the sun heard us instruct each other, *Whatever awaits, there must be committed intimacy.* Inside, the sun knew it could blossom with a warm golden light that pleasingly perfumes through thawed bodies opening to release natural musk.

18 MARCH

Once upon a time, Elena entered a grey building to meet Ernst in their apartment. During the walk towards the elevator and the elevator ride up three floors, she tried to empty her mind, to be suspended until she literally was in Ernst's arms. *How can anticipation be so painful,* she thought as she tried to empty her mind.

But only the dead can truly bear empty minds. Elena sighed and thought of an old poem, or rather, the old beginning to a poem she'd not yet been able to continue:

> *To live*
> *is*
> *To ache*

She knocked on Ernst's door. She intended that before their meeting ended that day, she would know why agony simmered deep within their eyes, occasionally welling to visibility.

"His name was Samuel, or Sammy. He was my best friend while I was growing up in Pacifica."

Elena raised her face from Ernst's chest. They were lying on their bed, resting from that day's "lesson." She gave them an encouraging smile. "Go on."

"We did everything together as youngsters: hiking, swimming, basketball, and other sports and games. We might as well have been siblings. My father didn't mind me spending a lot of time with Sammy's family. He was often overwhelmed by his own work duties and lacked much spare time."

From Ernst's expressionless eyes, Elena could tell they were looking back at their past.

"After his discovery, my father started spending more time with me, in part to dispute what he called 'undue influence' by Sammy's dad, Mr. Bellow."

"What discovery?" I asked after Ernst seemed poised to avoid continuing their tale.

"Afternoons can get quite hot in Pacifica. Mr. Bellow preferred skirts over pants. Helps with keeping cool, he said. But they weren't just skirts— they were crafted from colorful fabrics with gorgeously intricate patterns. I admired them—one day, I said so; he was wearing a skirt whose design made it look like a folded ostrich's wing, but more vivid with blue feathers, emerald stems, and randomly-scattered white and gold-colored sequins."

"I didn't know they had ostriches in Pacifica," I said into their long pause.

They shook their head slightly as if to lessen the pull of their memories.

"They're extinct now. But ostriches did wander through Asia from the Pliocene to the Holocene period. They've found fossils over 25,000 years of age. I learned all that from Mr. Bellow who designed some of his skirts to reflect his admiration of the animal. When I saw that particular skirt, I asked if he could help me make one for myself. He laughed. Sammy apparently was happy with his sports shorts. He said he was glad for the chance to create skirts with and for me.

"He'd started out with more sedate colors—the blacks and tans commonly found on ostrich butts. But he swiftly realized there was no reason to avoid color."

I felt a presence whisper its thought: *Wouldn't we all prefer to live in Technicolor?*

"Sounds like a wonderful being," I said. "You must have shared some fun times together!"

"Yes. Yes, we did. Until my father came home earlier-than-expected one day and caught me dancing in my room, dressed in my skirt. I was bumping my hips against the wall, emulating the latest dance craze called 'The Bump,' turned around and saw my father frozen by my bedroom door. I, too, froze. And as I followed his eyes slowly going from my waist down my skirt, down to my naked ankles, then up again, it was as if he, then I, were leaving behind the family we'd forged together after my mother died—leaving behind our family because I wasn't who he thought I was. By the time his eyes returned to mine, there was a chill in them I'd never seen before but which soon became familiar.

"My stick-up-his-ass father forbade me from seeing Sammy and his family ever again. And whenever he wanted to insult me, he'd use the phrase, 'Don't behave like a skirt' or "You're behaving like a skirt.' He took away my best friend, which only served to emphasize my loneliness after he also took warmth out of our relationship. It's as if spending more time with me also gave him more of an opportunity to know me, and he discovered he didn't care for much of who I was."

"It must have been hard." I struggled to find supportive words. "It's hard especially for children who still retain the openness to new experiences that living inevitably dilutes."

"He called me naïve. He said I lacked discrimination and, as a result, will be prone to making poor choices."

Ernst gently set me aside to stand.

"Enough of that," they said. "I'm thirsty. You?"

"Sure," I replied, watching them walk to the kitchen. I remained silent. I was familiar with how a moment of massive rupture can rear up swiftly and unexpectedly to devastate—at which words can be too weak to console. *We so often lapse to silence.*

When Ernst returned with a glass of water, they'd regained or pretended to regain equilibrium. They said, "Now you know why my wardrobe's mostly jeans and black t-shirts."

Trying, too, I replied, "Or why disco music is forbidden in your apartment?"

We both smiled. But as with other times, both of our smiles didn't extend much, didn't last long.

Nor did I say what I also was thinking—how it was a shame that empathy blooms best after the fertilizer of suffering.

3 AUGUST

Once upon a time, Elena entered Apartment 3J in a grey building that ceased to become a mere tile on an anonymous cityscape. *I shall be intimate with your space*, she thought at the walls as she accepted the stranger's invitation to move towards the living room. She sensed the walls quiver as if an earthquake hiccupped.

As she sat on the sofa, she felt the intentness of their gaze. They sat on a chair facing the sofa.

"What do you want?" Ernst said. They cut to the chase. It was their third meeting.

Elena looked at them, then around the room where paintings dominated the walls.

"I don't know you," she said as she returned her gaze to them.

"That's right."

"I suppose that means…" she spoke slowly at first, then firmed up her resolve and continued with a steelier tone, "I want everything."

They smiled, then replied, "You just got me."

She didn't smile back. She just said, "… including whatever you empty from yourself every time you make one of your paintings."

13 OCTOBER

Once upon a time, I went to meet a stranger; in this case, a person I once assumed was dead.

I was introduced to their existence by a gallery exhibition of their paintings, and I thought the works so masterful I assumed them to be dead!

To translate "falling in love" to "death" reveals something about me: I've long felt that all "masters"—as in those who've mastered their avocations—are dead. I suspect I held this belief because the world of the living is replete with flaws, a condition I meet with disappointment, regardless of my own flaws. But the dead cannot disappoint for long—if they or their memories only effect disappointment, they simply became forgotten. For me, the dead that remained a presence were those with admirable, *masterful*, qualities.

That I came to discover the artist still living, and then meet them, is a more clichéd matter. It's just another example of fandom, isn't it?

But what I did not anticipate was the role of aesthetics, and how they would push us both to embody these thoughts.

"Even abstractions are best when they contain muscle," they said.

Muscle.

"Fine," I said. "I'm willing to dance."

They laughed.

"Yes, Elena. Exactly. This, too, is a dance."

Any aesthetic philosophy, though, integrates the unknown. Whatever else I thought of what we experienced together, I realized that our personal beginning was appropriate. I began by leaving a subway tunnel's darkness to embark into sunlight, only to leave that sunlight behind when I came to stand in front of a grey, unfamiliar building. We all begin from darkness. Inside a grey building, a stranger waited for me.

19 SEPTEMBER

Once upon a time, she walked on black sand towards a grey building. She felt the warm grit slip between her toes. She felt barefoot despite the black leather encasing her feet. There is no armor against some memories, she realized as she felt sand lick a cat's tongue against her ankles.

She wanted to believe the stranger would help her want to be, and remain, open to whatever might surface from her past. Once, she had surfaced from between the thighs of a stranger into the arms of a cooing midwife.

"Look at this princesa!" a midwife had cooed. "Oh, Princesa: you will make the world fall in love with you!"

After learning of the midwife's words from her father, she'd judged the midwife to be a nitwit. The midwife should have known better than to attract the gods' attention with her compliments. The midwife should have erupted in dismay at her ugliness so as to make the spirits move on, *move on*...

Instead, the gods swiftly descended to hover as she flailed her tiny arms against their jealous breaths. Ultimately, they didn't touch her. But they did giggle over her mother dying in childbirth.

"I suspected your beauty"—once, these were the stranger's words after she'd entered their Apartment 3J. It wasn't her first compliment for her beauty, though theirs was oddly—or mischievously—worded. Her first lover, after depleting several wine bottles, once described her as with "silky hair that could form a kimono, full lips which need only pout to unlock a bank vault, skin of café au lait one could drink forever, breasts that embarrass pears, and legs long enough to shred a traveling man's tongue."

Like with many who came to possess immense wealth, boredom encouraged her former lover to think himself an artist, in this case a writer. But his words only repelled Elena into treasuring the many nuances of silence as well as becoming distrustful of those who made much of a physical beauty she did not consider an achievement when it was formed by biological coincidence.

Princesa is also smart, she thought as she smiled into the stranger's grey eyes. *You're smart to be careful around faces that irritate vain gods into casting curses.*

Smiling, she asked—casually as if she was thinking of something else— "What do you fear telling me?"

25 JANUARY

"Once upon a time, no grey building existed. Instead, dinosaurs roamed through the land."

"That's what's called a conversation non-starter," I said in response to their latest attempt to deflect my questions.

But their next deflection worked. They picked up a painting and turned its face towards me. They said, "I named it after and for you."

I forgot my question. I looked at my namesake: a monochrome gold canvas with a luster that allowed it to reveal the shadow of a viewer. I looked at my shadow—I looked at her.

Then she looked at them.

"Shhhhhh," they whispered as a tear began etching its trail down her cheek. "The color gold is banal unless it allows shadows, unless it's darkened by someone's life."

Decades later, I would whisper at this memory of reflecting only a shadow despite a face that could cause jealous gods to become so cruel they would kill her mother for giving birth to me, "A shadow can be reductive. Somewhere, someone died from Beauty."

6 AUGUST

Once upon a time, Ernst watched a woman approach their building. They were seeing her for the first time. *How will you translate into a painting,* they thought.

They remembered that thought when, some weeks later, she protested, "I am not your raw material!"

She was seated on their lap, her face against their neck. They moved her back until they were face to face. They insisted, "Look at me!"

She looked.

"What do you see?" they asked.

"You."

"Am I doing anything besides being focused on you? Am I sketching or painting while I talk to you?"

"No."

"So what else do you see?"

Elena looked at them, the intensity in their eyes, the slight smile hovering at the corners of their lips. And Elena allowed the tear to slip out before she replied, "Us. I see us...!"

They pushed. They insisted, "And?"

Elena closed her eyes before whispering, "You are holding me."

I thought, *You are holding me up.*

24 MAY

Once upon a time, Ernst watched from a window on their third-floor apartment as a long-haired woman approached their grey building. They watched her steps slow down as she noticed the red roses by the side of the building (they'd paid their building's management to plant the fragrant blooms). Then she looked up towards their apartment—when she looked towards them, her steps quickened.

No, they corrected themself as they fingered a scratch on their arm inflicted by Elena at their last meeting. *We are not strangers to each other.*

Not just another blank canvas, they thought as they turned to look at the paintings leaning against their walls. Once, they were all blank canvases. Under their hand, they all became things of value, at least as measured by those who've made them and their dealers rich.

Ernst turned their attention back to the woman now just a few steps from their building. They pushed away a wave of hair that had fallen over their eyes, partially blocking their sight.

"You," they whispered as if she could hear them. "You are the canvas who will react to each of my moves. You are a blank canvas that will look back at me."

They watched her pause, seemingly have a conversation with herself, but nonetheless continue: she raised her hand. Seconds later, they heard the intercom's music that they'd allowed her to program. David Bowie's voice lilted out, "Let's dance ...!"

3 FEBRUARY

Once upon a time, a building did not rise on the corner of 24th and Broadway. The area, strewn with used syringes, did not yet know the music of children's laughter or the rapid stiletto clicks of my eagerness to reach a stranger.

But context is unstable. Once, I asked the stranger, "How can the center hold?"

They didn't say, which would not have surprised me, "There is no center."

They replied, "The center need not hold."

Or is this a false memory? Should I remember the conversation as follows:

... context is unstable. Once, I asked the stranger, "How can the center hold?"

They didn't say, which would not have surprised me, "The center need not hold."

They replied, "There is no center."

1 MAY

Once upon a time, Elena approached a grey building. As she neared its front door, she fought the urge to look up at Ernst's apartment. By this meeting, she had learned that Ernst usually stood by their window watching her approach.

It wasn't actually difficult to quell the temptation to look up. Elena was wondering if she should continue visiting. Her right palm hadn't stopped tingling, if only in her imagination, since it slapped Ernst at their prior meeting.

In response to the slap, Ernst laughed. Then they looked at her with a smile. They replied, "I know you."

Recalling what they said, Elena did pause, turn around, and walk away from the grey building. She felt their eyes watching. She felt their eyes' lack of concern over her action.

I know you.

When she returned later that day, they greeted her with the same smile they showed after she slapped them. Diplomatically, they merely said, "You're late."

They continued.

22 SEPTEMBER

Once upon a time, Ernst stood by their window and watched Elena approach the grey building where they waited. They had longed for this day and others of Elena approaching their building—approaching *for* them. Every first sighting was a shock—each meeting could not accustom them to the next.

You mean so much more than you even realize, they thought. *You will provide the meaning of my life.*

But, first, Ernst understood, there must be a courtship. And the courtship had to be sweet for Elena, even as its process inevitably became tortuous for them. The intercom buzzer sounded. As they turned to open the door, they thought, *Our engagement must retain sweetness, Elena, even when you weep.*

Your story must *not be like mine...*

... my story, they thought, recalling their early days in New York City as an emerging artist—when their nights at a particular club featured them in a variety of colorful skirts that inspired others to give them their nickname: Peacock.

Dancing, whenever they caught their reflections against the club's mirrored walls, they felt authentic—they felt safe.

But the eyes starting to swirl in front of their inwardly-turned gaze weren't from the bird to which Charles Darwin referred when he said "no ornaments are more beautiful" in his *The Descent of Man, and Selection in Relation to Sex*. The eyes swirling were first that of Mr. Bellow's, then their father's, then Mr. Bellows's, then their father's... until Elena returned them to their reality with the collision of her knuckles against their front door.

5 NOVEMBER

Once upon a time, a woman approached a grey building to meet a stranger in their apartment. Elena was that desperate. Once, her steps faltered. But she determinedly picked up her pace again. *Might as well be killed by a serial killer,* she thought, *than live the rest of my life stunted by ignorance.*

Once, the woman insisted on Faith. She looked around the basement studio apartment where I chose to live and said, "I am not small and anonymous like you, Basement! I came from a family!"

Then she pointed at a framed photograph on the recycled door on brick stands that served as my desk and dining table. From the photograph, my father smiled at her. He was a teenager in the photograph, perhaps 16 years old; his face still lacked shutters from how he would live in the world. Even his eyes looked transparent, their violet pupils reminding her of the pelagia noctiluca jellyfish she once observed off of the coast of Pacifica.

Her father smiled even as she heard him ask, "Why are you hiding, child?"

"Of course, I was just imagining him talking to me. But I do that a lot," the woman told the stranger when she mentioned the incident.

"Imagine?" the stranger confirmed.

"Yes," I said.

"For you, that can be sad and weak," the stranger said.

"Imagination can make up for a lot of things!" she protested. "It can even offset loss."

"Not the way you're using your imagination."

I looked at them, my silence asking them to explain.

"Your imagination is allowing you to rest in your trauma rather than work your way through it."

I opened her mouth to disagree, to protest. But she lapsed into silence when she saw what was darkening their eyes: sorrow.

"Are you always living on the defensive?" they asked.

She didn't reply. She was pained to realize: their sorrow was over her.

But someday, Elena, Ernst silently promised as they brought her to the couch, *you will laugh more uproariously than you ever thought yourself capable. You will laugh frequently and robustly in the life you will come to forge.*

26 MAY

Once upon a time, Ernst stood by the window of their third-floor apartment to watch Elena approach the grey building where they both resided and made their paintings. *Life is work; work is life,* they often thought about their reality. From their window, Elena looked small. Elena looked ... fragile.

You come to me as a woman but you're still a child, they thought. *Elenita...*

The buzzer sounded. They moved towards the door. They thought, *You come to me as a woman but you're still a child. What, then, is my responsibility?*

Or, they thought as they waited for Elena, *should I just do again what I do and let you be the one to determine how you respond?*

Again. It didn't end so well the last time. So they thought again, *What is my responsibility?*

Suddenly, they felt tired. They regressed and split, enabling them to say and hear, *You and your whip only get involved when your "proteges" require a long time to get to their destinations.*

Then they laughed at the sunlight entering through their window. They laughed as the alternative would be worst—*Fortitude is exhausting. But, you learned this a long time ago.*

28 NOVEMBER

Once upon a time, Elena agreed to meet a stranger in their apartment. They shared their address by e-mail, the forum for their interactions prior to meeting. They gave some directions from the nearest subway stop as well as a brief description of their building's location: "surrounded by buildings of glass."

Elena became intimate with a space some few feet before the grey building's door. There, if a person paused as Elena often did during her visits, the person would see the grey building while also seeing it reflected in surrounding glass walls.

She called the area "The Portal" because Elena decided to believe that passing through it meant entering a parallel universe where she and the stranger would engage. "Engage freely," they once emailed. Elena didn't question their characterization though she wasn't sure such "free"-dom was possible. But the building's multiple reflections encouraged the thought of parallel universes. Much later, with increased self-awareness, Elena would admit the idea of a parallel universe was freeing for the implication her actions in the grey building would not be judged in the "real world."

Elena swiftly grew accustomed to greeting it, thinking *Good Morning Portal, Hi Portal, Hello You Inevitable Portal, Still Up Portal?, Darling Portal, Damn You Portal!* and so on. The nature of her greetings shifted with her mood based on what she'd recently experienced or anticipated next experiencing with the stranger.

That first meeting, when she first noticed The Portal's existence, Elena paused to note its space, smiled grimly, and greeted it with an *All right then! Surprise me, Portal!*

The Portal obeyed.

13 JULY

Once upon a time, a stranger stood beside a window watching a woman approach them by first approaching a grey building—both person and building were unknown to her.

They addressed her image, "You think me a stranger, Elena. Yet I know more about you than your name."

Nothing exists without context.

Once, they read a footnote in an essay by feminist poet and scholar Montana Ray. Ray cited Claude Levi-Strauss for noting it is "relationships among objects that result in a work of art."

Art cannot exist without context. But what makes Art is often the disruption of inherited context(s). *Dear Elena*, Ernst thought, *shall we disrupt the context a dictator wanted to enforce upon us?*

So much wisdom exists in footnotes.

So much life exists in the margins.

Yet I'm curious, Ernst thought. *What would it be like to blossom, fully confident your place is central and deserving of the attention you're confident you'll receive?*

16 OCTOBER

Once upon a time, Ernst watched Elena approach their grey building. It was their second meeting. Ernst took their eyes off of her to look at the new canvas they had placed on the floor near the window. Then they looked at Elena again. They kept looking at Elena even as the canvas appeared before their mind's eye. *I am looking at you,* they thought, *and wondering what you will look like.*

Elena, they thought. *I long to see you...*

As the intercom buzzer sounded, they turned and their foot unexpectedly caught a corner of the canvas, making it fall. They leaned over, picked it up, and set it back against the wall.

Not an omen, they told themself as they walked towards the intercom. *When you hurt, you can always make amends.*

Their finger pushed the button that unlatched the grey building's front door. *You can always make amends,* they thought again.

That will always be my job: I will make amends.

To their thoughts, they felt their back begin to pulsate. They imagined its scars welling up as if to meet the lash of a whip. They could feel their scars fearlessly proclaiming, *We can take more, as much as what you need to lash out, Elena. Gladly, we will bear them all.*

8 NOVEMBER

Once upon a time, Elena approached a grey building. She paused to look up at a window on the third floor. She couldn't see Ernst through the window glare, but she knew they were standing there watching her. She smiled as she threw up the thought, *You see me, Ernst. I know you see me.*

"It's what we all want, isn't it?" she'd later ask as they shared their bathtub afterwards. "Don't we all want to be seen for what we really are?"

"I believe some of us prefer to hide," they said, even as they smoothed away some frothy bubbles to see her more clearly.

"I guess it's a matter of trust," Elena said as she leaned forward to be closer to their hands.

Ernst didn't say anything, only let their hands do more roaming. But they agreed reluctantly as the thought brought a grey tint to the air, *Yes, it's a matter of trust.*

Trust, they thought again, then gentled their hands.

29 FEBRUARY

Once upon a time, it was the 29th day of February. As she was walking in a strange neighborhood toward a grey building to meet a stranger, she wondered if the events of the day could slip between cracks into a non-event.

"It's a good question," the stranger said. "But you should behave as if every day is February's last day during a leap year."

In response, her eyes dropped to their bared chest. Minutes earlier, she'd ripped off their shirt. Her eyes memorized the welt pulsing across their damp breast... until they tipped her face upwards to the smile lurking in their eyes.

They whispered and it was a jasmine-scented summer breeze: "The result won't always be a scar..."

She smiled as they emphasized their point. Sometimes, the result of risk is a kiss—open-mouthed for total exposure.

1 MARCH

Once upon a time, March began—the month that brought forth the Ides. First raised by the Romans as a deadline for settling debts, the Ides' history encompasses the Mamurula from ancient Roman religion that involved beating an old man clad in animal skins. This unfortunate ritual was intended to mark the transition from the old year to a new year, even as it evoked the Greek and Christian rituals of scapegoating—an animal symbolically burdened with the sins of others before being driven away. For me, settling old debts and starting life anew resonated.

This past December, she had passed through its holiday season with both extreme joy and extreme pain—the combination made her recall the two years she once spent in a stranger's embrace. *She'd memorized the red plum flavor of their blood.* She decided to embark on the cliché known as New Year's Resolution: she decided to write about the stranger everyday for the following year.

After two months of dutifully writing about the stranger, she paused to consider what she had managed thus far. She concluded: I can barely move past the beginning, that entry into a new neighborhood that contained a grey building where a stranger waited.

Beginning. Can I write a story as it unfolds, untainted by already knowing what happened? But I don't want to write reality this time, as I've done thousands of times through the form of a poem. This time, I want truth—what really happened—to be the author. Shouldn't this path be easier? There need not be the struggle to imagine; the story already occurred and one need only report it!

So what happened, Elena?

Once upon a time, Elena approached a grey building where a stranger waited for her.

She opened the door.

She entered.

So much joy. So much pain.

So many scars. Never enough laughter. *The bodily involvement of joy and pain.*

Bliss. Anguish.

Bliss...

She turned on the computer and pulled the keyboard closer to her. Once more, Elena began to write. Once, a stranger counseled, "Write your own reality."

That's possible, Elena thought, *when time bends for Kapwa.*

"Kapwa"—in Pacifica, its indigenous people used the term to reference how existence began as a ball where everything and everyone is part of each other, a connection that cannot be cut even after the ball exploded into fragments that spun away from each other and began time as a measure of separation. In Kapwa-time, existence is once again a unified ball, its cracks from the explosion disappeared into the seamlessness of peace.

Chapter 3 ·

Once upon a time, Elena approached a grey building to meet the person she'd learned to know as "Ernst Blazer" instead of "stranger." She wondered, *What are we creating?*

In her multi-layered novel *INSURRECTO*, Gina Apostol ends her first chapter with the statement: "Choosing names is the first act of creating."

Elena wondered if the novelist's theory is correct, having just seen "Bird Box," a movie whose Netflix audience surged for months upon release. Its primary protagonist Malorie, played by Sandra Bullock, temporarily refused to name two children, referring to both only by their genders: "Boy" and "Girl." But the two children were created—feeling fear, pain, joy, hunger, curiosity—before they ever would hear their names: "Olympia" and Tom." Indeed, nearly all humans are conceived ahead of their names—unnamed, they still exist.

They exist, but are not living—they are not creating, I told her or she told me.

What are we creating, Ernst, and what would it be called?

The questions made Elena pause. Standing still, ignoring the traffic around her and the distant music of children's laughter, she turned her gaze inward to consider: "What is something that is not created?"

After a few moments and despite being a poet, which is to say, cautious as regards any definitive answer, Elena answered herself definitively: "inheritance."

4 MAY

Once upon a time, a woman approached a grey building to meet a stranger in their apartment. She noticed some red roses blooming by the front door. Inhaling their promiscuous scent, she admired the red, waxy petals for their vividness as she pushed an intercom button. *I want to live my life in Technicolor!* When she heard the buzz that unlatched the door, she pushed it open and was immediately blinded by the sun.

The sun swallowed her. She felt herself tumble down its throat and land in a belly with walls of blinding light. She felt herself begin to disintegrate. She opened her mouth to scream.

She screamed herself into a different sun, this one just dawning outside her bedroom window. Heart pounding, she looked around. She was on her bed, damp and heaving breaths. Beyond the window, the sky was turning a benign, even pretty, pink. *Nightmare*, she thought.

As the sun evaporated darkness, as she felt her heartbeat slow down, she recalled her last words in the dream—what she'd been screaming. She had been pleading with the sun, *Wake me! Please. Wake me!*

Something was blinking red at the periphery of vision. She turned to see her alarm clock. It was time to rise. It was time to get ready. She had a meeting that day with a stranger in a grey building whose entrance was lined with red roses. She thought of an old poem where she'd written, *I want to live my life in Technicolor! Wake me!*

16 JUNE

Once upon a time, Elena approached a grey building where she knew Ernst waited. She imagined that they were waiting with much anticipation—they had ended their last meeting with words she'd kept turning over and over in her mind: *You redefine Bliss...*

From their apartment window overlooking the street, Ernst watched her approach. *Dear Elena,* they thought, *Bliss is not sustainable in all of its versions.*

They turned their thoughts inward: *And you will be a bastard for teaching her that lesson today.*

4 FEBRUARY

Once upon a time, no grey building stood on the corner of 24th and Broadway. For the grey building to exist, battalions of laborers dug deep into the earth, excavating their way through layers of dirt and stone to create a building foundation. The president of the construction company exhorted his workers whenever he visited the building site: "Let's offer not just a haven but a heaven to future residents! Let's first dig through hell!"

A cheesy pun that led to muddled as well as muddied words—but his message was clear: eager excavation of profits.

Broadway extended the length of the city, but its corner with 24th Street was in a neighborhood unknown to her for reasons related to its nickname, "Tartarus." My much used—thus, much loved—Wikipedia explains Tartarus as "the deep abyss that is used as a dungeon of torment and suffering for the wicked and as the prison for the Titans."

The nickname repelled her from visiting the neighborhood, though gentrification had smoothened much of its prior rough edges. The name repelled because it seemed to her that she'd already spent an exponentially large amount of her education on the Greeks. *The Greeks again?* scoffed the postcolonial pundits of the time to whom she was frequently introduced at the colleges where she adjuncted for a lowly series of wages. Yet there she was, she chided herself, walking up Broadway through Tartarus. When she reached her destination and felt joy as she raised a finger to jab at the intercom, she also couldn't help thinking how wise poets often end up asking, *What fresh Hell is this?*

Later, when she revealed these jumbled thoughts to the stranger, the stranger's hand paused before continuing to stroke her hair. She could see their eyes more clearly as they'd finally made time for a haircut. She liked their hair shorter for revealing more of the feelings lurking within their dark eyes—this time, kindness revealed itself.

"You do know," they said as they caressed away sodden strands from interrupting the sunlit ocean in her eyes, "the Titans' only survivors are their poetry..."

She closed her eyes but immediately replied because she felt the answer would please them, "As it should be."

But when she opened her eyes, she saw the opposite of joy in their eyes. In their eyes, she saw anguish rise. Too often does pain overcome kindness.

Anguish rose as they noted, "Poetry. Art. They exact huge costs..."

2 AUGUST

Once upon a time, Elena walked up a city's longest street where a grey building stood, deceptive in seeming to be anonymous among other such buildings. *I am here*, Elena thought as she stepped over sidewalk cracks, *to flesh out the gaps, the absences, that have come to form the primary motivations of what I do. I'd rather not wallow in what's missing. Surely life can be different—larger?*

Elena came to share her thoughts as she stood, nude, on a pedestal.

"Many assume that someone behind a mask contains much to reveal," the stranger replied. "But it may be the person who dares to be naked before

41

the world who contains much more to share."

"Hiding in the open," I said, then subtly stiffened my belly to make my breasts rise. Once, I peeked at a canvas-in-progress. Before they moved to block my view, I saw lavender, a golden crown of thorns, and the two letters "M Y."

Before they finally revealed the painting and its title, I'd already indulged in weeks of speculation—several times, I thought, or hoped, the title would be "MY LOVE."

Instead, Ernst, no longer a stranger, revealed that they had titled my portrait:

BLASPHEMY

18 SEPTEMBER

Once upon a time, Ernst stood by the window of their third-floor apartment to watch Elena approach the grey building where they already had spent a decade. In the middle of that decade, there was "another woman."

"What was her name? She's not just 'another woman'," Elena smiled to blunt any sting from her question.

"Of course," Ernst quickly replied. "Names are significant and her name is Madeleine."

They didn't say—admit—they were initially reluctant to share Madeleine's name as it evoked the pain of regret. Briefly, they thought to share their reason, but remained silent and allowed Elena to change the topic.

Later, seated on the fire escape balcony to her apartment, Elena looked up at the night sky. She did not see the stars camouflaged by the lights of yet another city that refused slumber. But in the folds of the dark sky where darkness contained varying shades of black, Elena saw the hair of another Madeleine—a woman whose presence was hidden by her lover to his friends and family, though revealed and immortalized today in Wikipedia. A woman who, like so many other women, existed outside the frame—Madeleine Knobloch, the lover of Georges-Pierre Seurat, the post-Impressionist painter who developed pointillism.

I know how you feel, Madeleine, Elena thought as she looked up at the hidden stars. *It's like my father's life. He'd led the opposition to The Dictator. But victors write history—because The Dictator prevailed, my father's life will be lost to history. My father will have his life pushed outside the gilded frame that bears the portrait of a fake royal with fake medals on his chest: a dictator who plundered a country and erased those who stood in his way.*

But then, more second-guessing. Elena lowered her eyes from the stars.

The Dictator, your ugly head pokes through my life again, she sighed. *I'm no better than Ernst to make Madeleine's life about you and not her.*

The Dictator, she thought as she reached for the bottle, *I don't want to live in your Aftermath.*

4 NOVEMBER

Once upon a time, Elena found herself entering a grey building to meet a stranger in the confines of their apartment. No one knew about her appointment, which naturally enhanced the danger of her position.

But one must have faith, she stubbornly told off the god whispering urgently in her ear. She'd also emailed herself the details of her meeting—*just in case I disappear,* she'd thought as she'd hit the "Send" button.

I hear you! she said when the god wouldn't stop lecturing on prudence. *You're a god—just use your thunderbolts or whatever to take care of me if something goes wrong!*

The god finally stopped chastising her when she stepped out of the elevator onto the third floor. *You see,* she proclaimed triumphantly, *both sun and sea have followed me!*

She shook her head—how could a god not know that life had taught her not to obey gods unthinkingly, that not all gods are worthy or trustworthy?

The walls shimmered with a brown-green paint. *I could be surrounded by trees even as I wade through a sea!* she noted to the silenced god whose disapproving presence she still felt.

"Kapwa-time, Elena," the stranger would come to whisper as their hands memorized every inch of her body. "When all is present..."

She opened her eyes to see a luminous blue sapphire sky as their ceiling. She quivered at the scent of sampaguita orchids invisible but nearby. She felt the warm kiss of a tropical breeze. From the corner of her left eye, she caught the scarlet wave of flame trees behind a sand dune.

"Yes," she replied. "No me or you—the time when the pronoun is only *Us*."

23 MAY

Once upon a time, she entered a grey building, waded through its sea, lingered through its forest, scaled its twin mountains, spelunked through its cave, traversed its fast-flowing river, crawled through its desert, and entered its Apartment 3J to look deep into the eyes of a stranger.

"No," they said in agreement as if she'd expressed her wonder out loud. "You are not home."

They smiled when she replied, "Then I'm in the right place."

They backed away from each other then precisely because they both knew the day would end with she mentally relishing the word, then physically gasping out, their name.

30 APRIL

Once upon a time, Elena walked towards a grey building. It was an apartment complex but on one of its corners was a music bar with a small sign. The sign held no words but presented the image of a female flamenco dancer.

The image caught her attention without affecting her pace. *The sign might be more effective if the image was just of the hands,* she thought.

"Why?" Ernst asked when she later shared her observation.

"I like how every inch of the *braceo* is controlled by the dancer," Elena said.

"You like the discipline?"

The question indicated knowledge: *braceo*, the arm work in flamenco, unfolds with resistance—the arms move through air that seemingly has become physical resistance, like quicksand.

"I like the discipline," Elena affirmed, even as she felt their conversation become about something else.

"I appreciate how the discipline is possible only due to resistance..." Elena continued, trying to show she also was not a mere student. "Resistance, but not for its own sake."

"Of course there's a goal," they said agreeably. "The beauty of the dance."

Elena looked at them. They looked peaceful on the bed, their hands behind their head. They had finished, but she was still straddling them.

"I admire flamenco dancers," Ernst said, almost idly. "They engage the arm muscles and control arm movement, often in an extreme manner. The result are powerful yet graceful arms."

"Ernst?" Elena said.

"Elena?" they replied.

Then they stopped toying with her. They said, "The dancers have to be fit. Their grace is possible because of their muscle."

Muscular grace. Afterwards, at certain times when the pain she inflicted on Ernst was most intense, Elena would counsel—comfort—herself by recalling how a certain grace can only be achieved through extreme muscular exercise. Then, once more, she would raise the whip.

14 JULY

Once upon a time, a woman containing a huge void walked towards a grey building. She felt the void contained within a large, black pot within her belly. The void simmered like mulligatawny soup in the cabin of an Alaskan mauled by a bear and now unable to return to tend, eat, savor...

Alaskan. Mulligatawny. Soup. Are you done being demented? I scolded her as we approached the building's front door.

Compassion, please, she replied. *I'm just nervous.*

No, you're just refusing to learn from Franz Kline.

What?

You're now throwing out a mental net to bring as many elements as you can to this encounter so as to dilute its intensity.

What does that have to do with Franz Kline?

When Kline made his black marks, he was focused on his black marks and not the contrast of the white field against which he painted or the space against which the marks were laid. He was focused solely on the mark. And the rest of it would just occur as a result of the mark. The stranger and your meeting with him are the marks—focus on them instead of bringing random elements to the experience.

As with many of her fears, she shared this internal conversation with Ernst. Unexpectedly, they said, "You were being silly, but for the wrong reason."

Then they made her gasp and she forgot the conversation for the lava their bodies were creating. It flowed off the bed, spread across the floor, seeped through the grey building's interior, flowed out into the building's exterior, crossed the street, and finally touched the earth (through the nearby park) to fuel the relief of arriving home. Home cannot be defined without a relationship to its earth, its homeland.

Afterwards, in their robe and sipping from a long glass chilled with ice water, she asked, "How was I silly in the wrong way?"

As if they weren't blotting blood from their arms where she'd scratched them—Elena was discovering how opening one's self sometimes meant losing control—they said coolly, "No need to imagine Alaska. No need to imagine. To exist is to contain context. That's Identity 101."

Then they threw away the bloodied towel and motioned her over.

She loved the taste of their blood. They knew that, and had left some for her.

She loved the way their eyelids flickered with each of her long, relishing licks.

28 FEBRUARY

Once upon a time, Elena approached a grey building to meet a stranger. For the next two years, they usually remained in the world they created within their apartment. But, once, she accompanied them to a dinner of collectors, dealers, and curators. Ernst's status continued to rise in the art world and, once, after some progress on her part that pleased them, they invited her. Inevitably, the affair engendered a poem—

"And what is seeing?"

Once, she asked them not to touch her hand as it laid next to theirs on white linen surrounded by crystal wine glasses, silver cutlery and purple lilies. It was a black-tie affair and her dress was cut low, translucent in wise places and unabashedly luminous. They complied with her desire, even an hour later. But an hour later, she saw the sheen break across their forehead from the effort of keeping their hand frozen when what they desperately wanted to do was take her fragile fingers and crush them until she fell to her knees. And during the fall, she would have bared her throat. The tendon would have leapt. "And what is seeing?" It is how they saw her notice the strain of their effort but remained silent, offering no reprieve so that the price they would extract later amidst twisted bed sheets would be high

*...the price extracted amidst twisted bed sheets...*Elena thought writing the scene would write it out of herself or dissipate its energy in the way novelists dilute the energy to write out their story when they talk about it too much to others.

But she failed: writing the first poem birthed an entire book of similarly-oriented poems. The book sold well, or as well as a poetry collection can sell. Critics also responded well to the book which bore the following blurb from poet-critic Alfred A. Yuson:

Elena Theeland's poetry hits us right in the gut. Or should we say groin, since it is at once scintillating, skittish and seductive. Primal in its experimentation, fugitive in its tactile manipulation of recalcitrance and romance, ultimately there blooms a hardcore quality to her corpus' radical engagements. None of the formulaic ploys is on show here; rather a robust desire to attach, if so subtly, vivid back stories that pique and shape our palpable interest with full-bloodied allure. The uniformly sensuous appeal of her wide-ranging work—from the lyric to the exegesic, to the imperial prose units—is served by no less than either a canny courtesan or a come-hither voluptuary. Or both. Universally is she betrothed.

Upon first seeing Alfred's blurb, Elena thought, *So I succeeded?* She put her finger on the beginning of the blurb and traced each letter as she re-read it again—attention, rarely awarded to a poet's words, demands savoring.

Then Elena thought, *Surely you succeeded, Ernst? Surely your fortitude was rewarded?*

Chapter 4

4 JANUARY

Once upon a time, a dictator approached the grey building where Ernst waited. Well, it wasn't literally The Dictator who approached. But to Ernst who was observing Elena, her figure cast a shadow on the sidewalk under the sun's all-discerning eye and the shadow was not of Elena but a man. The man's dark profile was familiar to Ernst whose prolonged and exhaustive research had caused them to memorize many images of The Dictator. Ernst saw The Dictator's shadow behind Elena. They also noticed her shoulders lifted and tensed by stress. Ernst concluded, *The Dictator took away your magnificence. But I will help you recover it.*

As Ernst heard the buzzer indicating Elena was pushing at the building's intercom, the painter in them thought, *The Dictator does not belong in your portrait.*

27 MAY

Once upon a time, a stranger watched her approach their building. When they heard their intercom announce her arrival, they said her name out loud: "Elena."

They watched her enter their apartment, how she dispersed space so that their furniture seemed a little displaced even as they knew they hadn't moved. Elena didn't seem aware that as she moved throughout the apartment, her fingers trailed across the surfaces of whatever she approached, then passed—walls, the top of the sofa and cushion, the coffee table as she leaned over to place her bag by its side.

But Elena was fully aware of what she was doing. When the elevator door had opened onto the third floor, she'd stepped out onto the reality of a luminous celadon ocean. *Be like water,* she counseled me as she approached the stranger's door. *Touch everything presented before you.*

Yes, I agreed. *I will touch everything in the stranger's world.*

My body shall be a voracious ocean: my flesh shall touch everything…

Thus, Elena was not surprised when they observed, "You're memorizing everything through touch."

Smiling, they added, "Will you do the same with me?"

She looked at the stranger, sitting opposite her on a chair. She said, "No doubt I won't limit myself to surface. I'm consistent that way."

The stranger's smile evaporated as they pondered her words. Then, suddenly, Elena felt tears well out because they replied, "Your consistency can be difficult. I am sorry that your father was brutalized before he was killed."

She bowed her head to meet her hands rising to cover her face. They stopped her hands. They were on their knees before her, pulling her hands down to her lap. Then they raised their hands to support her face. They didn't wipe away her tears. They said, "Remember: we are not to hide from each other."

She showed them then. With every ripple of her skin, every clenching of her wet lashes, every bite of her lips, her face showed them a man in a dim alley, his beloved Panama hat a few feet away from a face stripped of identity. The once well-fitting linen suit was not just dirty but seemed awkward around his body because so many of the man's bones were broken. His blood cloaked the entirety of the visible universe. And against his right palm, lying open in either supplication or acceptance, was a small black-and-white photograph: a younger Elena, so innocent her white teeth gleamed as she smiled at her father who'd so often raised his camera for her beloved image.

"He should be here instead of you," she whispered as she took back her hands. She wiped away her tears as she leaned back from them.

They stood and backed away.

"Water?" they offered.

"Please."

As they walked towards the kitchen, Elena composed herself. She looked around the room. She looked at the paintings stacked against the walls. *So many paintings,* she thought.

She looked at them returning to her with a glass of water. She thought, *I, too, will pursue this healing—this emptying even as the past will keep stubbornly and generously returning with its anguish.*

25 AUGUST

Once upon a time, a stranger stood beside a window watching a woman approach the grey building where they'd lived and worked for over a decade. They had not yet met in person, but knew things and suspected more things about her. After becoming an artist, they'd began looking for her. If they were going to make art, they knew they had to remake themself as not simply the inheritor of certain circumstances. They decided to meet her and, if needed, be available to help or improve the situation of someone their father had helped make an orphan. Once they found her—a discovery facilitated by the internet and overlaps between the art and poetry worlds—they began longing for the day when they would stand by a window watching her approach them. They relished the air connecting them by speaking her name out loud: "Elena."

To their eyes, Elena seemed to float as she approached their building. *She floats because she thinks no one is watching her,* they thought. With that thought, they corrected themself: actually—and so incongruously it's as if they were fictionalizing the matter—they had met once before.

They had been sitting on the corner of a traffic island on Baker and 5th Street. In front of them, a piece of dirty cardboard proclaimed:

PLEAS

It was one of their performance art happenings, but most of the traffic no doubt considered them a beggar who couldn't spell.

Elena had rolled down her window when her car stopped in front of a red light. She held out a $10 bill as she said, "To break agony's greed—that's my plea."

Her plea was also a confession bearing the type of honesty one can make only to strangers or others one anticipates never seeing again.

He recited his memorized response to those who engaged with him: "Art without a social justice component is ever at risk of not transcending masturbation."

Then they mumbled "Thanks" as they reached for the money. When their hands touched briefly, the universe shifted and they were no longer trading money on a dirty street for a dubiously-achievable goal. They were lying on a beach, under the shade of a palm tree. They were leaning over her laughing face, grinning at her. They had wanted the story to continue, or begin, but their shared touch was brief and they were soon back on the traffic island, watching her window roll back up, the light turn green, her car move away, and street cacophony return to their ears to erase the song of waves.

Elena: so I didn't imagine you, they thought as the intercom buzzed. As they touched the intercom button to open the building's front door, they began to smile. It's always interesting, they knew, when fallen angels meet each other in their human forms.

As they waited, they thought, *Elena, I wonder if you know who you are ...*

"Elena," they found themself whispering, "I wonder if you know who you are..."

Speaking out loud woke them. They could still sense their lips moving to form the words they'd been uttering in a dream. They turned their head to the surprise of light outside their window. They had overslept, a rare occurrence. They only overslept when they wanted a dream to continue—when they preferred the dream to reality. It happened rarely because, as they told themself with irritation as they rose from their bed, *You know better than to remain too long in dreams.*

As they moved on towards the bathroom and the rest of the implacable day, they berated themself: *Angels? Get real...!*

12 OCTOBER

Once upon a time, Ernst dreamt again as they could not stop dreaming.

"To be human is to dream," they heard Elena say before she appeared in their dream. She was borne in the arms of a muscular angel approaching their building. They stood in front of a window watching them. As they came closer, the angel disappeared and it was Elena coming nearer to them. Suddenly, Ernst coughed: Ernst suddenly felt a moment they were certain would happen. Someday, no, *soon*, Ernst anticipated, their mouth would be stuffed blissfully with Elena's dark, lustrous hair.

Soon, they salivated, they would learn the taste of the monochrome color gold.

26 JANUARY

Once upon a time, Ernst watched Elena approach their building. *There,* they told themself, *there is the past and present colliding.* Once, they smiled because they wanted to be optimistic.

Later, they would cradle her face and recall a poem she'd written about "the sweetness of damp cheeks." Their initial reaction to the line had been to wonder, *Optimistic? Or unrealistic?*

"Afterwards, the police found a note by Papa's body," Elena was telling them. The note presented the scrawled words:

HUNTER ORDERED

"You know," Elena said through her tears, "back then it didn't cost much to hire gunmen.

"My father was a good and accomplished man! His life was taken for 5,000 pesos! A hundred dollars!"

Gently, Ernst pulled Elena into a hug and rubbed her back as, together, they recalled "Smokey Mountain," a mountain of trash among the slums of a city where they'd spent their younger years. Elena was sharing how her dead father was discovered there by one of the slum dwellers who daily poked through Smokey Mountain for recyclables, discarded possessions they could use, and even food. By Smokey Mountain, an entire industry had arisen from "pagpag"—food scavenged from the landfill, boiled in hot water, then re-cooked with new spices. Sadly, the boiling never fully eliminated elements that would cause Hepatitis A, typhoid, diarrhea, and cholera—there are so many ways to abuse the poor.

As Ernst continued to caress Elena, they chided themself, *You already know what she's telling you.*

As Ernst breathed in the slight perfume—*jasmine?* they wondered—from her hair, they silently promised, *I will help you. I have been waiting a long time to help you.*

Elena pulled back and took a deep breath. Wiping at her cheeks, she tried to smile as she said, "I'm sorry for ruining your shirt with my tears."

You could never ruin anything of me...flowers should never be crushed, especially paradoxically for perfume...

Out loud, Ernst replied, "I will help you."

11 APRIL

Once upon a time, Ernst watched Elena approach their grey building. They allowed the curve on their lips as they noted her eager pace.

Ernst smiled as they recalled their last meeting—how gloriously she'd blossomed. They'd smiled as they'd noted the volcanoes erupting in her eyes. She'd already pleasured them, but when she pleasured herself, too, she pleasured them again.

Know what you want, Elena, they whispered as she neared their building's front door. *To know what you want is to know yourself.*

30 AUGUST

Once upon a time, I entered a grey building to meet a stranger. I had not yet met them in person but we had communicated by email. I had not met them, but I had met their paintings. Since discovering their works in a group exhibit at Xavier Young Ze Gallery, I followed their progress. I attended other exhibits or read about them. I also researched backwards, looking for their older works. An artist's progress interests me, and I wanted to learn about their aesthetic trajectory. But I didn't learn about their personal life until after our first meeting.

From their Wikipedia entry which had been updated since I first checked it, I learned that Ernst Blazer was born and grew up as a young person in Pacifica where their father Stephen Blazer served at the U.S. embassy. After realizing they'd spent their childhood in my birth land, I thought to apply the term "diasporic" to their work. It's a term I learned from too much exposure to academics and theory; I'm no stranger to academia as I adjunct-teach creative writing when not writing my poems. When I looked at Ernst's trajectory based on their exhibitions, I noticed that each of their exhibits was markedly different from each other—as if a different artist created the works in each exhibition. I felt this trajectory to be "diasporic" in that the path can relate to a dislocated person ever in search of a place that doesn't exist, a place some might call *Home*.

I thought Ernst Blazer the artist never found a home in any particular place. After growing up in Pacifica, they attended three different colleges in three different U.S. states before receiving their art history degree from Yale. They then traveled, lived and worked in several countries before landing in the city where I met them. For a person of this background and experience, I speculated, it's not unexpected that perhaps the only home the artist would find is in their art.

Naturally, I came to share these thoughts with Ernst. To all of it, they simply shrugged and said, "Sure, Elena. Why not?"

21 JUNE

Once upon a time, I approached a grey building in the Tartarus neighborhood. I walked with a steady pace, deliberately steady to help face what I was doing and what was about to happen. I thought, *What are the odds ... ?*

Ernst stood by their window watching me. They noted the deliberateness of my pace, notwithstanding uncertainty over what was about to happen. They thought, *What are the odds ... ?*

Both considered their meeting a collision of past and present. Both wondered what actions they had taken in the past that contributed to this collision. *Or,* both thought, *do we lack such control over our lives?*

The buzzer sounded.

They heard the knock on their apartment door.

A lifetime of thoughts spun across the movie screen in their mind as they looked into each other's faces. But their first thought was *Elena! Your eyes are grey!*

Then light shifted and so did the color of her eyes back to dark purple. They thought, *The body is capable of so many masks...*

For the rest of their life, they will remember how Elena's eyes reverted again to grey after the discussion turned to the unlikely odds of their meeting: they, the child of the one who ordered the death of her father; she the daughter of the one ordered to be killed.

That they would meet, that they would engage compulsively with each other over two years, that they would make love before fully comprehending the relevance of forgiveness—*what are the odds?*

"But not improbable in Kapwa-time," they would trade saying with each other in the grey building where Kapwa-time rooted itself. Not improbable at all.

17 OCTOBER

Once upon a time, you approached a grey building where I waited for you. *I've waited forever, Elena*, I thought as I watched you from a third-story window. *I've even waited in Kapwa-time where waiting should not exist.*

Kapwa-time—you asked me how I came to believe in this concept.

"It's rooted in indigenous Pacifican values, Elena. I learned of it from my nanny who joined our household after Mom died from a car accident. I wasn't even a year old. Nanny Priscilla became my second mother. Nanny Priscilla used to tell me stories before I'd go to sleep. Many were about Pacifica's indigenous culture."

"I'm sorry about your mother," you said. "You must miss her..."

"To this day. My longing puts a lie to that saying that one can't miss what one doesn't know."

"Do you know much about her?"

"Only what my father shared. She was from the Philippines who went to Pacifica for work. The Philippines sends many of its people abroad as it can't offer enough employment opportunities. My father met her as one of the janitors who cleaned the embassy's offices. She was college-educated but that was the only job she could find."

"I'd read somewhere about the Philippines calling its overseas foreign workers 'national heroes' for the remittances they send back..." You paused as you sensed the topic starting to become painful for me. Most children will miss a dead parent until their own deaths.

"So, was your Nanny Priscilla Itonguk?" you asked, referring to Pacifica's indigenous people as you changed the topic.

"Yes. And very generous. She possessed enough kindness to mother me. I grew to love her very much after she taught me love."

"What do you remember most about her?"

"Her openness, and yet acceptance of anything and everything. It seemed impossible to surprise her—she accepted everything that happened to her, including me and my father."

"She certainly sounds unusual..."

The warmth in your eyes showed you'd become positively predisposed towards Nanny Priscilla.

"Yes. She's the one who first counseled me about my unease over gender. She said that the idea of gender fluidity is not so unusual among her people. Among Itonguks, gender is based more on social function rather than physical sexual characteristics, which is how my father falsely characterized the matter. Nanny Priscilla's normalizing of my situation was quite helpful— it helped me cope with others who were less open as I grew up and when I entered the larger world, beginning with college."

I left unsaid: "It helped with dealing with my father."

The warmth in your eyes deepened as your appreciation for Nanny Priscilla increased. "She must have been a comfort, too, after your father forced you to separate from Sammy and Mr. Bellow?"

"Yes," I said, then laughed. "She wanted to see my skirt. She got quite mad when I told her that my father took it away and, I assume, trashed it."

I paused as our conversation brought back emotional memories of my beloved nanny. "That's when she told me the story of Lakapati, a transgender deity of fertility and agriculture. Lakapati lived during a time when there were individuals born with male sexual organs but who were seen and considered as women by society. They married other men, dressed in women's clothing, and partook of activities often associated with women, such as weaving. They were not considered abnormal but were thought of as people who were closer to the divine. Many became spiritual authorities in their communities."

I quirked an eyebrow at you as your smile began widening into a grin.

"Don't say it! No need to say anything," I laughed. "More often than not, Nanny Priscilla reminded me there wasn't anything divine about my behavior!"

As you also laughed, my memories deepened.

"I once asked her how she came to be so unflappable..."

"And?" you prodded gently, obviously curious.

I shook my head to return from the past to you.

"Nanny Priscilla said she accepted that life will always raise something or someone new, and that she cannot anticipate everything but must be open to what arrives. The world, she often said, *is* multiple and diverse. Therefore, the world, she often stressed, *must be accepted* as multiple and diverse."

"Indigenous and sophisticated," you observed.

"Yes. She certainly made me admire indigenous culture. Kapwa, she once said, means that despite diversity, *One is All and All is One.*"

9 NOVEMBER

Once upon a time, Ernst watched a woman approach a grey building. From the window of their third-floor apartment, they watched the woman intently; they saw how her pace slowed as she neared the building. *As she neared them...* Her pace was the opposite of eagerness. She was not Elena.

She was Madeleine, a woman they'd met before Elena. They characterized their relationship as "intense" in ways they found pleasurable, but their engagement ended poorly.

A relationship can end badly for many reasons: unrealistic expectations of each other, the wrong scent, naivete, cynicism...

But such reasons pale, Ernst understood, to a more determinant factor: their reluctance to take on emotional risks. They can never forget Madeleine's question at their last meeting: "How can you help me, or others, grow if you remain stunted?"

They were determined to change for Elena—a goal they rationalized to themself as something that also would benefit their paintings (though, whenever their mind went along these lines, they couldn't help mocking themself: *For art's sake? Who do you think you're fooling?*).

Ernst was determined that Elena would always approach their building with eagerness. For the two years they met with Elena, they never failed to watch each of her approaches. Elena, they thought the second time they watched her approach their building, *You must always be eager.*

Please... be always eager.

14 FEBRUARY

Once upon a time, she approached a grey building. No pots surrounded its austere entrance, pots from where flowers bloomed with thick, colorful petals perfuming the air with memories. As oenophiles can attest, scents become eternal through sharing memories—a means, in some cases, for creating relationships or achieving community. But no potted flowers cheerfully waved by the grey building. Later, when she observed this lack to the stranger, they replied, "Asceticism is freeing."

She turned towards the window so they wouldn't see her frown. They saw through her effort.

"What do you dispute," they said.

She sighed, then turned away from the winter sky for the grey in their eyes.

"I love roses," she said simply.

Briefly, they smiled. But no smile lingered as they hugged her closer. Against the nape of her neck, the stranger whispered, "Roses are ferocious—they know to integrate thorns."

27 NOVEMBER

Once upon a time, she walked from sunlight into a grey building's steel elevator.

"Well, yes," she whispered at her blurry reflection against the steel walls. "I'm also just making memories that will remain stubbornly even if, in my last hours, I shall be senile as I lie dying."

The stranger, though, made her feel silly for making decisions based on anticipated deathbed ruminations. Once, they left their bed to continue painting on the canvas they'd brought closer to their bed. They said, "Make memories for now."

To clarify their position, they paused their brush, ignoring the scarlet drips to the floor, to say, "Tomorrows are just illusions."

Jokingly, she reached for her notebook by the nightstand, as if to write down something about the moment. But when they turned back to their painting, she let the notebook slip to her lap as she watched them. She wanted to inhabit fully the present that contained them. For the rest of the day, the notebook page remained blank.

❦

She did not know that Ernst had departed for a memory's other world.

"Tomorrows are just illusions," they said, and the thought immediately yanked them back to the past.

"Dad!" they were saying, shocked. "Dad!"

Then they continued, "Stephen ..."

They continued with their father's name rather than "Dad," as if the linguistic switch would eliminate their father-son link. As if language, indeed, could create reality.

Later, they stepped back from the painting they were trying to finish. Looking at it, they concluded, unsurprised but with grimness: "Another failure."

22 JANUARY

Once upon a time she walked towards a building whose greyness, she thought, could be relieved by red tulips blooming on both sides of its doorway.

"I would have thought you'd prefer red roses," the stranger said when she later shared her thought.

"Yes, but just the color red would evoke my favorite flower," she said. "The reminder would suffice to plant roses in my mind. Meanwhile, tulips would be more unexpected."

"Unexpected only to you," they said. The moment was one of many that taught her about subjectivity.

Their lesson was harsher when, on her next visit, they presented her with a bouquet of red tulips. She didn't express anything but gratitude. But she knew they knew: she was disappointed despite the red's reminder of roses. There are limits to thoughts remaining thoughts when they should be embodied. In her mind, the roses preened, but as they slowly twirled each bloom lost petals until, too soon, nothing relieved the starkness of stems spewing forth thorns.

Later that day when she left the stranger's apartment, she took the tulips with her. She noticed the flowers' lack of perfume as she walked down the hallway, rode down the elevator, and walked out of the grey building. On the streets, she looked back once to confirm the grey building could no longer be sighted. Then she looked for the nearest trash can, and topped it with tulips.

"Hey!" she heard a startled passerby say as she walked away. But she did not look back at the flowers—the petals which failed to form her beloved roses.

20 MARCH

Once upon a time, she ascended through an elevator to the third floor of a grey building. The doors opened. When she walked out, she stepped out to walk on a sea. She waded for several minutes before she reached the entrance to Apartment 3J.

When she knocked on the door, flesh met steel. When they pulled her against them for their first embrace, steel met flesh. Both acts preceded other openings awaiting the future.

Right then, she was still knocking on the stranger's door for the first time. Painted a lime green, the door opened. Later, when she explained the green enhanced the presence of a sea in the hallway, they raised an eyebrow and said, "That was the color on sale when the landlord decided to paint all of the doors."

With that revelation, she began to see how the sublime can be affected by a cheap trick. Perhaps the stranger understood her sense of betrayal because at the end of their meeting, they said as a seeming non-sequitur to their discussion about their paintings, "To excavate truth, lies must crumble to become rubble tossed aside."

12 APRIL

Once upon a time, I wondered what would happen if I had brought a bouquet of red roses with me to meet a stranger in a grey building. I wondered, *Would the gift have accelerated intimacy?*

What a useless question, I realize now. Between us, intimacy spread swiftly enough to befit Kapwa-time: no beginning, no end, simply the eternal present. The poet Eileen R. Tabios is a strong influence on my work and, once, she wrote in a poetics essay:

> "...the moment, the space, from which I attempt to create poems: the human, by being rooted onto the planet but also touching the sky, is connected to everything in the universe and across all time, including that the human is rooted to the past and future—indeed, there is no unfolding of time. In that moment, all of existence—past, present and future—has coalesced into a singular moment, a single gem with an infinite expanse. In that moment, were I that human, I am connected to everything so that there is nothing or no one I do not know. I am everyone and everything, and everything and everyone is me. In that moment, to paraphrase something I once I heard from some Buddhist, German or French philosopher, or Star Trek character, 'No one or nothing is alien to me.'"

If the present the stranger and I created were an image, it would be of our first embrace, where the gesture was intensely formed by our bodies holding each other. We had held each other stubbornly despite the uncertainty flickering deep within our eyes.

15 FEBRUARY

Once upon a time, Ernst stood by their apartment window and watched a woman approach the grey building where they waited. *How did I get here?* they thought. They were unsure whether to be critical of themself or not.

Upon entering Apartment 3J, and not for the first time, the woman unbelted a grey trench coat before shrugging her shoulders lightly to make it fall behind her. She was naked except for a silk sapphire scarf knotted around her neck and a black leather belt cinched around her waist.

How did you get here? Ernst thought as they approached her. They looked into her eyes before they knelt: *sheen of dampness threatening to spill into a wave...*

Ernst knelt to pick up her coat. They rose and put it back over her shoulders. Surprised, she raised her hands to the lapels to cover her breasts.

Ernst walked away towards the window where they'd stood many times watching her approach. They looked back at her and said, "Elena, you should learn how to say No."

Elena turned her back as she lowered the coat slightly so that her arms could push through into the sleeves. She belted the coat as she turned back towards Ernst.

"But surely not to you, Ernst?" she said.

"We change, Elena. That's a good thing."

Elena gave them a confused look as she began walking away towards the door.

It pained Ernst to watch her, but they made themself continue to look.

"We change," they repeated, then clarified, "We grow..."

29 APRIL

Once upon a time, a woman approached a grey building to meet a stranger in their apartment. As her finger pushed at the intercom, she wondered, "Did I stalk you or did you stalk me?"

Months later, she asked the question of the stranger. They were in their bed. They had just raised a blanket over their bodies as they began to cool down. She had placed her palm over their heart to see if the question would affect its beat. But it stayed the same as they replied, "Did I please you or did you please me?"

Then they turned their focus to more pleasure.

But, later that evening, at the door where she was poised to leave, she turned around and placed a palm again over their heart. *The beat of horses galloping away from fear, or towards the needed water of a sighted river...* She smiled. But, mere minutes after leaving the grey building, she damned herself for continuing to feel pleasure from their encounters. For their father killed her father.

Chapter 5

10 JULY

Once upon a time, Elena approached a grey building to meet a stranger. Because of that stranger, she would come to meet Madeleine.

"Help me," she begged the surprised Madeleine after she'd tracked her to Scottsdale, a community accessible from the city through a commuter train. Fortunately, Madeleine's house was just 10 minutes of walking from the train stop. People on the train had been looking at her furtively, which made Elena suspect she was unsuccessful at hiding her anguish.

"Come in," Madeleine offered after Elena blurted out, "Ernst! I'm their..."

Elena couldn't find the words to describe her relationship with Ernst but understanding darkened Madeleine's green eyes when she mentioned Ernst's name. She raised a pale hand to push thick blonde hair away from her face before gesturing to invite Elena into her home.

Elena entered a large foyer where a chandelier cheerfully sparkled. Madeleine motioned her towards a living room on their left. It was a room that belonged in *Architectural Digest* with its plush sofas, inlaid wood floors, soft and lushly-wrought cushions etcetera etcetera with windows overlooking lovely views of a lush rose garden.

"Oh, I love roses..." Elena whispered as she sat on the sofa that Madeleine indicated.

"Something to drink?" Madeleine offered.

"Not tea..."

"Of course not. The topic, after all, is Ernst," Madeleine said. Smiling, she walked to the mahogany sideboard that featured a silver tray with crystal decanter and glasses (*an arrangement*, Elena thought later, *accommodating*

63

those not tasked with maintaining metals that tarnish). She poured a dark-red liquid into both glasses and brought them over to Elena. Elena took one of the glasses.

"Toast?" Madeleine asked.

Elena just looked at her.

"A joke! Don't mind me!" Madeleine said as she backed up to sit on a chair facing Elena.

"One: you don't seem confused over my presence. Two: you're quite cheerful," Elena observed. "I don't need to ask you questions. Just give me answers."

Madeleine sipped at her drink, then replied, "Do you like my house?"

Surprised, Elena looked about the room—noting, too, the preponderance of silver bibelots—and said, "Sure...?"

"She's in school right now but don't you think my daughter is lovely?!" Madeleine pointed at a silver-framed photograph of a girl photographed amid laughter, a missing front tooth only adding to her charm.

"Sure," Elena repeated.

"And my outfit!" Madeleine stood and turned around to show off her yellow fluffy sweater and tight black jeans accessorized by high-heeled ankle boots and a necklace-scarf ingeniously fashioned from woven safety pins. Elena recognized it as a sculpture made by a Dutch artist whose name she couldn't recall, but whose work also once festooned the black dress of Ernst's art dealer.

Elena remained silent, which didn't discourage Madeleine from saying as she sat down, "My outfit deserves appreciation—it's carefully curated, so to speak. I didn't just roll out of bed to put on a sweat suit."

Elena sighed before asking, "Your point...?"

"My point: I am happy!"

"I am happy," Madeleine continued, "even though, once, I was as morose as the self you've brought into my house. I am also capable: whatever I've done with my life has been effective in putting me into nice clothes, setting me up in a lovely house, raising a happy child, and making me greet most days with cheer so that I leap out of bed every morning eager for the day to unfold."

"Ernst..."

"Ernst," Madeleine said, leaning towards Elena, "helped put me on this path. If you're unhappy, confused, angry, frustrated or any such combinations of the above, it will pass. Ultimately, Ernst will uplift you, not make you fall!"

Madeleine sipped more wine, smiled as she relished its taste, then continued.

"The public knows them as an artist. But, privately? Well, if you've wielded a whip, you know."

Madeleine paused.

"Do you know?"

Elena didn't say anything.

Madeleine watched as a tear surfaced. Gently, she reached over with a fingertip and wiped it off Elena's cheek.

"Ernst would never whip others. But sometimes they teach others to wield the whip."

Elena whispered, "At first, I found it unfathomable. It's not something I'd ever thought about, let alone thought about doing."

"Yes," Madeleine said, nodding her head. "How does wielding a whip make you feel?"

"At first, to be frank, repelled. Then nervous."

"And now?"

"Empowered."

But then Elena burst into more tears. Trying to regain control, she tried to joke, "Ridiculous—how one cries over the matter of empowerment."

Madeleine sighed. "True. But not when Ernst…"

"Yes," Elena said, wiping her cheeks after Madeleine paused for a while. "It's difficult to continue."

Madeleine breathed deeply and straightened up. She looked at Elena squarely.

"No. Let's continue—let's say the thing for what it is. Ernst allows themself to be the whip's recipient to redeem their father's past."

They stared at each other. Articulation often transforms what may be amorphous to undeniable reality. For a while, Elena didn't know what to say. When she did, it was to raise a less important point.

"That's why I looked for you, came to you."

Madeleine nodded. Then she said slowly as if she was choosing her words carefully, "It can be difficult to continue something that helps you but not the one bearing the brunt of the healing, especially if they choose not to see it that way."

There were more conversation, more tears and soothing, a break for the bathroom, and so on before Madeleine showed Elena out of her door. What Elena did not see, though she turned around once to wave at Madeleine, was how Madeleine shut her door, entered her living room, and looked around for comfort by resting her gaze on various cherished objects and then the photograph of her child.

"Of course there will be scars," she whispered as her gaze lingered on her daughter's face. "But can one understand, let alone appreciate, joy without also knowing its opposite?"

Then she sent a thought out to accompany Elena towards the train station, to enter the train and travel with her to the city, to depart from the train and catch a subway, to float up from the belly of the subway station and traverse a path that, soon, will make it approach a grey building. The thought will bypass doors and float up three floors before hovering in front of a window to Ernst's apartment. The thought will look through the window while delivering its hope: *Good luck, Ernst, in making sure Elena's last thoughts of you will not wallow in dismay.*

Meanwhile, Madeleine couldn't help but remember the last words she'd flung at Ernst: "You need to share yourself, too, Ernst! You create damage when you fail—when the most you offer is your back! After me, don't think you can keep using your difficult upbringing as an excuse!"

She mentally spat back the reductive statement Ernst had used during their interactions: *Unless you want to wallow in victimhood, no excuses. No excuses.*

5 APRIL

Once upon a time, Elena approached a grey building to meet a person who was no longer a stranger. Their name was Ernst, and they seemed to like smiling at her. When she first met them, they usually presented an unreadable face. Once, she asked, "Do you ever smile?"

Elena would learn that it wasn't that Ernst avoided smiling. They had trained their face to remain impassive and a smile—like a frown—was simply a crack they did not want to allow.

"Emotions are for showing, not hiding," Elena said.

In response, they looked at her for a while, as if they were trying to decide whether to share their thoughts. Elena quirked an eyebrow, and it made them smile. It also made them share their thoughts, but it wasn't what Elena expected.

They said, "Dictatorships have long, wide-ranging aftermaths. Their effects are often unknown until they occur. When I was young and grappling with my family's history in Pacifica, I often had to push through my feelings to get to some insight that was hard to attain. Initially, I learned the wrong lesson—that emotions are best kept hidden in a dictator's aftermath."

"The wrong lesson? You are harsh on yourself," Elena said. "You were younger, not the more mature person you are now as you approach your forties."

"More mature, but I still have to learn what Nanny Priscilla tried to teach me—to open myself to others."

Elena reached for them then, placing a palm along their unshaven cheek. She didn't mind its roughness, especially when they added as they leaned closer to her caress, "It's becoming easier with you."

24 SEPTEMBER

Once upon a time, Ernst watched Elena approach their building. As the intercom announced her arrival, they looked around at their current crop of canvases propped up against their walls.

"Well, she'll surely provide some relief from you all," they announced out loud to their paintings.

Their current series was not going well. They were making paintings by using single-hair brushes because one of their dealers, during some idle chitchat, had insisted "the painters of ancient India and China have done all that can be achieved with single-hair brushstrokes."

Not with monochromes, they'd thought. But, so far, their dealer was right. Their paintings to date were titled "Derivative 1," "Derivative 2," "Derivative 3" and so on.

"You disappoint me. I thought you'd be different," they mock-chided "Derivative 12" as they passed it on their way to the door.

Ah, Elena, they thought as they opened the door, *Please be different.*

"Elena."

Silently, she entered. When she didn't smile at them, her countenance heartened Ernst.

Usually, they thought, *they smile at the beginning...*

15 JUNE

Once upon a time, Elena approached a grey building to meet a painter, Ernst. At their last meeting, they had shown her a painting, a monochrome of a tan color so pale she initially thought it to be an untouched, bare canvas. *You showed me a painting but there was nothing on it to see,* she thought. Her steps faltered as the thought surfaced. *Or maybe you were painting nothingness?*

Shortly after entering Ernst's apartment, she said as she stared at the painting, unchanged since their last meeting, "If this is nothingness, you've painted my life."

She heard silence, and turned around for Ernst's response.

"You're surprised," she said as she looked at their frown. "I'm surprised you're surprised."

"Elena, the good thing about a painting is that it can be changed," they said, approaching her. "I can paint something there, perhaps a man, perhaps your father. I can even avoid painting a hat to avoid the need to paint a shadow that would obscure the man's face."

They both turned to look at the painting.

"If your life has been nothing, or nothingness," Ernst said, "you can still change it."

Ernst went towards their brushes, and picked one up.

"Here," they said, offering it.

"What do you mean?" Elena asked, startled.

"I want you to change this painting. I want you to be the one to change it."

Elena smiled and accepted the brush.

"Sure, I'll play. But changing this painting won't change my life, Ernst."

Ernst just made a shooing motion with their hand, and walked towards the living room area.

"Go on. I'll catch up on some research, then catch up with you."

Years later, as Elena looked at The Dictator's grandson hugging her daughter, she thought, *But changing that painting—wielding that brush!—did change my life, Ernst. How did you know?*

She remembered not adding figures onto the painting. She'd only changed the color. From the color she'd interpreted as nothingness, she had painted the fortitude of an oval luminescent green—like an emerald island floating in a blue sapphire ocean.

Jewels. *I want to live my life in Technicolor!*

28 MAY

Once upon a time, Ernst opened the door to their grey building. As they waited for Elena, they wondered, *What do you know, beautiful stranger?*

They weren't surprised by the arc of their engagement, but they were surprised by several of the details that would create the arc. One, in particular, made them laugh—

Elena stepped off the bus that let her out on Hamilton Avenue, the city's primary shopping strip. She hurried in and out of the stores looking for a particular scarf, looking for what they hadn't known they'd suggested she obtain (obviously, they couldn't control her interpretations). At one store, two sales women looked her up and down, then traded belittling eyes with each other. Elena wondered if they were mocking the belt of stainless steel circles she'd cinched around her waist but outside her black blazer.

"It's outdated!" she'd protested when Ernst discovered it deep in her closet. It was their first visit to her apartment but they proceeded to explore every inch because, by then, she'd given them the right to explore as much of her as they cared to know.

"The metal circles will be useful," they'd said. Then they watched intently as she blushed.

Later, the metal circles provided a useful handhold as she stood on tiptoes. The belt was wrapped around a beam. One by one, slowly, her clothes fell to puddle around her ankles.

Afterwards—oh, how she loathed the waiting!—they wiped the sweat from her body with the long scarf she'd eventually found in a small boutique on Hamilton Avenue: sweat, not blood.

"From my country," the store owner smiled as she spread out the scarf to reveal a profusion of colorful, wide-petaled flowers Elena couldn't identify.

"Do you have a scarf with roses?" Elena asked.

The vendor shook her head. Because of her sad eyes, Elena purchased the scarf. As Ernst used it to dry her off, they asked, "What kind of flowers are these?"

"I don't know. I didn't ask," she whispered. Then she opened her eyes to look at Ernst as she said. "What's the point of knowing? Isn't it enough that they aren't roses."

"Elena," Ernst said, their eyes suddenly like pieces of grey slate under rain. "A scarf painted with roses *still* would not be roses."

Ernst flung away the scarf and she teared up from their disappointment. As she wiped away her tears, she saw the boutique owner's sad eyes: grey as the building in which she met a stranger who received her trust. *Such sad eyes*—from a type of grief, she suddenly felt, that could only be caused by knowledge.

24 AUGUST

Once upon a time, she walked towards a grey building where a stranger waited for her. In the stranger's apartment, 3J, she would try to surprise them as well as herself. Once, her wrists and ankles were pink for several days from the masking tape to which they'd surrendered.

The masking tape was used on just one occasion; the scarves were in another bag she'd forgotten to bring when she couldn't concentrate as she prepared for her next visit. Or, rather, she could concentrate only on the memory of their last meeting—the ziggurat tattoo on her inner left thigh throbbed in anticipation of seeing them.

Lacking scarves, they'd looked for alternatives and noticed the roll of masking tape on the nearby window ledge. Afterwards, she loathed the sticky residue it left on her flesh. Relaxing in the bathtub, they watched her reflection on the mirror. She frowned as scrubbing with soap failed to take off the masking tape's stickiness.

"I'll deal with it later," she finally sighed and turned to look at them.

"Good idea," they grinned. "Bath time!"

They continued to see her, wet and fragrant, as they began a new series of paintings that evening. The paintings all share the same palette: grey. At times, the monochrome canvases lean towards silver. At times they are less metallic and more matte. Once, the color seems to be on the verge of washing into white (*the white of a bath's frothy soap bubbles*, they'd thought). But, always, the paintings are grey.

Months later, she would see the paintings at their show at a new exhibition. A few hours before the opening, they gave her a tour, watching her face intently as she looked at each painting. They gave her space as she walked from one canvas to another, but followed her. Finally, she looked at them with a quizzical smile.

"I'm trying to see why each painting is named after me," she said softly.

They had named each painting "E #1," "E #2," and so on until the 13th painting, "E #13."

"I know the 'E' is for my name's initial," she said. "Don't deny it."

"I'm not denying," they said.

"So, why me?" she said. "And where *is* me in all that grey?"

"The masking tape was grey."

With robust enjoyment, they watched intently as, slowly, she blushed.

11 OCTOBER

Once upon a time, I entered a grey building to meet them. I would come to visit them numerous times and, per our agreement, each visit formed a new experience.

"Repetition," they stressed during our early meetings when they laid down the "ground rules" for our engagement, "should only occur in our memories—perhaps to serve as emphasis for certain moments. But let's. not repeat what happens in each encounter."

I agreed, though I'd already anticipated the moment when, at my tears, they would observe, "We're repeating ourselves."

After their New York show of grey monochrome paintings inspired by their experience with grey "masking tape," Ernst had another exhibit of newer work from the same series, as requested by a British dealer who saw their works at their New York gallery. The paintings involved grey as well but also featured brushstrokes of pink in a variety of shades.

They invited her to see that exhibit, taking care of all the flight and hotel arrangements for London.

"Thank you!" she exclaimed happily as she twirled in their hotel room, wanting to memorize every single detail of their suite. In particular, she lingered over the crystal vase of red roses on her nightstand. When she saw it, she looked at them and repeated, whispering, "Thank you."

As with the other exhibit, they gave her space to see during the opening, even as they followed her from one painting to another. She wore a red sleeveless and knee-length dress she'd found in the hotel closet.

"No need for other accessories, jewelry or stockings," they'd said as they handed her grey high-heeled shoes.

As she moved from one painting to another, she noticed that they again had titled the 14 paintings after her, starting with "E. #14."

She paused the longest in front of the last painting, lingering until they noticed that I was no longer paying attention to the painting but seemed to be trying to control my emotions. They walked over and, with their body, blocked the gallery crowd from my view. They tipped my head up and noticed the sheen in my eyes.

"What?" they whispered.

"Pink?" I said.

"Variations of pink," they agreed. "There is the more vivid scarlet in a couple of the paintings."

"These paintings are what you meant when you told me you wanted to paint me blushing!"

"Why does that upset you? Didn't you expect me to paint you?"

"I'm not just material for you, am I?"

Then, without waiting for them to reply, she straightened her shoulders and firmly said, "I am not your fodder!"

Despite the tear still slowly etching a scar across the blush powder on her cheek, they briefly smiled. They said, "That's right, Elena."

5 FEBRUARY

Once upon a time, she pushed open the heavy door into a grey building. She did not yet know, that first time, that she would come to repeat the pushing gesture against their chest in an encounter that would mix blood with tears. They had just finished saying, "My blood is yours."

"Look," the stranger said. "Your blood wept."

She raised her damp face from her elbows where she'd sought succor. They were lying on their bed, facing each other. She looked surprised.

She repeated slowly after them, "My blood wept..."

They raised an eyebrow as they looked at her. Then they stood and walked over to a nearby carafe.

When they returned to offer her a glass of water, they said, "You're welcome."

She took the glass. Before she sipped, she said, "What should I have thanked you for?"

They said, drily, before they turned to walk towards the bathroom, "Your next poem."

🌀 🌀 🌀

Entwined Hay(na)ku

When I bleed
I camouflage
Tears

୧୨

When I weep
I camouflage
blood

17 SEPTEMBER

Once upon a time, Ernst watched a woman approach their building. Air shimmered in front of their window pane, silvering the light. *Lovely*, they thought, before dismissing it. The effect usually happened when they looked through the pane with a glass wave pattern. They moved slightly to look at Elena through a clear glass pane. They thought, *Lovelier...*

They would come to share this moment with Elena as she protested against accompanying them to an exhibition of paintings by Lucas "Lucifer" Straight.

"Yuck. I have no desire to see his polluted landscapes," she pouted. Still, she put on her coat because they'd promised her lunch afterwards at Jack's Bistro whose French onion soup she always enjoyed.

"Have you ever seen his paintings?" they said, opening the door.

"Just reproductions," she admitted as she walked out. "But the images didn't pique my interest."

Elena still felt the pout on her lips as they arrived at the gallery, as they walked through the gallery doors. *At least lunch will be good*, she anticipated about the restaurant a block away from the gallery.

Lunch occurred after 5 p.m. Elena had insisted on staying until the gallery closed.

"What a revelation!" she said as she gulped down her soup. "Did you see his brushstrokes! Or, not see the brushstrokes! He didn't make a canvas with an image! He made the actual image! I swear there was a dimensionality to that fog he painted so that it felt like you could walk through it! I actually felt a slight shiver from its chill! And, while walking, I even felt the urgent care to be sure to step carefully around the wet debris on the ground! You had these visceral feelings about something physically real—you weren't looking *at* something; you were in it!

"But you couldn't see what's brilliant on the paintings until you actually saw them! The reproductions I saw couldn't capture the absences that made the paintings brilliant! He erased the sense of the painting as a painting!"

Reproductions often fail to live up to what they're imitating, Ernst thought as they listened to Elena's enthusiasm. They noticed her eyes had alit to translucent violet—*like seaglass*, they thought. As a child, they'd collected them from the shores of Pacifica.

After Elena calmed down, they said, "Have you ever compared what you see through wavy glass versus clear glass?"

Surprised, Elena replied, "No. Your point?"

"Sometimes, the imperfections of glass serve to enhance the prettiness of a picture one sees through it. A wavy area might hide a blemish. Or the wavy glass might effect a silvery sheen upon the image, making it look better. But clear glass presents the picture for what it is, blemishes and all. Some viewers prefer the more truthful image."

"Because it's more honest?" Elena said. "Like, 'Truth is Beauty and Beauty is Truth'?"

Ernst just smiled and dropped the topic when the waitress arrived with their main courses; hungry, Elena also was diverted easily by the flavorful coq au vin. When Truth and Beauty next arose in the future, the references would occur through Elena's anger.

"It's not true, or always true! Truth can be Beauty, but so can a Lie!" Elena hissed. "Right now, I wish I was hearing you tell me my father died from a single bullet shot, not from days of prolonged torture!

"That, Ernst, would be beautiful!"

Ernst let her rage. *There's a time for everything,* they thought as they simply watched her after she rejected their embrace. But they also understood, sighing deeply inside without breaking the impassive façade they showed to Elena, *Sometimes, time runs short...*

3 NOVEMBER

Once upon a time, Elena entered a grey building to meet a stranger. Whatever she was thinking, she was not anticipating that before the day ended, she would recall one of the ghosts haunting her dreams: BeeBee, The Dictator's son who continued Pacifica's demise.

Marc "BeeBee" Con and his father were forever graffitied upon her memory through a particular photograph. They, along with their family, military advisors and other supporters, stood on a balcony of their palace watching masses of marching protesters. The protesters presented the maelstrom of society: businessmen and garbage men, students and professors, socialites and their maids, nuns and mothers, artists and mothers, grandchildren and grandparents. About them all, BeeBee urged his father, "Kill them! Bomb them all!"

His father, The Dictator, stayed silent as BeeBee embarked on a tirade— "Who do they think they are?" etcetera and all spicily interspersed with a young, spoiled, and privileged boy's obscenities.

Elena's father might still be alive were it not for The Dictator and his henchmen. But on that day, too late for Elena's Dad but thankfully not for many others, The Dictator improbably said, "No. I will not kill these people, *my* people."

Elena recalled the balcony image when Ernst observed, "Humans are interesting. So much of our monstrous behavior are inexplicably part of being human."

Minutes earlier, Ernst also had shared, "I no longer have parents."

Surprised, Elena said, "You're an orphan, too?"

Ernst turned away as if to ignore her question. But they paused, looked back at Elena, and softly said, "It was tough for my father to understand how his 'son' was not a man."

Their tone was the softness of cotton laundered over a thousand times, just a breath away from fraying.

After returning home that evening, Elena discovered that Ernst wasn't actually an orphan. They simply had disavowed their parents. Wikipedia and other online sites were stuffed with encomium about these "pillars of the community" in St. Louis. *There are so many ways to lose a parent,* she thought. *So many ways to lose.*

With his second wife, Ernst's father stared at Elena from her computer screen. She felt as if she'd met him before, then realized he and Ernst shared similar eyes. Like Ernst's, his eyes were dark with impassivity; splash a certain slant of light against them and the result would be walls. In one snapshot, he smiled during a fundraising dinner honoring him and Ernst's stepmother, but his eyes were unchanged from another snapshot of him "sadly" (according to the caption) looking at the empty shelves of a food bank he was about to support with a new donation.

What did you teach your son about feelings? Elena wondered. *As someone whose existence came to be denied by his own child, how did you teach Ernst how to feel?*

As no one answered, Elena thought back to earlier that day. She was watching Ernst contemplate a painting-in-progress for nearly an hour without moving. When they finally lifted their brush, they smeared a careless red brushstroke against the yellow canvas. She heard them whisper, "Light is rarely pure."

20 DECEMBER

Once upon a time, Elena approached a grey building to meet Ernst. As they always did when they met, Ernst watched her approach. *Yes!* they thought, then grinned. They discerned something new in her walk that day: a swagger to her hips.

They heard the intercom and turned eagerly towards its sound. When Elena walked through their door, they said, "This time, I'm at your service."

Elena smiled as she walked slowly towards them.

"Yes," she said. "This time, it's my turn..."

From them, she received a training no one else could have given—a training crafted from trying to redeem their past that included their father and his actions. Their training also reflected a technique long proven for its effectiveness: they merely opened the door. They opened the door slightly, but she had to be the one to walk into the space of her potential—she had to enter by herself. She had to be the one to push the door open, wide open.

18 OCTOBER

Once upon a time a grey building loomed over her footsteps. She looked at it and warned, "You'd do best to remember: I once advised Rapunzel to cut her hair and braid a rope for her escape!"

Then she remembered: Rapunzel was in a world in her mind. But in this world where the grey building loomed with a waiting stranger inside, her body was in play. Her flesh was at risk.

"But at risk not simply to pain," the stranger reminded her as they slipped a button from its keyhole, "You're also at risk to rapture."

She'd drafted so many prose poems about the Rapunzel in her mind— prose poems, not verse, as she couldn't bear to *break* any of the lines about Rapunzel struggling to free herself. She titled the first poem of the series "Rapunzel, Enrapt," and it began

> She locks the entrance to the turret containing a thousand diaries whose papers are yellowed and leather covers cracked. Then she feeds the key to an alligator. She is outside where ants clamber up the velvet folds masking her thighs (she actually scents grass!). She understands gloves are old-fashioned but has resigned herself to certain constraints: it takes time for the ink stains on her hands to fade. But she has crossed the moat. As she peers at the stolid, grey tower that she once draped with her hair, that a man once climbed, she shivers but smiles.

She stopped writing the Rapunzel series when, finally, her Rapunzel knew enough to reach out for … rapture. She titled the series' last poem "Against Disappearance," and it ended on the path where Rapunzel danced away from her ex-tower:

> … she lifted her skirts and skipped down a gravel path whose unknown destiny she did not mind. She danced with a swath of silver butterflies who appeared from nowhere and lingered over her smile. Until an old male dwarf from another fairy tale

popped his head from behind a boulder by the bend of the path and asked, "Who are you?" She proclaimed with glee and pride, "I am Rapunzel." To which the dwarf replied, "Nonsense: Rapunzel has long hair!" And she laughed and announced as she twirled in a circle so that her skirts flared high to reveal her bare legs, "I cut my hair, braided it into a rope, and used it to escape my turret!" Amazed, the dwarf said, "How did you think of that unusual idea?" Rapunzel stopped her dance, fixed a cold stare at the dwarf and hissed like Clytemnestra: *When women control their destinies, they are only exercising a law of nature. How dare you be surprised!*

Chapter 6

Once upon a time, Elena entered a grey building, rode the elevator to the third floor, entered Apartment 3J, then enacted several acts with Ernst—all of which they'd experienced with each other before but which provided so much pleasure that they didn't mind the repetition. Afterwards, a dialogue ensued:

"Has The Dictator ever done one thing good?"

"One thing."

"Oh?"

"Remember when he was young—before he embarked on his path of destroying the country who birthed him."

"Yes?"

"When he was young, Pacifica had a different name."

"Yes: DoveLion."

"And I see you pronounce it correctly: *duh-vee-li-on*. But by the time he embarked on politics, people were pronouncing it as the combined English words of *duv* and *ly-on*... ."

"Because U.S.-American colonialism brought English and the colonizers found it too easy to pluck out the English words of 'dove' and 'lion' from the name. As with many elements touched by colonizers, degradation occurred..."

"Exactly. So as a blow against colonialism, The Dictator called for a national referendum to change the name to Pacifica, and managed—without even much bribing—to persuade most to vote for the new name."

"Sure, but every good thing turns bad with The Dictator, doesn't it?

When he and his minions came into power, they started dividing the people between them and others. They called themselves 'Lions' and the people they subjugated 'Doves'."

"This makes me think of that novelist Gina Apostol who wrote about 'naming' as the 'first act to creating.' They divided the people and, as a result, spun off a new name to add to 'Doves' and 'Lions.' A name both sides would ascribe to each other.

"A new name?"

"Yes. A name that's the opposite of Kapwa: 'Other'."

It doesn't matter who spoke what. Sometimes, there are other matters than identity.

3 DECEMBER

Once upon a time, a woman approached a grey building to meet a stranger. The stranger watched her from their third-floor apartment. For a moment, their minds melded to think the same thought: *dance is difficult in quicksand.*

27 JANUARY

Once upon a time, a woman approached a grey building to meet a stranger. The stranger watched her from their third-floor apartment. Neither had expected to end up in a certain tango—a complicated dance unfolding as they parsed the difference between *fodder* and *father.*

Elena, they thought.

Ernst, she thought.

She opened the door. They let her in.

Ernst, she thought.

Elena, they thought.

She was lying face down on their bed, waiting for them to return from a phone call. They lay next to her and started stroking every inch of her back.

"You see," Ernst whispered against her hair, "my father had done his job for so many years..."

Elena didn't seem to move, but Ernst could feel her body become more still as her muscles tightened.

"Did our fathers ever meet?" Elena kept her face turned away as she asked the question.

"No," Ernst said.

That's when Elena rolled over to look at them. She said, "What do you think is worse? That your father meet or not meet a person whose death he orders?"

Ernst felt their chest constrict.

"Perhaps what's worse is when their children meet and...," Ernst paused.

"And what? Fall in love?" Elena whispered.

Then she raised her voice.

"No, Ernst," Elena said, her voice firming. "What's worst is that my father was assassinated."

"Of course, Elena. That's the worst," Ernst said.

Elena rolled the other way and pressed her face back against their bed. They reached over and began stroking her back again. After a few moments, they felt her shaking diminish as she calmed down.

"Elena," Ernst whispered as they leaned closer to speak against her hair. "Elena, none of this is about being in love."

They held me then in a tight embrace as I began shaking again. They pressed their face against her hair and opened their mouth. They felt hair begin to enter their mouth. They welcomed the feel of damp silk against their tongue. They opened their mouth wider.

Elena, they thought.

Ernst, I thought.

"Elena," they simply said.

They spoke out loud to feel her name physically shape their lips, to physically affect their body. They did not question the appropriateness of her shuddering: it's appropriate to protest whenever love is dismissed.

They repeated, "Elena..."

18 DECEMBER

Once upon a time, Elena entered a grey building. A seagull cackled in front of her before soaring to disappear into the sunlit sky. She felt a small fish nip at her right ankle as she proceeded towards the elevator. She raised her hand to trail fingers against the wall and felt the sun quiver. She surrendered her fingerprints to the universe. She became universe. She reached the elevator and stood before it. As its doors opened she heard an invisible someone whisper, "You are universal, yes, but now it's time to be specific."

By entering the elevator, Elena understood she agreed. As she pushed the button for Apartment 3J, she said to the sun who crowded in with her, "Specifics..."

She felt light shimmer as the sun cheerfully embraced her. *Yes*, the sun replied, *specifics can never be overrated*.

Interesting, Elena thought, *the sun's voice sounds familiar...*

31 AUGUST

Once upon a time, Elena entered a grey building, walked down a sunlit path, and entered an elevator where she heard the sun speak.

"Specifics can never be overrated," the sun said, and while Elena would come to think frequently about that statement for many years, right then she focused on the sound of the sun's voice—it sounded familiar.

She quickly scrolled through her memory but couldn't identify the person whose voice sounded like the sun. She forgot about the matter until it surfaced again in a meeting months later with Ernst.

"Specifics can never be overrated," she lashed out at Ernst. They had just confirmed their father's complicity in directing the assassination of Elena's father. But in rushing to explain, they tried to focus on their father's motivations including what their father hoped would result from the murder.

"Stop," Elena ordered. "I don't want to know your father's opinions. Right now, I want to know exactly how my father died. I want all the details, every single detail."

"There's nothing in those details that would reveal any useful information. They would only hurt you."

"Stop," Elena repeated. "You don't have the right to manage that information, or the right to determine what would be helpful or not in my healing.

"I want to know everything. It was *my* father who died: specifics can never be overrated!"

"Specifics can never be overrated," Ernst repeated slowly, as if the saying of the phrase helped them prepare to respond.

Shocked, Elena raised a palm to ask them to pause. She repeated the sound of Ernst's voice through a mental loop and confirmed, yes, it was the exact sound she'd heard months earlier in the elevator. Ernst raised an eyebrow questioningly. She lowered her palm. Softly, she whispered, "Go on..."

Ernst went on. They meticulously described how Elena's father died. Their description was so specific Elena had no problem visualizing the death scene, no matter how much it hurt. Just as the sun illuminates everything within its glare without discrimination, Ernst detailed all that they knew about their father's actions.

Ernst's tone was distant because they wanted to be distanced from the narrative leaving their lips. Still, at one point, they faltered. They were detailing a rape. No, Elena's father wasn't raped. He was forced to rape. If he didn't rape, another expendable Anonymous—this one kneeling in the corner of the room with lips around a gun another torturer held—would die. The rape victim was worse than young. She was "very old, too old, so old..."

"...his last words to my father's goons were..."—here, Ernst paused to wet their lips. They'd been speaking for a long time.

"Continue..." Elena said even as they spoke up again.

"His last words were," Ernst said, "'Never forget you agreed not to touch my family. The last survivor of my family: my daughter Elena.'"

Upon hearing her name, Ernst saw a future painting in Elena's eyes: an implosion, a sinkhole of emotion so painful it overcame all the defenses that Ernst had thought in past months to strengthen within Elena. Erase or dilute idealism? Check. Erase or dilute magical thinking? Check. Strengthen fortitude at engaging with painful topics? Check. So many more tools, all to thicken Elena's psychological spine. Yet, such is the power of a name—unexpectedly, Elena saw her name, herself, in that space so long unknown to her. So unknown she'd mistakenly assumed it to be an *Other* from herself. One need not be in Kapwa time where all is one and one is all—her name specifically was called out in those vile moments of her father's dying.

Specifics. Can. Never. Be. Overrated. Elena thought as she fainted.

I fell and fell and fell in the darkness of my faint. When I finally felt something solid catch and stop her fall, I opened my eyes. She saw Ernst's face, suddenly older than what she recalled seeing at the beginning of their meeting that day. She heard her father say the words, *My daughter Elena.* She closed her eyes again. *Damn you, Ernst,* she whispered. Then I chose to continue falling.

5 JANUARY

Once upon a time, Elena approached a grey building. That day, as Ernst watched her, they closed their eyes before opening them slightly into slits. It was as if they didn't want to watch, but felt compelled. Ernst noticed the pace of her approach. It was not halting, nor interrupted by the occasional pause. Slowly but steadily, Elena approached. Still, there was no lift to Elena's steps. Ernst easily discerned the lack of eagerness.

Of course, they thought. *Why did I think you'd always be eager to meet me? To meet me with the* gusto *most found among the innocent?*

Once, there was a period when Ernst often wished they had been born in different circumstances. No Pacifica. No spy father. No CIA. They ceased when they accepted the uselessness of such thinking. But after meeting Elena, they began thinking again about a life not steered from its beginning towards a certain direction because of their father's identity. Once, they revealed those thoughts to Elena—they asked, "Do you believe in parallel universes?"

"Sure," Elena had cheerfully replied. "What's good enough for physicists is good enough for Moi!"

After Elena learned the identity of Ernst's father, the next time Ernst raised their wish to have been born in different circumstances, she said, "There are no other universes besides the one in which you are who you are and I am who I am."

Elena could not have given a more cruel response, especially as she wasn't trying to be cruel.

"Just being realistic," she added unnecessarily.

"The next step is yours," they said.

She only looked at them, then gathered her coat and bag to leave. To their relief, she said, "I'll see you at our next meeting."

On her way out, she quietly opened and shut the door but the modest click felt like a gunshot. Ernst thought, *I will do anything to erase the loneliness in your eyes, to wipe away the grey ever-threatening to shutter away your lovely purple...*

While they were orphaned differently from suffering their parents' deaths, Ernst understood the particular nature of orphanhood—the implacability of its loneliness, how it simply refuses to be appeased.

26 NOVEMBER

Once upon a time, long before Elena would approach a grey building to meet a stranger in their apartment, she was a child still living in the country of her birth. She was not yet experiencing what everyone, not just diasporics, must suffer through—that any "homeland" after the first is unstable, and the first was not birth country but womb. She was not yet alone with the kind of loneliness that propelled her to meet a stranger in their home where no one could track her if, say, the stranger was a serial killer. She was still enjoying the paradise where loneliness was alien; she lived with a father who loved her and doted on her, his beloved child.

After they no longer were a stranger to her, Ernst would describe her father as a "moralist."

"How do you know?" Elena asked, surprised.

"That's how my father described him."

More slowly, Elena asked, "I thought you said your father never met mine?"

Ernst's voice also slowed its pace to match Elena's. It was as if both were tip-toeing through a minefield of facts.

"Right. They never met."

"But you said your father called mine a moralist...?"

"Circumstantial," Ernst said, their voice turning abrupt as they stood from the chair facing Elena on the couch. "He said that's how folks described your father."

Ernst moved towards one of their paintings standing up against the wall.

"I'm not sure this is ready to send out to the gallery," they said as they perused the portrait of a man in profile. The man also wore a fedora and the hat's shadow further darkened the man's face.

Elena walked to stand next to them. She looked at the painting but said softly as they both pretended to inspect the painting, "You didn't really answer me. How did your father come to know or be interested in my father?"

Specifics can never be overrated...

They looked at her. They looked at her anguish.

They checked their watch. It was nearing 5 p.m., a time they had set for her departure in order to allow them to spend the evening working on their paintings. All muses are jealous.

But they looked at her again. They looked at her anguish.

"How, Ernst?" she repeated.

Gently, they took her hands and guided her to the couch. They made them both sit. Then they answered her question.

They could feel the world outside their apartment obviate bright sun and luminous sapphire sky to become grey—sky, buildings, cars, other people (even the children playing at the park), birds, trees, grass and so on. All *felt* grey.

And as they informed her, the agony even made Ernst at one point attempt the diversion of a disquisition on U.S. imperialism and how its growth consistently damned individual lives, like how their father the "American diplomat" sacrificed her father the "late-in-life rebel scholar." But Elena steely guided them back to the specific topic of her father.

And so they informed her. And as they informed her, the phrase "collateral damage" showed its ugly face.

And as they informed her, Ernst also did something they hadn't anticipated as they found themself more agonized than they expected from Elena's pain. They mentioned their father's father—a grandfather they knew mostly as a grey photograph of an old man. Despite its age, the photograph still revealed a face lined and made gaunt by cruelty. They also knew their grandfather as a scar inflicted on their father's back.

"Those scars are from my career as a patriot," their father once said after Ernst commented on them. They were in the locker room of their father's club, preparing to play squash.

"Well, except for one," their father continued. "See the one slashing across my latissimus dorsi? That's from your grandfather."

"What did you do to deserve that?" young Ernst had asked, their eyes trailing along the scar's furrow.

"Huh. Probably something stupid like existing," their father replied with no bitterness, just the matter-of-factness of a person who'd lived a long and experienced life.

But the tale only made Elena weep harder.

"Your grandfather whipped your father? But evil begets evil, Ernst!" I whispered. "So what about you?"

5 MAY

Once upon a time, Ernst watched Elena approach their grey building. Beyond the window, all of the world looked as grey as her trench coat. But even the morning's somber palette did not make them anticipate that before the end of their meeting that day, she would ask them, "Evil begets evil—I get that, Ernst! So what about you?"

When they could finally speak, they replied, "But I am here for you, Elena."

They reached for her hands, drew them down from her bowed face and towards them. She looked up at them. To her tear-stained face, they stressed, "I rejected my family, Elena."

They stilled her face when she would have looked away. They stressed again, "I rejected my family, Elena. But that's not all I did. Elena, I looked for you. Elena, I am here for you. And I will always be here for you, as I was never not here for you."

4 APRIL

Once upon a time, Ernst watched Elena approach the grey building that they'd come to consider with affection for hosting their engagements. They watched her pause to coo over a baby in a stroller pushed by smiling woman—they thought, *What utter aliveness in your face...!*

I promise you, they thought, as they watched her laugh with the baby's mother, *the title of your story will not be mine—what my father called your father and too many others:*

COLLATERAL DAMAGE

21 MARCH

Once upon a time, Elena approached a grey building. As ever, Ernst watched her approach from their third floor apartment. She wondered as she watched her finger punch at the intercom, *Will today be the last day?*

Will today be the last day? she thought as she walked through the door.

Will today be the last day? she thought as she walked down the hallway.

Will today be the last day? she thought as she watched her finger call for the elevator.

Will today be the last day? she thought as she entered the elevator.

Will today be the last day? she thought as the elevator doors opened to the third floor. The ocean was particularly present that day, its waves reaching up towards her thighs.

Will today be the last day? she thought as she stood in front of Ernst's apartment door, the sea agitating around her ankles.

Finally, as the door opened to reveal Ernst, she thought, *Will today be the last day?*

Her eyes traveled towards sky and snagged onto Ernst's face. She looked into Ernst's eyes and saw a cloudless blue sapphire sky. Sky embraced Elena as she thought, *No, today will not be the last day.*

She walked towards Ernst and stepped into the sun.

29 MAY

Once upon a time, Elena approached a grey building. As usual, Ernst watched her from the window of their third-floor apartment. Were there a bystander able to see them both, the image would lack revelation. Both characters' concerns were not all visible. Ernst needed time to melt the impassivity on their face. Elena needed time to dampen the eagerness in her eyes. Nothing useful, after all, can be forged in illusion. Or, nothing useful that lasts.

Or so Ernst thought as they pushed the intercom button that opened the building's front door to Elena. Once, a different lover told them in a neutral tone that befitted observation more than criticism, "You work with others to maximize their self-awareness, but not so much yours."

Months later, long after they'd ceased sculpting their face into impassivity when first greeting Elena at their meetings, they realized they didn't anticipate one thing: what would replace their mask. They'd anticipated the pain, but not the thing that would replace the defensive wall to which they'd become accustomed upon their face.

What does a falling mask reveal? When Ernst revealed their father's identity—the identity of the person who ordered the death of Elena's father—they were prepared for Elena's reaction. But they weren't prepared for their own tears—how, without impassivity walling them back, the tears welled up unexpectedly like non-sequiturs.

Man up! they could hear their father scold. In the past, during a variety of circumstances, in response to their father's cold directives, their body always tried to stiffen its spine, firm its lips, clench its fists, and otherwise become the steel their father demanded. They didn't always succeed—sometimes they felt themself crumple.

Once, through my own tears, I raised her hands to cup their face. Their

87

tears leaked through my fingers.

"Sshhhh, Ernst," Elena whispered. "You are not your father."
Sshhhh...

23 JUNE

Once upon a time, Elena left a grey building feeling stronger than when she'd entered that same building earlier that day. But she still felt fragile, and entered a café for some bolstering coffee. As she sipped from her mug, she wrote a poem. She had been thinking about poeticizing the notion of color as narrative. But as often occurs in poems, the words left behind the poet's intention. Elena wrote:

That Sudden Affinity

How to freeze each inevitable stutter of love—Let us commend encaustic for protecting the fragility of paper—Meditation, if conducted deeply, must harvest pain—

Radioactive yellows and reds make plastic flowers inappropriate for marking grief. But how else to see them by roadsides when traffic passes swiftly? To see—

The past is thick, and the present thin

Tears / not diluting the martial energy of a gaze

Absence a singe

Pushkin / grieved because Beauty exists

True love / is never chaste

But love is also / a source of difficulty

: : :

Sudden affinity for tender hours

Chapter 7

Once upon a time, Elena approached a grey building to meet a stranger. Elena would replay that walk in her mind frequently over the years. Often, she wondered what would have happened if she'd veered away before reaching the building's doors.

Do I need to have experienced Ernst to experience you, my Love? she occasionally thought as she watched her child grow. It was a rhetorical question she swiftly dismissed. Instead, whenever the question arose, she paused to relish:

> *I am a mother. I have a child.*

13 APRIL

Once upon a time, Elena entered a grey building for the first time. She anticipated that meeting a stranger in their apartment would create, among other things, complications. But she did not anticipate that one of them would be the naming of a daughter she would bear after she and the stranger stopped meeting in a grey building.

Faustina, Saturnina, Carmen, Adelfa, Pilar, Matea, Isabel...

Faust? Please no..., she chided herself, and continued ruminating.

Elenita...

She's not a junior of you, she chided herself again. She was surprised the option of "Elenita" even surfaced when she always thought children

91

should not be named after their parents—especially with diminutives—as she thought a parent's greatest responsibility should be to guide a child into independence, including—or perhaps especially—away from the child's parent(s).

Trinidad, Mungan...

Mungan? Promising, she thought about the heroine of the Iliganon epic of Mindanao, Philippines. The Philippines was the nearest country to Pacifica. Some historians believe that in ancient times both territories were one.

Amy...

Amy? So benign. Not sufficiently fraught with various significances, she thought, then reconsidered. *Perhaps I should wish such lightness for my child!* before reconsidering again. *Forget about it; to be my child is to be moody—I just know it.*

Sol, Mila/Milagros, Isabel/Ysabel, Teresa, Estrella...

Sol. Milagros. Sun. Miracle. Getting there, she thought.

Maruja...

Maruja. Or Cristy? she thought. To refresh her memory, she looked her up online. From her cherished Wikipedia:

> **Maruja** is a Filipino comic book character created by Mars Ravelo. It is about an immortal love story about two people whose love for each other transcended a century. Written by Mars Ravelo and illustrated by Rico Rival, it was a story that dealt with reincarnation, beginning with the ill-fated love story of Maruja and Gabriel during the Spanish era and ending with their reunion one hundred years later.
>
> Maruja and Gabriel were madly in love with each other but Maruja's parents disapproved of their relationship because of their class differences. Maruja was forced to marry Rodrigo, the captain of the civil guards, to ensure their fortune. But right after the marriage, the same night, she took her own life with a promise to Gabriel that they would be reunited someday. One hundred years later, Maruja was reincarnated as Cristy. She sees flashes from the past, memories that are not hers. She connects all the pieces together and was finally reunited with an aged and dying Gabriel.

Possible, possible, she thought. *I like that stubbornness of love—that love that refuses to be erased...*

Orchid or some other flower name.

Sonnet, or another kiss at poetry.

Ann...

Later that night, Elena woke with a start. She was sitting straight up in bed, the covers flung from her. When she felt pressure dissipating from her lips, she knew her dream ended with a kiss. *Cristy Maruja*, she thought as she lowered her hands to her belly and started softly rubbing its bump. *Cristy Maruja.*

When she felt tears drop onto her hands, she mocked herself for their predictability. *Yes, Ernst,* she thought out to the night air and all the creatures she knew were masked by darkness, *I long for time's reincarnation if it means being together again. There are many ways to be a father, to be a parent. I shall choose to see you in my child.*

31 JULY

Once upon a time, my mother entered a grey building where she met a stranger who came to influence my naming. I felt sorry for her after she told me the story of my name. I also discovered she'd made an error. Mine, no doubt, was not the first time a naming occurred from a mistake. But while my name's error was benign, I couldn't help thinking how worse things have unfolded from an erroneous or misguided naming—clarity can be so important, even as it can be difficult.

My mother said she hadn't wanted to name me with a diminutive as she felt them to be diminishing. She thought she'd avoided that when she named me after one of two characters "whose love for each other transcended a century," according to her beloved Wikipedia. But "Maruja" is also a Spanish diminutive of Mary, the Christian mother of God. Many Pacifican women are named Mary, Marie, Maria, and Maruja as a result of Spanish Catholicism. As with the Philippines and other nearby countries, Pacifica was not untouched by Spain's colonial forays during the 15th to 19th centuries.

When I discovered Maruja's etymology, I never thought to withhold it from my mother whose devotion to the truth is obsessive. And perhaps I also didn't withhold the information as payback for her unseemly eagerness, or so it seemed to me, to strip away any illusions I might hold about the boys, then men, with whom I fell in love. *Isn't to love inherently to have an illusion?*

Not if you truly see the target of your love, I could imagine her responding.

Well, who's being the idealist versus realist here?

"Always see the thing for the thing itself, not what you'd prefer," she often counseled with no irony, paraphrasing a favored artist who can be paradoxically opaque in his works, Jasper Johns. So I told her about the diminutive aspect of my middle name. Vacationing in California, we were walking Malibu beach to admire the sunset. At first, I was confused by her response. Her eyes teared up, before glazing to look at the waves behind me.

I heard her whisper, "Of course. Of course..."

When I asked her to explain, she only said, "Things are so often not what they seem..." before she literally waved away the topic with her fingers. Instead, she shivered and whispered, "I'm suddenly so cold!"

I had to veer off from her and our conversation to return to our car for a blanket. I returned to see her plopped down on the sand and facing the ocean, her knees pulled up to prop her face. Gently, I placed the blanket around her shoulders. She looked up at me, smiled, and patted the sand next to her. I sat down, then put my head on her shoulders like I used to when I was a little girl. We sat together like that for several minutes, looking at the sun dancing its gold-orange rays across the water.

"Pretty," I said as I used to when I was a little girl.

"Yes, pretty," mother agreed. I could hear the smile in her voice.

But after a few moments, joy ended as my mother continued. Tears suddenly dominated her voice.

"Once, someone called me *Elenita*..."

1 SEPTEMBER

Once upon a time, someone who is not my father stood by a window watching my mother approach a grey building. They didn't yet know that the woman would become a mother. The thought didn't cross their mind because they rarely thought of children. As my mother said they once told her, "Kids are a preface that doesn't interest me. I'm interested in how people behave at the peak of their prowess."

They added for emphasis, "I don't like prefaces of any sort."

Her mother said she immediately understood Ernst's reaction as she flashed back to what they'd shared about their childhood difficulties. *Such a gorgeous feathery tail wrapping itself around Mr. Bellow*, Elena recalled about the bird that became doubly-extinct for Ernst. But it was a memory whose beauty could not overcome, for Ernst, the pain of childhood—that prefatory period before someone begins fulfilling their potential.

"Would they have disapproved of your choice to become a mother? Would they have disapproved of me?" I asked my mother. I had thought frequently about asking her those questions before I actually did.

But I was nervous, and so waited until Mom was recovering from an illness and sleeping, drugged, on her bed. I asked only because I thought she wouldn't hear me.

But perhaps she did hear, and was just unable to reply. The next morning, awake though groggy, she said after her first sip of her coffee, "I often think we humans are born in grandeur by being born whole, and it's just the living that chips away at us and makes us fragmented and smaller than we can be."

I smiled weakly. Then I urged her to rest and asked about which book I might bring her for distraction.

Thinking about the incident now, I realize her statement always seemed familiar and suddenly remember the source of its familiarity. I've heard her say to many young poets who sought her counsel, "We're all born poets. It's the living that can suck poetry out of our lives."

Yes, my mother is a poet. And her saying that I have taken most to heart and can never forget is when she said, in response to skipping one of her award ceremonies so that she could cheer me from the sidelines of an unimportant martial arts exhibition, "I'm a poet and that comes with a certain lifestyle, including the occasional prize if one is lucky—it's a mark of the generally insecure poetry world that it privileges awards. But I don't want to sacrifice my only child for poetry's demands—poetry is a role for which I never wish to apologize."

"But this is just a practice event," I said. "The important one is next month. You can see me then, too, performing kali. Participants will be limited to those who've already received the black belt."

"Nonsense," she shooed away my concern. "I want to see every one of your shining moments. All of them are important."

My mother made me happy. She wanted to know, to *see*, everything about me.

9 JULY

Elena entered a grey building, entered its elevator, then entered the room of a stranger waiting for her. Over the ensuing months, the same question kept popping up in her mind—more frequently after first meeting the stranger, then slowing down in frequency, but continuing to lurk until it articulated itself again. Even after decades, the question still occasionally surfaces: *What if I'd never entered the grey building?*

But I did enter the grey building, thought Elena after the question arose again while she was on the front row of the auditorium at her daughter's school. Cristy was in fifth grade and she was performing in a school play. Cristy was playing a grape.

Cristy played a grape sundered from its bunch. She rolled on the floor as she played a grape falling away from her siblings (as well as Mom, Dad, Grandma, and Grandpa, from what Elena could determine from the loose plot). As Cristy moved towards stage-left away from her family clustered together on stage-right, Elena felt her chest tighten. Soon, she was fumbling in her bag for a Kleenex.

Precious Cristy Maruja, she thought as she quickly wiped away her tears.

95

May you never be sundered from people who care for you.

Elena was among the first to rise in the standing ovation of family and friends applauding the tween actors. *Thank you, Ernst,* Elena thought. *Without you, I would have remained stuck in my mind and not entered the world of the body that gave me my precious child.*

Thank you, Ernst. With each clap of her hands, Elena thought, Thank you, *Ernst.*

28 APRIL

Once upon a time, Elena approached a grey building. From their third-floor apartment window, Ernst watched. They noted the quick clip to her steps. *A woman on a mission*, they thought.

They soon learned that mission.

"Will you give me, us, a baby?"

While Ernst did not expect the question, they weren't surprised by it. Nor was Elena surprised by their answer: "No."

"I'm not surprised, but I'm not sure why I'm not surprised. Can you explain your answer?"

"Please," Elena added when Ernst shifted their gaze to behind her shoulder and didn't speak.

They looked back at her, then leaned over their kitchen table where they were sharing coffee to kiss her gently. Their lips were warm.

"Elena, I believe that when you become a parent, it's important that you do it because you want to be a parent, not because of your desire or love for who would be the other parent."

She frowned.

"Why not? Why can't a child manifest love?"

They smiled and said, "Isn't this also what we've been working on—your identity, including knowing what you want, rather than an identity based on another?"

"Oh," she said. "I thought you rejected the idea because you weren't planning to be around forever."

Ernst laughed before replying, "Elena, *you* are *not* planning to be around forever."

"Really?"

Ernst stopped laughing, but their eyes retained their smile.

"Or, I can answer differently...?"

"Please do."

"Kapwa-time, Elena: this moment *is* forever."

4 DECEMBER

Once upon a time, Cristy learned that her mother visited a stranger in a building many times over the course of two years. To this discovery, she first responded with tears.

For several minutes, and despite Elena's attempts to comfort her, she merely sat on her chair across from her mother with tears silently waterfalling down her cheeks. When she finally spoke, she whispered as if each word scalded.

"Mom. To begin this relationship with a stranger, you must have been so damaged ..."

Elena reared as if she'd been slapped. She, too, teared up.

"Yes," she whispered back. "So much has happened and it was a long time ago. But, yes, when I went to Ernst I was... fragmenting."

16 JULY

Once upon a time, Elena told her daughter many times, she approached a grey building to meet a stranger in their apartment.

"Don't ever do this!" As a mother, she naturally stressed this to Cristy Maruja the first time she told the story.

Cristy would come to repeat the story to her children, and their children to theirs and so on through the generations. The story did not stop with Ernst. The story continued on to June12.com. Began by Ernst, June12.com was continued by Elena and later both Elena and Cristy.

"We can't overcome what we inherited if we only focus on our pain," Ernst said. Then they revealed how, for years, they had funneled much of their profits from their art works into buying and maintaining internet domains and other sites, of which June12.com was the first and organizer of the rest. Directed by several brilliant drop-outs from Silicon Valley and staffed with volunteers around the world, June12.com's network sought to disrupt the narratives of Pacifica's political and economic elite whose actions were geared to maintaining control while failing to uplift most of Pacifica's people. As with the neighboring Philippines—and many other countries throughout human history—it's proved difficult for ruling politicians to overcome the conflict of interest in also being in charge of overall economic growth: the elite usually only cared for their own and not others.

Elena did not need to ask for an explanation about the network's name. It was the day Pacifica declared independence long ago, a declaration ignored by its colonizers.

"Yes," Elena replied, her eyes beginning to light up for the first time since Ernst shared the intersecting fates of their fathers.

Oh yes, Universe, she thought as she turned around in Ernst's arms to look through the window by which Ernst had watched her approach numerous times. *Universe, I am awake!*

Here we come, Pacifica! Against The Dictator's regime, we proclaim Independence!

28 JANUARY

Once upon a time, Cristy remembered, her mother entered a grey building numerous times over the course of two years to meet a stranger who became her godparent. She thought of Ernst as "godparent" because her mother told her that their guidance helped Elena to grow and eventually blossom into a mother. Nor did she have a father; Elena said she'd used a sperm bank when she needed to become pregnant.

"A sperm bank?!" Cristy naturally questioned when she became old enough to interrogate Elena more deeply about her absent father. When she was younger, Elena had simply explained that her father "could not be around," implying he had to live in another place.

They were seated together on the couch in Elena's living room. Elena held Cristy's hands as she began the talk for which time she thought had finally arrived.

"Using a sperm donor allowed me to be in charge of my life," Elena said. "I just didn't want to allow another person to affect how I might live."

Elena squeezed Cristy's hands as she continued. "And look at you— looking exactly like me! Black hair, similar complexion, and even the same violet eyes I got from my father, your grandfather. If we weren't of different ages, we could be twins!"

Cristy smiled—she adored her mother and liked the idea of being twins. But her smile faltered as she asked, "But doesn't a child affect how you want to live your life?"

"It does, doesn't it?" Elena replied with a look of affection on her face. "Ah well, then I'm just like—or, rather, am *also*—that traveler Walt Whitman: full of contradictions."

Contradictions, Elena recalled Ernst once whispering to erase her tears, *don't exist in Kapwa-time.*

9 AUGUST

Once upon a time, her mother entered a grey building numerous times over the course of two years to meet a stranger who became her godparent.

Cristy often thought of Ernst whenever she logged onto June12.com.

That morning, she was entering the site to coordinate the latest online assault on The Dictator's son, Marc "BeeBee" Con. *Least I can do*, she often thought, as she infiltrated another of BeeBee's websites. On it, she and other volunteers around the world put up excerpts from porn movies BeeBee secretly financed, images of BeeBee's Panamanian and Swiss bank accounts, photos of him hunting "exotic" animals on the Damul tribal region he'd taken for his own Disneyland as its indigenous peoples were shunted away to parts unknown, and his less-than-stellar grade reports from a college attempt at Princeton.

Cristy thought again, *Least I can do! You think you can just hop on an elephant to meander back into the presidential palace that was your childhood playground because your father aborted our country's democracy!*

BeeBee had become enamored with one elephant and called him "Republican" after the U.S. party of the ex-President who began developing hotels along Pacifica's coastlines. BeeBee was also running for President after the interim leader The Dictator had allowed when BeeBee was still too young to hold office. It was no secret to June12.com that BeeBee believed or hoped that enough time had passed for the voters to ignore his father's dictatorship with the help of bribes to lower-level politicians across the country. *Corruption is nothing but predictable*, BeeBee was caught observing in a private video recovered by June12.com. *Especially in a poor country*, someone off-camera guffawed. BeeBee, whose family already had plundered millions into poverty, laughed right back.

Your Dad killed my Grandpa and fuck you and your family! Cristy huffed as her finger clicked on the On button for sending a photo of tuxedo buttons and cufflinks repurposed from a rosary; the rosary's beads had been crafted with stolen diamonds by BeeBee's mother. The Dictator's wife preferred to stay out of Pacifica, choosing instead to enjoy the proceeds from The Dictator's thievery from their real estate properties worldwide (June12.com would discover she favored their chateaux in Provence, penthouse apartment in Manhattan, townhouse in London, and beach house in Malibu). The Dictator was happy to finance his wife's prolonged sojourns outside Pacifica since that worked best for maintaining a variety of domestic mistresses.

Yet you still dare to claim your colonial Catholic faith, you hypocrite! Cristy thought as her fingers remained busy on the keyboard.

"Christy?"

"Sorry, was I talking out loud?" Cristy asked as she turned towards her mother who'd just entered the kitchen.

"More June12 stuff?" Elena asked as she moved towards the coffeemaker for a refill.

"Of course! Oh—want to know what happened to MotherF Melda's diamond rosary?"

Cristy nicknamed BeeBee's mother "MotherF" as she knew Elena didn't like hearing the whole word. After everything her mother had experienced, Cristy was usually amused by her prudishness.

Elena wrinkled her nose and said, "I'm sure I'll learn it all the next time I check on June12's website. Right now, I have to prepare for tonight."

"Good idea. Must have your priorities right!" Cristy enthused.

Elena was preparing for a reading to launch her latest poetry book, *HIRAETH: Future Last Tercets*. Cristy approved of Elena focusing on her poetry. She had told Elena when she took over managing most of June12. com, "You have others helping you. Wouldn't Ernst agree that if you allow The Dictator to take over your time to the detriment of your own poetry, then The Dictator won?"

"Oh you're so smart!" Elena had replied before kissing Cristy's cheek.

And Elena had also thought, *Oh Ernst, you're so smart!*

She could hear them whisper to repeat a promise they'd made long ago: *Whatever happens, the results will not be banal—not boring like my father's wardrobe."*

11 NOVEMBER

Once upon a time, a woman approached a grey building to meet a stranger in their apartment. She didn't know that by taking this step, this risk, she would bear a daughter who, in turn, also would bear her redemption.

Cristy came to learn of the cause-and-effect that began because Ernst wanted to create something better from out of their father's history of malevolence as required by spy craft.

"That's such a huge pressure," Cristy said. Ernst was a frequent topic as they prepared dinner together—a time when both could try to relax through the motions of preparing a meal.

Elena turned from the stove where she was checking on one of the few dishes she'd managed to learn: pork belly adobo. She looked at her daughter with a raised eyebrow.

"Pressure on you?"

"Yes! Ernst wanted to let you know what happened to Grandpa so that you wouldn't be mired in always wondering what happened. Obviously, it was horrific, but it would have been awful for you to spend the rest of your life wondering if Grandpa had left the family of his own decision rather than knowing he hadn't wanted to leave the family but was kidnapped."

"So how do you relate that to feeling pressured?"

"Well, you always said knowing what happened helped heal you and strengthen you into becoming a mother. But all that would be for nothing if I, your child, can't do something worthwhile. But here I am, 23 years old, and

I don't know what I want to do with my life!"

Elena turned back to the stove to hide her smile.

"You know, this adobo is not difficult to make. But I didn't learn it until my late 30s," she said. "Most 23-year-olds haven't yet figured out their lives, Cristy. Just know that you're worthwhile because you exist."

"I don't know what that means," Cristy muttered.

"Don't feel pressured to make Ernst's decisions worthwhile," Elena said. "They didn't even know that you would exist when we met each other and continued meeting."

"But they did continue engaging for your sake?"

"No doubt. But they probably had other reasons."

"Like?"

"They didn't discuss them all with me."

"But if you had to guess?"

Elena paused to consider Cristy's question. Slowly, she said, "No doubt they also had to reconcile events in their and their family's lives."

She looked at Cristy.

"Perhaps they also did it because they needed to forgive their father."

Cristy raised an eyebrow.

"What, dear?"

"Mom, maybe they needed you to forgive their father before they could even consider doing the same."

Elena paused, the adobo ignored as she considered her daughter's speculation.

"You think Ernst was looking for a way to reconcile with their father—to forgive him?"

Cristy shrugged before replying.

"Did you hear about David and Louise Turpin in California? They were just sentenced to life imprisonment for the years of abuse they inflicted on their dozen children. Beatings, getting shackled to beds, malnutrition, cagings, no access to bathing,... beatings... for years and years!"

"Yes, how can one not hear of their plight? The news is full of their coverage."

"But did you know that just before their sentencing, two of the children provided testimonies..."

"No, I didn't hear of that."

"Well, despite years of abuse, the two children said that their parents truly loved them, and that they forgave them and loved them as well."

Elena looked at her daughter. She repeated her question, "You think Ernst was looking for a way to reconcile with their father?"

Cristy shrugged again before replying, "It takes a lot for a child to reject a parent."

25 SEPTEMBER

Once upon a time, a grey building was approached by a woman whose multitudes contained a desire for simplicity. Simplicity, like a small mound of white rice next to the most delicious adobo made on the planet. Delicious, and simple to make. Here's a straightforward recipe:

> 1:1 soy sauce and vinegar
> 1-2 bay leaf
> 1 tsp pepper corn
> 3 garlic cloves
> cut up pork belly

> Dump everything in the pot, turn on the heat, then observe.
> When you can't smell the vinegar anymore, it's done.

Adobo can be made with chicken as well but, trust me, pork has more savory potential. When it comes to adobo, I prefer pork belly for its fatty, melt-in-your-mouth tenderness. I have read that one can easily substitute pork shoulder for its benefit of being a leaner cut. But I'm Pacifican—when it comes to luscious fat, I see no reason to minimize. Here, I'm no different from the rest of my people. Notwithstanding the travails and sufferings that mark Pacifica's history, no dictator can eliminate the people's passion for a well-lived life. It's also the people's weakness: bribes can do much to achieve ... a well-lived life.

Some Pacificans try to deny the simplicity of a great adobo dish by topping off the dish with a boiled quail's egg. Not a single diner has ever mocked the attempt—it may be pretentious (no boiled egg will ever mask the simpleness of adobo) but, as well, it's harmless. As regards harmless matters, Pacificans are not just easy-going but, given the country's history, easily forgiving.

Or, perhaps the predilection for forgiveness elides the issue. Perhaps the matter is more that a recipe elides the issue at hand: hunger, such that one becomes grateful for food in any form. Perhaps the issue is that simple: hunger.

12 MARCH

Once upon a time, a woman approached a grey building to meet a stranger in their apartment. She knew it to be a risky move, but she was also bolstered by her faith in Kapwa. *All is One, One is All*, she thought and the thought, as always, steeled her whenever she did or made a decision to do something uncertain if not questionable.

Yet, even after what she came to experience with Ernst, Elena would be stunned years later to see the visitor her daughter brought to her home.

"Mom!" Cristy exclaimed as she ran over to give Elena a hug. "I've brought a surprise!"

Cristy beckoned someone from the hallway. A slim, handsome man approached with a shy smile. His black hair looked like velvet and dimples flitted in and out from his cheeks. He and Cristy reached for each other's hands. Turning to Elena, Cristy said, "Mom, this is Paul Romuel."

Elena's smile faltered as she heard the name.

"Welcome, Paul," she heard herself say, though her voice seemed tinny. She felt like she was talking underwater. She coughed to clear her throat and her mind.

"Paul Romuel?"

"Yes," he said. "That one. You're not the first to react that way."

Of course not, Elena thought. *Your grandfather was responsible for the deaths of so many people...*

"Do you know my family? Cristy's family?" Elena asked.

Paul's smile dimmed. Dimples disappeared.

"No, it's okay," he said to Cristy who seemed about to intervene.

"Yes. I know you're asking a specific question so I want to say that I know what my grandfather did to your father."

"Yet you're here, standing in my living room," Elena said. Before she could continue, Cristy interrupted.

"Mom. He's not his grandfather! Paul is not The Dictator!"

"Obviously, Cristy," Elena said. But before she could speak more, Cristy interrupted again.

"Mom. *All is One, One is All.*"

16 SEPTEMBER

Once upon a time, Elena entered a grey building and rushed towards Ernst's apartment. Impatiently, she ignored the sun, sea and sky to think *Hurry! Hurry!* as she mentally urged the elevator to arrive.

From the elevator, she ran to Ernst's door and knocked rapidly on it. Soon, she was banging on it. *Hurry!* she thought again. But even as her knuckles began to hurt, the door remained implacably shut.

When she saw her blood on the door, she stopped. She stepped back, bringing her right knuckle to her mouth. She looked at the shut door as she licked blood.

"Ernst," she whispered. "You weren't supposed to make me bleed for you ..."

Years later, Elena recounted the story to Cristy.

"Why wasn't Ernst there that day?" Cristy replied.

"At our prior meeting, they'd described their father's role at your grandfather's murder. I said I never wanted to see them again and rushed out. After I calmed down that night, I realized that it wasn't their fault."

"But they weren't there at your next visit?"

"Fortunately, they arrived back at their apartment while I was still in the hallway. By then, I was crying, just looking at their bloodied door.

"They came over, looked at their door, reached for my knuckles and kissed them before hugging me.

"Then they said that the last thing they'd ever wanted was for them or their family ever again to cause me or my family to shed blood. *Never again.*"

"Wow. That's almost romantic," Cristy said. "But I'm sure it wasn't."

Cristy reached over to embrace her mother. As Elena leaned into her hug, she whispered, "No. It wasn't romantic at all."

6 FEBRUARY

Once upon a time, Elena entered a grey building to meet Ernst. When they opened the door to his apartment, she smiled at them.

"You're smiling. That's a relief," Ernst said, returning her smile.

She leaned up to kiss them, then said as she walked towards the living room windows, "The person who forgives will benefit as much as who is forgiven."

The sunlight was generous as it flowed through the windows. Elena turned her face towards the light. Like a cat, she warmed herself in the sunlight, purring as the chill left her bones.

10 OCTOBER

Once upon a time, a woman approached a grey building to meet a stranger in their apartment. The woman did not consider herself a strong risk-taker, aggressively curious, or any other description that might explain why she'd decided to meet the stranger in a potentially dangerous situation. *But here I am!* she thought, watching her hand rise to the building's intercom. When her hand extended out from her coat's sleeve, she tried but failed to ignore her naked wrist, *Well, maybe they'll fatten you up,* she thought dourly.

Elena's meeting with the stranger would plant many seeds. One was named Cristy Maruja.

"Got it!" Cristy yelled at her computer screen, both hands rising as if to signal a football touchdown.

"What is it?" Elena's voice announced her arrival. She hung her coat on a coatrack and moved towards her daughter.

"No less than 'The Marquesa' by Goya!" Cristy proclaimed as she jumped up to give her mother a hug.

"Tell me," Elena encouraged, her voice affectionate as it usually was when she addressed her only child.

"Remember I told you about Mina, Khardosshi's granddaughter? And how she'd loathed having to deal with the aftermath of Khardosshi being the money bagman for all sorts of loathsome characters, including The Dictator?"

"Yes...?"

"Well, she discovered which of Khardosshi's houses held 'The Marquesa'—it was hanging in a pantry in a London townhouse! She passed on the word. And I passed it on to June12.com and their network has helped the Commission recover it!"

Cristy referred to the Commission of Government Goods whose staff was searching the globe for what The Dictator stole—monies or those assets financed by The Dictator's thievery.

"I'm glad you're happy," Elena said.

Her understated response made Cristy pause. She looked at her mother.

"I know the value of 'The Marquesa' comes nowhere near the $10 billion or so that The Dictator's family plundered. But we plan to publicize this discovery as loudly as we can—it will be useful for highlighting The Dictator's thievery and that other assets exist out there which were acquired with their victims' monies!"

"l understand," Elena swiftly replied. "I don't mean to minimize its significance. I'm very happy Mina cooperated and helped reveal the whereabouts of Goya's painting. I do understand that its discovery will be helpful against The Dictator's son."

Cristy smiled.

"Yes. BeeBee has no business running for President today, as if The Dictator's victims and their families would so easily forget what happened during the dictatorship."

She turned back to her computer.

"I have to write Mina. She might be helpful with other stolen assets."

"Don't worry about me. Go back to your work," Elena said. "I just brought you some dinner you can reheat later as I know you're busy. I'll unpack it into your refrigerator."

Cristy's fingers paused on the keyboard.

"Oh, but can you stay for dinner?"

Elena looked back at her daughter.

"Of course I can stay," she said. "Now go back to your work. I brought a book to read while you work—the latest volume in Karl Ove Knausgaard's brilliant if maniacal series, *MY STRUGGLE*."

Of course I can stay, Elena thought again. *I will always be here with you and for you.*

For the rest of the afternoon, she pretended to read. But she actually just watched Cristy at work. Once, Cristy raised her voice to share what she was addressing: "You know, technology is impacting what tyrants and dictators can get away with. Look at the 'Panama Papers'—now we can trace where people have hidden ill-gotten goods! Inexpensive, limitless digital storage and fast internet connections will digitize the revolution against thieves and corrupt politicians!"

She's happy. She's fulfilled. She has goals and knows what to do to achieve them, Elena thought.

Or, Elena thought as she recalled Ernst, *she knows what to achieve because she's identified her goals.*

25 NOVEMBER

Once upon a time, Elena approached a grey building where Ernst waited. A year ago, Elena had approached the grey building for the first time, and Ernst had watched her approach for the first time.

Will this sense of trepidation ever go away? Elena wondered as she entered the building.

"I didn't stop being nervous for a long time," Elena recalled to Cristy as they prepared yet another meal whose cooking process became a memory feast over her time with Ernst. "But it was all worth it. I have you!"

"I hope it was worth it," Cristy said. "I'm meeting with one of BeeBee's representatives this afternoon..."

"Are you sure it's not dangerous?" Elena interrupted her.

"I set the meeting for the lobby of the Chelsea. Several of the June12 folks will be scattered about. In fact, Alvin Querrer, the new director of June12. com, will be videotaping from behind a huge potted tree or whatever he finds to camouflage him."

"I don't trust BeeBee and his cohorts."

"Me too. But what choice do we have?"

Mother and daughter lapsed into silence as they contemplated the events of recent days. Despite the efforts of June12.com and many others who thought like them, The Dictator's son won the recent presidential elections. It was a victory with the usual rigged ballot boxes and disenfranchised blocs of voters. But the margin was too huge for BeeBee's victory to be challenged.

"President BeeBee—what a tragedy," Elena sighed. "I can't believe a majority voted for him. The Dictator's victims are their parents' generation! It's not something they can forget from an absence of witnesses or evidence!"

"Well, let's see what he has to say," Cristy said. "Obviously, he knows his father killed my grandpa, your father."

🐚

"Obviously, your President knows his father killed my grandfather," Cristy repeated to BeeBee's representative before they even sat down at the plush couches tastefully placed throughout Chelsea's large lobby.

"Nice to meet you, Cristy Maruja. My name is Herb Gonzalez," he responded, ignoring the edgy tone of Cristy's greeting. "Shall we sit?"

Cristy stared at Herb. He was about her mother's age, tall and slim, crowned with a full head of hair though silvered, and possessed eyes that displayed both warmth and a full knowledge of suffering. It was the latter that made her sit down.

She shook her head at his offering of refreshments. Her voice was sea water solidifying to steel as she asked, "How does your President plan to kill me?"

22 DECEMBER

Once upon a time, Elena approached a grey building to meet Ernst in their apartment. It would be their 20th meeting. She was amazed there was a 20th meeting, and that there likely would be more.

Years later, Elena would tell her daughter, disbelief etching her words, "Who would have thought my encounters with Ernst would lead to you, and then The Dictator's son contacting you?"

Cristy had just summarized her meeting at the Chelsea with BeeBee's representative, Herb Gonzalez.

"Go over his plans for you again, please," Elena said. Both were seated at Cristy's dining table. They both ignored the dinner before them as Cristy updated Elena.

"Well, when BeeBee is ready to go public with his plans to reform the government left behind by The Dictator, I'm supposed to be part of the announcement—perhaps the one to present his plans through the internet."

"A status conferred on you because of June12.com and..."

"Yes, and because of how Grandpa died—how The Dictator killed your Dad."

"Well ..." and again Elena couldn't continue.

"Yes, well! Not exactly how I'd like to gain credibility for any role— through Grandpa's death!"

As Elena remained speechless, Cristy sighed and picked up her fork.

"We might as well eat," she said. "C'mon, Mom, before the food gets cold."

Elena picked up her fork, only to put it down.

"But would your participation do any good?"

"For whom?

"The people represented by June12.com?"

Cristy frowned.

"You know, except for the actual volunteers, I don't know who June12.com represents. I always thought it represented principles rather than people."

"Hm. Interesting." Elena nodded, then served herself some chicken though she had no appetite.

She wasn't sure why she didn't share her misgivings over Cristy's answer. She recalled how Ernst once said, "Principles are useless without people believing in them."

"Yes," she had replied, "Like how poems would be useless without anyone to read and experience them."

19 OCTOBER

Once upon a time, I met you in a grey building, Elena thought. She'd never stopped thinking about Ernst though the years multiplied their distance from the period they shared in the grey building. Now, Elena thought about them more frequently given her daughter's unexpected activities.

When Cristy helped expand June12.com, the group's vision was to "clean up" in the aftermath of The Dictator's rule over Pacifica. Their activities ranged from looking for The Dictator's and his family's assets that were plundered from their country to filing suits on behalf of The Dictator's victims and their families to, more recently, disputing the recent campaign of The Dictator's son to win the Presidency. Though they failed in the latter, they also were not surprised. The country was locked in tribal politics and The Dictator's tribe members stubbornly retained their support of The Dictator who, after all, diverted a majority of national tax revenues to their areas for infrastructure and other social services mostly lacking elsewhere in the country.

But the son apparently turned his back on his father despite years of enjoying the benefits of his father's reign. When he became old enough, BeeBee ran for the leadership of Pacifica. The Dictator encouraged it in the manner of royals, including (or, especially) self-anointed royals who expected their progeny to be the rightful heirs of privileges they'd amassed. But BeeBee only ran for office so that he would be in a stronger position someday to dismantle his dictator-father's legacy.

"It's not unusual for dictators' children to live in a bubble," Paul explained to Cristy, shortly after they met at a June12.com protest outside the United Nations. They and a few others had ended up in a bar afterwards. Paul sought her out and asked her to join him for dinner the next day. Charmed by the cheer that never left his eyes as well as the smile ever tilting up the corner of his lips, Cristy agreed. Recalling their meeting to Elena, Cristy explained, "I needed more joy in my life and Paul just seemed like such a happy person."

But Paul swiftly revealed himself. While attracted to Cristy, he'd initially sought her out for her June12.com affiliation. Not wanting to deceive Cristy, he revealed his goals during their first date. He thought June12.com could play a role in his and his father's attempts to overthrow the still strong remnants of The Dictator's rule.

"My father was raised in the heavily-guarded residences of our family, attended the top boarding schools in Europe, vacationed in luxury resorts around the world, and so on. I did, too, when I was growing up. For both of us, returning to take up adult lives in Pacifica was a shock—we'd been protected for so long from the poverty and abuses of my grandfather's rule. But my father couldn't and didn't do anything for a long time; The Dictator's influence had hardened among the military and other politicians who were well-paid for their loyalties. It wasn't until I, too, expressed misgivings about the growing misery surrounding us that he finally decided to do something to improve conditions for Pacifica's people."

"President Marc 'BeeBee' Con shall begin with land reform!" Cristy proclaimed on Net-TV. She had just finished sharing BeeBee's vision. A first step was to address one of Pacifica's most difficult problems, the ownership of much of the country's real estate in the hands of a mere ten families. The country's economy revolved significantly around agriculture, and the ownership by mostly absentee owners created an infrastructure of poor farmer tenants. BeeBee planned to spread land ownership to more farmers.

"As we all know, much of land ownership resulted from the current owners' ancestors having collaborated with colonizing forces. As their reward they were given land. But their historical collaboration was against the country's interests and it's not fitting that they and their families should continue to be rewarded by their lack of true patriotism!"

Oh Cristy, Elena thought as she watched her daughter. *I hope you and your generation indeed will do better.*

Lead on, Daughter! Lead on!

17 DECEMBER

Once upon a time, Elena approached a grey building to meet Ernst in their apartment. They had been meeting in their apartment for nearly two years. *That long, Elena?* she asked herself. *What's the endgame?*

Elena did not expect that the "endgame"— the significance of her engagement with Ernst—would not be hers but her daughter's.

Lead on, Daughter! Lead on! Elena thought as she watched her daughter on Net-TV. Improbably, Cristy had become the new spokesman for Marc Con, The Dictator's son and Pacifica's new President.

Watching her daughter on her computer screen, Elena caught a familiar face behind Cristy. The camera was panning the crowd behind her and the caption identified him as the president's only son, Paul Romuel.

Really? Elena remembered when she confronted Paul in her living room. Cristy had just introduced him as her new boyfriend. *Really?*

6 JANUARY

Once upon a time, Elena approached a grey building to meet Ernst. They were waiting for her in their apartment. Once, she asked them why they mostly met this way.

"How about lunch sometime at a lovely restaurant? Or afternoon tea at the Excelsior where I can softly sing you the words to the songs never verbalized by the jazz trio?"

"I don't do tea…"

"You mean, you prefer us to end in your bed," she teased.

But Ernst didn't smile. They said, "I want us to meet this way because, someday, you will recall what we experienced together from a distanced light. Someday, you will need the consistency of details as infrastructure to hold you up, to make you continue, through your memory's… rough spots. Details like how we usually met."

"How do you know the future?" she replied. Elena had thought to continue teasing them but the mood didn't hold. Without waiting for their answer, she asked the question she should have asked first.

"Rough spots…?"

"It's what happens," Ernst said, "when an individual's story is never just about the individual."

Elena remembered this conversation as she confronted Paul in her living room.

"Why are you here?" she demanded, even as she tried to soften her tone. "I can't believe you're here simply as my daughter's boyfriend!"

Cristy began to speak but Paul lifted a hand.

"It's okay, Cristy. It's okay."

To Elena, he said, "I didn't expect to fall in love with your daughter. But I did and my love is genuine."

"But?" Elena interrupted.

"Yes, there is a 'but'," Paul conceded. He turned slightly so that he could face both Cristy and Elena.

"Actions, especially like my grandfather's, can have long-lasting repercussions. My grandfather, as The Dictator, not only made his victims suffer but also the descendants of his victims. As with my father, Marc Con, I want to make it up to as many of his victims and their families as possible."

"How?" Elena asked, her tone still wary.

"My father will do what he can to dismantle the political structures The Dictator implemented during his rule. But The Dictator was also the greatest thief among the 20th century tyrants. He's hidden billions and billions away in slush funds all over the world. My father and I are The Dictator's heirs. While my father works internally within Pacifica, I will find those funds hidden outside the country and divert them back to help Pacifica's impoverished population."

"And June12.com's networks will help him," Cristy added into the silence with which Elena responded.

Elena looked at her daughter even as she directed her words at Paul.

"It's unusual for the powerful and wealth to dismantle the source of their privilege," she said.

"I agree," Paul said. "But things have deteriorated too much; the gulf is too wide between the wealthy elite and the mostly impoverished population. My father and I believe Pacifica's reached the tipping point where it's no longer safe for the elite as they also become overdependent on the military or private armies to exist safely. If The Dictator and his supporters had been smarter, they would have, fine, stolen from the people but left enough for others to survive better than how they've been coping for decades."

Elena raised an eyebrow in surprise as she directed her gaze towards him.

"I actually appreciate the pragmatism of that analysis," she said. "Of course, human history shows how despots rarely achieve such a nuanced point of view. Absolute power corrupts absolutely."

"True," Paul said. "Maybe it's just human nature, and why we're the most dangerous, if not deplorable, species on the planet."

Elena gave a brief nod as she looked at Paul more closely. She looked him over as if to memorize every detail about him.

Breaking the silence, Cristy said, "Apparently, when The Dictator was forced out of Maharlika Palace by the Yellow Revolution, a lot of the records to his holdings were destroyed while his minions destroyed evidence of other things. Other things, like the contents of bedrooms turned into torture chambers..."

The Yellow Revolution was unprecedented, formed from an unexpected groundswelling of the population who had had enough of The Dictator and joined together to march to the Presidential residence. The revolt joined prostitutes with nuns, janitors with businessmen, students with teachers, artists with cops and so on—all marching towards Maharlika Palace and calling for The Dictator's ouster. The crowds came up against soldiers in battle gear. The soldiers looked at the crowd, then joined them. Less than 24 hours later, The Dictator and his family were led out of Maharlika Palace and the country by supporters of the U.S. who safeguarded their departure. The Yellow Revolution would come to inspire other so-called "People's Revolutions" in other countries suffering from tyranny, from former Soviet bloc countries to the Middle East where the "Arab Spring" blossomed.

"Bank account numbers, passwords, bank locations and so on are unknown today as The Dictator didn't release them from his mind before he died," Cristy said. "Paul contacted us and we agreed to work with him. It's easier to get banks to cooperate if a legitimate account signatory, like The Dictator's heir, is involved."

Elena continued to look at Paul as she replied, "So that's the theory..."

"Oh, but it's more than theory, Mom! With Paul's cooperation, we've already taken about $250 million out of The Dictator's Seychelles accounts," Cristy said.

"Really...?" Elena said as she turned back towards Cristy.

"Really, Mom!" Cristy replied happily. "We can trust Paul!"

Elena smiled as she agreed, "Well, a quarter of a billion dollars is not peanuts."

Turning back to Paul, Elena said, "So you're interested in redemption?"

"Redemption—yes, I suppose that's as apt a word as any. It's not hard to think of redemption when you grow up in my family," Paul replied. "It's not hard to think of redemption whenever I leave my family's residences to drive through the streets of Pacifica where the toll on the people can no longer be anything but obvious."

"Redemption won't bring back my father," Elena said, but already in a softer tone.

In an even softer tone, Paul agreed, "It won't bring back your father."

16 FEBRUARY

Once upon a time, a woman approached a grey building to meet a stranger in their apartment. The woman could not have foreseen that, because of this stranger, she would meet the grandson of The Dictator who had caused her to become unmoored. She was unmoored without her family: her mother who'd died at her childbirth was unknown to her and her father became unknown after he was assassinated with the help of The Dictator's ally, the CIA.

"Whatever I do won't bring back your father," Paul conceded to Elena.

"That's all right," she chose to soothe The Dictator's grandson. "I still managed to have a good life."

Yes, it's a good life, she thought as she looked at her daughter who was in love with The Dictator's grandson.

It has to be a good life. I am a mother. I have a daughter.

Elena paused her thoughts, before continuing, *And perhaps I will also have a grandchild because my daughter loves you, grandson of The Dictator.*

Elena placed a smile on her face, opened her arms wide, and beckoned Paul to enter her embrace.

"My daughter loves you and she does not love without reason," Elena told Paul as Cristy beamed.

As Cristy joined in the embrace—"Group hug!" she joyously proclaimed—Elena thought again about Ernst.

This, too, is because of you. Thank you, Ernst.

30 MAY

Once upon a time, an emerald island laid upon a blue sapphire ocean and both glowed under the beam of a 24-carat sun. The gilded description—emerald island, sapphire ocean, 24-carat sun—could begin a fairy tale. But not for this situation—we might as well begin:

> *Once upon a time, a dictator ruled over an island and plundered its resources and its people because he only pretended to be benign.*

"'Benevolent dictator'? What a joke!" Cristy snorted. "He sure couldn't maintain his 'benevolency' for long! It took, what, one week after roclaiming martial law for the University of San Toma to become a jail for his political opponents?!"

"That was his slogan," Elena said. She was telling Cristy one of the many stories she recalled about Pacifica. "That's how he rationalized his regime during its early days. He would point to the models of Mustafa Kemal Atatürk of Turkey, Josip Broz Tito of Yugoslavia, Lee Kuan Yew of Singapore, and France-Albert René of Seychelles."

"It's amazing how so few of these tales are on the internet," Cristy often said about many of Elena's stories. "The Dictator's family did an effective job scrubbing the net of anything useable against them."

"Well, I'm sure you and the rest of the June12.com volunteers will redress all that," Elena said encouragingly.

"I hope so. I can't believe how many of these stories aren't known by my generation!"

"And mine, which is worse!" Elena said. "My generation experienced

The Dictator's rule and yet there's this deliberate amnesia on the parts of many! Again, that's where you and June12.com play a critical role. It's great that you're getting a lot of volunteers to interview people, to elicit the oral histories that you can transcribe into documents that will be available for libraries, schools and other means."

"Yes, our recruitment efforts are going well," Cristy said. "But let's you and I continue with our own oral history. Our family's history. Tell me about my grandpa..."

Elena closed her eyes, then began, "My father was a good man..."

She breathed deeply, then opened her eyes. She looked at Cristy as she continued, "Your grandfather was not perfect, but he was a good man and, as with many during the dictatorship, that was his undoing.

"Under The Dictator, evil begets evil and goodness begets death."

Cristy pursed her lips.

"Evil begets evil? I suppose. But aren't exceptions possible?"

Elena reached over to smooth away some hair strands that had fallen over Cristy's eyes—yet another moment that reminded her of Ernst. Once, she'd preferred hiding her eyes while they loved to reveal them.

"What exceptions, dear?"

"Evil begets evil," Cristy said, haltingly at first but then more firmly as if she was willing it to be true, "unless redemption surfaces."

Chapter 8

7 MAY

Once upon a time, an emerald island laid upon a blue sapphire ocean and both glowed under the beam of a 24-carat sun. *Emerald island, sapphire ocean, 24-carat sun*—a fairy tale next should unfold. Instead, an island boy grew up to be an *adurag*, a man-eating eagle-devil ever reconnoitering greedily over the island paradise known as "Pacifica."

On an emerald island set upon a blue sapphire ocean under the beam of a 24-carat sun, the baby Mateo was born. He was quintessential baby: plump, big eyes round with humor or wonder, the softest pink flesh, silky wisps of hair, and a gurgling laughter that invited others to join in with their own smiles, grins and laughs. To meet baby Mateo was to fall in love.

But the baby grew up to be quintessential dictator, complete with made-up military uniforms festooned with invented medals for honor and bravery. He over-excavated his paradise island's natural resources. He plunged most of the island's citizens into poverty. He exported much of the country's wealth to become jewels for his wife and luxury residences around the world for his family and supporters.

The baby did not retain his name after he outgrew his infancy. It started simply when he raged against a captured rebel, "You are an insect, too small to utter my name, to even know my name!"

That's when he interrupted his rant to consider what he'd unthinkingly uttered. He considered what he said, liked it, and ordered the appropriate proclamations that no one would be allowed to address him or refer to him by name. Instead, he would be hailed only as "The Dictator." Decades later, psychologists and political scientists would write lengthy papers on how foregoing his name allowed him to become more inured to the effects of his dictatorship—that is, the loss of his name helped him become inhumane.

As a poet attuned to linguistic nuances, Elena also pointed out to Cristy, "Note, too, how he wasn't called 'dictator' but 'The Dictator.' The *The* facilitates the distancing and elevation desired by the dictator's self-pedestalling ego."

On that emerald island, The Dictator ruled and, as often occurs in a tyranny, most tried to live without catching his attention. But as also often occurs in a tyranny, a small number tried to save the island paradise by overthrowing the cruel regime. One of these rebels came to The Dictator's attention when the rebel crafted an ingenious propaganda plan against his rule. The rebel understood the power of the name. He didn't refer to him as Mateo but by various diminutives of the name that diluted The Dictator's image. Not *Mateo* but

> *Matty!*
>
> *Matetito!*
>
> *Mateteo!*

Mateteo! had the unfortunate meaning in one of the island's dialects of "monkey's butt hole," which popularized the use of the monkey's image on various flyers, graffiti and other outlets of anti-dictatorship propaganda. Of course, it wasn't the monkey's face that was featured... and, often, copious amounts of excrement were featured flowing out of its hole with as much generosity as the volume of The Dictator's ego-propping "fake news."

To The Dictator's frustration, *Mateteo!* well exemplified the potent use of humor as a strategy for belittling the powerful. The scholar Nerissa Balce once said, "I teach 'Race and Humor' in my university. The theory of humor I love to share is the theory of inversion—the reversal of power. We laugh when the cruelties of the world are exposed. We laugh when the powerful are made fun of, and they're taken down by a joke. Fascists hate humor because humor threatens their order, the order that they want which is that they're on top."

However, *Mateteo!* also had the unfortunate effect of drawing The Dictator's attention to the rebel who conceived of the highly-effective humiliation strategy: when the insult first started surfacing in Queza, The Dictator even caught allies—and some of his own guards!—joining the national snickering. He vowed to punish Mateteo's rebel-author. That witty rebel was Thomas Theeland. He had a daughter, Elena.

19 JANUARY

Once upon a time, an emerald island laid upon a blue sapphire ocean and both glowed under the beam of a 24-carat sun. *Coral motus* ringed much of the island's circumference like a sandy fringed shawl; beneath its surface and before many hungry Pacificans were forced to forage offshore, a variety of sea creatures and fishes frolicked in blue but also gin-clear waters. Under starlit skies, it was possible to spot bioluminescent plankton in the sea. Presiding over the island was the peak of Mount Itonguk from where, according to indigenous mythology, the Itonguk people descended to become the island's first human inhabitants by walking down a rainbow. During The Dictator's reign, not many Pacificans bothered to climb Mount Itonguk for the incongruous winter-like beauty of its peak. There, an icy climate abounded despite the island's location in the tropics. In other parts of the island, verdant jungles hosted other wildlife in a number so varied not all have been given names by humans. In the island's interior, awe-inspiring limestone formations rose starkly from rice fields. On one part of the island's western coast, rock arches and a hundred caves presented an eyelet pattern whitened by sea salt over the years.

In Pacifica, the darkness did not emanate from the land or sea that accomplished exactly what they were supposed to do to create a paradise. In Pacifica, the darkness simmered within its people.

Thomas Theeland turned away from the street with its puddles of half-naked toddlers, exhausted mothers in loose dresses, and makeshift gangs of teens with time their only possession. With dark-brown hair, medium height, muscled but wiry frame, and his most compelling characteristic of violet eyes hidden behind darkened sunglasses, he could melt in a crowd. But he stood out with his pressed pants, neatly tucked shirt, clean-shaven face, and a slim leather briefcase. He turned away from the street of wary eyes to enter a dim alley. He had been instructed to go there for a meeting. As also instructed, he looked for a wooden pig by a door.

He saw the pig. Its oversized snout was almost as large as its body. *More proof,* he thought, *of the world losing all sense of proportion.*

But before he moved deeper into the alley, he paused, struck by a thought. He made a slight turn, as if to return to the street. But he merely stood there as he considered what he'd observed: the street, despite its people, was neat. There wasn't an inch of debris despite its path of broken concrete.

In desperation, he came to share that observation with his captors. When he'd reached the pig—atop its huge snout leered the cheap entertainment of a scrawled moustache—the door opened to release four men. They grabbed him and started pummeling him. In desperation, he gasped, "The street was clean! No trash on it!"

Yes, that non sequitur made the men pause. They looked at each other and laughed.

One spoke for them all, "You're facing your death, man! What are you babbling about?"

Thomas replied between wheezes, "The people are poor. They're exhausted from hunger. You can tell by the dim stains under all of their eyes. Yet they keep the street clean. They pick up their trash!"

One man muttered, "Crazy" and started to beat him again. But another raised a hand to make him stop.

The man said, "I'm curious. What's the significance to you of clean streets?"

"One becomes a killer when hope has died," Thomas said. "But people don't have to give up hope, like those people of that street. You don't have to kill me just because someone told you to do so."

The men looked at each other and shook their heads. The man who had questioned Thomas reached over and slapped his forehead with the back of his hand.

"Fool!" he said. "The street lacks trash because it's picked clean—there may be the stray bit of food, and paper, cardboard and metal parts can be sold to the recycler. You think they care about keeping streets clean? Fool—they became garbage scavengers *precisely* because they lack hope."

Yet the conversation triggered something in the questioner that made him order the other men to cease the beating. He gave another order that resulted in Thomas being tossed in the back of a car and taken away. With eyes nearly shut from his beating, Thomas could no longer observe the streets they passed.

But his ears could still work and, once, Thomas heard the man who sounded like the one who questioned him.

"Hope!" he snorted before muttering in disgust, "Classic—how people who've never experienced poverty become poverty scholars. Try having them explain how this trained engineer with a Ph.D. became a thug!"

Thomas heard the others respond with their own sneers. One said, "Hope is useless without a full bank account."

Another added, "... and an authentic and big, fat pig in the yard waiting to be barbecued!"

Thomas passed in and out of consciousness to the music rapped out by those who'd forgotten the feeling of full-bellied satiation: *BAAAH-BEE-CUE! BAAAAH-BEEE-CUE! BAAAAA...!*

8 JULY

"Once upon a time, an emerald island laid upon a blue sapphire ocean and both glowed under the beam of a 24-carat sun"—this began one of Pacifica's most popular childhood tales. The story inspired a common chant that transcended its beginnings to become a toast at celebrations and parties:

Emerald island!

Sapphire ocean!

24-carat sun!

Let's have fun!

Thomas learned the chant from his Pacifican mother who had married a Texan. In Houston where he was raised as a child, his mother taught him as much about Pacifican culture as she remembered, interspersing the tales into the more common children's stories surrounding them: Grimm's *Fairy Tales,* Aesop's *Fables,* and, of course reflecting local color, Edward O'Reilly's cowboy folktale *Pecos Bill.*

As he had done many times before in moments of stress, Thomas mentally chanted as he rocked back and forth to the car's speedy pace over ill-maintained and often broken streets: *Emerald island! Sapphire ocean! 24-carat sun! Let's have fun!* After a rough turn that threw him against the legs of one of the men who promptly kicked him away, Thomas thought, *What a perversion. The only person having fun in this hellhole is that adurag, The Dictator…*

14 APRIL

Once upon a time, an emerald island laid upon a blue sapphire ocean and both glowed under the beam of a 24-carat sun. *Emerald island, sapphire ocean, 24-carat sun*—from such treasures, a fairy tale should have unfolded into a happy ending.

"My name is Rob. I promise you that your family will find your body."

"Well," Thomas coughed out through the blood, "that's not what one wants to hear just before dying."

The man who schooled him on how Pacifica's streets remain clean, replied, "It's something. I still don't know what happened to my parents."

Thomas looked at him. He looked at the other three men surrounding him.

Dead eyes. Deadened eyes, Thomas thought. *Except in yours, Rob. I see your anguish.*

To experience pain means one can still feel… and the possibility one might still be redeemable.

Thomas looked directly into Rob's eyes. He could barely talk, but whispered loud enough so that Rob could hear: "Rob, I forgive you."

27 APRIL

Once upon a time, Elena dreamt she was walking on an emerald island down one of its streets towards a grey building. It was daylight but what she saw in the sky behind the building was a full moon. She paused and raised a bare arm. Against her skin, she saw the silver of moonlight instead of a sun's golden glow.

What does this mean? She thought. Looking towards the building, she wondered, *Has Ernst stopped waiting for me there?*

24 JUNE

Once upon a time, an emerald island laid upon a blue sapphire ocean and both glowed under the beam of a 24-carat sun. *Emerald island, sapphire ocean, 24-carat sun—a fairy tale next should unfold.* Instead, an island boy grew up to be the adurag demon of the island paradise known as "Pacifica."

"Pacifica was paradise for me," Ernst said. "But we were expatriates from the U.S. and the dollar went a long way. You didn't have to travel far from our compound to see the distress on the streets. The Dictator and his family were high maintenance—they wanted all that they could squeeze from the people."

"Yes, the dollar was potent," Elena said, frowning. "It supported The Dictator and your father's decision to assassinate my father."

"I suppose I could say my father didn't decide, just followed, orders. But I accept that no one needs to follow immoral orders."

Elena didn't say anything. Ernst, too, became silent. *We're so often lapsing to silence.* For the moment, there was nothing to say.

17 FEBRUARY

Once upon a time, an emerald island laid upon a blue sapphire ocean and both glowed under the beam of a 24-carat sun.

"I once marveled at how Pacifica's lush colors never infiltrated my father's consciousness. His wardrobe could have at least benefited from their surroundings," Ernst said as they took Elena's hand into theirs before turning over to look up at the ceiling. Elena sat up on their bed to look at them.

"What did your father usually wear? He surely could not have worn pin-striped wool suits in that heat?!"

"Not dark, wool suits. But he wore khaki slacks and white shirts. Every. Day."

"Everyday? Well, no wonder you admired Mr. Bellow's vivid, technicolor skirts!"

"I learned to associate my father's bland uniform with the kind of lifestyle—the kind of life—he wanted to press upon me."

"Oh?" Elena was surprised by the conversation's turn.

"Yes—a life tied to conformity, as well as an unimaginative view of the world. So paradoxical, given his life as a spy."

"Perhaps it was his spy work that made him wish for you what he considered 'normal'?"

At Elena's theory, Ernst merely grunted.

"You wanted something different," Elena said to encourage them to continue after a long pause.

"I think so. I wanted not to be as boring or predictable as him. And not as close-minded. I began reconsidering what I knew, or what he'd taught me. I suppose I began then to consider identity—even though it was sparked by simply not wanting to emulate him.

"Besides, I'm biracial—only half-white. I had another parent to consider, a mother from a different culture and whose values might differ from his. I knew nothing about my mother's background, but what I did know was that her background was different from my father's."

"Why didn't you know much about your mother? Didn't your family stay in touch with her family in the Philippines?"

"No. None of us knew anything about her relatives. Orphaned at a young age, she was raised by Catholic nuns as their ward. By the time I came to make some inquiries, the nuns had passed."

"How sad," Elena said, squeezing their hand and regretting her question.

Ernst drew in a deep breath, then continued. "But the point remains: my mother's culture is different from my father's. Despite my father's conservatism, that he married my mother proves differences can co-exist, can manage relationships with each other.

"I chose to be gender fluid since that's more accurate to reflecting me, or the me I wanted to be—wide-ranging, multiple, open... everything that was the opposite of my father's tightly-clenched position on identity."

After a few moments, Elena said, "I'm glad."

"Oh?" Ernst looked at her.

"I'm glad because the person you forged yourself to be is the person I needed to learn from, to help me."

"You help yourself, Elena," they said before accepting her kiss.

"You know what I mean," Elena replied, smiling.

They kissed again.

17 JULY

Once upon a time, an emerald island laid upon a blue sapphire ocean and both glowed under the beam of a 24-carat sun. *Emerald island, sapphire ocean, 24-carat sun*—the stuff of fairy tales.

"You know, Pacifica really was a paradise," Elena said, reaching for the mug of tea Ernst had prepared. She didn't feel like drinking tea, but she felt chilled and wanted the warmth of the mug.

"Sure. Before The Dictator," Ernst said, just to say something and keep the conversation rolling. Before speaking just then, Elena had been silent for several minutes, staring out the window but clearly seeing only the past.

"The Dictator," Elena repeated, nodding her head. "It's painful how his effects go beyond Pacifica. Here I am, years later in an American city an ocean away and I'm just *ravaged* because of something The Dictator once set in motion."

That's when Ernst asked what they'd long been curious to know ever since they discovered their father's role in Elena's family.

"After your father died, what happened to you?"

Elena looked at them, an old hurt in her eyes.

"Unlike most Pacificans, we didn't have a close-knit family. I don't know Mom's relatives. It was just Dad and me," she began. "When he died, some of Dad's acquaintances took me in, but only to prepare me for adoption by a family in the U.S."

Elena paused and looked down at her mug. Its warmth failed to dispel the cold she felt in her fingers.

"Instigated by my father?" Ernst asked. They thought they knew to what Elena referred, but wanted to hear it directly from her.

"Yes. I suppose your father must have felt some guilt over creating an orphan. He pulled strings to get me adopted by a U.S.-American family."

Elena put the mug of tea back on the coffee table. As she leaned back against the couch she said, "There was a time in Pacifica when I never would have had to leave. Other Pacificans would have taken me into their homes, as they did with any orphan. To reflect Kapwa."

"It must have been a tough transition. You didn't just lose a parent but a country."

Elena nodded.

"So, you have an American family, too—the folks who adopted you?"

Elena shook her head.

"It didn't last," she said.

"Please don't tell me you were placed with bad people," Ernst said as they reached over to hold Elena's hands. Their concern matched the warmth of their hands and aborted the shiver lurking just under her skin.

"Oh no, they—Stuart and Leny Pearson—weren't bad," she replied. "But I didn't have a chance to know them as much as I could. Once puberty hit, I began asking and kept asking them to let me go. After some time of being a problematic child, they reluctantly agreed, surrendering me to the state and its foster care system. I just went from one family to another until I aged out.

"I didn't know, of course, how problematic the foster care system is. Had I known, perhaps I would have stayed with the Pearsons."

"I'm sorry," Ernst said.

Elena shook her head at their apology. "It's not your fault."

She continued, "Many years later, I researched international adoption issues as well as older child adoption and learned that about 25% of older child adoptions fail. And part of the failure is not necessarily due to abuse or a so-called 'poor fit'. Adoption begins with loss, and the adoptee often grieves the loss of her biological parents by taking it out on whoever adopted her. Unfortunately, to the young child, there may seem no one else to blame but the new parents. In some cases where the child is rehomed rather than placed in foster care, the child may not have the same problem with the new family because the child took out most of the loss issues on the first set of adopters."

Squeezing her hands, Ernst said, "It sounds like you've learned a lot about adoption."

"Yes. It led me at one point to volunteer for Safe Children, the orphan advocacy group."

"Great—you turned your unhappy experiences to something good."

Elena smiled. "At one point, I felt like I would have gone under were it not for the kids I met through Safe Children. Someone once said I was 'saving' them when, actually, they were saving me. They were giving me a reason to find value in my life.

"Anyway, exploring adoption issues was my first step towards eventually investigating my past."

Ernst said, "I suppose you didn't expect to stumble onto me during your search."

"No," Elena agreed. "But that ball was in your court, wasn't it? It was up to you to ensure we would 'stumble' across each other?"

"I won't dispute that," Ernst said. "Because of my father, The Dictator, Pacifica, and even how art demands maximizing self-awareness, I searched for you."

"Here we are..." they both said simultaneously. They smiled at each other. But the smiles were brief and quickly faded away.

20 MAY

Emerald island

Sapphire ocean

24-carat sun...

Ernst muttered under their breath. Elena, who had returned from the bathroom, finished it for him: *Let's have fun!*

"What a joke, right?" Elena sighed as she looked for her purse.

"It need not be a joke. It shouldn't be a joke!" Ernst said.

Elena looked at Ernst.

"Why do I think you're concocting something?" she said.

"Elena, I think we've just discovered June12.com's newest slogan! That childhood rhyme beloved by Pacificans before The Dictator's reign made joy evaporate from Pacifica!"

Slowly, Elena chanted softly as she considered Ernst's idea: *Emerald island, sapphire ocean, 24-carat sun....*

"Brilliant," she concluded. "I'll inform the volunteers and our network. Before The Dictator, there was a Pacifica. And after The Dictator, there will continue to be Pacifica—may it return to Paradise!"

22 MARCH

Once upon a time, an emerald island laid upon a blue sapphire ocean and both glowed under the beam of a 24-carat sun. But a dark cloud came to rise from paradise. The cloud, named Mateo Con, diminished light as he reigned over the island as The Dictator.

"Despite their darkened times, honest people persevered to guide Pacifica back towards sunnier times. Of course, many of them died.

"I say, 'Of course,' because my father's story was the story of too many Pacificans," Elena said. "That's what I was told by the social worker who first introduced the idea of adoption. She called the situation 'sad but nothing special'."

"*Of course*," Ernst stressed, "we know that *not* to be true, right Elena?"

"Yes." Elena smiled. "Dad was special. What happened occurred to many but each individual was special.

"But it took me a long time to come to that conclusion. *Of course*, I'm glad I did, as it was my refusal to just accept him as just another of The Dictator's victims that fueled my search for what happened to Dad."

"And I'm glad you began your search, Elena," Ernst said. "Both of our searches led us to each other, and now you will continue June12.com."

Elena paused.

"What do you mean? I'm happy to work with you on June12.com, Ernst. But won't we continue together?"

Ernst stood and walked towards the kitchen.

"I need some water. You?" they asked.

"No, thanks."

When they returned, they stood there for a while, watching Elena. She watched them back, then raised a questioning brow. But she didn't say anything, unsure as to whether she wanted more details. She thought, *Are you going somewhere, Ernst? Will you leave me, too?*

"Elena," they said. "I am very sick."

15 SEPTEMBER

Once upon a time, an emerald island laid upon a blue sapphire ocean and both glowed under the beam of a 24-carat sun. But has there ever been a paradise that wasn't interrupted if not cut short?

Elena thought she and Ernst had come to create a modest secret paradise in Ernst's apartment, in a grey building. But...

21 OCTOBER

Once upon a time, an emerald island laid upon a blue sapphire ocean and both glowed under the beam of a 24-carat sun. On the other side of the world, I once left the darkness of the underground subway for the street that led to your grey building.

That day, I rushed towards you.

That morning, I'd woken with a jolt to find myself seated upright in the middle of my bed, both my body and the linen damp with my sweat. My fingers were itching, as if they were still stroking the scar over your heart in the nightmare I'd just left.

I rushed towards you.

As soon as I walked through your door I tore off your shirt.

"No foreplay," you joked even as your eyes glimmered with concern.

"No scar," I gasped as my palm confirmed the lack of a scar over your heart, or anywhere else on your chest. Your warm hands held me then against the stolid strength of your existence, your heartbeat as strong and consistent as the fortitude of your support.

Later, after I'd explained myself—the nightmare that made me retch into wakefulness—you whispered directly into my ear as my face was pressed against your neck, "Silly girl. My scars are not visible."

Years later, I'd whisper back against this memory: *Wrong answer, Ernst. I wanted to hear you say, "Silly girl. I don't have scars."*

You weren't supposed to have scars at all, Ernst. You were supposed to be invincible—so invincible you would always be there for me.

3 APRIL

Once upon a time, an emerald island laid upon a blue sapphire ocean and both glowed under the beam of a 24-carat sun. But has there ever been a paradise that wasn't interrupted if not cut short?

Elena thought she and Ernst had come to create a modest secret paradise in Ernst's apartment. But, there, Ernst said it: "Elena, I am very sick."

Elena watched them take a sip of water. It seemed the act occurred in slow motion. Slowly, they raised the glass to their mouth, opened their mouth, took a sip, and then swallowed. As soon as they swallowed, time crashed back to its normal pace which was too fast.

"Creeley's Disease," they said.

Elena felt her hands fold around her belly as she felt the news punch her there. Creeley's Disease originates from a brain tumor that ultimately impairs memory and harms a person's ability to carry out daily activities. While the tumor remains tiny, its afflicted display no symptoms. But it's only a matter of time before it grows large enough to damage its host. Its victim will suffer in part from memory crunches, as distinguished from memory lapses, where the diseased does not forget events but "scrunches" them together as if they all occurred simultaneously.

Ironic, Elena thought. She'd grown accustomed to idealizing Kapwa and Kapwa-time. *How bludgeoning*, she thought as she hugged her belly, *to be reminded—yet again—that the ideal is not always real.*

"How much time do you—do we—have?" Elena asked. She spoke slowly, as if she wanted to force time to slow down.

"A few months. I waited to tell you," they said, looking sadly at her. "We have much work to do. Our time is limited."

"Time wouldn't be time if it were not limited," she said, then wondered why she replied that way. It was utterly meaningless.

"Love," she forged forward. "Love transcends time."

They smiled.

"Agree with me," Elena urged.

To the plea in her eyes, Ernst replied, "I agree."

They added, "How can one disagree with such a lovely baby..."

Elena paused, wrinkling her brow.

"... such a lovely baby...!"

She wondered if the disease had begun to speak for them.

"I'm no baby!" she pretended to scoff to test their faculties.

"Oh, but you're a baby! A lovely baby! Bay-baaay! Ba-by bay-bay..."

They coughed. As if the coughing returned them to their senses, they said, "I agree. Love transcends time."

Elena, relieved, ignored their earlier ramblings and repeated with a smile, "Love transcends time."

29 JANUARY

Once upon a time, an emerald island laid upon a blue sapphire ocean and both glowed under the beam of a 24-carat sun.

"I will meet you there," Elena whispered to Ernst on their deathbed.

Despite their dissipating life-breaths, a grin brightened Ernst's face because of Elena's gift: a colorful scarf she'd draped over their chest to mask the biliously-lime hospital gown they wore. Unfolded, the scarf revealed a peacock's flamboyantly-spread tail with wide open eyes.

"You've lived your life in Technicolor!" Elena proclaimed when she gave it to them.

Forcing back her tears, Elena sang and chanted,

> *Emerald island*
>
> *Sapphire ocean*
>
> *24-carat sun*

and the last line as she amended,

> *We will have fun!*

Elena made sure Ernst's last life experience was joy. She made sure the last expression on Ernst's face was a smile.

> *Emerald island*
>
> *Sapphire ocean*
>
> *24-carat sun...*

10 AUGUST

"Once upon a time, an emerald island laid upon a blue sapphire ocean and both glowed under the beam of a 24-carat sun. Ernst has returned there—to Pacifica when it was an island paradise."

Elena wondered if that was too cheesy. *Probably*, she thought. But she hit the *Send* button anyway to announce Ernst's passing to the June12.com network.

The news wasn't a surprise—Ernst had spread the news about their illness as soon as they informed Elena.

"We have much work and need time to transition you as my successor," they said after revealing their diagnosis.

Elena didn't bother to ask, "Why me?"

Instead, she affirmed, "It's my way back. Back to Pacifica."

"I'm glad you recognize that," Ernst said. "And, of course, it's the least my family can do for yours."

"My family?" Elena said. "I'm alone now."

"Not forever, Elena. I know you. Someday, you will be a mother. And you will mother the new nation Pacifica will become."

"Really? How can you know that about me?"

"There's so much love in you, Elena," Ernst said, watching their hand rise to touch her cheek as if on its own volition.

Elena rubbed her cheek against their hand.

"Yes," she said. "One should bring the past into the future through love."

13 JUNE

"Once upon a time, an emerald island laid upon a blue sapphire ocean and both glowed under the beam of a 24-carat sun. That is your reality..."

Elena woke with a gasp. She was sitting straight up on her bed, the bed linen damp and strewn about her as if she'd wrestled with them in her sleep.

She knew she'd been dreaming about Pacifica but couldn't remember the owner of the voice last speaking to her.

"I would have thought it'd be you, Ernst," she said out loud to the dimness. "But the voice was female..."

Uttering Ernst's name, she realized it was the first time she'd spoken their name since their funeral. She recalled another dream: once upon a time, Elena had dreamt she was walking down a street towards a grey building. It was daylight but what she had seen in the sky behind the building was a full moon. She had paused and raised a bare arm. Against her skin, she had seen the silver of moonlight instead of a sun's golden glow.

What does this color mean? she had thought. Looking towards the building, she had wondered, *Has Ernst stopped waiting for me there?*

She had been in that state where she knew she was dreaming and yet continued to dream instead of waking up to reality. She had been walking down a street towards a grey building to meet a stranger there in their apartment.

She had sensed her preference for dreaming rather than facing reality. *Why?* she had thought. *Why do I not want to wake?*

What is my reality?

Elena laid back against her bed and turned to curl into a fetal position. Tears leaked out as she mumbled into her pillow, "This. This is my reality. A world so cruel it contains the bludgeoning reality of your death, Ernst. A world so cruel..."

But as I fell into the succor of sleep, I thought I heard the music of children's laughter and Ernst's voice. They were also laughing. Then I thought I heard them chide, "Tsk, Elena. In Kapwa-time, it's always time for laughter!"

14 JUNE

Once upon a time, Elena approached a grey building after the two-year period she'd spent approaching this same building to meet Ernst. When she neared The Portal, she slowed her pace. She was not eager to reach the front door as she knew what would happen—it would be unusual for someone to rush towards disappointment.

At the front entrance, Elena did not raise her hand to push at the intercom button for Ernst's apartment. She merely stood there and looked at the button with its label, "Apt. 3J."

When she finally looked away from the door, an hour, perhaps two, had lapsed and she looked up at the sky. It was as grey as the building.

She turned around and began walking away from the grey building. She walked under a grey sky, feeling all of the buildings around her to be grey. Soon, the air, too, turned grey. She walked in greyness for the rest of the day as she paced the length of a city swaddled in grey.

When night fell, she saw the grey retain its shade against night's blackness. She sat on a park bench watching grey retain its tone over people, passing cars, dogs being walked, a cop who watched her but decided to move on, surrounding buildings, sidewalks, what would have been browning patches of grass, a plastic bag blown across the street by a stray breeze, street lights ...

"Are you okay?"

Elena heard the concern more than the words and turned her face towards the voice. A young woman holding an umbrella was looking at her. The woman then moved closer so that she also could hold the umbrella over Elena.

"It's starting to rain. You should get out of the rain. Do you have somewhere to go?"

Elena smiled and felt herself say the necessary things to alleviate the woman's concerns. She also stood to illustrate that, yes, she will leave the onslaught of rain. The woman offered to share her umbrella's shelter but Elena shook her head, saying she was going the opposite way. When Elena turned away from the woman to leave, she noticed the world was no longer grey.

She turned her face upward to feel the rain. She felt her face as a compilation of nerve endings and the sensation of water drops brought her back to the world, as it inescapably was, around her.

She parted her lips to lick at the wetness brought by rain. She thought of the many times she had willingly parted her lips for Ernst. And with that recollection, she knew Ernst need not evaporate. She could bring Ernst's presence back into her life whenever she wanted to remember.

Like, she thought as she walked towards the street corner, *when I pause before a street light waiting for red to turn green, I can remember you in your kitchen, slicing red and green bell peppers to put into an omelet you cooked for us one afternoon. We were pleasantly tired from making love. And we made love again after we each devoured two omelets.*

Elena licked her lips. Then she parted her lips to whisper against the soothing rain: *I remember you, Ernst. I remember you in a world whose greyness you taught me to both accept and repel.*

Chapter 9

"Once upon a time, an emerald island laid upon a blue sapphire ocean and both glowed under the beam of a 24-carat sun—wow! It really is like the way it was described in the children's fairy tale!" Cristy said as she looked out of the airplane window.

On the aisle seat, Elena smiled at her daughter's enthusiasm. She smiled wider when she glimpsed Pacifica through the window. *How heavenly,* she thought, *to see Pacifica and my daughter seeing Pacifica for the first time.*

"Yes," Elena said. "It will be good for you to see Pacifica—to see where it all began. To see the people and the country for which June12.com is fighting. Principles are not abstract."

Cristy turned to look back at her mother.

"The embodiment of principle," she said thoughtfully. Brightening, she added, "Where it all began, yes. But we are still defining what that 'it' is, right Mom?"

Then she laughed. She announced, "Here's my version!

> *Emerald island*
>
> *Sapphire ocean*
>
> *24-carat sun*
>
> *It has begun!*

135

22 AUGUST

Once upon a time, an emerald island laid upon a blue sapphire ocean and both glowed under the beam of a 24-carat sun.

"This heat!" Cristy exclaimed. "How can people get used to it?!"

Elena smiled. They had just exited the airport terminal and were waiting by the edge of a sidewalk for their ride.

"The heat from a 24-carat sun," Elena said, raising her face towards the sunlit, blue sky. She felt her pale complexion begin to blossom warmly into pink rose petals.

Just like the sunlit hallway, Elena thought, *in a grey building where, once, Ernst constantly waited for her.*

15 SEPTEMBER

Once upon a time, an emerald island laid upon a blue sapphire ocean and both glowed under the beam of a 24-carat sun.

Cristy and Elena escaped from the tropical heat into Tata Romeo's dimly-lit house. There, despite the tropical heat, Elena felt a chill overcome her body as her father's former chauffeur recollected her father's last days.

"He was so tense," Tata Romeo spoke softly as his eyes glazed into that look that showed he was looking inward at the past.

"Where was he going? Who was he meeting?"

They were discussing the day Tata Romeo drove Elena's father to a meeting that would begin the end of his life.

"I'm not sure. I was only his driver, and really just a kid at the time," he said, turning his grey eyes on her. The cataracts were on the edge of fully overcoming his sight. "But it also doesn't matter much, does it?"

"What do you mean it doesn't matter?" Cristy interjected.

"Whatever your father's story was, it was no different from those who also rebelled against The Dictator. He died from his efforts, but so did many other thousands, hundreds of thousands, like him."

Tata Romeo's eyes began to glaze over again into the past but cleared quickly back into the present. He whispered as he raised a trembling hand with fingers thinned to resemble claws, "You should both just focus on the larger story. A story that is still unfolding. After all, who's in power now?"

A glimmer of hurt darkened the greyness in his eyes. He said, "They took away my parents. Salvage..."

He lifted a finger to wipe away a tear that had leaked out to dampen his cheek.

"He's dead now. But should The Dictator, that thug, and his family still remain in power?"

7 FEBRUARY

Once upon a time, an emerald island laid upon a blue sapphire ocean and both glowed under the beam of a 24-carat sun.

"We're leaving. We're returning to New York," Elena announced as they left Tata Romeo's house.

"What? We're supposed to meet the resistance here," Cristy said, walking faster to keep up with her mother.

"Skype or Zoom will do. There's nothing here for us. Let's do what we want to do through June12.com, which we can do from anywhere in the world as we work the internet."

Elena stopped, turned, and looked at Cristy.

"I know you wanted to see Pacifica, learn more about the island fueling our activities. But Pacifica is not the paradise it is supposed to be until we finish June12.com's work. So let's focus on that!"

"But..."

Elena raised her hand to stop Cristy. Curtly, she said, "Look around. What do you see?"

Cristy obeyed, looking about from where they'd halted on the sidewalk. The "sidewalk" had lost its concrete long ago, remaining mostly as dirt and stones. The few people around moved sluggishly as if to preserve energy. Her eyes stuck on an image that could have symbolized the destructiveness of The Dictator's and his heirs' regimes: a naked toddler with bloated stomach sitting listlessly against a wall. Cristy swallowed hard as she looked back at her mother.

"Not exactly a paradise, is it," Elena said, then continued walking towards their hired car.

When they reached the car, Elena ordered the driver as she opened the door, "The airport. As quickly as you can. We're leaving this, this... this complete opposite of Paradise."

2 SEPTEMBER

Once upon a time, an emerald island laid upon a blue sapphire ocean and both glowed under the beam of a 24-carat sun.

"It's amazing, and depressing," Cristy said as she looked out of the window of the airplane ascending away from Pacifica. "How can something that looks so beautiful from a distance look so ravaged up close?"

She would have looked back towards her mother but Elena encouraged her, "Keep looking out. Pacifica retains its beauty from the sky and I want you to hold that image in your mind, despite what we saw on its broken streets."

Cristy looked down through the window. The island gleamed as it offered luminous degrees of green under sunlight. But soon, the emerald began to fade. When all she could see was the grey of clouds, she fell back against her seat and closed her eyes.

Elena saw the grey against the window and sat back, too. *Grey, like a building I once approached, at first with trepidation and then with anticipation,* she remembered.

Elena thought, *Ernst, at least you didn't see what Cristy and I saw—what happened to our beloved Pacifica.*

Elena thought, *Ernst ...*

20 OCTOBER

Once upon a time, an emerald island laid upon a blue sapphire ocean and both glowed under the beam of a 24-carat sun. But humanity interfered.

Many people silently hoped the island would return to paradise after The Dictator died. But his legacy was long-lasting. The Dictator's son now ruled Pacifica.

"You told me your father wanted to make amends! To help Pacificans recover from his father's—The Dictator's!—reign," Cristy was hissing at her computer screen.

Elena lifted her eyes from her book to pay closer attention to Cristy's Skyped conversation.

"That's what my father promised," Paul said from the computer screen. "Give me some time to figure it out. I'll get back to you soon."

Cristy pushed back from her computer with a frown, looked at her mother, and rolled her swivel chair over to Elena who asked, "What happened?"

"A group of Pacifican June12-ers met with BeeBee at his request. It was supposed to be the first of several meetings to discuss how to dismantle The Dictator's apparatus throughout Pacifica. But they were arrested!"

The mother and daughter looked at each other, a shared worry staring from each other's eyes.

"It's on us," Cristy whispered. "They only agreed to meet with BeeBee because of our recommendation."

Before Elena could speak, Cristy suddenly stiffened.

"Oh no! I'd given Paul the contacts for other June12 networks!"

She lunged back to her computer screen and began typing furiously.

Elena let her work—she knew Cristy had to alert every June12-er on Pacifica to go into hiding. BeeBee's betrayal didn't surprise her—it always seemed too good to be true that The Dictator's son would give up the privileged lifestyle with which his father cosseted his family. But Elena did wonder whether Paul, The Dictator's grandson, was also corrupt. *How many generations,* she thought, *will The Dictator damage?*

26 SEPTEMBER

Once upon a time, an emerald island laid upon a blue sapphire ocean and both glowed under the beam of a 24-carat sun. But humanity interfered.

"We don't know if Paul betrayed us," Elena said. "Sure, he had to help set up the meeting but it could have been his father who was playing him and us."

"The two had to be in it together," Cristy said. "Otherwise, the father would be using his son."

"Well, don't wait in letting the other June12-ers know. Their lives are in danger."

What else have I dreamt? Elena thought. *Why didn't I consider the difficulty required for a child to betray a parent?*

The planet was full of other dictators besides Pacifica's Mateo Con. Once, Elena read an article interviewing Peony Jingwah, the daughter of the strong-armed ruler of United Teemor. Despite her father's rapacious reign over their country and the privileged upbringing that Peony and her siblings enjoyed as a result of their father's thuggery, Elena momentarily felt sorry for Peony. Peony was being interviewed in England where she attended Oxford. A reporter and political scientist major for the university's newspaper had asked tough, unrelenting questions about her father's dictatorship.

"We didn't really see much of that," Peony kept saying to the reporter's litany of human rights abuses. "We were just children, and he was a good father. He was loving, kind, playful and generous."

Smart enough to attend Oxford and yet so stubbornly blind, Elena thought. But it requires fortitude for a child to reject a parent.

"Would BeeBee Con actually repudiate his own father?"

Elena didn't realize she spoke her question out loud until Cristy turned to her to reply.

Cristy said, "As you've often said, Mom: *Power corrupts.*"

Both also thought, and one said, "There's nothing so sticky-stubborn as the power of privilege."

9 OCTOBER

Once upon a time, an emerald island laid upon a blue sapphire ocean and both glowed under the beam of a 24-carat sun. But humanity interfered.

His eyes were red—it seemed as if The Dictator's grandson had cried recently.

"He mentioned the Mafia, the cartels of South America, others... ," he spoke from the computer screen at Elena and Cristy. "He said families have imploded from less."

Paul coughed, or pretended to cough. He continued, "He said I was too young to have known my grandfather. So he said he didn't blame me for knowing him only through how he's been portrayed by the media. He said, 'Don't be embarrassed because The Dictator was your grandfather.' He said, ... "

Paul broke off, seemingly unable to continue. Cristy put her hand on the computer screen, as if she could reach through and comfort him. Impatiently, Elena moved her hand away so she could see Paul more clearly.

"So BeeBee used you, his only son, to penetrate June12.com?" Elena asked. She thought she knew the answer but she wanted confirmation.

He didn't say anything. But he nodded.

"We'll get back to you," Elena said curtly and turned off the Skype connection. She turned to Cristy.

"Have you alerted everyone whose names you'd shared with Paul?"

"All except one," Cristy said. "We're still trying to find Susan Tinto."

"Good," Elena said, relief lightening the furrow on her brow. "But you can stop trying to find Susan. Just help the others go underground or leave Pacifica."

"Why not Susan?" Cristy said, surprised.

Elena looked at Cristy, momentarily silent as if she was trying to choose her words.

"Susan Tinto was never part of June12.com. I included her on the names you shared with Paul because she's one of BeeBee's most favored and trusted advisors. Now, BeeBee will go after her as he will believe she betrayed him. An apt revenge for the planner of the massacre that decimated the Damul tribe because BeeBee wanted their land for his own Disneyland."

Sorrow dimmed Cristy's eyes.

"You knew to plot against Susan Tinto by using Paul? You've become Machiavellian."

The same sorrow dimmed Elena's eyes. To become adept at fighting wars is not by itself praiseworthy—it's another hallmark of losing innocence.

"But how did you know BeeBee was just using Paul, his own son?" Cristy asked.

"I didn't. I just didn't trust them," Elena replied.

From many past and future conversations, Elena repeated, "Power corrupts."

1 NOVEMBER

Once upon a time, an emerald island laid upon a blue sapphire ocean and both glowed under the beam of a 24-carat sun. But humanity interfered.

"All managed to escape Pacifica, except for one," Cristy told Elena. They were bent over Cristy's computer.

"Jose Bedia," Elena read from the email.

"Tortured. Body found separated from head," Cristy continued reading. "On the beach, by the charred remains of his boat."

As they scrolled up his image, both women froze at a sign pinned on Jose Bedia's torso:

"As in Star Trek, there's always a 'Lieutenant Expendable'—

Here he lies with your lies."

"Mofas," Cristy muttered. The Dictator was known for loving the "Star Trek" television series, and his affection must have been passed on to his allies.

Elena straightened up and stretched. She went to the couch where she sat down.

"It's going to be another tough drawn-out fight," she said, rubbing between her eyes.

"Well, we are certainly prepared to continue," Cristy said. "I just got another email. Jose's friends all agree: 'June12.com can persevere. While tragic, BeeBee's henchmen found just one of us. There remains plenty of us for the battle.'"

"And Jose Bedia's death might even persuade others to join the fight against The Dictator's son," Elena said. "But it's a paltry benefit of martyrdom, the waste of a young and brilliant mind. Jose Bedia was valedictorian at University of Pacifica."

Cristy paused and looked at her mother.

"Are you okay?"

"Just tired," Elena said, summoning a smile for her daughter. "Don't worry."

Cristy replied, "And don't you worry, Mom. BeeBee—and even Paul if he is with his father—will learn that the rebellion is not comprised of expendables."

Elena sighed and leaned back against the cushions.

"Yes," she said, remembering another time with Ernst when she heard the same words she now shared with her daughter, "Everyone matters."

"Don't mind me," she added, closing her eyes. "I'm just going to take a brief nap. I didn't sleep much last night..."

As Elena dozed into slumber, she felt a soft kiss that expanded into Ernst's face. She heard them say, *Everyone matters...*

3 NOVEMBER

Once upon a time, an emerald island laid upon a blue sapphire ocean and both glowed under the beam of a 24-carat sun.

But paradise is difficult to maintain; humanity interferes. Many Pacificans grew afraid of The Dictator. Many thought they could survive The Dictator's abuses if they hung on long enough. Many became inured to the sight of a malnourished toddler lying on the sidewalk, the toddler's bloated stomach the only reprieve from thinned limbs.

But a determined minority didn't lose sight of right and wrong.

"If The Dictator thought he could reign forever through his family, he can witness his error from hell," Cristy said, grief and determination hardening her face.

"Have you heard from Paul?" Elena said.

"No," Cristy replied, her brow furrowing.

Elena hurt for her daughter. The longer Paul's silence extended, the more likely that he had been a willing participant in BeeBee's attempts to destabilize June12.com. But before Elena could go over to hug her, Cristy turned back to her computer.

"I've got to get back to work. New plans must be made."

Then Cristy paused, looked up from her computer and said, "Thank you, Mom."

Surprised, Elena replied, "For what?"

"You and Ernst formed June12.com," Cristy said. "It will matter, Mom, what June12.com has done, is doing, and will do. We've recovered much proceeds of The Dictator's thievery from the Pacifican people, we've continued to make the world aware of the abuses there and some countries have adjusted their policies for supporting the regime, and we've provided hope and resources to those in Pacifica involved in the rebellion. It matters, Mom."

Elena smiled and said, "I know, Dear. And it will be you and your generation who will continue the fight for as long as it takes to make Pacifica a paradise again."

Cristy smiled back, though her smile quickly faded.

"Right," she said, determination steeling her voice. "Plans must be made. New plans."

12 NOVEMBER

Once upon a time, an emerald island laid upon a blue sapphire ocean and both glowed under the beam of a 24-carat sun. All of the June12.com rebels assumed Pacifica, before The Dictator's reign, was a paradise.

But even during the original *Star Trek* series, thought Elena after she was reminded of The Dictator's favorite television show, the crew of the starship *U.S.S. Enterprise* never discovered a paradise in any of the different worlds they encountered in the galaxy. The closest was a world named Talos IV where its residents could live out their desires. But it was all based on illusion, as practiced by the Talosians.

Is Paradise an illusion, too, among humans? thought Elena. *Is the Pacifican paradise an illusion, a myth?*

It's been so long... can I trust memory?

5 DECEMBER

Once upon a time, an emerald island laid upon a blue sapphire ocean and both glowed under the beam of a 24-carat sun. All of the June12.com rebels assumed Pacifica, before The Dictator's reign, was a paradise.

But even if, once, Pacifica was a paradise, Elena thought, *has there ever been a successful return to paradise? Adam and Eve never returned...*

"Perhaps the answer is irrelevant, Mom," Cristy said. Elena had just shared her musings about Pacifica as paradise.

"There's a rebellion going on against The Dictator and his descendants. If our rebellion must be fueled by a belief that Pacifica can be a paradise if unshackled from their hold, I'm okay with it."

"Even if it's a false belief?" Elena said, her brow wrinkled.

Cristy smiled before replying, "I don't call it false, Mom. I call it *Faith*."

23 DECEMBER

Once upon a time, an emerald island laid upon a blue sapphire ocean and both glowed under the beam of a 24-carat sun.

But no one there lived happily ever after.

Not even The Dictator who took away everyone's happiness. When one is powered only by power, joy becomes irrelevant.

24 NOVEMBER

Once upon a time, an emerald island laid upon a blue sapphire ocean and both glowed under the beam of a 24-carat sun.

"I have to wonder," Elena said to Cristy after both returned to New York, "about how our visit to Pacifica affected you."

"What do you mean?" Cristy said, looking up from her computer monitor.

Elena knew that when Cristy responded that way she usually required more time to consider the question.

"Well, seeing the state of Pacifica today could depress anybody..."

Cristy thought about it, unconsciously inclining her head.

"I suppose it could make our goal seem farther away. Even if we overthrow The Dictator's family, there's been so much damage..."

She drew in a deep breath, and continued more firmly, "But the extent of the damage we saw only highlights the importance of what June12.com is trying to do. In fact, I'll be passing on my photos to the network. It will be depressing, but I hope the images firm up everyone's resolve that we must all work harder to overthrow The Dictator's family and legacy!"

Elena watched as Cristy returned her attention to her computer. She watched her daughter's fingers type furiously on the keyboard. She thought, *I am so proud of you. You and others like you are Pacifica's future, not The Dictator. I am so proud of you.*

But maternal pride was cut off by another memory of Ernst—always! These memories of Ernst! In this particular memory, Ernst had just turned their head away from a painting-in-progress to look at her. They looked at me to emphasize, "There is no past, present, or future in Kapwa-time. It's all now."

26 APRIL

Once upon a time, an emerald island laid upon a blue sapphire ocean and both glowed under the beam of a 24-carat sun. According to a myth so old people assumed its truth, it was a paradise.

No one knew who created the myth, but it was easy to believe that ancient Pacificans never intended what the island became: a generator of images like a shriveled baby watched avidly by a hovering vulture; a corpse strewn by the roadside difficult to identify as its face, teeth and fingertips had been obliterated; an alley perpetually dampened by sewage; a corner edge to the capital city's boundaries colonized by a mountain of trash which, in turn, generated its own neighborhood of t-shirt masked pickers salvaging what they can for food; hospitals with shelves nearly always empty of medicine; beggars everywhere; so many flies over so many sores on malnourished bodies ...

Whether or not it was ever a paradise befitting its creation myth, Elena thought, *I do remember a land where I was happy as a child, a time when I had a father.*

I remember when people can open doors to leave their houses and the first thing they would see were not beggars. Not the thin mothers and their big-bellied babies. Not girls in mini skirts and high-heeled plastic shoes. Not the absence of pet dogs many could not feed... or long since ate. And not men as many were "salvaged" or in hiding.

Elena shook her head to clear the images from her mind. She saw her daughter working with other volunteers through the internet to dilute the power of The Dictator's family. Her eyes suddenly welled up with tears, though she raised a hand to brush them away furiously. *Pacifica,* she thought, *you deserve better.*

11 AUGUST

Once upon a time, an emerald island laid upon a blue sapphire ocean and both glowed under the beam of a 24-carat sun. According to a myth old enough that people assumed its truth, it was a paradise. The wish—the desire—ever simmered in Elena's subconscious...

They heard a knock on the door. Startled, Elena and Cristy looked at each other.

"Are you expecting anyone?" Elena asked.

"No," Cristy said as she stood and walked towards the door. She opened it and immediately stepped back. Paul Romuel stood in their apartment hallway. Shadows from insufficient sleep and shaving weathered his face. His wrinkled clothes suggested he hadn't changed clothes in several days

"How'd you get into the building?" Cristy said, surprised.

"May I come in?" Paul said, as if understanding Cristy's question was not on point.

Cristy just stared. It was Elena who walked towards them and said, "Come in, Paul."

Slowly, Paul entered and walked towards the living room area. He paused and looked around as if he'd never been in their apartment before. He noticed Cristy's computer and the mess of paperwork around it and on the floor by her chair.

"Still busy," he said, turning to look back at them.

Elena motioned him to the couch. Elena followed him to sit in a nearby chair. Cristy moved towards them but remained standing. Paul had never seen her in this state—stiff arms ending in fists alongside her rigid stance, lips thinned, and eyes flaring out a heat he could feel singeing his face where she directed her glare.

"Never mind the chit-chat. Why are you here? And are your father's soldiers close behind?"

Paul closed his eyes as if to shield himself from Cristy's anger.

"No, no soldiers," he said, then opened his eyes.

"Talk," Cristy ordered, still not bothering to hide her anger.

"First, I want to say I'm sorry. I'm so sorry I left you..."

"Never mind all that," Elena interrupted. "You can go into that later with Cristy. The more important thing is to explain what happened and what you're doing here now."

Paul shook his head briefly, as if to reset his own thoughts.

"Let me begin by just noting that I was pressured all of my life to be the heir to my grandfather's stolen throne," he said, his eyes traveling back and forth between Elena and Cristy. "When I met Cristy, it was part of a plan for me to penetrate June12.com and help my father bring it down. I wasn't yet strong enough to dispute my father."

"The Seychelles funds...?" Elena couldn't help herself from asking.

Paul grimaced before he replied, "$250 million is a lot of money, sure. But my father thought the funds expendable if it brought down the rebellion and June12.com. The Dictator had squirrelled away billions and that stash just continues to make more money from illegal but lucrative investing around the world."

Slowly, Elena whispered, "The rich really are different..."

Then Elena shook herself away from the topic. "Never mind that for now. What was happening with you?"

"At first, I went along with my father's plans," Paul said. "But while I pretended to support my father, I could not forget the horror I felt when I first returned to Pacifica after graduating from Princeton. I looked around and really saw how the island was a paradise only to my grandfather's family and our supporters. And for the first time, I could not ignore the other elements that had been walled away from me while I was growing up."

"Like?" Elena asked even as her mind drifted back to what she said during her and Cristy's visit. Like *a shriveled baby watched avidly by a hovering vulture; a corpse strewn by the roadside difficult to identify as its face, teeth and fingertips had been obliterated; an alley perpetually dampened by sewage; a corner edge to the capital city's boundaries colonized by a mountain of trash which, in turn, generated its own neighborhood of t-shirt masked pickers salvaging what they can for food; hospitals with shelves nearly always empty of medicine; beggars everywhere; so many flies over so many sores on malnourished bodies ...*

"Jose Bedia!" Cristy's harsh voice interrupted Paul. "It's unfortunate that whatever change of heart and mind you experienced, you didn't experience it soon enough to save Jose Bedia's life!"

Paul inhaled deeply and looked sadly at Cristy.

"Yes," he agreed. "I was too slow. Nothing can excuse my betrayal of him and the other Pacifican members of June12.com. I was too slow to come out of my lifetime of being brainwashed.

"I can share that I made arrangements for his family to be taken care of. And everything I do for the rest of my life will be in atonement, too, for having helped facilitate his murder."

Elena and Cristy looked at each other. Elena turned back to Paul and asked, "Why are you here?"

"My father doesn't know that I believe our family is wrong. He thinks I'm in Barcelona for a brief vacation. I'm here because I want to help June12.com overthrow my father. I can be useful—my father trusts me after I gave up the Pacifica-based members of June12.com."

After a few moments, Elena said, "You look tired, like you haven't slept."

Paul nodded, but said, "That's not important. I want to offer my services and help create a plan to oust my family out of Pacifica once and for all. Our family has done enough damage to what once made Pacifica a paradise for everybody and not just a privileged elite defined by their support for The Dictator."

Elena stood and gestured at the hallway leading to the bedrooms.

"Why don't you get some sleep? It will give me and Cristy time to discuss you and your proposal with others from June12.com."

They watched Paul as he walked towards the bedroom he'd used before in what seemed like another lifetime long ago, long before they saw for themselves the current plight of Pacifica and long before Jose Bedia's death.

"What do you think?" Cristy said as the bedroom door closed.

"I think," Elena said slowly, "parents always seem to damage their children."

"In other words," Cristy said, "you don't know what to say?"

Elena asked, "Do you?"

We so often lapse to silence.

You're still in love with him, Elena thought as she motioned Cristy to share the couch with her. She encouraged her daughter to lay her head on her shoulder as they sat there for a brief rest. *I know you will want to give him a chance—I will let you, but also task several people to monitor him, to keep him under watch.*

Darling, Elena thought as she held her daughter, *Power corrupts.*

1 JUNE

Once upon a time, an emerald island laid upon a blue sapphire ocean and both glowed under the beam of a 24-carat sun. According to a myth old enough that people assumed its truth, it was a paradise.

But what happens when paradise becomes a dream deferred? The poet Langston Hughes once answered that question by noting several possibilities: shrivel, fester, odiously run, stink, crust over as hardened sweet syrup, or sag as under a big burden.

Pacifica's rebels opted for the poet's last noted alternative: explode.

Chapter 10

Once upon a time, an emerald island laid upon a blue sapphire ocean and both glowed under the beam of a 24-carat sun. Once upon a time, a dictator destroyed a paradise.

Over time, many of the waning paradise's citizens escaped to various parts of the world. Unfortunately, Pacifica's diaspora meant that The Dictator was able to maximize his abuse on those who remained. Cristy's and Paul's twin sons, Enrique and Gonzalo represented the fourth generation of rebels against The Dictator's rule, continued by his heirs after even he transitioned to dust. Not even dictators can overcome their mortality—it's a reality that can benefit other parts of the planet where no saviors are impending, but not yet a benefit Pacifica could enjoy.

As Paul had joined June12.com and been The Dictator's only grandchild, The Dictator's rule was continued by the twins' fifth cousin, Remedios "Remy" Con.

No doubt, all three cousins were raised on the same childhood rhyme:

> *Emerald island*
>
> *Sapphire ocean*
>
> *24-carat sun*
>
> *Let's have fun!*

All Pacifican children were raised on the rhyme. In bad times and bad times, children kept being born.

"Liberation didn't happen for my generation," Elena told her grandsons.

"Nor for mine," Cristy added.

They were seeing off Enrique and Gonzalo as they prepared for another infiltration into Pacifica. It was no longer enough to conduct the rebellion through the internet.

"Don't worry," the twins soothed their mother and grandmother.

"We have the Kali-ans on our side for blowing up that damned dam," said Gonzalo, the more talkative one. He referred to the tribe living by a dam Remy's government was building in the center of the island. The dam threatened the environment and the Kali-ans' way of life. It was also unnecessary, simply a means for one of Remy's companies to profit through bribes given by the multinational company awarded the construction mandate.

"The Kali-ans have set up the necessary network to bring us to the dam and then out of the country after we do our job," Gonzalo said.

"With this and other June12.com plans to make doing business highly unprofitable, we will irritate Remy out of her bank accounts and office!"

Enrique grinned. Often content to let his brother do the talking, he added, "It's fun to irritate our greedy cousin."

Then, he began chanting,

> *Emerald island*
>
> *Sapphire ocean*
>
> *24-carat sun*

Gonzalo joined him in the last line which the mischievous twins had amended to

> *The fun has begun!*

As they burst out laughing, Elena shook her head over how the childhood rhyme had become bastardized by the June12.com rebels into verbal graffiti mocking The Dictator's family's rule. *Wouldn't it be nice,* she thought, *if that childhood rhyme became one of innocence again? No malnutrition, no pedophiliac sex trafficking, no abuse and neglect for the children ...*

What would it take, Elena thought, *to introduce innocence again to Pacifica?*

She felt a nudge from Ernst. She edited herself, *What would it take to introduce wisdom?*

18 JULY

Once upon a time, an emerald island laid upon a blue sapphire ocean and both glowed under the beam of a 24-carat sun. According to a myth old enough that people assumed its truth, it was a paradise.

"Three water buffalos died. We didn't know the *carabaos* were there and we'd already triggered the dynamite with just a one-minute timer to allow us to escape its blast."

Elena and Cristy could see the sorrow on Gonzalo's face shimmering from Cristy's computer screen. They tried to share his sorrow, but couldn't just then as they felt too relieved that he and Enrique were safe.

"We're so sorry to hear that," Cristy said. "Come home soon."

As they ended the too-quick transmission, the women turned to each other.

"What's wrong?" Cristy asked, looking at her mother's face.

"You said, 'home.' You said, 'Come home soon', to come home to New York," Elena said. "Has enough time passed so that the boys no longer consider Pacifica their 'home'?"

Cristy understood what her mother was saying. But she didn't have time for a conversation that would calm Elena down. So she said after a quick look at her watch, "You're talking like an old woman!"

Surprised, Elena replied, "Old woman?"

"Yes. All fretful and the like. But there's no point in discussing this now. Let's focus on overthrowing Remy and her minions!"

"Yes, I suppose," Elena said as she watched her daughter gather up her bag and coat. "And you're off to...?"

"To visit Paul before I get caught up tonight on working."

Elena didn't say anything else as she watched her daughter leave. Cristy's busy schedule meant she couldn't visit Paul as much as she desired. The doctors said Paul was a "vegetable" after the beating delivered by his father's goons. But Cristy maintained faith that he could still recover.

"He just needs to rest, Mom," Cristy had insisted when they'd moved him to hospice. The hospital doctors hadn't felt there was anything else they could do.

"To want to kill one's own blood, one's own child!"

Cristy's eyes greyed into steel.

"He's not dead yet. But his sons will circle back to him and those who keep extending their grandfather's cruelty. My sons will redeem our family."

"Your sons are just fourteen."

"They've passed puberty, haven't they?" Cristy said. "They're old enough to understand what they have to do."

Pacifica—once, you were a paradise, Elena thought as she heard the door click shut, bringing her back to the present. *Now, your children grow up quickly to become soldiers. I remember your blue sapphire ocean but, in my dreams, they've taken on the color of red. Red, the color of blood. Red, the color of melted rose petals...*

23 MARCH

Once upon a time, an emerald island laid upon a blue sapphire ocean and both glowed under the beam of a 24-carat sun.

As Elena watched Pacifica—its human and animal creatures as well as the land—suffer under Remy Con, or "Dick Three" as she was nicknamed by June12.com, she occasionally paused her day to breathe out a message towards the sky, *When I join you again, Ernst, it will be in a paradise.*

I will see you in the paradise lost to both of us in this lifetime.

"Mom!"

Cristy's scream jolted Elena out of her reverie. She bolted towards the living room from the panic she heard in her daughter's voice.

"What's happening?"

Cristy turned from the computer screen with an anguished look.

"Enrique never made it to his airport rendezvous with Gonzalo. Gonzalo isn't leaving yet; he's staying to look for Enrique!"

It felt like a forever, Elena would later think about how she and Cristy froze, locked in a mutual stunned gaze as they contemplated how Enrique would fare if his cousin Remy captured him.

The horror was a forever.

9 FEBRUARY

Once upon a time, an emerald island laid upon a blue sapphire ocean and both glowed under the beam of a 24-carat sun.

Enrique was missing. Pacifica was an island but The Dictator and his family had created a maze of tunnels and rooms underground throughout its terrain. Though a finite space defined by the Pacific Ocean, it was a large island and Elena and Cristy knew Enrique may as well have evaporated if he'd fallen into the hands of Remy the Dick Three and her minions.

Once, members of June12.com discovered one of the tunnels. They entered and walked through it as far as the tunnel extended. It extended into a room of bones. The bones were new, which meant the tunnel and room had been used recently. The disappearances that began under The Dictator were continuing under Remy's rule.

Enrique was missing and the horror was a forever.

21 AUGUST

Once upon a time, an emerald island laid upon a blue sapphire ocean and both glowed under the beam of a 24-carat sun.

No glow existed underground. Enrique woke to find himself slumped against a wall in a dark room, his hands tied behind his back.

The door exploded. Given the darkness of the room, the sudden light to Enrique's shocked eyes seemed like a burst from an exploding 24-carat sun.

"Hello brother..."

Relieved, Enrique heard Gonzalo's voice.

"What took you so long?" he complained.

"Reception's unclear underground. I had to test several tunnels before the chip on your belt caught onto my locator to lead me here."

The June12.com rebels had learned the hard way to embed their members with chips as too many were being caught or kidnapped by the military. The locator chips had decreased "salvage" by half since sympathetic Western powers gave the technology to the rebels.

For a moment, by the brief light of Gonzalo's flashlight, the twins looked into each other's eyes.

"This island's a pain in the ass," Gonzalo said as he helped his brother stand.

"No disagreement there," muttered Enrique.

When the twins had briefly locked stares, they had seen the same things in each other's eyes: deep-seated frustration and immense anger.

Belaboring the point, Enrique spat out, "This rebellion's going on too long! Dick Three's got to go down!"

"So many words, brother? But, yep," Gonzalo replied. "No way can Pacifica afford a Dickhead Number Four!"

Chapter 11

29 JULY

"Once upon a time, an emerald island laid upon a blue sapphire ocean and both glowed under the beam of a 24-carat sun."

That was a passage in a *Washington Herald* article that heralded what sparked a new myth in the century containing Enrique's and Gonzalo's lives. When it happened, they were no longer 14 but 34 years old. Twenty years...

Here, it would be clichetic—and appropriately distressing—to note more descriptions of the suffering, the violence, the tortured deaths, the missing, and the aborted lives and songs that paid the price for years, then decades, of what Enrique and Gonzalo wrought from the terrain they inherited. Here, even Ernst would agree specifics are best set aside—or, simply, insert here a description from any of the many ways humans have waged war against each other, of which history ill-advisedly but generously contains many examples. My cherished Wikipedia contains a long list of revolutions and rebellions, beginning with the circa 2730 BCE Set rebellion during pharaoh Seth-Peribsen's reign in Egypt and including the shortest war in recorded history, the "Anglo-Zanzibar War" (as a "final act" of that 45-minute war in 1896, Britain demanded the Zanzibar government reimburse it for the shells it had fired—oh, how obnoxiously can victory expand arrogance!); the list ends with Pacifica's overthrow of The Dictator's family, right after the ongoing Algerian protests. Here, an editor would ask a question that I would consider, given human history, to be irrelevant: "How did they achieve a coup?"

Does the answer matter? It's a mere technicality.

The better question would be: "How will the successful coup matter?"

There will be dictators; there will be rebellions. Again. There will be dictators; there will be rebellions. Again—even with the occasional surfacing of justice, there again will be tyrants. Perhaps suffice it to say, the *Washington Herald* article also mentioned something historic: the twins became the first co-presidents of a country, following the successful but brutally costly coup they managed against The Dictator's regime.

Perhaps suffice it to say—though it be just a momentary surfacing of justice when measured against the entirety of human history—the twins pulled off this historic detail: *Peace.*

Under Presidents Enrique and Gonzalo, their faces prematurely wrinkled and brows furrowed by the toll of battle, Pacifica began rising from The Dictator's darkness. The myth will circle around itself to bring forth Paradise and end where it began—Kapwa-time.

Kapwa-time. Yet it's not only a cultural belief. Various physicists have long proposed time is not linear. Some call time a dimension of spacetime and, thus, does not pass because spacetime doesn't. Instead, spacetime simply continues to exist as part of the universe continuing to exist. The past, present and future exist simultaneously such that any event, once occurred, continues to exist somewhere in spacetime. It's a controversial concept, but backed by Albert Einstein's theory of relativity.

There are reasons why certain beliefs become archetypal. Like, Kapwa-time backed up by physics.

Kapwa-time at work: Once upon a time, currently, and in the future: an emerald island sits upon a blue sapphire ocean and both glow under the beam of a 24-carat sun.

3 SEPTEMBER

Once upon a time, an emerald island laid upon a blue sapphire ocean and both glowed under the beam of a 24-carat sun.

As peace began to succor Pacifica's ravaged land and people, a rumor began. It began as a white feather floating down and through the window of the National Administration Building. The dove's message, as some interpreted the new portent, inspired some advisors to the Romuel presidents to suggest that the country revert back to the country's indigenous name: DoveLion. Pronounced *duh-vee-li-on.*

13 NOVEMBER

Once upon a time, a poet was compelled to write a poem about the history of an emerald island set upon a blue sapphire ocean, both glowing under the beam of a 24-carat sun. Hours, days, months … into writing it, the poet realized she was in the middle of a poem that will end only when she dies. The final poem may be considered an appendix—say, "Appendix I"—to Elena's story. All stories bear appendices, notes, footnotes, and postscripts, whether or not they will be available to be read. Until that particular appendix bearing Elena's poem is available, here is an excerpt from the poem-in-progress, a list poem whose numbers, too, rebel against an inherited order:

The Return of DoveLion
By Elena Theeland

7: I forgot there is a country somewhere on the opposite of where I stand on this earth, a country whose scents stubbornly perfume my dreams.

46: I forgot discovering the limited utility of calm seas.

3: I forgot the light burned and we never shaded our eyes.

78: I forgot children learning to trick hunger with cups of weak tea.

97: I forgot I began drowning in air.

51: I forgot lowering the flag of a country I despised. I forgot lowering the flag of a country I loved.

82: I forgot narrowing the focus always reveals something else.

101: I forgot you were the altar that made me stay.

72: I forgot feeling you in the air against my cheek.

138: I forgot your body against mine introduced the limits of sunlight's expanse.

142: I forgot greeting mornings as an exposed nerve.

158: I forgot the empty chair that awaited us, its expanse the totality of an alien world still unexplored.174: I forgot suckling wine from your lips, then biting, then swallowing *earth, leather, currants, gravel, tobacco, oak and plums* to release the same voluptuous tears familiar to Elizabeth Barrett and Robert Browning who loved through 573 letters before bearing a son they nicknamed with much affection, "Pen."

160: I forgot how Beauty dislocates.

179: I forgot you falling asleep in my skin to dream.

478: I forgot regret is a Kingdom with unknown borders.

344: I forgot how exile can sa[l]vage.

658: I forgot the logic of amnesia.

1,034: I forgot the anguish of knowledge.

1,104: I forgot love stutters over a lifetime.

901: I forgot the poem whose page was a glass pane etched with words—that paper would be too soft a field for your hand leaving my waist.

1,167: I forgot my poetry is going to change the world. I forgot my words are healing. I forgot my words are holy. I forgot my words are going to lift you—all of you!—towards *Joy*.

II. THERE ~~BECAME~~ IS

Chapter 12

8 OCTOBER

Once upon a time, I left the darkness of the underground subway to find myself on the street that led to your grey building.

I left the dark for light. Then I left the light for your darkness. Then, light.

I didn't know who or what I was addressing but I breathed out, *Please ...* then stepped forward towards the light.

15 APRIL

Once upon a time, I left the darkness of the underground subway to find myself on the street that led to your grey building.

You were waiting for me in Apartment 3J, as you would wait for my visits over the next two years. That day, you waited with as empty a mind as you could muster.

"I didn't want to set a paradigm for what would happen between us," you later explained.

I was less open-minded. I left darkness with a goal: I wanted light.

I wanted illumination on everything. I wanted light to flood my life, what had become to it and of it, so that I could move forward with the rest of my life in non-blinding clarity.

I wanted to recognize what next would unfold as it unfolded. I wanted transparency, for which I knew I had to wipe away the dust and cobwebs that covered my past. Is not the past always the light bulb that illumines the room of the present, where the future next would unfold?

I wanted, *needed*, light. I wanted light flaring up every second and inch of my past. If the tool to do so needed to be a bomb, I speculated fantastically (for such was the desperation of my need), I accepted it. I recognized, *Light costs.* Why should light be any different from what comprises life? Living costs.

Some time during our first few meetings, I would say to you, *Radiance penetrates. There is no blasphemy.*

30 JANUARY

Once upon a time, I left the darkness of the underground subway to find myself on the street that led to your grey building.

I wanted the light you contained within you.

But it wasn't easy. Once, I protested.

You replied, "It's not fair. But it's logical for your life to be difficult." *See the matter for what it is.*

25 JUNE

Once upon a time, I left the darkness of the underground subway to find myself on the street that led to your grey building.

Your Apartment 3J became my new country.

8 MAY

Once upon a time, I left the darkness of the underground subway to find myself on the street that led to your grey building. I made this trip so many times for two years.

Within the walls of that grey building, you asked so many times, "What do you want?"

So many times, I failed to articulate what I wanted, what *exactly*—as you emphasized—I *wanted. I* wanted. *I wanted.*

To push me, you once noted, "Be a child" in the way children are frank and truthful because innocence precluded them from being any other way.

But there was that one occasion when, instead, you noted *severely*: "You are no longer a child."

14 SEPTEMBER

Once upon a time, I left the darkness of the underground subway to find myself on the street that led to your grey building. For two years, you waited for my arrival—my multiple arrivals.

At that first meeting, you promised, "I will always wait for you."

But that didn't mean you didn't push me. You pushed me, not to be a better person but, to be the person I was meant to be. You waited, but also pushed me to become.

"But what am I meant to be?" I once pleaded through tears of frustration.

You looked at me and said simply, "What you want yourself to be."

"That's not helpful!"

"It's on point," you said, remaining cool. "It's about desire, Elena. But you have to want, which means you have to identify what you want. Desire is the ultimate fuel, but it's useless if its target is not identified."

I sighed before saying, "Knowing what to want? It's not that simple, is it? That seems...difficult."

"Sure," you agreed. "It *is* difficult. That's why most people drift."

You raised a hand to touch my cheek. You caressed it as you bludgeoned verbally: "You've drifted so far through most of your adult life. That's neither a compromise nor a privilege that you want."

"Now you're telling me what I shouldn't want?" I protested. "How do you know what I want?"

"You're here, aren't you?" you said.

Yes, I was *there* with you, Ernst. But time was required for me to admit that meeting you in your apartment was not what I wanted—no matter how much I came to look forward to our meetings, no matter how much desire I felt.

Yes, I was searching for something else. I wanted something else.

19 MAY

Once upon a time, I left the darkness of the underground subway to find myself on the street that led to your grey building. When I began my second year of leaving darkness for your light, I was resentful. On the one-year anniversary of meeting you, my steps slowed on the sidewalk as I thought, *Another year with you, another year of an incomplete me.*

It wasn't your fault that I needed you. But in that moment, I resented you, and even your loving generosity for making it easier for me to be with you.

Then I looked up towards your windows and saw you there, standing and looking down at me, waiting for me. It was compulsive: simply, my steps *quickened* towards your light.

I *quickened* towards you.

12 JUNE

Once upon a time, I left the darkness of the underground subway to find myself on the street that led to your grey building.

At our last meeting, I'd left you sodden on your bed, the mattress half off its frame. You couldn't muster the energy to make your lips grin, though your eyes did. I knew what you would have said had you been able to speak.

You would have said, "Be proud of yourself."

Years later, there would be a moment when I would be holding my twin grandsons for the first time, one cupped within each hand. My heart would be full and I would be speechless with love: *Gonzalo! Enrique!* In that moment, I would hear you whisper, *Be proud of yourself. Self-confidence generates its own effects—it can be useful.*

Be proud of yourself.

There are so many ways to define *fertility.*

8 JANUARY

Once upon a time, I left the darkness of the underground subway to find myself on the street that led to your grey building.

I walked in a daze towards your building. As soon as I reached your building's front door, I went so far as to lay my finger against the buzzer to your apartment: 3J.

I walked towards your grey building. You see, I wanted to forget you were dead.

I looked at my finger on the buzzer to 3J.

I memorized the image of my finger on the buzzer to 3J.

I didn't allow my finger to go further. I lowered it, turned around, and walked away from the grey building. It was no longer your grey building. Apartment 3J was no longer your home, our home. *Or my country...*

I looked back once, before turning the corner that would erase the view of your grey building.

I looked back and saw the difficulty of losing one's delusions—I was still calling it "grey" as if it was concrete: I forced myself to acknowledge it for what it actually was: a building formed by glass and steel. It reflected the world outside of it, and the world was not grey.

I was no longer grey.

I was just someone who missed you very much. I was just human.

31 OCTOBER

Once upon a time, I left the darkness of the underground subway to find myself on the street that led to your building.

Your building was no longer grey. As I approached, it revealed itself for what it was: a steel and glass skyscraper not so different from other skyscrapers that erupted throughout this city. It revealed itself for you no longer lived in it. Without you distracting my eyes—and mind's eyes—I could see it for itself, not project the grey silk curtain I once draped around the two of us as if we could hide from the world. As if I could hide from myself.

The building's glass mirrored its environment. I saw my reflection upon its walls. Without you in the building, I saw a sad woman—like someone who missed her lover, which is what I was.

But I also saw a strong woman. I saw her strength in the fortitude that steeled her spine. She stood straight, that woman. She was anchored firmly on ground, on earth, even as her face was raised towards the building's third floor, the direction towards the sky. She was not grey. She was like that image of the ~~Pacifican~~ DoveLion human standing on ground and with the top part of her body also touching the sky. *In that moment of that image, everything is connected so that there is no past, present or future but only a single time where everything across all ages is One.*

In Kapwa-time, the woman I saw on the glass building's mirror-walls whispered, *we are never separate. Ernst, there is no need to miss you. We are One.*

23 NOVEMBER

Once upon a time, I left the darkness of the underground subway to find myself on the street that led to your building of glass and steel.

Ernst, I whispered at my reflection, *I have a child now.*

Specifically, I looked just to the right of my reflection as if you stood next to me. I whispered at our reflections since I could so clearly see there the image of your face with its lips tilted slightly to hint at a hidden amusement.

Ernst, I whispered, *I have a child now. Her name is Cristy Maruja.*

Ernst, I continued to whisper, *I didn't need to rely on someone else to give me a child. I decided for me. I gave myself my own child.*

And I am proud of myself.

15 DECEMBER

Once upon a time, I left the darkness of the underground subway to find myself on the street that led to your building of glass and steel.

I reached the building close enough to see my image against its mirror-walls.

Days later, someone would find the token I had slipped off my body and placed against the edge of the building, behind a planter that presented freshly-planted tulips (the latest gardener obviously had not yet received the wisdom of flowers). Someone would find it and be baffled by a lace-edged garter embroidered with roses, tiny but in full bloom. Its perfume still would be discernible: a musky scent of desire and nostalgia. A scent of a treasured memory, and its treasured future.

"It's been a while, yes," I whispered towards my reflection's right ear. "I've been busy helping a new friend.

"Bill has an interesting background. Remember the immediate aftermath of dictator Ceausescu's fall in Romania? Remember how, among other things, they discovered the plight of so many orphans neglected and jailed in orphanages? Well, Bill was one of the fortunate who were adopted out of that situation. Now, as an adult, he's starting to grapple with the effects of his background."

I broke off my whispered update to you when a voice behind me asked, "Who're you talking to?"

I turned around to see a young boy looking at me, his head tipping as he looked at me with confusion.

"Oh, just me," I said with a laugh, pretending to make light of the situation. "I often talk to myself and when I see my reflection I usually talk at it!

"But it's just me," I said, bowing down towards him. "I was just talking to myself."

Frowning, the boy backed away. With the concern of the innocent, he advised before he turned and ran away, "Don't go crazy on yourself!"

I laughed as I straightened up. I turned and looked at your building of glass mirrors and steel.

"Great advice, right, Ernst? Don't go crazy?" I whispered at where I imagined you to be.

But the spell had been broken. Inadvertently, and with the help of an innocent child—a synchronicity I duly noted and appreciated—I'd articulated reality versus my desire for an imagined reality. All along, I'd been talking to myself.

2 APRIL

Once upon a time, I left the darkness of the underground subway to find myself on the street that led to your building of glass and steel.

When I arrived at your building, I put the duffel bag on the ground, opened it and began rummaging. First, I took out the components of a lectern and placed them on the sidewalk. Then I put it together, all the while watching my reflection against your building's glass wall. Then I took out a slim book from the bag and straightened up. I positioned myself in front of the lectern. I placed the book on it, opened it to find the first poem, then looked at my reflection—towards the right of my reflection—and announced, "Dear Ernst, I just received a copy of my first poetry collection. I hope you enjoy it."

For the next few hours, I read every poem in my just-released book, *Beyond Life Sentences*. I began writing many of its poems after I ceased visiting Ernst in the grey building—after Ernst no longer waited there for me. Of course, I dedicated the book to them. One of the poems was inspired by the sculptures of Richard Tuttle, an artist Ernst introduced to me. Tuttle's sculptures move me—they have a powerful impact despite the deliberate meagerness of their material: pencil marks, the gallery wall against which the art was installed, wire, shadows, a nail and space.

The Wire Sculpture

The shadow is thin but what slices air is thinner. The press of approximation is confidently approximate. It does not matter to the naked eye. What is solid is what is not visible. Once more, you look back at the sculpture. But the light has changed with the progress of the hour. You leave and dwell instead on the simmer deep within your belly. How a shadow's imperfection humbles you. How a shadow foretells a life you want to possess versus the life that folds itself around your awkward steps

Some people stopped to listen; some people tried to address me between poems; some people ignored me and kept walking to their version of the day they wanted to unfold; some people clapped; some people snorted—I ignored them all to read to and for you. This was the one time when you couldn't challenge me by saying, "Don't ignore the world."

In reading my poems to you, I ignored the world, Ernst, and gave only you my attention. I focused, Ernst, only on you. With poetry, I saw, Ernst, only you. *I see you.*

18 FEBRUARY

Once upon a time, I left the darkness of the underground subway to find myself on the street that led to your building of glass and steel. You no longer lived there, but I still considered that building "yours."

I brought you my first book, *Beyond Life Sentences*. I would not have transcended my childhood had you not helped me to face it, then reject the prison it sought to wall around me.

"Beyond Life Sentences"—these, too, are your words. Once, I asked why you searched for me to help me. You replied, "Because I am my father's child. And I wanted to go beyond inheritance. Inheritance should not be enforced."

Then you said as if you were exhaling from relief, as if you had waited a long time to say what you next said: "My father was among the CIA's best operatives—among the most proficient spies who will ever work for the United States. I am deeply sorry for what my family did to your family."

2 JUNE

Once upon a time, I left the darkness of the underground subway to find myself on the street that led to your building of glass and steel.

I did not know it yet, but someday I would discover that, when on my deathbed I recalled your building, its image would be of glass and steel. That image—that I don't recall the building as grey—would fill me with immense joy. I saw the thing as what it was. *I see the thing as what it is.*

9 JANUARY

Once upon a time, I left the darkness of the underground subway to find myself on the street that led to your building of glass and steel.

I did not know then that, someday in the future, I would write a poem about dictators and, in the midst of it, recall your building. From that recollection, I would not mention the word "grey," and the poem would bear the line, *Steel bends to form a heart.*

18 MAY

Once upon a time, I left the darkness of the underground subway to find myself on the street that led to your building of glass and steel.

I started sweating after a few steps on the sun-ridden street. The heat prickled at my flesh and made me think of my skin. I thought of the tattoos you left every time you touched me. I felt your hands' imprint against my body, long after your hands had left my flesh.

The tattoos burned through my skin to the other side where flesh touched blood. The tattoos exist, but they're now on the other side of my skin, embedded deeper within me. That's why the tattoos are invisible to others, while I see them only by feeling them.

Once, I explained all this to you—how you generated tattoos.

In response, you snorted.

"Elena, what did we discuss about distinguishing between reality and desire?"

But after you transitioned, once you no longer lived in the building that I still visited, I sent you a message in a mental bottle tossed into an ocean's infinite unknown. *Reality is overrated.*

Reality, Ernst, is that you are dead, I thought as I arrived at your building. *Desire, Ernst, is that I feel you embedded within my flesh, and that I still visit you.*

When I heard you snorting again, I pushed back. *I'm not crazy. I understand reality, Ernst.*

I approached the building close enough to touch it, to put my hand against glass. *I understand reality quite well, Ernst,* I said as I looked just to the right of my reflection.

Desire, dear Ernst, is my reality.

26 JUNE

Once upon a time, I left the darkness of the underground subway to find myself on the street that led to your building of glass and steel.

I walked towards your building.

I arrived at your building.

But your building was just a building.

Your building was just a building.

I walked away from your building of glass and steel, utterly dumb to my presence.

I walked away. I walked down many blocks away from your building. Once, I glanced at the side of another steel and glass building as I passed it. My steps faltered. I thought I was walking on my legs encased in high-heeled boots. But the reflection I saw was of a woman on her knees, moving forward on her knees, and with her face bowed onto the palms of her hands.

I looked down my body and, yes, I was walking on my legs. But when I looked at the glass building, the image stubbornly reflected back a woman moving forward on her knees. In some strange empathy with the image, my knees began to hurt. My body hurt with the image of a woman leaving her altar.

24 MARCH

Once upon a time, I left the darkness of the underground subway to find myself on the street that led to your building of glass and steel—to your Apartment 3J.

I visited your building many times after you no longer resided there, after your light no longer obviated walls between a "grey" building and the rest of the world where Pacifica glowed beyond the horizon.

Then, once upon a time, I stopped.

I stopped.

Sometimes, a building is just a building. *See the thing for what it is…*

Chapter 13

6 JULY
Once upon a time, a dictator made me an orphan.

4 SEPTEMBER
Once upon a time, a dictator made me an orphan.
>To be an orphan is to be a vessel of need.
>To be an orphan is to be a vessel of need that can never be filled.

19 JULY
Once upon a time, a dictator made me an orphan.
>To be an orphan is to be unsure.

9 MARCH
Once upon a time, a dictator made me an orphan.
>To be an orphan is to be unsure.
>To be an orphan is not only to be a victim. One can transcend victimhood. But one will always feel unsure—a feeling that can be buried deep within the orphan's psyche, especially if the orphan *wants* to bury this feeling. But that strain will never evaporate; it will simmer within the orphan, highly vigilant for a crack that will allow it to surface. When it surfaces, it will not be like a charming buttercup blossoming yellow from a sidewalk crack. When it surfaces, it will be like the repellent pus of a popped pimple, staining and clinging to whatever it touches.

Once, you asked me to move in with you—to live amidst steel and glass. But I passed, though I wanted to say Yes, because I could not trust that joy was something possible for someone like me.

This, you understood.

I hurt from this knowing: you had paid your own price for your ability to empathize with someone who felt happiness to be an impossibility.

While lucidity is a worthwhile goal, knowledge can inflict pain.

8 FEBRUARY

Once upon a time, a dictator made me an orphan.

My mother died at childbirth, my birth. My father earnestly explained over and over that I did not cause my mother's death—but this is a matter one can understand intellectually without resolving emotionally. There was a time when I remained fragile against the occasions when something reminded me or forced me to think, *My mother is dead because I live.* I was unmothered. Then The Dictator made me an orphan.

Lilies make me cringe.

Once, I met Lily Montvale (oh this impossibility of forgetting her name!). We were both second-year students at Marymount High School. I was new to the school, to the neighborhood. It's clichetic how I, the transfer student, was eating lunch by herself in a corner of the cafeteria. Lily approached and introduced herself. A month later, I was giving her a silver (well, fake silver) necklace carefully wrapped in some second-hand but still useable giftwrapping paper that my foster Mom collected. Lily was surprised but accepted the gift and said she would open it when she got home after school. The following day, she didn't avoid me, but she didn't go out of her way to meet me. The same unease unfolded the next day, and the next, until we naturally (or so it seemed) drifted apart. Nor did she ever mention my gift.

To this day, I cringe when I happen upon lilies. The necklace had featured a tiny lily pendant, its silver also fake.

But I was not surprised by Lily's reaction. It was as if I'd expected her response—her diplomatically-hidden discomfort, if not disdain. I didn't speculate that something else might have caused her cool response—after all, she didn't acknowledge the gift but neither did she make fun of me. I merely assumed that I wasn't good enough for Lily, my first crush, my youth's romantic—privately impassioned—desire...

This is all to say, when The Dictator made me an orphan, he created someone who would never be surprised by bludgeonings—who, indeed, would expect life to be a series of blows on someone already weak, wounded, and felled on her knees.

I managed to rise. But that very first time, when Ernst opened their apartment door to me, I was malnourished and there was no split between my body and my psyche. Sometime during that first meeting, Ernst took my wrist. They circled its diameter with two fingers. They said, "Elena, this is not acceptable."

The Dictator made me an orphan. Nothing shortcuts time. It took months before I could agree with Ernst, "*This* is not acceptable."

12 AUGUST

Once upon a time, a dictator made me an orphan. But such did not prevent me from being a mother.

Shortly after giving birth to Cristy, I held her in my arms. I gazed at her face and memorized a miracle. In between cuddles and kisses, I breathed out a promise to the same air from which The Dictator's heirs breathed sustenance on the other side of the world. I promised, *If I don't make you pay, my daughter will. If my daughter does not make you pay, her children will.* I breathed out the promise that created families of soldiers and saviors. I breathed out a revolution. I breathed out the revolution that will make Pacifica rise again from the ashes created by The Dictator Mateo Con.

I bore a child for Pacifica.

Yet.

Seeing and feeling my newly-born Cristy in my arms caused time to hiccup. I did not expect the sudden enchantment from her slight but oh-so-solid and warm weight! I looked at her pink face, leaned in closer to breathe in her sweet scent, and suddenly second-guessed myself. *Surely,* I thought, *it's not fair to apply my dreams upon this child? Surely she should be the one to determine her dreams, to determine how her life unfolds?*

But I shook off these questions. The deed was done, and I did it for Pacifica. I'd borne a child—I did it for Pacifica. I would start there—I had no choice. I shook off the questions that would distract me from decisions made by me and many others long ago. I existed with a particular context: Pacifica. I bore a child for Pacifica. I did it for Pacifica. The deed was done.

Chapter 14

Once upon a time, a dictator made me an orphan.

I was not the first, nor will I be the last, orphan to be warped by my circumstances. I told those who asked that I didn't want to rely on the existence of a male partner or lover to become a mother. True enough. But I wanted to birth a child to avenge my father who was killed by a dictator—I wanted my flesh to cause the downfall of The Dictator and the heirs to his cruelty. I wanted to overthrow his regime. I would have wanted to do it myself but was limited by mortality—The Dictator's own mortality as well as the toll aging would take upon my body. I thought artificial insemination convenient for preventing someone else, my child's biological father, from getting in the way of my goal. Was that sick? Or was it an act of fairness to not involve someone else who was not invested in Pacifica in the same manner I was and who, consequently, might be uneasy with my decisions? Perhaps it's even an admirably disciplined way to enhance the likelihood of my strategy's success as there would be no one to check the path I'd determined for my daughter? I considered these questions but, ultimately, I shook them off. A dictator made me an orphan—such, I believed, can excuse a few dysfunctional acts.

A few dysfunctional acts—to be an orphan is also to over-rely on the euphemism. Euphemisms distort reality and, by doing so, offer relief from pain, even if only temporary. Euphemisms—the occasional aspirin for misery.

17 JUNE

Once upon a time, a dictator made me an orphan.

She was clinging to my ankles. I had transformed the body of a successful stock market trader who'd walked through the door in a bespoke business dress cut from dark blue wool and fuschia silk. Where there had been a confident stolidity, there then laid by my black leather boots a melted heap of wet flesh. But when she looked up at me, bliss from her widened eyes adored me.

"How did you know?" she whispered.

My heart gentled its blood rush as my face remained impassive.

"You told me," I said.

"I never told you..."

"Not with words," I said. Had I explained, I would have added, "Your body spoke—the tremors, the pace of your breathing, the sudden glistening of sweat, the directions the corners of your lips curved, the clenching, the uncontrolled widening or narrowing of your eyes, the gasps and moans, the baring of your neck for more exposure..."

A dictator made me an orphan—that stark statement more than suffices for certain decisions I wouldn't have made had I not once visited a steel and glass building. Afterwards, in response to Ernst's death, I picked up the dominatrix's trade.

I worked as a professional Mistress for two years, the same amount of time I'd spent with Ernst. I was proud of what I accomplished—I, to my deep satisfaction, became known as "The Healing Dom." Only I knew that to get to this position, Ernst had to help me first to heal myself.

There are many types of dominatrixes and submissives. My experience with Ernst taught me the type of dominatrix art that I practiced. I thought of my clients as "patients." I gave them the experience they desired which was not submissiveness so much as the release of control—"so freeing," as one of my patients sighed with pleasure.

As The Healing Dom, I also never caused my patients to bleed. The whip was an absent presence.

I actually became an expert in shibari, an artistic form of sexual bondage that dates back to the Japanese Edo period (1615 to 1868). Back then, samurai warriors bound captured enemies with jute or hemp rope and used intricate knots to symbolize power. Known as Kinbaku ("tight binding"), the practice more recently became popularized within the domination/submission world. The practice typically requires two participants; one takes the dominant role as "Top" and the other takes the submissive "Bottom" role. These "Top" and "Bottom" descriptions are deceptive—which my poet's perspective appreciates—as it's the Bottom's desires that guide how the engagement unfolds.

While each session is unique, the Top will tie the Bottom in a basic harness that will lay the groundwork for more intricate knots. These basic knots must be tied correctly since they play a key role in ensuring that the Bottom remains comfortable throughout a session, especially through the suspension phase. Moving on from the initial harness knots, the Top can become more creative with the knots they use and will often transition the Bottom into a suspended position. During suspension, the Bottom's body can release endorphins—a type of mood hormone that works as a natural painkiller and provides a rush commonly known as a "runner's high." Once the Bottom is securely suspended, the Top may continue to tie different variations of knots and move the bottom into different positions.

My favorite element is the karada ("rope dress") that allows me to tie an intricate structure of rope around the body in a complex web-like fashion. A rope dress uses around 10–15 meters of rope and involves multiple passes of rope from front to back around the body to build up the characteristic diamond-shaped rope pattern. In some cases, a rope harness may extend beyond the torso, into diamond-patterned webs that extend down the length of the arms or legs. Discovering my affinity for the karada made me long to take up the practice of wardrobe design, but I filed that notion for the time when I will see Ernst again. I plan to design a futuristic peacock wing-flare for their skirts.

I also once served—yes, I considered it "service"—for a month at a certain center (to remain unnamed) in Tokyo. There, I donned the stereotyped uniform of a British nanny (as imagined by the center's sartorially unimaginative director): ugly black dress, white apron and cap, dark stockings and great-for-standing thick shoes. With similarly-clad women, I welcomed some of Japan's most important figures from the business and political worlds—all men—and saw them undress from their Milanese custom-made suits into the swaddle of oversized cloth diapers. We helped them into oversized prams. Then, for a very expensive hour, each nanny slowly pushed her pram along the edges of a large room. It wasn't a park setting, but the sound of birds was piped into the room. For an hour, we simply pushed our oversized infants round and round within the fake-park room.

At the end of the hour, we stopped and leaned over the pram, often to wake the men as we reminded them it was time to leave their quilted hiding places. All of the men wore the same expression: with lines relaxed, their faces projected *Peace*.

All happily left the club fortified for their next efforts to dominate their worlds. I ignored at least five marriage and 20 mistress proposals that month (no surprise: mistresses are preferred). A dictator made me an orphan, and

I ended up in a scratchy, polyester outfit swaddling naked politicians and CEOs in Supima cotton diapers. What a world.

30 OCTOBER

Once upon a time, a dictator made me an orphan. From that beginning, I came to learn from you, Ernst. With your help, I broke through the context predetermined by The Dictator—I am more than his Aftermath.

With your help, I came to recognize that no child is responsible for the life she inherits. Through you, I came to see myself as more than a victim.

Ernst, I could wish you had lived long enough for me to reciprocate your gift. I could wish to have helped you overthrow the belief that you needed to become others' "whipping boy" as karmic atonement for your father's actions as a CIA spy.

But we know there's no need for me to wish such a thing, don't we, Ernst? We shall meet again in Kapwa-time. Then shall I help you heal yourself, as you have helped me heal myself.

9 MAY

Once upon a time, a dictator made me an orphan.

I was 11 years old when I was adopted by Stuart and Leny Pearson. In their charge, I was often ill-humored. Before beginning my search for a sperm donor, I paused. Before hitting "SEND" on the email that began the process, I thought of the Pearsons. I imagined their smiling, though worried, faces on my computer screen. I paused and mentally apologized to them.

After apologizing, I promised that in what I would do to The Dictator, my actions also would exact revenge for the pain The Dictator caused them. *My adoption failed with you*, I thought towards my memory of the Pearsons, *and it wasn't your fault. It's just that a dictatorship has such a wide and prolonged impact—the effects of its abuses bring their acid to the most unexpected parties.*

As proven throughout human history, cruelty's privilege is to be careless.

1 APRIL

Once upon a time, a dictator made me...

31 JANUARY

Once upon a time, a dictator made me an orphan.

This meant that, inevitably, the first time I fell in love the relationship would not work out. Or the second. Or the third. Or the fourth ...

To orphans, desire is sometimes difficult, fraught... Some orphans avoid emotional attachments. Their troubled beginnings trained them to live defensively. To desire is to risk.

But you, Ernst—you rewarded my desire.

16 APRIL

Once upon a time, a dictator made me an orphan.

I tattooed my father's name across my left arm. Whenever I raised my wrist to check the time on my watch, I'd see my father's name. I often checked the time even when I already knew, or did not need to know, the time.

I tattooed my father's name across my arm. I welcomed the pain of its inscription. I felt the pain to be appropriate.

I tattooed my father's name across my arm. I manifested his presence on my flesh.

I tattooed my father's name across my arm. I caressed his name daily.

I tattooed my father's name across my arm. And, still, I was made an orphan by a dictator. And, still, I remained an orphan.

28 SEPTEMBER

Once upon a time, a dictator made me an orphan.

By the time I first visited Ernst in a building I initially considered "grey," I had one overstuffed storage container under rent. It contained items I acquired, then collected, over the years. I could not bear to give away or dispose of most possessions unless their long-term storage involved worms or mold.

"Hoarding," yes. But the matter for me was simply one of never ever being separated from anything that had been part of my life—from the most mundane pencil to the sublime white leather boots I adored but never wore to the hanger broken but covered with a once pretty sateen fabric to a used plaster leg cast to my first bikini to my last owned box of cigarettes after I stopped smoking to a doll from Pacifica to a silk scarf from Italy to a birthday card from a former foster sibling to the hard-earned college degree. If an item contained the smallest iota of sentimental value, I refused to discard it. I deliberately treasured each item.

But that strategy, too, failed: I remained cocooned in loneliness. Objects can never replace human companionship, let alone a parent. I remained an orphan.

If art surfaces from the relationship between objects, as Levi-Strauss noted, then the storage container presented an artwork entitled "Futility."

14 NOVEMBER

Once upon a time, a dictator made me an orphan.

Such a beginning allows certain anomalies to be logical. Like anticipation quickening at the sight of a whip.

14 DECEMBER

Once upon a time, a dictator made me an orphan.

Thus, to my younger mind, confusion was a state of normality.

After Ernst, an unwavering focus.

I became a sniper and, The Dictator, you never left my sights.

17 JANUARY

Once upon a time, a dictator made me an orphan.

I was so confused that, once, I dreamt The Dictator was my father. I woke with a shudder. But as I thought about that obscene possibility, I was fascinated as much as I was repelled.

7 OCTOBER

Once upon a time, a dictator made me an orphan.

I was born with six toes on my left foot. My father said it was a genetic trait and that his sixth toe was cut off when he was a baby. He said I could cut mine off, too, but, he said, the procedure was easy enough that he wanted the decision to be mine.

Nothing was decided about my sixth toe before I became an orphan. After I became an orphan, I kept it. I kept it because it was from my father's flesh and blood. I could have cut it off but never did. Not only did I not want to create a new "orphan" from that limb, I did not want it relegated to what would have been its logical fate: the trash.

Many orphans are treated like garbage. More than 200 million orphans exist worldwide—they comprise a parallel universe with which most people's lives rarely intersect. But they exist, and often exist in ways shocking by normative standards. I suppose Ernst's father saved me from a worse fate: he found a family to adopt me and put an ocean between me and my father's murderers.

But sometimes, those who understand they were just a fate's blink away from living life in a landfill can become the most determined, the most stubborn, the most hard. Even if they go through a period of fragility—which for me was too long a time—they can come out of their fragility stronger for having been broken then patched. Then *Kintsukuroi:*

the Japanese pottery tradition's lyrical beauty of patching broken pots with gold.

Once, I told Ernst, "My capacity for *Faith* is hard-earned."

I was the sixth-toed orphan whose cracks revealed gold within myself—gold for the resilience of my birth country. That gold will be the legacy of warriors I will help to overthrow The Dictator and his legacy.

Thank you, Ernst.

22 NOVEMBER

Once upon a time, a dictator made me an orphan.

But I was not born an orphan. I knew the experience of being parented. That my mother died at my childbirth only made me treasure more my father and his earnestness at parenting me. His earnestness helped dilute the weight of my mother's presence as absence.

Then I knew the experience of, and the damage of experiencing, the agonizing news, then permanent knowledge, that my dear parent was murdered.

The sum of these events was not just grief over my father's death but sheer loathing at my state as an orphan. Loathing. Loathsome!

All the more fuel, I promised myself, for what I would come to do to you, The Dictator. *I will trash your legacy. I will burn your legacy.*

The Dictator, you should not have made me an orphan. The Dictator, you should have killed me.

7 DECEMBER

Once upon a time, a dictator made me an orphan.

In one of many dreams about The Dictator, I had a choice between becoming Chinese, Colombian, Spanish, Norwegian, English, French, Greek—in that dream, nationality would affect how I was to become a murderer. I intended to kill The Dictator.

First, I thought of capturing him and burying him alive—there are two ways, one with and the other without oxygen. The first is a straightforward execution. The second is more insidious: to be buried in a coffin or its equivalent but with air piped in so that you can last days or weeks. During that time, you are fully aware you are buried alive—perhaps it's a chance not only to face fear but the sins or regrets of your soon-to-end life. This manner was famously used to punish the Vestal Virgins of ancient Rome for losing their virginities. It was also used by the Chinese and Europeans, the latter mostly for punishing women as men usually were more mundanely beheaded.

Second, I considered applying the "Colombian Neck Tie" where the victim's throat is sliced open and the tongue is pulled out through the open wound. Used during the outbreak of La Violencia, the Colombian civil war, it's also been adopted by today's drug kingpins for intimidating others.

Third, I contemplated the amusingly-named "Spanish Tickler." Crafted from sharp iron spikes resembling claws, said Tickler ripped flesh away from the bone. Historically used on thieves and unfaithful wives, it creates a slow death. The Tickler was attached to the end of a long stick then used to gash victims' backs as they hung from their wrists. If you didn't die from the wounds, you would die from the infection caused by the blades which were rarely washed to keep the chances of infections high.

Fourth, I considered the "Blood Eagle" from Nordic legends. Its manner was to cut the victim's ribs by the spine, breaking the ribs to make them resemble wings (albeit blood-stained), then pulling the lungs out through the wounds in the victim's back. The last phase was to sprinkle salt on the wounds. Famous victims included King Ælla of Northumbria, and King Maelgualai of Munster. I liked the sound of this Blood Eagle, but that poetically-named method may remain the stuff of legends: to my dismay, I learned that in reality the victim would lose consciousness from blood loss and shock as well as immediately suffocate when the lungs were ripped out. If I applied this method to The Dictator, he wouldn't make it alive to be salted. For The Dictator, I desired salt on his wounds.

Fifth, I considered burning, and thus learned the importance of pacing. Historically, burning was a common execution method reserved for crimes like treason, witchcraft, and heresy. The victim was tied to a stake to burn. But from a medical point of view, in a huge fire the victim would die from carbon monoxide poisoning before flames consumed him. But if the fire was small, then over hours the victim would die slowly, first his legs, then torso then vital organs. Sometimes, for mercy, victims were strangled (by hanging) while being burned to reduce the dying process to a few minutes. Of course we all know burning's most famous victim: Joan of Arc. Needless to say, my fire for The Dictator would be small.

Sixth, I considered a method whose description curved my lips into a smile: "slow slicing." This was also known as "Ling Chi," translated as death by a thousand cuts. Used in China from the 900AD until it was banned in 1905, Ling Chi utilized a knife to remove portions of the body over an extended period of time. This method was reserved for crimes such as treason and killing one's parents—the latter synchronistically makes it most fitting for The Dictator. At times, victims received opium as an act of mercy— obviously not relevant were I to choose this way of execution. But, sadly, this method has drawbacks: it's not possible to remain conscious or even alive after one or two severe wounds so that dying might take only 15-20 minutes.

Uh, huh. For The Dictator, I wanted a slower death, slower than the pace of an injured snail.

Seventh, and for seemingly meeting my requirements for a slow death, I considered the "Brazen Bull." Naturally, I had to go Greek as they provided the foundation to Western civilization: the "brazen bull." This bronze bull was invented by Perillos of Athens, who made it for Phalaris, the tyrant of Akragas, Sicily, as a new way to execute criminals. It was hollow with a door on one side. A criminal was locked inside the bull, under which a fire was lit. The victim then would roast to death. Significantly for its design, the bull also was fashioned in a way that converted the victim's screams into sounds which were similar to the bellowing of an aggravated bull. Amusingly, Perillos was thrown inside the bull to test out its sound system, as Phalaris set fire underneath it. Before Perillos could die, Phalaris freed him, only to exercise the alternate execution method of throwing him off a cliff. Amusingly again, though, when Phalaris was later overthrown, he was killed through the brazen bull—a fine example of what can occur when justice isn't blind.

Eighth, once more I contemplated the Greek ways. For The Dictator, I swiftly became enamored with "Scaphism." Here, the victim was stripped naked and tied to two narrow boats. He was forced to eat milk and honey until he developed a severe bowel movement and diarrhea. More honey was rubbed on his exposed appendage to attract insects. Left to float over a stagnant pond, his feces would accumulate within the container, attracting even more insects to eat and breed on his exposed flesh. Soon, his body would become gangrenous and stuffed with burrowing insects. The victim would be fed each day, so that he didn't starve or dehydrate to death, prolonging the torture. Finally, the victim would go into delirium before dying. For The Dictator, I adored this method.

Ninth, I considered the genius of the Chinese with their bamboo-based torture whose advantage seemed to include providing the slowest death. This method involved growing a bamboo shoot through a victim's body. The sharp, fast growing shoot would puncture the victim hanging above it and then, for several days, completely penetrate the victim's body until it emerged through to the other side. MythBusters tested out this method and found out that a bamboo shoot can penetrate through several inches of ballistic gelatin in three days. Ballistic gelatin is considered comparable to human flesh, and the experiment supported the viability of this form of torture.

Finally, I considered "Hanged, Drawn and Quartered" because I'd heard of it more than once, but never really knew what the phrase meant. Googling, I learned that HDQ or, as I cheerfully nicknamed it, "Headquartered," was used in England as the penalty for high treason. Convicts were first tied to a horse and dragged to near death. Then they were hanged (but not killed), castrated, had their organs removed, chopped to four pieces (quartered), and then beheaded. Their remains were shown in public in prominent places of London (including the London Bridge).

When I woke from my dreams, I realized they reflected my insomniac internet surfing on the topic "TORTURE lengthy ways to die." In my dreams—but also in real life—*I became a sniper and, The Dictator, you never left my sights.*

In my dreams, I never decided on the "best" torture mechanism for The Dictator. Just as well: it was time to stop dreaming. It was time to stop dreaming about revenge. I knew it would take years, decades—indeed, generations—for justice, and my revenge, to unfold. It was time to stop dreaming. It was time to act. It was time for real-life action. It was time for my revenge. It was time to become pregnant.

I became a sniper and, The Dictator, you never left my sights.

Chapter 15

Once upon a time, a dictator made me an orphan.

Naturally, I paid attention to his only child.

I tracked his only son over the years—I did not want to blame the child for his father's sins but tracked him until he became an adult when he would reveal his character. Would he grow up to be as cruel as his father? Would he grow into the privilege that cocooned his youth, for instance believing he deserved all the wealth that his father created by stealing from others? Or, would he have the capacity for objectivity and self-awareness such that he would reject his father's abuses? Would he have the capacity for justice? Yes, that last question should make us all snort. Absolute power corrupts et al tediously.

I wasn't in a position to do something about the dictator's son. Marc "BeeBee" Con grew up during the time I was battling the alcoholism, bulimia, and other demons that unsurprisingly resulted because, once, a dictator made me an orphan. But being significantly younger than The Dictator meant that I also paid attention when his son gave him a grandson.

A dictator made me an orphan. I began tracking the life of his grandson. I may have been too young to do something about his son's ascent to power. But there was a grandson—I believed I could still do something to topple The Dictator's house and relieve the stranglehold of his family on Pacifica. I believed. I had to believe. Then Ernst guided me to see my strength. Thus, did I come to have *Faith*.

A dictator made me an orphan. In turn, I tracked the life of his son. Then I tracked the life of his grandson.

189

Chapter 16

19 FEBRUARY

Once upon a time, a dictator made me an orphan. In turn, I tracked the life of his son. Then I tracked the life of his grandson.

As no less than the Old Testament might put it: there was begotted a dictator, Mateo Con; Mateo Con begot Marc "Beebee" Con; Marc "Beebee" Con begot Paul Romuel...

The gods, indeed, possess warped senses of humor. The Dictator's grandson fell in love with my daughter. My daughter brought into my clutches The Dictator's flesh and blood.

Ignoring reason is often a luxury for the privileged. One sees this in gods, dictators, hedge fund investors, spymasters, scions of oligarchs and powerful politicians, among others. Many behave as they please, knowing no one dares or can afford to challenge them. Decency is rare among those who know they can behave as they wish. Many gods played cruelly with me until one decided to show mercy: that god who must have imbibed so much alcohol he became compassionate enough to allow me and Ernst to find each other.

I considered my obsessive, almost life-long tracking of The Dictator's family to be perfectly logical. I considered revenge to be perfectly logical.

24 DECEMBER

Once upon a time, a dictator made me an orphan. In turn, I tracked the life of his son. Then I tracked the life of his grandson.

My daughter did not know that I perversely welcomed the entrance of The Dictator's grandson into our life.

When Cristy brought Paul into our apartment, I was speechless—that speechlessness was an act. I could have spewed forth a torrent of obscenities about Paul's father and grandfather. That speechlessness allowed me to harness my scrambled wits to present the front of being reluctant, but willing, to allow Paul a chance to see if he could work with other June12.com volunteers for a better Pacifican future.

How my mind raced. How I mentally ordered myself: *Keep. Calm.*

I was willing to wait and see. And continue tracking The Dictator's presumed heir. The Dictator made me an orphan: I tracked the life of his grandson.

20 FEBRUARY

Once upon a time, a dictator made me an orphan. In turn, I tracked the life of his son. Then I tracked the life of his grandson.

Then The Dictator's grandson gave me grandchildren. Ahhhhh, The Dictator: *I became a sniper and you never left my sights.*

25 MARCH

Once upon a time, a dictator made me an orphan. Then The Dictator's grandson gave me grandchildren. Ahhhhh, Dictator: *I became a sniper and you never left my sights.*

Once, The Dictator, you made me laugh.

An orphan, I was intimate with the blackness of night and the monsters it camouflaged—no laughter existed—all the more reason I treasured light.

But, The Dictator, when I received news of my daughter's pregnancy with your grandson, I laughed. The Dictator, I laughed long and hard into the black, black night.

17 APRIL

Once upon a time, a dictator made me an orphan...who cringed at every sound.

Once upon a time, I lived in an apartment I chose for being the size of a closet. I burrowed within its walls. I chose an apartment that could cocoon me. Within its walls, I cringed at every sound entering its cracks from the outside. A dictator had made me an orphan.

But. That period didn't last. Because *Ernst*...

Once upon a time, a dictator made me an orphan. But with Ernst by my side, I cracked a black whip into the black, black night. Because *me*...

Once upon a time, a dictator made me an orphan. Oh, black night. *Oh, darkness...*

10 MAY

Once upon a time, a dictator made me an orphan.

Against an inner thigh, I carried the tattooed image of a ziggurat. Lovers consistently asked about it. Until Ernst, I never revealed its truth: I wanted a temple to camouflage what was underneath—cutting marks.

Once, a dictator made me an orphan. Once, I often cut my body to remind myself to feel.

Once, I tattooed over the remnants of blade edges with the only image I could conceive to mask several paralleling lines: a temple. I graffitied a temple against my skin though I did not yet know where to place my faith. I had not yet started visiting a grey building where, unfailingly, Ernst waited.

10 JUNE

Once upon a time, a dictator made me an orphan.

I have known night as a body. I have cut this body. Night bled.

Night bled out more darkness.

A dictator made me an orphan. Night bled.

Night bled around me. The darkness was interrupted when it was penetrated by light. A pale arm extended itself toward me, then cupped its palm around my elbow and lifted me up. Night receded as Ernst's father took me away, took me away, took me away...

I've sometimes wished that I looked back before I lost my birth land. It would have been nice to see Pacifica, still green, before clouds erased the scenes from our airplane window—to see the emerald island glowing under the sun. But I couldn't have seen past my tears anyway. I was Lot's Wife without having looked back. *Dear father, your demise left me frozen, my psyche a salted wound...*

After Pacifica, I stepped off the plane into the country Pacificans called "America" though it was only one of many countries in the two American continents. I stepped off the plane's steel ladders into snow.

Winter froze my tears into icicles against my face—the first of many lessons I would learn in my new country on how not to cry.

27 JUNE

Once upon a time, a dictator made me an orphan.

I associate orphanhood with the cold, the chill of tears freezing against my fragile skin, then penetrating to enter my veins and eliminating the heat from my blood.

The body can get so cold.

Thus, did I learn to stop crying.

13 AUGUST

Once upon a time, a dictator made me an orphan.

For years, I never cried. But I rediscovered crying with Ernst.

"Tears are paradoxical," they said. Then they pushed my face away from their shoulders so we could see into each other's eyes.

"Tears often surface from pain or grief or stress," they said as they raised a finger to wipe away the wetness on my cheek. "But crying also removes toxins, kills bacteria, elevates our mood by reducing a person's manganese level..."

Confused, I asked, "Manganese...?"

"Manganese. Yes. Don't interrupt my brilliant lecture."

"Now," they continued. "Emotional tears—those formed in distress—contain toxic byproducts, far more than tears formed from irritation like when an onion makes you cry. Crying removes those toxins from our body that form from stress. Like a natural therapy or massage session, but cheaper."

"Crying is cathartic. It lets the devils out before they wreak all kinds of havoc with the nervous and cardiovascular systems."

They checked my face. I'd calmed down, distracted by their lesson on tears.

"Elena, do you know what tears allow us to do?"

I shook my head.

"Tears improve our sight, Elena. Tears improve our health, enabling us to see better."

17 MAY

Once upon a time, a dictator made me an orphan.

By definition, an orphan is one who's lost both parents. One day, I thought to consider: what is the term for someone without a country?

Research revealed the terms "expatriate" and "stateless person." But research also revealed

persona non grata

unacceptable person

undesirable

I remembered these terms as, under Ernst's tutelage, I began sloughing off what I inherited. *Persona non grata, unacceptable person, undesirable?* I scoffed. Words matter, and these made me all the more determined:

The Dictator: I will be a sniper and you shall never leave my sights.

3 JUNE

Once upon a time, a dictator made me an orphan.

I wept. Then I saw quite clearly. I had made a family. I had created my redemption: Cristy, Gonzalo, and Enrique.

The Dictator, I kept you in my sights. I took you down. I took your legacy down.

Not right away. It took three generations—fortunate for me as I would not have lived long enough to witness another generation. But I took you down, and lived long enough to see your demise.

Now, Gonzalo and Enrique rule—no, *guide* the citizens of—Pacifica. And reality is becoming myth:

Emerald island

Sapphire ocean

24-carat sun…

16 JANUARY

Once upon a time, a dictator made me an orphan. But I have family now.

How fun, The Dictator, to retire the whip my grandsons never knew I wielded. Happily, my story shall be the unknown myth ever simmering within the myth recuperated by Pacifica's new Co-Presidents:

Emerald island

Sapphire ocean

24-carat sun…

Let's have fun!

Once upon a time, I left the dimness of an underground subway station to emerge into sunlight. I walked down a street towards a grey building where Ernst waited for me.

I brought them my dream of an emerald island set upon a blue sapphire ocean, both glowing under the beam of a 24-carat sun.

A dictator made me an orphan.

I brought Ernst a broken self. I emerged from our engagement with each other whole, my cracks soldered with the *Kintsukuroi* gold of sun, light, lucidity.

So much lucidity. So much light.

I was filled with so much light I could harness darkness without being diminished. I knew night as a body. I cut that body. Night bled forth more darkness. I inhaled it all to know its darkness more intimately. Still, my light remained undiluted gold.

I was young. I became old.

I was fragile. I became old.

I was hurting. I became old.

I was ignorant. I became old.

I was fearful. I became old.

I was victimized. I became old.

I was collateral damage. I became old.

I was an orphan. I survived, thrived, became old.

8 MARCH

Once upon a time, a dictator made me an orphan.

A. Dictator. Made. Me.

The Dictator. Birthed. Me.

But I stopped The Dictator.

I. Stopped. The Dictator.

Ultimately, I made me.

I. Made. Me.

I MADE ME.

III. THERE ~~WILL BE~~ IS

Chapter 17

24 APRIL

Once upon a time, I woke up.

I woke up and I was old.

I was old.

5 JULY

Once upon a time, I woke up and I was old.

Age is a leveling element. Old, I became no different from my peers regardless of our disparate backgrounds. As with them, my neck was stiff. As with them, my back ached. As with them, my knees were weak. As with them, my sight was impaired. As with them, my hearing faltered. As with them, my breath was short.

Age is a leveling element. Oh, how I welcomed its effect of a seeming normality: suddenly, I was like other people.

5 SEPTEMBER

Once upon a time, I was old. All of my beloved German Shepherds long had predeceased me—one of existence's biggest flaws is the short life span given to dogs. By choice, I lived by myself to avoid distractions from my memories with Ernst.

Decades later, every moment from my two years engaging with Ernst is as clear as a diamond. But not an FL-grade diamond. Instead, a fracture-filled gem. Diamonds are formed deep within earth under extreme heat and pressure. What many of its fans don't know is that it is possible to treat the imperfections and discolorations resulting from its creation. One can drill a pathway to an internal inclusion with a laser beam, then pour acid into the tunnel to bleach the inclusion. Also, fractures in a diamond can be filled with a clear glass-like material to make them less visible.

I appreciate the process of improving a diamond's clarity. Diamonds, like humans, are not born perfect. It can be a painful process for a human to become lucid. Drill, then bleach—certainly apt metaphors for the road to lucidity. Go deep, then eliminate distractions or Plato's shadows to focus.

I was old: with experience, I could see more.

29 SEPTEMBER

Once upon a time, I woke up and I was old and I could see more.

I saw Pacifica and realized what my favorite poet Eric Gamalinda once wrote: "It need not take more than one person to bring the world to ruin."

But I also saw it only requires one person to change the path of what seems like the world's unrelenting process of ethical decay. Much can be accomplished through, for example, redemption.

Awake, I realized I would not be what I became without someone attempting redemption. Stephen Blazer followed orders to have assassins kill my father in support of The Dictator—the United States and all empires before and in addition to this young country too often discount morality in determining which regimes to support, and Stephen Blazer was a loyal soldier. But he also moved me out of suddenly dangerous territory to give me a future in his country, in the diaspora.

Ernst Blazer tried to offset his father's sins by helping me cope with the effects of The Dictator making me an orphan.

Cristy Maruja embodied my hope beyond abstraction as she helped fight The Dictator's regime which had murdered her grandfather and orphaned her mother.

Gonzalo and Enrique—and the many they persuaded to follow them—achieved the goal for which many before them suffered or died: Pacifica as Paradise.

It need not take more than one person to destroy or save the world. But many people formed my "I" and it's exactly like a bedside story my father used to lull me to sleep as a child. He said it's a fairy tale indigenous to Pacifica. Our favored tale always ended with my father delivering the parable's conclusion to our mutual satisfaction:

A bunch of sticks, tied together, is stronger than an alone stick.

Once, before leaving Pacifica, I visited a friend's house for a sleep-over. Her parents told us the same bedside story but concluded with the line more commonly used among Pacifican families:

A bunch of sticks, tied together, is stronger than a single stick.

I preferred my father's version. To be alone is often to be lonely. It's often better to be among others—to belong.

A bunch of sticks, tied together, is stronger than an alone stick.

10 JANUARY
Once upon a time, I woke up.

Old and awoke, I recalled my father's moral to my favorite bedtime story: *A bunch of sticks, tied together, is stronger than an alone stick.*

Who knew *Hope* could be reasonable?

20 JULY

Once upon a time, I was old.

To be old is to pause and look back.

To be old is to consider what one has learned and what gems of wisdom one can share with others.

To have aged into wisdom is to realize there are as many ways of learning—and growing old—as there is variety in people. To be old and wise is to know that "elder" does not automatically mean "sage."

To be old is simply to be old.

12 SEPTEMBER
Once upon a time, I woke up and realized, *I'm old!*

Since that first realization, I've laid in bed each morning, not in a hurry to rise. As thoughtfully as I could manage, I considered what the day presented that might make me want to leave my quite comfortable bed.

Once, I woke and rushed (to the extent my old body could rush) out of bed, propelled by the question facing me:

What is reality?

—a question with many first cousins:

Did I dream Ernst?

Did I dream an island paradise called Pacifica?

Did I dream an earnest, single parent who was my father?

Did I dream a daughter? Did I dream my *daughter?*

Did I dream the blessings of twin grandsons?

...

I rushed out of bed as if the answers were written across the bathroom mirror, hanging in my closet, or waiting for me beyond my bedroom door. That morning brought a litany of questions broken only when, to my immense relief, I was visited by a lovely lady who would know to say about herself, "Mom, it's Cristy—your daughter."

Recognizing—remembering—Cristy, I felt myself walk back vigorously from the cliff's edge overlooking insanity. *Insanity*—what an aggressive word. Let's call it *frailty.*

With lucidity's return, I then scolded myself. *Ernst, Pacifica, my father, my daughter, my grandsons who now rule Pacifica—they are real! You old woman—they are* all *real!*

Fortunately, that incident happened only once. I was old enough to foresee the onset of dementia. But I was still at the point where I could proceed forward with lucidity. Nor did I need my one-time lapse to understand: we are all fragile—without memory, we are nothing. *Fragile...*

10 FEBRUARY
Once upon a time, I woke up and I was old.

That's when I began to feel the recurrent sense of having stepped into a story that I thought was about me, only to discover the story was about something else—someone else.

27 JULY
Once upon a time, I woke up.

Occasionally—usually in the initial throes of waking, whether from a night's sleep or nap—I felt that sense of living a story that I thought was about me, only to discover the story was about someone else.

At first, I thought it was dementia starting to show its presence. But after much consideration of this effect, I began to wonder. I wondered, wandered, wondered until I came to conclude: I felt this sense because, for some reason,

I was dissatisfied with how life had proceeded thus far. Despite demolishing a dictator's legacy, despite Pacifica healing towards the return of paradise, I was dissatisfied.

What an irritating conclusion. Absolutely irritating.

15 NOVEMBER

Once upon a time, I was old.

So much unfolded in my lifetime, and did so against the odds. What was the likelihood of my grandsons, the grandchildren of an orphaned, single mother, wrestling a country away from a dictator's family and guiding it now towards a healthier development?

I should have been happy. To be old was to see the successful— and lovely!—blossoming of my dreams: a paradise of an emerald island laid upon a blue sapphire ocean and both gleaming under a 24-carat sun. As I considered my age, I thought of the elders throughout Pacifica's villages. There, many were respected for their wisdom—sometimes, their wisdom translated to the ability to foretell aspects of the future. But while old, I must lack their wisdom. I was waking up from sleep increasingly irritated—as if I'd dreamt something I did not want to see. I thought about raising my trembling hand to wipe away the curtain of fog hiding the truths revealed in my dreams. But something stayed my hand. A foreboding.

Oh Elena. You wake up old, and, suddenly, you lack courage?!

Wisdom is earned—often, it requires courage.

31 MARCH

Once upon a time, I was old, but...*I did not want to die.*

Fortunately, I chastised myself as soon as that irrelevant thought erupted. It is irrelevant since we all die. What's relevant is what's causing me to think that way—I could tell it's a distraction from something more difficult to face.

One might think there would be no death in Kapwa-time—where there's no past, present, and future. Not true. Death would exist as much as life, concurrent with each other. As Ernst's Nanny Priscilla and physicists have noted, if we were to look down on the universe, we would see all of time and events spreading out in all directions—none would be canceled into a past or erased as a future act still to unfold.

Kapwa-time does not discriminate—it presents all.

6 OCTOBER

Once upon a time, I woke up old.

Old, I understood I would die soon, which is to say, I would not be able to affect things anymore. I was too old.

Or, was I?

I set aside the bedcovers and began to rise. I left my cushy bed. Slowly but surely, I moved my feet to the floor and stood. Slowly but surely, I walked over to my dresser where I pulled out its bottom drawer. I reached into its depth, past some linen and other material rarely used, took out a folder, and brought that folder with me to the kitchen where I planned to peruse its contents.

But, first and foremost, I prepared a cup of coffee.

Old, I understood my priorities: try to start the day, *ideally*. For me, that included a cup of coffee. Coffee with its kick.

To get started, sometimes the old do need to be kicked.

2 MARCH

Once upon a time, I woke up and I was old.

It was time to consider, *reconsider*, the past. I looked at the file in my hand. After first reading its contents long ago, I'd ordered myself not to read it again—I'd hoped only one reading might allow me to forget what its papers revealed. Well, I didn't forget. But avoiding the folder over the years allowed me to live less painfully with their knowledge.

But I was old. It was time to open the file again.

I opened the file. I began turning page after page until I came to the document that revealed the initiator of so many deaths—so much pain, so much grief. I looked at that piece of paper—I thought how easily its old, flimsy sheet could crumple if I chose to close my hand into a fist. But I was old—I had to look at the words it contained as I was running out of mortal time. So I looked.

Ah, yes, I thought. I was surprised I felt nothing as I read through the words whose existence manifests life's deep unfairness. *Ah, yes. Good morning, Mother. We meet again.*

23 OCTOBER

Once upon a time, I woke up and I was old.

My mother never became old.

My mother died giving birth to me.

I'm glad.

I'm glad my mother died giving birth to me.

Chapter 18

21 NOVEMBER

Once upon a time, I woke up and I was old.

The pages seemed as old as my wrinkled fingers slowly turning them within their file folder. Brown, brittle and flaking off in some corners, the pages seemed too fragile to hold their burdened past with its heavy secret.

It's a paradox how the fragile can contain so much.

8 DECEMBER

Once upon a time, I woke up and I was old.

My mother died giving birth to me. That did not mean she never lived.

I wanted to confront her life. I was old, hence, running out of time. But though I was old, the pain caused by my mother remained fresh. Once, I thought to write a poem so as to elide the pain. A poem is good for many things, including camouflage. I wrote:

> "Power
>
> corrupts absolutely"—
>
> you provided proof.

Your life proved

"Absolute corruption

powers."

The only thing to admire about that poem is its form: a "rippled mirror hay(na)ku." The hay(na)ku is a tercet with the first line being one word, the second line two words, and the three line three words. Variations, such as my poem's rippled mirror, are allowed—even welcomed— by its inventor Eileen R. Tabios. The poem elides because no specifics are lined out. But, as most good poems will effect, it moves me—the poem instigates me to attempt anew to face my mother's life. Perhaps the poem's reference to "power" refreshed my resolve. Or, perhaps it was the verb "corrupts."

Power corrupts—the reminder returned me to facing my mother's life. I took a deep breath, and, with exhalation, resolved again that I would be the aftermath determinedly, stubbornly, even bravely looking back.

13 DECEMBER

Once upon a time, I woke up.

Did my age mean I only live as an aftermath to the past? I was old. Was it my curse, then, to live the remaining days of my life as, simply, *aftermath*?

I looked at my fingers, stilled against the pages as they lay on the kitchen table.

"Elena," I spoke to myself and I spoke out loud. "When the aftermath looks back, the witness becomes more than aftermath. It's quantum physics: the observer affects what is observed. The observations cause ripples and the observed is also observing for more crosscurrents..."

As I spoke out loud, I watched the air in front of me as if the words were visible objects floating out of my mouth. I didn't see words, of course. But what I unexpectedly saw was my reflection on a mirror hanging against the wall. It was an antique mirror with the glass rippling within its frame. When the glass ripples, any reflection is inexact. I saw my reflection and I saw a distorted face—in that distortion, I saw identity still unrealized despite my old age, as if I was still looking for myself. Yet while my face was distorted, my eyes were reflected within a brief stretch of straight glass so that their reflection was accurate. In those eyes, I saw a fragile determination to continue. Never, I thought, has determination been so fragile.

19 AUGUST

Once upon a time, I was old.

I caught my eyes in the mirror. In those eyes, I saw appropriate fear. Evil always should be feared. I saw sadness. Evil always generates grief—for itself and those it touches. But in my eyes I also saw a fragile determination to continue.

I picked up the pages in the file that bore an old secret: my mother, Patricia Santos. I picked up the pages and looked for my mother. First, I looked at her sole photo in the file. My mother's hair was black and pulled back from her face to reveal the stubborn set to her jaw, oversized pupils like coal colonizing the rest of her eyes, and a tiny scar etched on her forehead over her right eye. She also bore the flat nose of the Pacifican peoples, but hers tipped up unexpectedly for a bewitching endnote. She looked young, but she bore a face of experience. Despite the evident stubbornness, the coal dominating her eyes, and the scar, my mother was beautiful. Her beauty was not conventional but my father once described her face as bearing "a vivacity that made it difficult for the viewer to look away." As well, not evident in the portrait of her face was a body well suited to beauty pageants with their skimpy bathing suits and thigh-baring evening gowns. My father had summed her up as a "charismatic, erotic presence."

I knew it was her life—her choices—that threatened now to weaken me, despite everything I had done to redeem myself of the blood we shared.

"Aftermath," I ordered myself, "look back now and *survive*."

29 OCTOBER

Once upon a time, I was old.

Scientists say long-term memories are subject to fading and repeated recollections are helpful for preserving them. For decades I refused to think about what my father revealed about my mother. I didn't want to remember.

But I didn't learn about the science of memory until I was a young adult. By then, I had gone over and over in my mind what my father disclosed in the file he left for me and which the Pearsons handed over before we parted ways. Its revelations were painful for contradicting the warm feelings I'd long felt about the mother I never knew. After all, when I was younger, my father always insisted she would have loved me if she'd lived. Continually recalling what my horrified reading revealed must have solidified those shocking revelations deep in my memory before I was able to bury them. Decades later—older—when I unlocked the door in that deep cave of my brain where I'd stored knowledge about my mother, a toxic typhoon of dank water rushed towards me. The memories rushed back gleefully—these memories were sadists: they reveled at the chance to overcome me, to take away my life-preserving breaths.

I fought.

7 MARCH

Once upon a time, I woke up.

I sat at my kitchen table looking through a file I hadn't opened in decades. I looked through the pages looking for the only photograph in the file.

Patricia Santos made me freeze. When I came across her photo, I felt a chill from the middle toes—they were the longest—of both feet begin to spread through my body. As my mother looked at me, the chill froze my ankles, froze my knees, froze my thighs, froze my very warm vagina, froze my belly, and turned my scalp into a tundra from which icicles came to replace my hair. Of course, my mother also chilled my heart.

Suddenly, I found myself smashed against the floor. *But of course,* I thought, as I slowly realized what happened, as I slowly struggled to rise. *After I'd first read through my mother's file, I also had fainted.*

At least I'm consistent, I thought as I put my hands on the chair from which I'd fallen. Pulling myself up, I thought, *Whenever I remember you, Mother, I always respond with a desire for oblivion.*

> *I respond to you, Mother, with a desire for thought to cease.*
>
> *Mother, how it pains me to think of you.*

18 APRIL

Once upon a time, I woke up and I was old. I had been unmothered all of my life. She died giving birth to me.

After reading my father's file on my mother, I ceased grieving over the abstraction I'd labeled "mother." Indeed, I was glad my mother died before she could mother me. I was horrified at my gladness, but I was glad.

I was glad I'd never suckled at her breasts. I was glad I'd never slept in her arms. I was glad I'd never sipped from a cup she held before my lips. I was glad she'd never changed my diapers. I was glad she'd never brushed or stroked my flimsy infant hair. I was glad I'd never experienced her dressing me. I was glad she'd never rubbed sunscreen on my uncovered limbs before she took me outside to play. I was glad we'd never played together. I was glad we'd never laughed together. I was glad I never experienced Patricia Santos through her kisses, her hand lotioning my infant body, her teaching me new foods, or her telling me a bedtime story to shift me into sleep. (I also realized I could have been making false assumptions about her willingness to behave as a devoted mother.)

Stories. I was mostly glad she never had a chance to tell me stories. I would not have wanted to be a captive audience for tales from such a creature. The sweetness of her words would not have masked her nature and my sleeps no doubt would have contained a multitude of nightmares.

We create life trajectories from the stories we are exposed to as children. I was glad Patricia Santos, by being dead, was dumb to me as a child.

15 JANUARY

Once upon a time, I woke up and I was old. It was time to experience a different type of light, another dimension of illumination.

First, I had to throw off the heavy cape that had smothered me all of my life, that made me intimate with gloom. Patricia Santos, my black smothering cape—I reached out with trembling but determined fingers to fling her off of my flesh.

Next, I had to survive. I knew the test of surviving my past: at the end of trading this darkness for light, would I laugh?

Chapter 19

11 MAY

Once upon a time, my mother was a young girl. She had not yet slashed her black marks against the world she'd swiftly come to consider a mere canvas for her foibles and desires. The world was not yet something she'd made, but one she'd simply inherited.

It's hard for me to believe this so I kept whispering as I considered and reconsidered the past: *once, my mother was actually innocent.*

How difficult to believe in the intersection of two elements: my mother and innocence.

16 MAY

Once upon a time, my mother was a young girl. What moves a person from innocence to monstrosity? It can be something benign, as it was in my mother's case: a compliment.

Her hair: bla-di-blah. Her eyes: bla-di-blah. Her cheekbones: bla-di-blah. Her skin: bla-di-blah. Her nose: that improbable tilt usually unknown among Pacificans who mostly display noses flattened into a broadness that matched their smiles.

Someone, then many someones, called her "beautiful." Inevitably, she began participating in that ubiquitous activity among Pacificans: the beauty contest. She became Miss Magnolia Soap Bar, then Miss Palm Oil, then Miss Sun-Soaked Province, then Miss Bla-di-blah several times, then Miss Pacifica and, finally, Miss Universe. Yes: Miss Universe—there was even that ridiculous moment when the comedian-host misread the card noting the winner's name and made my mother First Runner-Up to Miss Colombia. The whole arena gasped in disbelief—so blah-di-blah beautiful was my mother. When, minutes later, the host returned onstage to correct himself, all unanimously nodded—even the egotistical Miss Colombia. It was that unthinkable to anybody that my beautiful mother would lose a beauty contest.

I wondered if she would have fallen so low were she not blessed—or was it afflicted?—with an immense beauty rivaling historical or fairy tale figures like Helen of Troy; Aphrodite and her human model, the courtesan Phryne; Cleopatra; Bathsheba; Snow White's Evil Queen; Herod's great-grand-daughter Berenice of Cilicia; Salome; Grace Kelly; Farah Fawcett; Wakanda's Princess Shuri; and Kim Kardashian.

But unlike her admirers, my mother did not consider her beauty a goal or an achievement by itself. She cared about her loveliness only as a means to power.

Patricia Santos provided yet another reason for the universe to cease its culture of affording privilege to people for something they did nothing to achieve, in this case, physical attractiveness endowed only by genetics instead of merit. To consider my mother is to acknowledge how a one-word compliment corrupted a young girl. Her moral downfall was to hear herself called "beautiful."

There are so many ways for Beauty to cost.

4 JULY

Once upon a time, my mother was young and innocent.

When historians come to dissect Pacifica's history, many will note how Patricia Santos was no different from many politicians whose ethical degradations mirrored political ascension. The process would be banal were it not for the suffering of their victims. For Patricia Santos, the process began with Pacifica's most popular pastime. Pacifica was no different from the Philippines, Venezuela, Thailand, Colombia, and other poor countries: the beauty pageant was a rare source of succor for people whose days were stuffed with hunger, abuse, and other ills imposed by corrupt or incompetent politicians. As proven by human history, corruption and incompetence easily slips down slippery slopes to cruelty. To be poor is inherently to receive cruelty.

But even the most venal tyrant was happy to allow the people their beauty pageants. Why not? Dictators enjoyed the spectacle, too. Some even used the pageant terrain as their own hunting ground for pleasures too predictable to bother specifying.

28 JUNE

Once upon a time, my mother was young and innocent.

But she decayed so swiftly behind the toned façade of her nubile body. She was no longer innocent when she entered her first beauty pageant at age 13. She competed for the title of Miss Teen Earth of Pacifica. The country's schedule was stuffed with competitions for almost any category any Pacifican could imagine, such as "Miss Teen Sun Rising of Pacifica" sponsored by the country's largest insurance company, Sun Rising. The company brochure proclaims, "Sun rises you away from problems if you are insured!"

There preened "Miss Windswept Pacifica" sponsored by the island's premier kayak rental company, Windswept. As well, "Miss Arroz Caldo," sponsored by popular congee maker, AC Yum. Not to be overlooked was "Miss Coco," sponsored by coconut oil exporter Coco which would cease operations when its coconut fields were destroyed by a Chinese mining company whose bribes fattened The Dictator's account in Dubai. Many more beauty pageants—Pacifica can never have enough—and Patricia Santos won all that she cared to enter.

In Patricia Santos' case, the "Earth" in the first title she won referred to the pageant held in the land of the indigenous Itonguk tribe. Years later, historians would shake their heads over Patricia Santos betraying the very tribe which gave her a second home, then supported her into national prominence through the crown that proclaimed her Miss Teen Earth of Pacifica.

21 FEBRUARY

Once upon a time, my mother was young and innocent. As I considered her past, I marveled at how someone can lose innocence so swiftly.

Patricia Santos didn't win her first beauty crown by being beautiful. In any world that contains politics, even beauty does not suffice.

My beautiful mother won despite another candidate being the frontrunner—a powerful politician's daughter. The pageant sponsors certainly understood they could not allow anyone but the politician's cross-eyed but spoiled daughter to be the winner—the pageant also had been timed to coincide with her 18th birthday.

However.

"Now, now, Patricia," the congressman said as he pulled up his pants. He kept his eyes glued to Patricia's breasts—*oooomph, those juicy large cherry nipples!*—as he tried to soothe his young lover.

"Don't now, now me, Gago!" Patricia replied, rising to sit up from the bed. The act emphasized her breasts, overlarge for her frame but without a single droop. "Do you see that hole in the ceiling?"

The congressman plucked his gaze from her breasts to follow up to where Patricia pointed. A slight crack gleamed against the dark ceiling, situated next to a light fixture.

"Every time we met here, we were videoed. Every time. Even when I rode you around the room, spanking your fat butt to keep on going. How would your constituents like that?!

"And when I made you drink my..."

The congressman raised his hands in surrender.

After my beautiful mother donned her first rhinestone crown and slipped on her polyester beauty pageant sash, she never mentioned the politician's name in any of her Thank you speeches. Instead, she took the good Lord's name in vain by fake-tearfully proclaiming, "It's all due to God."

4 JUNE

Once upon a time, my mother was a young girl with a father. My grandfather didn't live in Queza, Pacifica's capital city where my father worked and raised me. My few interactions with my grandfather created only one memory I could retrieve when I began thinking again of Patricia Santos: a grimace.

Once, I saw my father give a small carton box to my grandfather. My father said, "Here are some of Patricia's things. I thought you might want them returned to your home."

This implied my mother had taken objects from her childhood home when she left her family for the capital. Perfectly understandable. I've always wished I had more objects from my own childhood home, but didn't have time for such packing when Ernst's father rushed me out of a country that suddenly turned dangerous for me.

But I remembered my grandfather saying, "No need. I don't want reminders. I'd rather forget she ever existed—that I had a role in creating her existence."

I never knew my grandfather—with hindsight, I thought he might have avoided me because I was his daughter's child. Because I never knew him, I could feel sorry for him only in the abstract. But I was sincere in thinking, *Poor Grandpa*. He must have loved Patricia Santos when she was still so young she didn't know alternatives to innocence. How grievous it must be to move from the immensity of parental love to preferring amnesia.

26 JULY

Once upon a time, my mother was young. As I looked back, I saw that I'd been conflating youth with innocence in the same way people created jewelry featuring Baby Stalins and Baby Hitlers—yes, I've witnessed these ill-conceived gems on the coat lapels of people I've passed in New York's underground subway systems. A multiplicity of creatures, indeed, passed through the Big Apple's bowels.

As humans, we want our babies and youth to be untainted with evil. We can understand how some people grow into monsters based on their lives' circumstances. But is it foolish to assume that monsters cannot be born?

I remember one tale about my mother's childhood. My six-year-old mother was brought to a fiesta by her relatives. At this neighborhood party, she was invited to join the company of other children who were tasked with creating a Pacifican dessert, the *biko*. Made of sweet rice cooked with coconut milk and baked with a shaved coconut topping, the *biko* provided incentive for teaching the children to work together.

But the baked results were egregiously sweet, rendering them unpalatable even to the parents who wanted to eat heartily with effusive compliments to encourage their beloved youngsters. Subsequent days of conversations and questionings within individual family households revealed how a certain six-year-old had told each of the children that it would be nice to include an extra cup of sugar to heighten sweetness.

"There can never be enough sweet," the children consistently recited to their parents—recited, as if the passage was something they'd heard more than once. Patricia's childish subterfuge resulted in ten extra cups of sugar.

It could not be ascertained whether Patricia was ever addressed—*Who wants to bother chiding a six-year-old?* perhaps most if not all of the parents thought.

But what was most interesting about this tale was how it came to be known—and then finally reach my listening eyes through old papers in a file. The story was revealed by a highly amused Patricia Santos herself. The occasion was another award dinner concocted by her supporters to laud her during a highly-publicized event.

"It's never too early," Patricia noted in her storytelling, "to teach our youngsters that sweetness can mask darker elements of human nature ... or monsters.

"We should banish forever those fairy tales," she concluded, "that end with that ridiculous statement: 'And they all lived happily ever after.'"

6 SEPTEMBER

Once upon a time, Patricia Santos was young and innocent. During that period, she might still have been an infant, unable to talk or talk—but during that time she was innocent. To preserve her innocence, I wish she would have remained immobile and dumb.

"What a waste!" some might express as regards her fall.

But her riposte is too easy to imagine. It would begin with a lilting laugh spurred by pure amusement. Then she would undoubtedly exclaim—not hard to imagine as I read these words first from her correspondence to a journalist she later threw in jail—"My dear, to live is to lose and that first loss is of innocence."

That was my mother: *To live is to lose innocence.*

2 FEBRUARY

Once upon a time, my mother was a young girl. How does a young girl first come to know that their youthful beauty can be a source of leverage over an older, powerful man? It's an old story, but what wasn't clear to me is that step over the threshold that separates innocence from knowledge.

One night I woke with a jolt. I woke up in a seated position in the middle of my bed, covers strewn off of me, and my flannel nightgown damp with perspiration. I was usually cold—old people usually are—but that time I felt heated. My dream had burnt me.

My dream burnt. I dreamt the resuscitation of an old memory...

...fists bleeding and yet continuing to punch. I was hiding in a closet, peeking through the slats of its flimsy door. I was aware of the door's flimsiness. I was worried the door wouldn't protect me from the scene I watched with wide and horrified eyes. I felt myself begin to whimper and hurriedly crammed a fist into my mouth to stifle sound.

The door did protect me from the fight. But I didn't yet realize how eyes can take in all of what one sees, take it in and bury it deep within one's self to stay buried until, perhaps, one is approaching one's death bed.

Seated there, feeling the heat from a dream dissipate until I was shivering again from a more familiar chill exacerbated by the sweat drying to ice my skin, I went over my dream: my usually calm father beating an old man. I was struck by the old man's age. Being old, he surely was much frailer than my father and I remembered first considering his age before wondering why my father was hitting him. The old man wasn't fighting back; he simply had his hands wrapped around his head as if to protect his face.

Then I heard my father shout. It explained everything. My father shouted, "She was four years old! She was your niece—your blood! You were her uncle! She was four years old and that's when you began ...!

"And then you passed her around to your gago pals?! Like a bottle of cerveza to be shared with your stinky fish pulutan?!"

I fainted. I fainted before I could hear my father recite what was my grand-uncle's crimes.

What an old story: the damages inflicted within families, often with zero witnesses to their occurrences—and this specific tale also hearkening another old story, misogyny. (Misogyny—a trait so deeply embedded in culture it's often not perceived or articulated such that it often lapses into the parenthetical).

I never knew my mother's relatives—perhaps my father did not want to risk his daughter with those who abused or did not protect his wife.

And perhaps that is how and why my mother became a monster, I thought as I lay back against the bed, pulling the covers over my shivering limbs. But I quickly rejected the notion: many such victims—and there were many; about one in ten children were sexually-abused before their 18th birthday—don't end up abusing others, or certainly to the extent my mother did.

It doesn't matter, I thought as I watched night leave my bedroom window. Soon, daylight would enter to chase away the dimness and the dreams it brought. It doesn't matter: *Mother, I still don't forgive you.*

Once upon a time, my mother was a young girl. Irrelevant. Notwithstanding the impossibility of my existence without her, I wished that my mother had never been born.

20 NOVEMBER

Once upon a time, my mother was a young girl. But that's not an excuse. Once, I was a young girl, too. I have never killed anyone.

Nor did my mother just kill someone.

My mother executed genocide on an entire tribe: the Itonguk tribe who once lived outside of Pacifica's capital, Queza—remote enough to have no lobbyists in the capital but not remote enough to escape attention for its diamond reserves.

30 MARCH

Once upon a time, my mother was a young girl. Like many children, she loved to play. Her favorite game was *apis*. It's a simple game using three bottle caps connected together by string. Children would take that make-shift ball and kick it to each other with their toes. Others would catch the bottlecaps ball with their own toes before flinging it back or throwing it to someone else, depending on how many were playing the game. The goal was to keep the ball in the air as long as possible. The loser was the player who let the ball fall.

My mother could play *apis* for hours. She did so most often within the embrace of the indigenous tribe who lived near their home, the Itonguk, the same tribe who invented the game.

One could recite a long description of the many enjoyable hours spent by Patricia Santos within the Itonguk tribe's embrace. But their generous warmth did not protect them: not a single Itonguk survived Patricia Santos' desire to establish power in Quetza shortly after arriving in the capital. Setting up and maintaining her power base required the funds created by selling Itonguk diamonds.

My mother was once a young girl? It didn't matter. If my mother was born innocent, that fact simply did not matter.

23 APRIL

Once upon a time, my mother was a young girl.

She must have experienced love.

She did experience love. *Ag mano po, Itonguk*. Blessings to you, Itonguk.

She'd felt love—how could that experience, that knowledge, be insufficient to turn her away from acts of such... *cruelty*?

I loathed my mother's blood flowing through me.

I loathed my mother's blood flowing *gleefully* through me—the specific glee felt by the amoral.

11 SEPTEMBER

"Once upon a time, my mother was a young girl."

I kept repeating that statement, rolling it around in my mind, whispering it, screaming it loud after checking nobody was within earshot, silently mouthing it as if to sense the words' physicality against my tongue ...

But I couldn't dispel the sourness of the sentence. If I repeated it often enough, I'd find myself hurrying to the nearest sink or toilet feeling as if I was about to vomit.

My mother: sour.

9 JUNE

Once upon a time, my mother was young. Her youth wasn't wasted on her. She wasted her youth.

There is no youth in evil. There is simply evil.

Chapter 20

30 SEPTEMBER

Once upon a time, a man and a woman competed for power. One was a dictator. The other was my mother.

3 MARCH

Once upon a time, a man and a woman competed for power. One was a dictator. The other was my mother.

"Elena Theeland?"

I didn't recognize the voice, but I confirmed my identity over the phone since... *Why not?* I thought. *I'm old. There aren't many calling an old lady...*

She said her name was Margie. She said she was a secretary to one of Ernst's former attorneys. She said Ernst had instructed I receive any of their papers that related to Pacifica. She said that something was overlooked when her former employer retired and the file transfer to the firm which took over her employer's clients was messy and bungled. She said she came across Ernst's files for me and though it'd been years her conscience couldn't let her just ignore its existence. So, she said, she looked for me, found me, and now wanted to confirm my address so she could send me Ernst's papers ...

So many voices clamoring from the past, I thought. But I gave Margie my address.

Then I waited.

16 NOVEMBER

Once upon a time, a man and a woman competed for power. One was a dictator. The other was my mother.

I opened the Federal Expressed package sent by Margie. I watched my hands slowly but determinedly cut the tape with scissors, then open the box. I noticed how my hands did not shake.

A younger me, anticipating long-sought answers in the package, would have had her entire body quivering, her hands shaking as if dancing a salsa. But I was old. I just wanted... to get it over with, whatever *it* was. I wanted to know, be felled to my knees by the knowledge if such would be its effect and so be it; but at least I would know. I was old—there was no longer any time for uncertainty.

9 DECEMBER

Once upon a time, a man and a woman competed for power. One was a dictator. The other was my mother.

I started reading through the files sent by Margie. It didn't take long for its first revelation: my mother had not loved my father.

I was not surprised—can a monster, after all, love?

But I was surprised by its second revelation: my mother had loved... Ernst's father.

I couldn't decide what surprised me more—that my mother had loved Stephen Blazer, or that she loved anyone.

Can a monster love?

12 DECEMBER

Once upon a time, a man and a woman competed for power. One was a dictator. The other was my mother.

How amazing to me that my mother actually loved somebody beside herself. And it wasn't my father. Patricia Santos had loved—*supposedly loved? I began to doubt again the association of love with my mother*—Stephen Blazer, whose letter to Ernst I began reading from the file:

> *Dear Ernst,*
>
> *You don't know, as I write this letter, how you saved my life. Fatherhood, having a child, saved my life.*
>
> *I looked at the world I helped create, and decided that it wasn't a good enough world for you to inhabit. It took me a*

> *long time, too long a time, to realize my complicity in creating such a fucked-up world, but I got here—crawled here to this point of facing my complicity.*
>
> *And so, for you, my only child, I decided to attempt to dismantle this world—a world I'd first helped create. I began by remembering that I'd chosen my career, after all, with one abstract but sincerely-felt motivation: to do good.*
>
> *I have not done much good.*

I stopped reading. I tore my eyes from the page and lifted them to the window where light entered from an outside world. I thought I was too old to be responding so intensely to words on a page written by a stranger, but there it was: the pain rising. Soon, I predicted, I would be anguished.

World, I thought, *what mysteries you contain.*

> *World: what pain you contain …!*

26 MARCH

Once upon a time, a man and a woman competed for power. One was a dictator. The other was my mother.

I returned to the letter written by Stephen Blazer to his child, the love of my life—I'm old and so can say it freely now: *Ernst, the love of my life*:

> *I have not done much good. Not only did I help create this world but I strengthened its evil pillars and foundation…*

I lifted my eyes away from the page. *To live is to be complicit,* I thought.

Then I determined, *I should just try to read through once, just once, without attempting to consider what I'm reading. Otherwise, I might die before I finish the letter!*

28 OCTOBER

Once upon a time, a man and a woman competed for power. One was a dictator. The other was my mother.

> *I have not done much good. Not only did I help create this world but I strengthened its evil pillars and foundation…*

If someone were to look back at my life, that person could judge me a 20ᵗʰ century cliché from the genre of thrillers we both love to read: a white male growing up in a privileged lifestyle, an Ivy league schooling, CIA recruitment for my facility at languages, an athleticism that made me Letter in five sports, and an affinity for guns as first discovered by a grandfather who loved to safari hunt in Africa. A cliché.

But there's no need to criticize me for that background—it's not something for which I should be judged. Kids don't make, only inherit, their initial circumstances.

What I should be judged for is ...

Well, you should be the one to decide how I should be judged. Let me just tell you what happened.

I looked up—I looked away again from the page. *You old woman,* I thought, *can you only make it through five paragraphs?* I took a deep breath, then looked down to continue reading:

... Let me just tell you what happened.

Years into my career as a spy, I was assigned to the U.S. Embassy in Pacifica. The position had several attractions— back then it was paradise. My expatriate position came with a good home and staff which included your beloved Nanny Priscilla to help me when your mother passed. Pacifica, by U.S. foreign policy standards, was also deemed a "sleepy" place—nothing of import happened there. I thought I could rest there in peace, away from the sins I'd committed elsewhere and around the globe.

No doubt it was that judgment of Pacifica's unimportance in the U.S.' perspective of world affairs that facilitated the abuse our country would perpetrate on this island. To make a long story short, when rival factions battled for control of Pacifica, we Americans mostly laughed. We laughed as we considered the Pacificans, to quote my boss, "children tormenting each other on the playground."

CIA Deputy Director Ed "Ludwig" Smith ordered me to keep an eye out and make sure whoever ended up being "the Biggest Bully on the playground was someone who also would play with us." Ludwig got his nickname by promoting it because he deemed his birth name—"Ed"—boring and

unimpressive. Ludwig already knew the power of language.
He thought "Ludwig" more scary, more appropriate for his
CIA position.

Understanding language, he also made sure always to
talk about Pacificans as America's" younger siblings"
which effectively infantilized them to his CIA bosses and
the politicians to whom they reported (he once told me he
learned the tactic from its use in the Philippines where we
Americans ascribed the term "Little Brown Brothers" to the
Filipinos as we colonized them).

As I kept an eye on the Pacificans, my vision stumbled, then
latched on to the most beautiful woman I had ever seen. My
eyes latched on to her and never let go. But that wasn't the
punch line. What was significant was that she looked back at
me, and kept looking.

Her eyes latched on to me, and never let go.

18 AUGUST

Once upon a time, a man and a woman competed for power. One was a
dictator. The other was my mother.

Or so I'd long assumed. I discovered from Stephen Blazer's letter: a man,
a woman, *and* another man competed for power. One was a dictator. The
other was my mother. The other was Ernst's father.

But as soon as I identified the third party, I realized I got it wrong. The
third was not Ernst's father, Stephen Blazer. The third was his employer, the
United States' Central Intelligence Agency. The third was the CIA, befitting
the obscenity of this ménage a trois.

24 OCTOBER

Once upon a time, a man and a woman competed for power. One was a
dictator. The other was my mother.

Ernst, Patricia Santos fell in love with me. (Candidly, perhaps
fall in lust rather than love is more accurate, but allow me this
gloss on memory—it exacted such a high price!) Neither I, nor
my CIA bosses, could have predicted this flukey outcome. I'm
easy on the eyes (as are you) and that undoubtedly facilitated
things. But it would be hard to separate my physical or other

charms from another important detail she'd known about me before we even met. One of her contacts had revealed me to be the CIA liaison in the U.S. Embassy. She wanted to recruit the agency to her cause of becoming the new head of Pacifica.

The CIA was intrigued. Patricia Santos actually was a legitimate possibility for leading Pacifica, thanks to her widespread network of supporters bought to do her bidding. By the time we met, she had parlayed her beauty into much wealth, thanks to the support of lovers and former lovers from Pacifica's wealthiest families. But others also supported her: as history has consistently revealed about human nature, poverty often makes people small. Poverty rarely uplifts. Thousands of Pacificans relented or compromised to offer Patricia Santos: Give me bread. Let me kill for you.

"Wouldn't it be interesting," Ludwig thought, "if the husband of the next leader of Pacifica ended up being, through a surrogate, a CIA man... ?!"

Unfortunately for Ludwig, I wasn't available—or refused to be available—for this purpose.

"Why not?!" Ludwig shouted, ready to go off into one of his prolonged rants.

I cut him short with one word. I replied, "Ernst."

Ludwig shut off his glare: I had said the one thing that he knew he wouldn't be able to argue against. He knew I wouldn't sacrifice my family life—you. You, my child, saved me from being used for yet another CIA plot.

But I did agree to find a replacement and help persuade Patricia Santos to commit to him instead in exchange for the CIA's support. After reviewing the ranks of our spies, I and the CIA found the man for Patricia Santos to marry—he was Pacifican-American which made his choice even better: Thomas Theeland.

Here, I had to raise my eyes again. Thomas Theeland. My father. I raised my hand to press against my heart. There was a roar in my ears and I could feel my heart pounding rapidly. My father. My father was planted by the CIA to marry my mother! I looked at Stephen Blazer's letter in horror. I had no choice: from pure self-defense, I fainted.

13 SEPTEMBER

Once upon a time, a man and a woman competed for power. One was a dictator. The other was my mother.

The CIA thought to stack the odds by helping my mother grab power. They gave her one of their top intelligence agents, my father. They offered Thomas Theeland as her spouse with the idea that he would be her conduit to the CIA, including the CIA's wide variety of assets that would bolster her regime. As for my father, he didn't mind returning to the birthland of his mother who had married a U.S.-American. He was open to staying in Pacifica, whether on a temporary or more permanent assignment, depending on how his relationship with Patricia Santos developed.

I no longer had the chance to question my father—so I will never know whether the sex was just for fun, or because the CIA might have thought a child would help boost Patricia Santos' attractiveness to family-oriented Pacificans. In any event, my mother's pregnancy was also analyzed—then welcomed—for its perceived merits.

> *Yes, Ernst, Patricia became pregnant and the CIA thought that only made her more valuable as an asset. But even the CIA could not prevent how a woman might die during childbirth. Still, the CIA was stuffed with strategists— someone came up with the idea of Thomas Theeland taking over Patricia Santos' network to battle The Dictator. He provided a potent figure: a native son returning from the diaspora, the rebel widower with the infant daughter of The Dictator's primary opponent.*

> *The Dictator still managed to become Pacifica's leader, but for a time Thomas Theeland led the rebellion against him until he, too, lost his life.*

Again, I looked up from Stephen Blazer's letter. Momentous and historic events were being described. But I was only human. In response to what I'd read so far, I could only whisper—repeat—a very personal question at the ignorant air: *Did my biological father love me? Did my father truly love me?*

14 JANUARY

Once upon a time, a man and a woman competed for power. One was a dictator. The other was my mother.

There was much to say about their story. But as I observed, it didn't take long for the story to stutter to a stop so that, for a long moment, the story could be about love—its existence or not, its sufficiency or not. *Did my father truly love me?*

How pathetic, I thought. *Human nature is consistently so pathetic: we center ourselves in whatever story we might stumble across.*

27 MARCH

Once upon a time, a man and a woman competed for power. One was a dictator. The other was my mother.

Then they engaged in a ménage a trois with the CIA.

How could there possibly be a happy ending to this sordid tale?!

How could there possibly be a happy ending?!

> *My Ernst, such a sordid tale indeed. And there I was, right in the middle of it, knowing I was fully implicated because I took advantage of a woman falling in love with me.*
>
> *And as soon as I write that—"a woman falling in love with me"—of course I paused my pen. I'm not a fool: I knew it was significant that I also represented a powerful agency that Patricia Santos thought could work for her benefit. Still, I complied with Ludwig's and his bosses' orders. I promised Patricia I would be available to her even as I encouraged her to marry Thomas Theeland for CIA access.*
>
> *I told her, "You don't have to choose between me and Thomas."*

I groaned an old person's groan: a low, raspy groan, an ugly groan. Then I groaned again...and again...wanting to mimic the world as it has been for me: ugly, ugly, ugly...

15 MAY

Once upon a time, a man and a woman competed for power. One was a dictator. The other was my mother.

Then my mother—like so many women before her—was felled by biology. She delivered a child, only to die during the process. What is the significance that she delivered a daughter instead of a son? Is it because, as human history proves, most women—even my mother—can rarely retain power and often return to a state of weakness? There are exceptions, but they are exceptions. Fortunately, the examples are increasing: Cristy Maruja, that Leni Robredo who recently became president of Pacifica's neighbor, the Philippines,...

But I was digressing. I felt my thoughts try to scurry away from the inescapable fact that I was created through the global politics of world-order domination. My dark-humor tendency peeped, *Dear CIA, Send child support...*

...only for me to realize—the CIA did send child support. Stephen Blazer's conscience may have spurred him to act on my behalf, but the CIA also intervened:

> *When I informed Ludwig—informed, not asked permission— that I would be extricating Elena from Pacifica to ensure her safety, he snorted. I expected that snort from Ludwig. But he didn't get in my way. In fact, he had the agency facilitate legal and other logistics to smooth Elena's immigration to the U.S. to an adoptive family. I believe he even had the CIA check the home studies of Stuart and Leny Pearson to ensure they would be a good family for Elena. Months later, when I would have a chance to ask Ludwig why he had been so helpful, the bastard replied, "The CIA helped create her. Maybe she'll end up returning the favor and become one of our most effective spies when she grows up."*
>
> *Bastard. He went on, "It's intriguing to reconsider the meaning of a home-grown spy..."*
>
> *Not to worry, Ernst. I made a fist, pulled back my fist, and punched the beeejeeezus out of him.*

I wanted to faint again. But this time, I didn't. I reaffirmed my identity— the identity I made for myself versus the identity I could have inherited: I was the orphan turned sniper to take down a dictator. I birthed a warrior who, in turn, birthed the sons who reclaimed an island from its polluters to turn it back into a paradise. I could withstand whatever else was floating in the muck of the pages before me.

I stood up and stretched. I looked towards the window and saw the bright light unfolding from a new day. I breathed in, and breathed out... deeply. Then I sat back on my chair and took up the next page. I began reading again.

It's paradoxical how so many savage secrets can be contained within the flimsy hold of a Manila folder. Bureaucracy, indeed, is one of humanity's greatest and most effective armies.

23 FEBRUARY

Once upon a time, a man and a woman competed for power. One was a dictator. The other was my mother.

> *Ernst, there you have it. Somewhere in this country is a girl, or woman by the time you read this letter, named Elena Theeland. I don't know where you will be at in your life by the time you read this letter. But her family is inextricably linked with ours. Perhaps this discovery will be meaningful to you, perhaps not—your life is yours and I don't mean to tell you how to live it. I am done with telling other people on how to live their lives.*

The letter stopped there abruptly. It had seemed longer, but I realized when I turned to the next few pages that they were blank. There was no ending signature, which implied that Ernst's father may have intended to continue writing.

Ernst's father never used the word "son." He only referred to Ernst with their name or as "child." Did he plan to but never got around to discussing rapprochement, to discussing Ernst's gender fluidity? Did Ernst hope so when they stumbled across their father's letter? *I am done with telling other people on how to live their lives.* I began to grieve, too, over how Ernst and their father never managed to reconcile. We humans are so often our own worst enemies.

The letter's ending also affirmed that all of Ernst's actions towards me had been of their own volition, under the influence of no one. And, that's when the tears surfaced like a flood—not when I learned of the CIA's involvement in my life, but when I was faced with how Ernst chose to involve themself in my life.

"I see you, Ernst," I whispered through my tears. "I will always see you, just as you have always seen me."

Chapter 21

3 JULY

Once upon a time, I was a child who was insignificant to the machinations of the power-hungry. To be hungry for power is never to be satiated. The world whirled around me as a child too young to understand what I was forced to experience: no mother, the often inexplicable need to go into hiding, the death of a father, the arrival of a stranger with sad eyes who would gather me into an embrace to be put into a car, then into a plane, then onto earth inexplicably covered with a cold, white dust.

I never lost the chill introduced by snow—it obsessively threaded its way through my veins and continued circulating until I met Ernst. They warmed me up until, finally, I could leave the accompaniment of sweaters. It was their presence that had alerted Ernst.

"It's a hundred degrees outside," they said, their eyes tracking my sweater as I lowered it onto the couch.

"I know. But I'm usually cold regardless of the temperature."

Months later, I would come to raise my face from their damp chest and whisper, "You heat me up…"

They laughed as they replied, "Vitamin B is amazing!"

No doubt, but I preferred to think it was Ernst. My sun.

7 SEPTEMBER

Once upon a time, I was a child who was insignificant to the machinations of the power-hungry. I was no different from the more than 200 million orphans around the planet who lived in a universe parallel with the rest of the world. Our universe rarely intersected with the *normative* universe—as children we had no votes, no voice, no control over the forces who wrecked our lives and held many of us without reprieve. To be orphan is to be insignificant—to be invisible.

Ernst said I could remain a victim or revolt. They held my hand as I took my first steps away from what chilled me and kept me frozen ever since I left Pacifica.

Then I let go of Ernst's hands: I inhaled deeply and breathed out fire—not dragon fire which remains myth but bombardier beetle fire which is real. Rubbing my belly to ignite stored hydroquinones and hydrogen peroxide, I hotly birthed the revolution.

5 JUNE

Once upon a time, I was a child who was insignificant to the machinations of the power-hungry.

I remained insignificant for a long time. Once, I told Ernst, "I've wasted so many years feeling…small."

"No," they said firmly, pushing me away from their chest where I'd buried my face. They looked at me directly and sternly as they said, "All those years were not wasted. They total a sizeable amount of time that will strengthen your hatred at what caused you to be lost and unmoored for so long. Don't you want to change the world created by The Dictator even more because you suffered for so long?"

Time, I thought as I looked at the mirror's reflection of my old face, *There's never enough time.*

I remembered saying that to Ernst as they began to die: "There's never enough time!"

"Sometimes," they'd said as their hand reached for my cheek. "But sometimes, there *is* enough time—when I see what you've become and continue to become, I know the time was sufficient for us."

The feel of their fingers against my cheek—I still felt it long after their death, often surfacing from the most random events like a breeze, a jolted awakening as if they'd inhabited a recent dream, the sound of distant piano notes as I crossed a hotel lobby, the image of a cheerful scarf peeking out from a passerby's tightly-belted trench coat, the faint music of children's laughter, or the scent of roses. I had faith the sensation—*their fingers against my cheek*—will be among the last sensations I would feel before I, too, closed my eyes for the last time.

Then, Kapwa-time—I will always feel *their fingers against my cheek.*

29 MARCH

Once upon a time, I was a child who was insignificant to the machinations of the power-hungry.

Fortunately for the world, children grow up.

Unfortunately—disastrously—for the world, children grow up.

To be adult is to defend. To be adult is to wreak revenge.

The world, as ever, turns: it blisters on its own spit.

8 JUNE

Once upon a time, I was a child who was insignificant to the machinations of the power-hungry.

To become adult is to damage one's self. The wounds and then the scabs paradoxically strengthen the child for the inherited world that is always damaged.

Some children don't survive, of course. But I wasn't one of them.

I survived, and I survived strong enough to conduct my own damage. *I saw you, The Dictator.*

But was I strong enough to overcome my genealogy—my father, the CIA?

And I was so old...

4 OCTOBER

Once upon a time, I was a child who was insignificant to the machinations of the power-hungry.

Perhaps that's at least one accomplishment to admire in my mother? That she did not consider her youth a reason to be insignificant? That she decided at a young age to be a monster?

Old age has addled me, obviously. Deciding to be a monster is never admirable, at any age. That I even thought it admirable for a second illustrated how off-kilter I became upon discovering the CIA is also DAD.

I existed because the CIA exercised its power. I wasn't even the goal, just a side-effect of spies doing what they do in an attempt to manipulate the world. Do some spies become spies to distract themselves from their mortality? So many ills arise from man's desire to be GOD.

22 JULY

Once upon a time, I was a child who was insignificant to the machinations of the power-hungry.

I existed because of the CIA—how many ways can identity be a rug suddenly yanked from under your feet so that all you can do is fall, and plunge brutally?

11 FEBRUARY

Once upon a time, I was a child who was insignificant to the machinations of the power-hungry.

My father was the CIA—shocking. The discovery certainly shocked me. But it occurred to me as I rose from where I was felled, as I uncurled from my fetal position, that this probably didn't make me special. The more I considered the matter, the more I believed I wasn't unique. The question was not if but how many: how many children have been birthed by the CIA?

10 SEPTEMBER

Once upon a time, I was chewed-up gum smashed flat against the sole of a shoe—a child insignificant to the heavy treads of the powerful or the power-hungry. I felt my naked self unwrapped. I was plucked. I was bitten. I was chewed. I was masticated—depleted of anything that made me sweet and worthwhile. I was spat out. Then I was stepped on. And stepped on. I was flattened by those not even seeing my existence as they nearly erased proof I once walked on the same planet from which they wrought more privileged, flavorful lives.

There are plenty of us: we were all judged as expendable, once upon a time.

We pockmark the planet like scabs or sores, depending on how we cope with our histories—do we thicken skin to push memories deep within the psyche, or do we fester until we erupt? In either case, our coping mechanisms reveal their failures through depression, criminality, aborted bonds, too intimate relationships with bartenders and postal workers, and behavior most would consider abnormal. I, for one, joyfully demolished a dictator's legacy.

I sat there waiting, pruney nose twitching as I sensed the church basement walls emit decades-old dust. After several meetings with other expendables, pardon me, *former* expendables, I was still waiting for shock to dissipate—I even would have welcomed a tediousness to begin recurring—over how everybody's story consistently began in anguish.

Such is the downside of Kapwa-time—when there's no past, present, or future, pain remains forever fresh even as hair whitens to a cumulous cloud and flesh attenuates to crepe paper. I was a grandmother, yet I remained forever the unmothered then orphaned young girl from decades ago.

"I couldn't hide my mestiza skin. Clearly, I was fathered by a white man,"

Estrella was saying. She's about my age, though it's hard to become more specific as everyone after 70 collapses time into one word. No, that word isn't "old." That word, denuded of time, is "ageless."

Estrella seemed to be remembering childhood memories as if they occurred just yesterday.

"My skin made it harder to find work, to feed myself and my mother. We may have lived in a slum but I suppose they, too, had their standards—any rare opportunity was hoarded for those they felt were of their own kind..."

Estrella was born in Laguna, Pacifica's fourth largest city. Laguna was on the other side of the island country from its capital, Queza. But the CIA's reach covered the entire island floating in its namesake, the Pacific Ocean. While pale skin made Estrella a target for neighborhood bullies and difficult to hire, it also made her a choice asset as a prostitute. It was an easy—a logical—consequence: by colonial beauty standards that are as difficult to evolve as for gold to rust, pale skin is often privileged. Pale Estrella did what she had to do to feed herself and her mother who'd become bedridden from whatever STDs she'd received from a CIA spy once stationed in Pacifica. Estrella called her biological father "Spy" as she and her mother never knew his real name.

"Spy left Mama and me without notice. Mama said queries would be futile as we didn't know his true identity," Estrella said, looking down at the hands clasped tightly around each other on her lap.

"But I tried to find him after I came Stateside, courtesy of another American I met at the U.S. embassy. Spy must be dead by now, but I still wouldn't mind knowing who he was—it's difficult not knowing a parent. But knowing something about him would be better than this total void within me. I'm hoping our sponsor will help."

"How did that American get you over here? U.S immigration's been tight for the past hundred years," asked Lola from Nicaragua.

"I was adopted," Estrella replied, looking up. She stood and went to the side table where a coffee urn awaited. She kept her back to us as she reached for one of the chipped mugs.

I swiftly reached to touch Lola's hand before she continued speaking. When she looked at me, startled, I raised a fingertip against my lips to silence her, to prevent her from asking for more details.

Later, as the meeting was breaking up, I motioned Lola closer to me. I whispered, "I'm sorry to hush you earlier. I didn't want you to embarrass Estrella."

"What do you mean?" she whispered back.

"Estrella was adopted—that was possible because she was just 15, a year under the age when the U.S. no longer allows international adoptions. But she was adopted by a man who used her as a sexual slave for himself and the other males in his large family—from his father to sons who, quote, needed to lose their virginities, unquote."

"Wow," Lola said. Then she added, "What an old story..."

Yes, an old story: there were so many of us expendables. There were also many ways to become expendable, though some ways get repeated more often. Sexual slavery was a popular choice.

But our group was "special," according to our sponsor. We were part of a support group with a name utterly lacking in music, as clunky as any moniker ever concocted by a paper-pushing bureaucrat: "The CIA's Clandestine DNA." Inevitably, the clunker was shortened for lexical manageability to "The CIA's CDs." It didn't take long for the junior clunker to become simply "CDs." We CDs were those birthed as a result of CIA activities around the world. I and Estrella represented Pacifica, but there were also those born in Saudi Arabia and other countries in the Middle East, Zimbabwe and other countries in Africa, Uzbekistan and other countries in Eastern Europe, Ireland and other countries in Western Europe, Venezuela and other countries in South America, the Philippines and other countries in Asia, et-tedious-cetera. The CIA's reach was tediously extensive.

Such an improbable support group! I thought, not for the first time, as I looked at the CDs still milling about in the basement of Manhattan's Methodist Church. It's not unusual for many of us to delay leaving the basement to return to a world that considered us abnormal... if not expendable. At our first meeting, I'd shared my thoughts with Nadine during the coffee and tea session that ended each meeting.

"Improbable?" Nadine said, quirking an eyebrow, its fullness depleted by time but subsidized with black eyebrow pencil—a hint of fortitude that I appreciated. From Burundi, Nadine had introduced herself by mocking her name which meant "something my mother felt despite her circumstances: 'Hope'."

"Why would it be improbable? There could be hundreds in this basement and thousands waiting in line outside!" Nadine said.

"I'm not surprised people like us exist. But I'm surprised that a 'support group' arose from our shared links with the CIA."

"Yes. That's something," Nadine said noncommittally. "It's decent for the CIA—"the new CIA," as they call themselves—to sponsor this, even though it's a secret group and they made us all sign confidentiality agreements.

"I find it helpful, you see, to have some sense that I'm not alone in existing because of, what would you call it, geopolitics? To be born that way rather than because two people fell in love and decided to parent a child together."

I nodded. Then we silently looked around at the others scattered about the room. About half were as "enduring" as Estrella, Nadine, and me, but there also were younger CDs, including a few in their twenties and thirties.

Perusing the other CDs, I thought, *We're so often reacting with silence, lapsing to silence. But what else can one say? What can one say to lift the heaviness in this room, this world—the heaviness cloaking us all, ever threatening to smother all light?*

6 MARCH

Once upon a time, I was a child who was insignificant to the machinations of the power-hungry. I wasn't the only one.

"Why are you here?" I asked Nadine at the next meeting. "I mean, I think it's unusual to be at a meeting like this. How did you come to be here?"

She took her time looking over the box of donuts someone had brought, before picking up a glazed sugar one with her napkin. She took a bite, chewed and swallowed.

"I'm not sure. I wasn't sure before attending my first meeting. I'm still not sure as I continue to attend," she said slowly. "Perhaps I'm just trying to normalize my situation—that it's not so unusual to be born because of—and I'm beginning to really loathe this word—geopolitics, rather than because two people fell in love and decided to parent a child together.

"And you?"

"Do you know if your parents sincerely loved you?" I replied. It wasn't on point to her question, but she followed smoothly.

"Sure," she said. I thought I saw her eyes soften for a moment. But when I looked more closely, I thought I saw pity. "I know they loved me—they've both passed on now, by the way—because they told me so. And I have no reason to not believe them. Why wouldn't it be possible to love your own child, separate from how you might feel about the other parent? It happens all the time, right, with divorced parents who share children?"

I nodded, though I wasn't sure.

She asked again, "And you?"

"My mother died giving birth," I said, the shock of the words fresh again as if I hadn't said the thought out loud before, which I had in private many times in front of mirrors as if I was trying to see what the words looked like. "When I asked about her, my father said nothing would have prevented her from loving me. He called her 'strong-willed,' a trait he said would not be bad for me to inherit.

"And my father wasn't the type to express his love. But he behaved as if he did love me."

"Actions certainly can matter more than words," Nadine said. "What do you choose to believe?"

What did I choose to believe? I replied something about, sure, choosing to believe both my parents loved me. But it wasn't until Nadine asked her question that I realized hers was the right question: *What did I choose to believe?*

Was I choosing to believe, for one, that the CIA's formation of CD groups came from altruistic motivations? Or, more… geopolitics—if so, what was set at play by the CIA as regards the CDs?

Hefty questions. But I was old—too old to be anyone's toy, even Daddy CIA's. I shooed those questions away for others to handle—like the younger or next generation of CDs. I'm sure the CIA will create collateral damage for as long as it operates, and many will be children. But, for old me, I reverted back to a more narrow but more personal concern: what did I choose to believe about my parents?

Later, in the privacy of my bedroom, I pondered that question more. That's when I realized the answer had little to do with my father who I easily believed loved me. The answer related to my mother: *What did I choose to believe about her? Did I choose to believe she would have loved me had she survived?*

Can a monster love?

19 APRIL

Once upon a time, I was a child who was insignificant to the machinations of the power-hungry. I wasn't the only one.

One of the others, Nadine, was forged in Burundi, that country ranked by the World Happiness Report as the planet's most unhappy nation. She gave me the tip that would lead to my visiting a CIA underground archive somewhere in Washington D.C. I said "somewhere" as I was only allowed to visit it by being taken there with my scarf folded around my eyes.

Unseeing, I stepped off the plane. I was led to a car, driven in a car, then helped out of a car into a building, stepped into an elevator that descended (I was able to tell the difference between descent and ascent), walked out of the elevator into a room, helped into a chair—all before my folded scarf was taken off from my eyes.

I looked at the table in front of me. It was laden with files. More files from the tenure of Ed "Ludwig" Smithson.

Ludwig. I looked at his name and wondered, *How many ways can suffering unfold?*

12 JANUARY

Once upon a time, I was a child who was insignificant to the machinations of the power-hungry. Decades later, I confronted one of those influential to my creation, a CIA spymaster nicknamed "Ludwig."

As the grandmother of the current leaders of Pacifica, a U.S. ally, I was able to receive the necessary permissions for visiting the CIA archives that held Ludwig's case papers. His files covering his stint in Pacifica covered half of the table in front of me. I thought that a lot of paperwork but the soldier who unpacked the files from boxes onto the table commented, "Just these? Obviously not one of this spymaster's most important cases…"

There you go: Pacifica, the paradise, was deemed not particularly important by an objective observer. So much for the U.S.-American world view. Sighing, I thought, *How does one confront the dead?*

I answered myself, *Obviously with paperwork…*

17 AUGUST

Once upon a time, I was a child who was insignificant to the machinations of the power-hungry. Decades later, I confronted Ludwig, the man who ordered my father to marry my mother and the man who ordered his murder. My nose twitched as I read through his old files, as if my very body was in physical protest against even the slightest scent from my odious past.

My flesh, the front line for my self-defense against the world, knew to recoil.

4 MARCH

Once upon a time, I was a child who was insignificant to the machinations of the power-hungry. That point kept being emphasized as I read through Ludwig's files of his "Pacifican Operation." Among other things, "PO"— as Ludwig also called the operation because the initials apparently encapsulated his feelings about it: "Pissed Off!"—was not about Pacifica. It occurred on Pacifica but it actually had to do with a neighboring country, Indrasia:

> *When our man in Indrasia, President Torpe, lost his reelection to the leftist Leo "Papa" Mircos, our interests started to be threatened by the self-proclaimed "People's Papa."*

I could hear Ludwig's snort as he wrote his report…

> *Papa cancelled the U.S.-Indrasia Treaty that allowed U.S. warships to be stationed at Indrasia's Naca Port in exchange for favorable export arrangements of its coconut products to*

*the U.S. This was disturbing as China's interests in the region
are no secret, and they apparently provided a ready market
for Indrasia's coconuts.*

I anticipated what came next: that as part of deflecting China's leverage, the U.S. stepped up its influence over neighboring Pacifica. *What an old story*, I thought, as I read of the U.S. ignoring another country's rights to self-determination to put its "own man" in Pacifica, though it was to be the woman who was my mother.

What an old story. I thought I knew my life. But it turned out I began life by being birthed in a story not at all about me.

25 OCTOBER

Once upon a time, I was a child who was insignificant to the machinations of the power-hungry. Because. Everything. Is. Political. And. Everything. And. Everyone. Is. But. A. Cog. To. This. Systemic. Obscenity.

17 NOVEMBER

Once upon a time, I was a child who was insignificant to the machinations of the power-hungry.

I was so insignificant that nobody cared to be concerned about the effects of a child believing she was the daughter of a monster. Ah, Ludwig— so irrelevant was my life to you!

From Ludwig's files, I learned that I had a half-sister. I learned that my father, knowing Patricia Santos was in love with someone else, had no compunction having affairs with other women. I learned that my father impregnated one of them. He was known as a "moralist" but, as history shows over and over again, morality rarely survives all challenges—and my father apparently enjoyed sex. I skimmed over the passages of Ludwig chiding him for his "sex addiction."

My father's "Girlfriend #1" (as Ludwig called her) was pregnant at about the same time as Patricia Santos. I started reading slower—breathing deeper—as I learned that the other woman's baby was born a day after Patricia Santos' daughter. I learned that Patricia Santos' daughter was born frail, with health problems Ludwig couldn't bother specifying. But what Ludwig revealed was how, with Patricia Santos dying from childbirth, there was no one to protest when the two daughters traded places so that the healthier one could receive the benefits of being Thomas Theeland's legally-acknowledged daughter, from better care to future private school education afforded only by the elite in Pacifica. Girlfriend #1 was willing to give up her daughter to offer her a better life without endangerment from her Itonguk blood. Patricia Santos' daughter was merely given to a paid caretaker—both of their names, insignificant to Ludwig, were not inscribed in his files.

I could hear the ocean singing into my ears. No doubt it was just blood rushing as I comprehended the significance of what I was reading. *Breathe...*

I continued reading to learn that after my father's death, Stephen Blazer took both children out of the country. I learned that my frail sister became even sicker and died during the plane ride. I learned that the child who died was the true biological daughter of Patricia Santos.

Breathe...

From Ludwig's files, I learned that I was not the daughter of Patricia Santos—a belief I'd held for most of the over 80 years spanned so far by my life.

Breathe...

I learned that I was not the daughter of a monster.

Breathe...

I learned that I was the daughter of a stranger but before I could turn additional pages to learn Girlfriend #1's name, I fainted again in self-defense—my long-held and cowardly habit of seeking unconsciousness in times of stress.

Chapter 22

Once upon a time, I was a child who was insignificant to the machinations of the power-hungry. Consequently, it took over eight decades for me to discover that my believed ancestry was a lie.

I was insignificant to the power-hungry whose concerns did not accommodate the collateral damage of a child sent off to live a life based on a lie. The powerful rarely cares about the side effects of their decisions, collateral damages which usually remain invisible to them—effects like a confused person moving back and forth between reality and dream state until she entered a grey building to meet a stranger.

I woke from my faint with one question on my quivering lips: who is my mother?

I raised my head and torso from the desk where I'd slumped in faint. *Who is my mother?!*

I was old. I was dying. I didn't want to die without knowing whose womb expelled me into this cruel, cruel world.

> *How many ways exist for one to be motherless?*

1 OCTOBER
Once upon a time, I was a child who was insignificant to the machinations of the power-hungry.

I was born motherless. The random equation of who survives or dies

249

during childbirth could not be controlled by even Ludwig. But more than eight decades later, in an anonymous room deep within the CIA Archives, Ludwig still would be able to exercise power: he took away the mother I thought was mine.

After learning about Patricia Santos in the file my father left for me, I spent most of my life ignoring Patricia Santos. I willed myself to forget her existence—that she was someone to whom I could point as my mother. But Ludwig's secrets not only made my chosen amnesia unnecessary—Ludwig also took away the *someone*—even if a monster—who I could point to— even with much loathing—as my mother. Suddenly I didn't even have that someone who had inhabited the space defined as "mother." I looked about the walls of the CIA archival room, a windowless room, and saw the yawning mouth of outer space. I felt unmoored as I floated in blackness without a single star to guide me.

I slapped myself.

I could feel myself faint again and, impatiently, I scolded myself: "Enough histrionics!"

Then I slapped myself again. I needed to see my way through this next great loss. Ernst had taught me: identifying or defining a loss offers a means to diminish its impact.

I turned my face back towards Ludwig's files. I could feel both cheeks burn from my hand's imprint—it was the least of my concerns.

19 NOVEMBER

Once upon a time, I was a child who was insignificant to the machinations of the power-hungry.

Then there I was, an adult—nay, a senior citizen!—still witnessing how insignificant I was to the machinations of the power-hungry. I. Felt. My. Insignificance. with every word I read from Ludwig's Pacifica files. There I was as a baby, as a toddler, and as a tween. There I was being brought out of my birth land to the United States. There I was beginning my life as an American under false circumstances: that I was to be my father's child who'd been procreated with Patricia Santos instead of my biological mother.

There I was reading that my biological mother was insignificant, too, to the machinations of the power-hungry.

I began reading faster and faster. I was eager, of course, to learn the identity of my mother beyond the insult of "Girlfriend #1." Faster I read until, there... *There*, my trembling finger pointed at my mother's name on the page. *There*, was my first introduction to my real mother.

Her name was... not revealed. Her name presented itself as a word hidden behind the slash of a redacting black marker. If I were less careful, I would have reared up my head and howled like a lost wolf at the black steel ceiling. I wanted to howl!

I was a wolf lost in the wilderness and I wanted to howl!

Howl I would have if I hadn't thought that the move would bring in some CIA handler who might interrupt my read of Ludwig's papers.

Instead, I lowered my face to my mother's name as if I wanted to kiss it. Perhaps I did want to kiss it. But as my eyes neared the page, I saw that the redacting pen had been careless—it did not quite hide the first letter of my mother's name. Was Pacifica so insignificant even the anonymous CIA staffer wielding the redacting pen couldn't be bothered to do well at this administrative task? Peering at where the redaction ended, I discerned that my mother's name began with the letter "B."

"B," I whispered out loud. I repeated the letter, "B," as if its sound might bring my mother to me—materialize suddenly in front of me like some character being transported from that old television and movie series, "Star Trek."

"B…"

I chanted the letter for a minute or so. But, of course, my mother did not appear. I remained motherless.

12 MAY

Once upon a time, I was a child who was insignificant to the machinations of the power-hungry.

B…had knocked on the door to Patricia Santos' and my father's residence. Thomas Theeland was the one who answered the door. Patricia Santos was not home but he invited her into the house to wait. Truthfully, he did not know how long Patricia would be gone, but he was sufficiently enthralled to want to spend time with B…

…who was described as "heart-attack and seizure-stroke gorgeous!" I could sense Ludwig snorting as I read my father's description of my mother in his files. But brushing aside the references to her complexion, to her eyes, to her hair, to her lone dimple, even to a slight scar on her cheek (from an apis stumble) that "only emphasized the surrounding perfection," Ludwig came to learn that B…was a surviving member of the Itonguk tribe. She had been visiting a neighboring tribe when the slaughter occurred. B…didn't know where to go for answers, so she visited Patricia Santos who was still publicly known as a friend of the Itonguk.

My father shook his head. He was truthful when he gave her the news: Patricia Santos had given up the tribe for the diamonds in its tribal grounds. He was truthful when he said, "Patricia will kill you, too, if she discovers your existence. The only way for your tribe's lands to be transferred to the company she set up for this purpose is for every Itonguk to be dead."

Ludwig didn't go into the details of what B... must have felt—the shock, the grief and so on. His words were dry. But the story was hot—it burnt me as it must have burnt my mother. And I, then, also succumbed to the hot tears and shaking that tore through my body, as they must have torn through my mother's.

B... B... B... Mama.

10 DECEMBER

Once upon a time, I was a child who was insignificant to the machinations of the power-hungry.

People who become powerful are usually hungry for it. Sure, there are exceptions, but they are exceptions. Indeed, power belongs in the same insatiable category as being rich or being thin. One can never be enough. One can never be too powerful.

Ludwig and his masters, the CIA and its masters—not one among them considered the child whose presence was barely acknowledged. On a "just in case," Ludwig had found it convenient to present me as a child of Patricia Santos instead of an Itonguk woman. To acknowledge my true mother would be to acknowledge the Itonguk had not been totally decimated. Such would upend the relationship they had set up with Patricia Santos whose power had been bolstered by the funds from liquidating the Itonguk's diamonds.

The duplicity existed past Patricia Santos' death. To ingratiate themselves with The Dictator, the CIA informed The Dictator about Patricia Santos' stolen diamonds and resulting demise of the Itonguks. The Dictator didn't care about the Itonguks but the information provided a nice bit of propaganda for bashing those who had opposed him. The tale also amused him—for its entertainment value, he allowed the CIA to use Pacifica as the agency wished, including maintaining a port on part of Pacifica's coastline. The port helped the U.S. Navy conduct whatever it needed to conduct on behalf of U.S. policy throughout Asia.

What an old story.

It was such an old story I was bored as soon as I read about it. I started reading even faster to answer my primary question: what happened to B...? What happened to my mother?

24 FEBRUARY

Once upon a time, I was a child who was insignificant to the machinations of the power-hungry.

I started reading even faster to answer my primary question: what happened to B...? What happened to my mother?

But didn't I already know the answer even as I looked for the answer?

Of course I did. I knew the answer.

My father, who had fallen in love with B..., tried to deflect the CIA goons. But he, too, was insignificant to the machinations of the power-hungry.

Ludwig agreed to let her live for only as long as my father was able to control her. At first, he did. No doubt he counseled, "B..., don't reveal your tribal ancestry. That would endanger you."

But B...'s ancestors—my ancestors—called for respect, called for acknowledgment that, once, they existed and, in Kapwa time, still existed. So B... thought to create some sort of Itonguk Heritage Center that would preserve the history of her people. Of course, the Center would be located on tribal land. She labored for months over creating such a plan, and writing up a proposal. After finishing, she approached Thomas Theeland for advice and support.

"Have you forgotten what we discussed? We're supposed to keep quiet on your Itonguk connection!"

My father was incredulous. B... had just finished summarizing her idea after handing him a thick document describing the proposed Itonguk Heritage Center.

"Why would the government want to help out when they were complicit in taking over the Itonguk diamond reserves? You're not making sense!"

"I don't just have a 'connection' to the Itonguk, Tom. I *am* Itonguk—I can't keep denying my identity! I can't deny myself!"

"But the danger..."

"No, wait," B...interrupted. "Let me clarify my idea. It should work because you would propose the idea *specifically* because the Itonguks no longer exist! How can the Itonguks be a threat if they're extinct? Perhaps, later, I could be hired as its Director or at least a staff member."

Did my father pity her as he observed, "You've clearly thought this out..."

"Yes! You could propose the idea as a cultural heritage project. After all, no one in the government is denying the Itonguks existed. And they were the first peoples of Pacifica! So, as they are now non-existent—as again you would note—there'd be no reason for any of them to feel threatened by such a project!"

Perhaps the idea actually would have worked. But unbeknownst to B... who had visited unexpectedly to try rallying Thomas Theeland to her cause, Ludwig was on a survey-trip of the CIA's Southeast Asian operations. He had been meeting with my father when they heard the knock on the door and B...'s voice. From behind a bedroom door, Ludwig heard every word uttered by B, each word offered with so much hope...

"I'll think about it," my father said as he showed her out.

"Promise?"

"With a kiss!" my father said, before giving a loving kiss that he knew could be their last.

He shut the door, sighed, and turned around to look at Ludwig who'd come out of the bedroom.

"Take care of her—you know what to do," Ludwig said.

My father nodded. He knew what Ludwig expected him to do.

But not even the long-time CIA spy in him would let him kill the woman he had grown to love and who bore one of his daughters. There were other revelations in Ludwig's files. But, for the moment, I ignored them for the details of how Stephen Blazer, at Ludwig's orders, alerted The Dictator to my father's location so that they were able to abduct him, then torture him, then kill him. Then, after "taking care" of my father, Ludwig "took care" of my mother.

In the days ahead, when Elena would keep turning the story over and over in her mind, the same thought would keep inserting itself like a tiny mosquito with a huge bite: *What an old story—the machinations of those in power. What an old, old story.*

28 MARCH

Once upon a time, I was a child who was insignificant to the machinations of the power-hungry. Thus, did it take over eight decades to learn I was a surviving member of Pacifica's Itonguk tribe.

Aaaah, ancestors: you saw me lost, wandering in a concrete canyon. Then you sent me the dreams:

> *Once upon a time, I left the dimness of the subway system to break out into daylight. The sun accompanied me for the five-block walk required to reach the building where a stranger waited.*

> *Once upon a time, I entered a certain building and realized the world outside was grey when the sun accompanied me inside.*

> *Once upon a time,...I pushed open a door and walked into a hallway awash in light. I moved forward: I walked through light.*

Dear ancestors, you claimed me back. Suddenly I remember you so clearly.

Once upon a time, an emerald island laid upon a blue sapphire ocean and both glowed under the beam of a 24-carat sun. *Coral motus* ringed much of the island's circumference like a sandy fringed shawl; beneath its surface and before many hungry Pacificans were forced to forage offshore, a variety of sea creatures and fishes used to frolic in blue but also gin-clear waters. Under starlit skies, it was possible to spot bioluminescent plankton in the sea. Presiding over the island was the peak of Mount Itonguk from where, according to myths, the Itonguk people descended to become the island's first human inhabitants by walking down a rainbow. Atop Mount Itonguk, an incongruous winter-like beauty offered an icy climate. Somewhere, verdant jungles hosted other wildlife in a number so varied not all have been given names yet by humans. In the island's interior, awe-inspiring limestone formations rose starkly from rice fields. On one part of the island's western coast, rock arches and a hundred caves presented an eyelet pattern whitened by sea salt over the years.

Dear Itonguk...

Dear DoveLion, I remember you. I see you. I hear you. I taste you. I feel you: the warm sea holding up my floating body, the breeze under starlit skies, the earth and plants nuzzling my fingertips, the smoothness of limestone against my curious tongue—the body of a place embracing my body to welcome me home. I see you. I hear you. I taste you. *I feel you.*

6 JUNE

Once upon a time, I was a child who was insignificant to the machinations of the power-hungry. Thus, did it take over eight decades to learn Itonguk blood runs through my veins.

"How's the CIA doing, Grandma?"

"Never mind them. They are not the center of my story—our story," I snorted (as best as my feeble nose allowed) at the images of my beloved grandsons on my computer screen.

Because I knew my priorities, I added, "Now, let me see more of those great-grandchildren of mine."

Both Gonzalo and Enrique just had babies. Gonzalo and his wife Hope birthed a daughter, Grace. Enrique and his wife Rose birthed a son, Will. In Pacifica, the clan had gathered together at Elena's request. Cristy was part of the same long-distance conversation and added to the loving tumult as she greeted her sons and their wives and children.

After several heart-warming moments of cooing, waving and air-kissing the babies—Grace had pink rosebud lips! Will had a growing cowlick!—I got down to business.

"I read through Ludwig's files in the CIA Archives," I began. "I learned something new about our family—about us, all of us."

And I told them. After frowns of initial confusion and gasps of surprise, I'll always remember the dazzling smiles that erupted as my revelations impacted my beloved family:

First—

"We are not descended from that murdering bitch Patricia Santos." No need to mince my words; I was old and the babies were still too young to understand my vitriol.

Second—

"My real mother was an Itonguk tribeswoman, which means Itonguk blood runs through your veins. Our family is the continuation of the Itonguk bloodline."

It wasn't hard for me to be ignorant about our roots. Physically, the Itonguks looked similar to the rest of the island inhabitants. It was their lifestyle, attire, and cultural practices that differentiated them from Pacifica's other peoples.

We are Itonguk…! Several times, my descendants repeated the revelation in varying degrees of joy, pride and astonishment. Over what should be improbable, we were to remain astonished for a long time.

We are Itonguk…!

Our grins were so wide they hurt our faces. But we dazzled each other with our grins. As we had always done, we bore through the hurt of my mother—our ancestor—whose name we only knew as an initial. We bore through the hurt and dazzled.

    We are Itonguk…!

Nor did I need to know I was Itonguk for me to have set forth in motion my greatest achievement: the rise of a renewed Pacifica under the wise and kind guidance of my warrior Itonguk grandsons, Enrique and Gonzalo.

I did not need to know I was Itonguk to act to recover Paradise out of The Dictator's stranglehold. I behaved simply as what I am: Itonguk.

We are significant.

Chapter 23

1 JULY

Once upon a time, I was a child who was insignificant to the machinations of the power-hungry. But to become significant is to understand that significance is also a responsibility. Blood is not enough to claim Itonguk identity—to be significant for Itonguk culture and history requires teaching my descendants what it means to be Itonguk.

When I shared news of our true ancestors, I allowed my daughter and grandchildren to express and marvel, "We *are* Itonguk!"

But past the celebration of the news, it's time for me to teach them what Itonguk identity is—and that it is something to be earned instead of inherited. Rather, I won't teach them. I will learn with them.

"For the Itonguk, who we are—the languages we speak, the traditions we practice, our broader cultures—inform our identities far more than DNA," I explained to my family.

Fortunately, Ludwig's files include the document my mother gave my father about creating an Itonguk Heritage Center. Among its papers were the requirements for Itonguk citizenship whose concerns range over the environment, interpretations of as well as foretelling of weather conditions, engagements with animals, agriculture, interaction with others, and creation of communities. While its concerns are shared with other indigenous as well as non-indigenous peoples around the world, a specific and unique Itonguk element is the role of poetry.

Poetry?! Is that why I'm a poet?! Naturally, at first reading, the thought crossed my mind before I reminded myself that the matter at hand was not about me me me. I continued reading.

Written in five lines, the Itonguk poem, flooid, used to be inscribed on bamboo utilizing their precolonial script, the aknat. But Itonguk tradition does not preclude the flooid from being created through modern-day languages as well as written or typed on paper—my mother's report includes generous examples. There are many examples because the flooid is a key component of Itonguk culture—to be Itonguk is to create flooid. But to create the poems, one first must live out the events that would come to appear in the poems. The flooid is reportage-poetry, and what it reports must be an activist exercise of Itonguk values—a value system based on Kapwa, the interconnectedess of all beings across all of time.

Thus, the Itonguk poet who wrote about pollution first had to partake of activities alleviating such pollution before writing a poem like

The Great Grief

As plastic smothers
Oceans and forests miss trees
I grieve with you, Dear—
We drink polluted water—
"Ethics of entanglement"

Over time, the tribe's poems came to reflect the history of a people—specifically, what mattered to the people—or not mattered—at certain periods of time. While a review of its poetic records indicates what historically concerned the Itonguk, also telling are its poetry's silences on certain matters. During the 1900s, for example, when diamonds were discovered on its lands, not a single poem about diamonds exist from that period. The gems simply were of no concern or value to the Itonguk.

According to my mother's report, writing flooid encourages the Itonguk to participate in beneficial activities while also avoiding harmful occupations. For who would write poems about the damage one causes? Such was monitored by a non-negotiable requirement for retaining Itonguk citizenship: the Itonguk must write a minimum number of flooid poems per year, a number that begins with one for toddlers just learning language to 20 for adults. As a result, Itonguk festivals often featured good-natured competitions for most poems written per age category during the year—what a healthier occupation than the beauty contest when a flooid's existence relies on the condition precedent of a good deed!

Fortunately, I am optimistic about the continuation of the Itonguk people as I raised Cristy to include poetry as part of her life and my great-grandchildren were already being read poetry. However, I might have to threaten my grandsons.

"Whoah! Wasn't it enough that we led rebels to depose The Dictator's heirs? That we actually fought on the battlefield? Want to see my scars? Plus, I still limp today!" complained Gonzalo on my computer screen. Naturally, he spoke as well for Enrique who was frowning beside him. Nonetheless, I firmed my voice to set them to right.

"And, no! Don't order your staffers to write them for you!" I ordered the twins.

"We must carry the lessons we've been taught by our indigenous Kapwa—our interconnectedness with all that exists," I told my family. "Know how the shadows of History can be uncovered, acknowledged, and healed. With this new awareness, you will learn to dis-identify with the Story of empire, supremacy, and capitalism. You will write new stories. You will make different choices."

I added, "Yes, it is often heartbreaking to hold this awareness. It will be hard being mindful of Patricia Santos' attempts to decimate our tribe. It will be hard being mindful of how my parents and your ancestors were sacrificed for the political concerns of another country on the other side of the planet. But agony is the least of our concerns."

To be Itonguk is to earn it.

13 JANUARY

Once upon a time, I was a child who was insignificant to the machinations of the power-hungry. It required over eight decades to learn I was the only surviving member left of Pacifica's Itonguk tribe.

My ancestors never left me. They came through and revealed their faces just before I soon was to join them. They revealed it in time for me to share it with my—their—descendants.

Now I remember Ernst's last few words to me. Before they said, "Love transcends time," they had been uttering nonsense, calling me "baby..." I thought the disease was making them ramble. But that night after learning of my Itonguk blood, the incident returned to me in a dream. I heard them say more clearly:

"Oh, but you're a baby! A baby Baybay..."

The morning after waking from that dream, I called Cristy. I shared my latest dream involving Ernst's visitation.

"*Baybay*? I've never heard of it," she said.

"Can you research it in case it means something?"

"Through Wiki, I presume?" she said, jokingly referencing my persistent love for Wikipedia.

"I'm a diasporic and to be cloudygenous is to be yoked to Wikipedia!" I reminded her.

Thus, did we both learn that, once upon a time, when the Itonguks flourished in DoveLion, they were led by "Baybays." They were community leaders who guided socially and spiritually. Wikipedia really is marvelous. Because its elements can be entered by anybody, it's become the repository of some research conducted centuries earlier by Douglas Brown, an Australian seafarer. During his travels, Brown ended up in DoveLion where he met members of the Itonguk tribe. Brown's notes and diary entries later were inputted into Wikipedia by one of his descendants.

"Mom!" Cristy said. "Perhaps you're a Baybay!"

I would not ascribe the term to myself (honorifics should be left to others to make). But I am struck by learning how an indigenous person became a Baybay. Usually, that person had dreams and experienced life-altering events that led to a change of consciousness—beloved Wikipedia described it as "a spirit possessing the self." But it was not enough for the transformation to occur. The Baybay's education is lifelong and she, he, or they also had to engage in leadership acts on behalf of their communities—this explains why most are senior citizens by the time they don the mantle of Baybayism.

Sure, the Baybay's path seems natural and familiar when I consider the improbable ways my life developed as I felt the impact of my dreams—once, I even visited a stranger in a certain building. Still, I protested the term—and not from self-deprecation.

"Look here," I told Cristy, my finger pointing at a section of the Wikipedia entry on Baybay. "It says their indigeneity specifically means a linkage to land, to be part of a local space."

As Cristy leaned over the computer to read the reference, I continued. "I mean, I invented the word 'cloudygenous' for a reason. I'm in the cloud because I had to turn to the internet in the diaspora—that's been my 'place'."

Cristy looked at me. "Mom. We've taken back DoveLion from The Dictator. You're no longer in the diaspora!"

I looked at her. She looked at me. DoveLion. *Duh-vee-li-on.* Then we both laughed.

"All right. Fine," I said. "But there's no need to debate. I've never been interested in labels for myself.

"What I do know is how the world seems brighter after learning we have Itonguk ancestry. I feel lighter—I've even felt the slight hump of my back, just beneath my neck, straighten as if some heavy weight on my shoulders evaporated. For the first time in my long life, I believe I know who I am."

🐚

Discovering my ancestry also made me more grateful to Ernst for introducing Itonguk values like Kapwa-time. In Kapwa-time, all of time collapses. In that collapsed space, everyone and everything has always been, is, and will be connected to each other. There is no such thing as separation. There is no such thing as *Other*.

Ernst. *And Ernst is forever with me...*

Once upon a time, it was January 21 and we saw each other at a museum exhibition of an artist—her name, for names are important, is Gabby Slang—who privileged margins to centers. Gabby Slang painted small square paintings with pale centers but whose edges vibrated with vivid colors. She privileged margins because they border the unknown of unfettered possibilities: still unknown are what lies in the terrain outside of a painting's canvas. The poet Eileen R. Tabios understood this and so eliminated periods at the end of her poems to manifest how the poetry experience continues past the edge of the page. Ernst must have understood, too, by revealing the wide variety of colors on the thickened side edges of his monochrome paintings. And Gabby Slang understood this by making paintings that psychologically drew viewers' eyes towards what lives on the outside of the paintings' centered but meager territories.

When we discussed seeing each other at Gabby Slang's exhibition, you had observed, "It wouldn't be a good way to end—solitary, ever looking at the world, including looking at how others look at the world."

"You mean we'll end up alone, alone, alone?" I'd said.

You'd chided me for being histrionic—"the single word suffices."

But you'd also said, "Write your own reality!"

Ernst, I am writing this along the infinite cave wall of my mind, *There is no Other. There are no separations that create individuals. We are all One. Ernst—you are forever with me.*

Elena, they replied.

We looked at each other, then began to smile.

Elena, they said again.

Ernst, I said.

We kept saying each other's names as if we had not already memorized them, as if the shape of their sounds already had not entered our bodily memories.

Between saying each other's names, we behaved in unison: together we laughed, laughed, and laughed.

Elena, they said again.

Ernst, I said again.

We laughed hard. We laughed robustly. We laughed long into eternity.

Chapter 24

14 MAY

Once upon a time, I thought Poetry is a fairy tale. From that delusion, I came to stand in front of a building. Inside, a stranger waited for me in their Apartment 3J. That first time, what I mostly knew about them is that they were as curious as I am.

Once upon a time, I heard children laughing but turned my back. I was bored with innocence.

Once upon a time, I stood in front of a building dimmed by a sun in hiding. It would come to be a moment, it seemed to me years later, that froze in time. It came to be a mental object I would fetishize as I struggled to understand how I became a creature willing to meet a stranger for the first time in the privacy of their residence.

23 JULY

Once upon a time, I thought Poetry is a fairy tale. That is the last thing it is. Poetry is birthed and borne through the hardness of living. Only by becoming part of real lives can it then transform inherited realities into better alternatives. Poetry, as quietly observed by certain poets (the ones not obsessed with a careerism defined by publication credits), is not words but an alternative—and hopefully better—way of life.

I visited a stranger in a grey building because Poetry encouraged me not to shirk from possibilities. Nothing would have unfolded as it has in my life—including Pacifica's recent history of recovery and healing—if I had not, once upon a time, entered a stranger's embrace because it *felt* like the right thing to do. It felt logical. It felt right. It felt safe.

My ancestors had whispered, *They are safe...*

> *Once upon a time, ancestral spirits hovered (as they always did) over a woman gliding over one block after another towards her destination of a grey building. They never left her...*

To hear the whispers across generations, collapsing time—that is not an imagined fairy tale. *That* is Poetry.

16 AUGUST

Once upon a time, I thought Poetry is a fairy tale. How sad that I once thought this way—it reflects how far I'd come from my origins. From the poet's job of reading anything and everything, I stumbled across the writings of cultural anthropologists. One of these books, *The Light Sang*, was written by Dr. I.M. Lowe, an anthropologist who was once stationed in Pacifica. Dr. Lowe wrote about the Itonguk, and noted one of their many wise beliefs:

> *"We are all born poets. It's the living that can leach poetry out of our lives. Be vigilant."*

Long before I discovered I am Itonguk, this was the most common advice I shared with young poets. Coincidence? Not.

> *"We are all born poets. It's the living that can leach poetry out of our lives. Be vigilant."*

Be vigilant. The Dictator, Patricia Santos, Ludwig—they lost their poetry.
Be vigilant.
Until Ernst, I also had lost my poetry.
Be vigilant.

> *"We are all born poets. It's the living that can leach poetry out of our lives. Be vigilant."*

For Poetry is also devotion.

11 DECEMBER

Once upon a time, I thought Poetry is a fairy tale, only as real as in the moment of its telling and soon to evaporate after the oh-so-false if occasionally wistful "*... and they lived happily ever after.*" Like rain—its touch, then evaporation.

To live is to experience rain. I remember a particular rainstorm before I met Ernst. I was at a farmhouse in upstate New York where I used to house sit for an investment banker forced to travel frequently by his job. I remember listening to the rain all night. It was a soothing sound.

That morning, I walked out onto the porch to see the rain. It didn't stop for three more days. Yet, despite its consistent flow, it wasn't a harshly pounding rain. It was soothing. I wrote a poem about—maybe, *for*—it:

ALL NIGHT

the rain was soft

But morning reveals
the gravel washed out
the camouflaging mist
the empty flagpole

Morning reveals mourning—
the gentleness of cruelty

Why did I title the morning "night"? Why did I focus on bleakness? Or the deceptiveness of cruelty?

But of course I knew the answer: I was focused on darkness then. I was not yet attuned to light, and the lucidity that it brings.

When my poetry matured, it began to practice lucidity—the ability to see clearly. Poetry is not something one needs to make up (though some do). Poetry exists all around us, and often the poet's primary job is simply to see. *Lucidity.* Connect the dots from such connections to discern a formerly hidden narrative and way of life. Connect the dots to create a better way of life. *Lucidity.* Connect the dots to discern *Kapwa.*

It's also a good tool for battle. One does not become a dictator without allowing the darker facets of human nature to overcome more positive attributes. Contrast that with *Lucidity*—by understanding human nature's sources of (moral) corruption, lucidity strengthens those who battle such sources. It's why dictators don't mind diluting the quality of education given to those they rule; education facilitates lucidity. *Lucidity*—particularly helpful given the nature of assymetric warfare the rebel Pacificans had to utilize against the stronger forces of The Dictator's family and supporters. From the loveable Wikipedia:

> *Asymmetric warfare* can describe a conflict in which the resources of two belligerents differ in essence and in the struggle, interact and attempt to exploit each other's characteristic weaknesses. Such struggles often involve strategies and tactics of unconventional warfare, the weaker combatants attempting to use strategy to offset deficiencies in quantity or quality of their forces and equipment. Such strategies may not necessarily be militarized. This is in contrast to *symmetric warfare*, where two powers have comparable military power and resources and rely on tactics that are similar overall, differing only in details and execution.

Lucidity. For enacting effective strategy, Sun Tzu would have approved.

26 OCTOBER

Once upon a time, I thought Poetry is a fairy tale.

Obviously—so obviously—I was wrong. Whether with Ernst, with having a baby, with seeing grandsons take back Pacifica from The Dictator's grasp—all of these were possible by Poetry being embodied.

Poetry is not just atmosphere, or a feeling, or a sense...or a story. Poetry, too, is a body. As a young poet, I once "married" Poetry. In Pacifican culture, there is a practice during wedding ceremonies called the "Money Dance." Here, wedding attendees stand in two lines, one before the bride and the other before the groom. Attendees dance with the bridal couple for a few seconds before pinning money somewhere on their outfits—a symbol of the community helping to start out the newly-married couple's new household.

Some months after I ceased visiting Ernst in a grey building, I enacted a poetry performance in a pop-up gallery in New York's downtown Chelsea neighborhood. For my poetry performance, I wore a borrowed wedding gown. Audience members were given print-outs of my poems and they lined up to pin the poems on my voluminous skirt as bossa nova played. No human groom existed in my performance. I was setting up a household with Poetry and its human stand-in had yet to arrive from the future I would make with my new marriage.

When it comes to commitment, Poetry is everything and wants it all. Poetry would only give me a human stand-in—they who lived in a grey building—after I committed fully to it. Yes, Poetry proposed. Yes, I married Poetry.

30 JUNE

Once upon a time, I thought Poetry is a fairy tale.

But Poetry is not escapist, even when it can present a temporary space for reprieve. It's not entertainment (though it can entertain). Entertainment can be escapist, but when it ends one is returned to reality. Poetry never leaves reality—it takes everything on the chin, even darkness.

So many true stories could be judged improbable: Mick Myers, then a 67-year-old homeless man who ended up meeting his biological Mom for the first time because a police officer decided to help him create identification credentials in order to receive governmental health benefits; a church in Beatrice, Nebraska where all 15 members of its choir were late for different reasons, which allowed them all not to be in the area when the church exploded (several naturally mentioned "God's hand"); or James Bozeman, Jr. who won two multimillion-dollar prizes in the Florida state lottery from tickets he bought at the same 7-Eleven. Let's also not forget entertainer Rihanna's Twitter and Instagram accounts which left sufficient digital bread crumbs to lead to two separate arrests in Thailand, earning her the dubious honor of the "biggest accidental snitch since Fredo Corleone."

Or that, next door to Pacifica, the president of the Philippines would begin selling its territory to China, the children of the martial law dictator Ferdinand Marcos would remain viable politicians, and citizens would continue to self-crucify themselves for a god who betrays them with priests who refuse birth control to the poor whose children they rape.

How then is it a stretch that Poetry—with all of its flakiness, its weirdness, its surrealism, its (shall we just say it!) *magic*—is not different from reality? Reality is large enough to contain Poetry's possibilities, even what one may judge ahead of time to be extremely improbable.

25 DECEMBER

Once upon a time, I thought Poetry is a fairy tale. I held this thought for years. I held onto this thought because I was no different from any sad person on this planet—I wanted to feel what it would be like if "everyone lived happily ever after."

What might be considered Poetry's "fairy tale" aspect are its improbable-turned-real effects. But poetry, like all art, can embolden its recipient into something greater, even against the odds. The German filmmaker Florian Henckel von Donnersmarck clearly understood this as shown in his film *Das Leben der Anderen (The Lives of Others)*. Its plot, among other things, shows how Stasi Captain Gerd Wiesler decides not to betray writer Georg Dreyman after hearing Dreyman play "Sonate vom Guten Menschen (Sonata for a Good Man)" on the piano. Afterwards, Wiesler asks, "You know what Lenin said about Beethoven's "Appassionata": 'Can anyone who has heard this music, I mean truly heard it, really be a bad person?'" Prior to that incident, Wiesler had read Bertolt Brecht's poem "Memory of Marie A" from a book he'd lifted from Dreyman's apartment. Both experiences with art changed Wiesler, a member of East Germany's repressive intelligence and secret police agency, to become instead "a Good Man."

7 JUNE

Once upon a time, I thought poetry is a fairy tale.

> Because I found it easier to deal with fiction than reality.
> Because I confused imagination with fiction.
> Because I thought imagination and reality present a binary.
> Ultimately, because reality is hard.

2 OCTOBER

Once upon a time, I thought poetry is a fairy tale. Wrong. To be a decent poet entails no separation between life and poetry. Such a separation would put poetry simply into the fictional realm. Poetry is faith, yes, and Poetry is real.

This is how I initially came to visit Ernst: I saw their paintings and I thought they embodied what I wanted to do through words. From that recognition, I chose to have faith that meeting the artist was something I needed to do for my poetry, perhaps to improve my poetry. Art and poetry are different from their makers—Ted Berrigan once called the poem the poet's best self. Still, I chose faith, including faith in the poet—I sought a meeting with the maker of the paintings that I felt matched my poems. I sought to meet Ernst because, were I a painter instead of a poet, I thought I would be making paintings exactly like what emanated from their brushstrokes.

Among paintings, monochromes are paradoxical. They are exactly what you see—that single color—but interpretations vary because viewers are different from each other. The form speaks to me as the viewer is primary—whether or not the painter succeeded (as some monochrome painters wish to do) in erasing autobiography and/or personality by seemingly presenting nothing but a single color, the viewer's response is what uplifts the viewing experience. But by ostensibly painting nothing but one color, the painting actually pushes the receptive viewer to reach for significance, in turn enhancing imagination. During the first year of meeting Ernst, I wrote a 20-page poem based on one of their monochrome paintings. Its color is green and my poem skips merrily from the Irish shamrock to the heavens of the Ming Dynasty to bad news in Israel to racy jokes in Spain to how racecar drivers consider green cars bad luck. In the middle of our second year together, Ernst painted a red monochrome painting—they presented it with the question, "Is this a rose, Elena?"

In response, I wrote a poem "after" their red painting as I didn't want Ernst's painting to be a mere teaching tool—I wanted it, too, to fulfill one of art's potentials by being a source of inspiration. I wrote my hope into reality—

Firebird (after "Red" by Ernst Blazer)

Broadway clamored for her attention. A wet mist diffused the boulevard's lights. One road grappled north, the other south. In the darkness, hands appeared and disappeared, their movements lacking premonition. Some bore ragged paper cups for her favors; others bore folded currency for other types of favors. Once, a hand revealed elegant, red fingernails and she almost halted her firm stride through night.

A woman sang sadly into the earphones plugging both ears. Ecstasies, she once read, are too rare. But it was not happiness that lingered on the street she savored for its camouflage of crowds. There was no bitterness in her recognition. The destination, she recognized, would arrive at its own time, indifferent to organization. Life is generous with consistent surprises.

Before a red light, she chose to recall her memories of Rome. She had walked for hours searching for a restaurant hidden behind high stone walls. When she found it, she stepped onto a small area with censored lamps, light coming only from the glare of pristine white tablecloths reflecting a blood-red moon. When she was seated, she was the only woman there. The scent of cigars permeated the air. The Chianti was harsh on the palate. But she savored each bite of her bleeding steak, and the men left her alone. For these pleasures, she effortlessly held her spine straight.

Back in New York, she paused before a man's bowed back. Despite the dimness and the clinging mist, he kept painting the tango on a panel of the sidewalk. She could see the flare of the woman's skirt as the man shifted its direction. She could see the jealous faces of women seated among a watchful crowd—the resentment of the men attending them. The artist had not yet painted in the couple's faces, but she knew they would be stunning. She knew the woman's teeth would be white, the lips stained crimson. She felt the woman licking her lips, the thickened tongue sliding languorously

—all that from a single color. At the point of writing the poem, I also had not yet visited Rome. But because I desired the visit, I wrote of Rome—I was optimistic that one day I would be able to check the reality of my metaphor. One day, I did. All of my outfits during that vacation were belted by red leather. One wrist was encircled by radiant rubies. Another gleaming stone remained a secret from the world, hanging from a gold chain to nestle behind my clothing, bringing their red luster to nestle warmly between my breasts.

5 MARCH

Once upon a time, I thought poetry is a fairy tale.

It's not. But it also is. Poetry is so all-encompassing it contains contradictions. Because poetry is *also* a fairy tale, my life will end with me "living happily ever after"—

> *Elena lived happily ever after.*

Elena. Wikipedia says my name reveals a long, multi-layered history. It lives in many languages including Italian, Spanish, Romanian, Bulgarian, Macedonian, Slovak, Lithuanian, Russian, German and Medieval Slavic. It exists, too, in other scripts: Bulgarian, Macedonian, Russian and Church Slavic. It has at least six identified variants: Ileana (Italian), Ileana (Spanish), Ileana (Romanian), Yelena (Russian, Helena and Helene (German). It's spawned diminutives like Lenuta (Romanian), Lena (Russian) and Leni (German). It is popular in many countries including the United States, England and Wales, Bosnia and Herzegovina, Catalonia, Chile, France, Netherlands, Poland, Slovenoa, Switzerland, and so on.

I could go on and on about my name, Elena. Names related to mine include Elaine (Arthurian Romance), Jelena (Estonian), Eliina (Finnish), Elene (Georgian), Olena (Ukrainian), Elin (Welsh), Jelena (Serbian), and so on.

I could go on and on happily ever after about my name.

But how could I go on happily without knowing the name of the mother whose womb once cradled me lovingly and protected me from a less kindly world?

"B" is what I know. B can stand for many things including one thing I know I was not: Bastard.

How could I live happily ever after without having once shaped my lips to say my mother's name?

B.

No fairy tale ending exists for me, Mother, without knowing your name.

Chapter 25

21 APRIL

Once upon a time, I thought poetry is a fairy tale. Or not. (Why not, not? Life is contradictory.) Whatever. It is a tale, and a good tale requires names.

Sure, there are stories out there whose characters are unnamed and identified as what they do ("tinker, tailor, spy"), their physicality ("blonde" or "small hands"), their idiosyncratic tics ("fish eye eater"), even their hygiene ("Pig Pen" in Charles M. Schulz's *Peanuts* comic strip). These characters are often at a distance from the reader or recipient of their story—they are *at a remove* because they lack the personal connection enabled by a name. I wanted a closer relationship with my mother—I desired to know my mother's name.

9 SEPTEMBER

Once upon a time, I thought poetry is a fairy tale.

Why not?

If so, why couldn't I then imagine my mother's name? If I couldn't know it, why couldn't I create it?

Didn't I imagine expansively as a result of engaging with Ernst? Didn't what I imagine then end up being real?

Did I not imagine, birth, then mother, a child?

Is not Pacifica now safe and ruled by kind and responsible leaders, my grandsons? Is not Pacifica back to being a paradise?

Is not Pacifica reclaiming its indigenous name, DoveLion? *Duh-vee-li-on...*

24 JULY

Once upon a time, I thought poetry is a fairy tale.

It is, because poetry is supple.

Within its fairy tale, my mother would come to have a name. Her name would have diminutives like "Bell." It would have relations like "Bliss" and "Bless." It would be popular worldwide. It would exist in at least as many scripts as my name—Bulgarian, Macedonian, Russian and Church Slavic. As a word, it would be—*is*—prized.

What a horrible world I inherited. Nobel Prize-winning Czeslaw Milosz, who grew up in postwar Warsaw, thought of naming as a means of appropriating reality—"an act of salvaging reality from oblivion and nonexistence by placing it outside time in an ideal place—a poem," according to his editors Bogdana Carpenter and Madeline G. Levine. Indeed: I named my mother to salvage her reality out of oblivion.

I named her. A daughter named her mother because poetry can be, thus, *is* a fairy tale.

Because poetry is a fairy tale, I found my mother. Because I found my mother, I could name her. Because I named her, I could address her.

Because poetry is a fairy tale, I could tell my mother, "I love you..."

Later, I introduced my mother to Ernst, and Ernst to my mother. Kapwa-time: there is no past, present, or future; it simply is. I was am able to introduce Ernst and my mother to each other because my mother has a name.

31 DECEMBER

Once upon a time, I thought poetry is a fairy tale.

That is how my mother came to be named—this is our Happy Ending.

When I addressed her for the first time, I said, "You held me so briefly. But the memory of your nurturing womb was enough for me to feel you ever with me for the rest of life. I feel you in that space where there's no past, present or future—there's only a single all-encompassing moment where you and I are not separated."

I will not, as I long have feared, end up alone—this is our Happy Ending.

Then I called my mother by her name, again and again. And as I felt her name shape my lips, I began to smile. As I felt her name continue to shape my lips, I began to laugh. As the life we'd never shared collapsed into the life where we, holding hands, look at each other's immense love for each other, I laughed and she, too, laughed. Together, we ~~were~~ are joy—*this is our Happy*

Ending. We all—all of us—lived happily ever after.

I continued to call my mother by her name. With each sounding of her name, I heard a distant echo in the form of *Innocence*: the laughter of happy children. Again, and again, and—unashamedly histrionic—*again,* I called my mother by her name—*this is our Happy Ending.* With laughter blossoming my heart into an immensity exactly the size of the total universe, I called my mother:

Beloved

The End

APPENDIX 1

The Return of DoveLion
By Elena Theeland

7: I forgot there is a country somewhere on the opposite of where I stand on this earth, a country whose scents stubbornly perfume my dreams.

46: I forgot ancestral houses standing solidly despite their grounds ever shifting, bereft of gutters, dams and other structures to mitigate nature's tantrums or tears from a gentle rain.

47: I forgot the mud in monsoon season always sucked at the ankles, non-discriminating, a placid surface but camouflaging sharply-edged stones, gooooey, gooooey, gooooey and brown as the hide on rotten bananas.

93: I forgot appreciating a *delicadeza* moonlight as much as any long-haired maiden.

50: I forgot farmers who never lost their smiles as their skins grew permanently stained from water buffalo excrement spread over surrounding fields during days of absent storms.

65: I forgot elders who always grinned at me, unashamed their gums held no teeth.

3: I forgot the light burned and we never shaded our eyes.

46: I forgot discovering the limited utility of calm seas.

78: I forgot children learning to trick hunger with cups of weak tea.

80: I forgot fevers refusing to abate even when drenched with seawater.

82: I forgot narrowing the focus always reveals something else.

51: I forgot lowering the flag of a country I despised. I forgot lowering the flag of a country I loved.

12: I forgot the stance of cliffs meeting water.

97: I forgot I began drowning in air.

101: I forgot you were the altar that made me stay.

99: I forgot the spine bent willingly for a stranger's whip.

100: I forgot clutching the wet mane of a panicked horse.

101: I forgot night is unanimous.

102: I forgot how an erasure captures the threshold of consciousness.

103: I forgot how one begins marking time from a lover's utterance of *Farewell*.

110: I forgot learning to appreciate rust, and how it taught me bats operate through radar.

113: I forgot admiring women who refuse to paint their lips.

114: I forgot dust motes trapped in a tango after the sun lashed out a ray.

120: I forgot the colors of a scream: the regret of crimson, the futility of pink, the astonishment of brown.

122: I forgot your favorite color was water.

123: I forgot admiring Picasso's *Sleeping Nude, 1907*, for its lack of sentimentality.

124: I forgot aching for fiction that would not chasten my days.

128: I forgot becoming my own sculpture when I crawled on a floor to see color from different angles.

129: I forgot astonishment over a block of grey metal swallowing light.

72: I forgot feeling you in the air against my cheek.

138: I forgot your body against mine introduced the limits of sunlight's expanse.

139: I forgot longing for a sky without horizon, but acceding instead to the eye's clamor against the opposite of claustrophobia.

141: I forgot addiction to *Duende* for its intimacy with savagery.

142: I forgot greeting mornings as an exposed nerve.

147: I forgot the capacity to feel you in the breeze lifting my hair from their shyness.

148: *I forgot you wanted to see her seeing herself...*

149: I forgot you thought of me as you paced the streets of a city whose sidewalks memorized the music of my footsteps dancing away from youth into courage.

156: I forgot you also loved New York City for hosting those whose hair whitened prematurely in order to write books with titles encompassing *Purity, Smoke, Thrall, Shield, Brush, Mote, Sheen*—which is to say, *The Encyclopedia of the Om.*

157: I forgot you saw each virgin moon as a ruby you wanted for adorning my body.

158: I forgot the empty chair that awaited us, its expanse the totality of an alien world still unexplored.

159: I forgot how pronouns confused me. I forgot the "She" evolving into an "I" then back again, flustered before your gaze.

163: I forgot you startled the girl whose poetry elicits dragon scales from empathetic muscles.

164: I forgot a fabric named *Solace* and its availability in celery, parchment, black pearl, crème brulee, persimmon and sage.

168: I forgot linens called *Lamorna* or *Serge Antique* that offered themselves not as black or white but as toast and oyster.

171: I forgot the definition of optimism: "when sky turns blue, it becomes as physical as an organ."

172: I forgot waking from a dream of white heat to see sun-washed walls forming a room where silk and lace sculpted a milk puddle on terra cotta floors.

173: I forgot the rest of Greece, its national heat *waiting...*

174: I forgot suckling wine from your lips, then biting, then swallowing *earth, leather, currants, gravel, tobacco, oak and plums* to release the same voluptuous tears familiar to Elizabeth Barrett and Robert Browning who loved through 573 letters before bearing a son they nicknamed with much affection, "Pen."

160: I forgot how Beauty dislocates.

177: I forgot tea with a sculptor absentmindedly rearranging objects on a table to alter their relationships in and with space.

179: I forgot you falling asleep in my skin to dream.

180: I forgot you dreaming I saw myself seeing myself. Objectively, I saw the flowers of my forgotten birthland: *damas de noche*, named after a long-haired woman afflicted into paleness by the verb of *feel*-ing.

184: I forgot memory contains an underbrush.

185: I forgot the inevitability of ashes.

186: I forgot a water lily forms instantaneously.

171: I forgot laughter is not comprised of stars.

194: I forgot sentences like veins.

195: I forgot the Introduction as a permanent state.

212: I forgot the green stalks holding up *ylang-ylang* orchids—how their thin limbs refused to break from the weight of lush petals and overly-fertile stamen.

213: I forgot how the mountains of bones shared the pallor of thick, white candles burning in helplessly tin candelabras.

214: I forgot no metaphors exist for genocide.

222: I forgot my heartbeats succumbing to radiance after curiosity taught me to bait handcuffs and whips.

223: I forgot radiance must penetrate if it is to caress, and its price can never reach blasphemy.

225: I forgot the sun hid from what I willingly bartered for *Lucidity.*

235: I forgot you holding me up against a steel door, radiated by a generous halogen.

239: I forgot how one can sag into night as if night was a lover.

224: I forgot the rice fields, sometimes melancholy at dusk, sometimes a rippling mirror of a sunset's maidenly blush.

248: I forgot never craving kindness.

249: I forgot photographs overcome by sepia and certainty demolished by screams.

260: I forgot seashells sleeping on windowsills.

286: I forgot that, sometimes, the world should be veiled.

295: I forgot part of mortality's significance is that wars end.

298: I forgot the taste of your mouth was song of licorice.

289: I forgot releasing breath to describe milk transformed by your scent.

319: I forgot the salt of expired matchsticks.

320: I forgot unfamiliarity with the edges of my body.

323: I forgot place became person.

349: I forgot your hands paused before my black brassiere.

350: I forgot you reminding, "Honey, angels may fall but they never die."

351: I forgot to be an angel is to be alone in a smudged gown, fingers poking through holes burnt by epistemology.

352: I forgot drinking from wafer-thin crystal whose cracked rims snagged lips into a bleeding burning. I forgot my skin was ruin.

420: I forgot the pleasurable tension of avidity.

446: I forgot reading lips through a mirror.

447: I forgot the seams caused by bindings.

452: I forgot capturing light through algebra.

466: I forgot moonlight revealing itself as broken.

467: I forgot the noiseless convulsion.

478: I forgot regret is a Kingdom with unknown borders.

495: I forgot a breakfast of rain.

524: I forgot rain arriving aslant like premature memory.

498: I forgot you losing all Alleluias.

526: I forgot freezing light into words by spreading lavender ink across thick cream paper.

529: I forgot the stench of spilled wine.

583: I forgot eyes widening to pull in more of the world.

344: I forgot how exile can sa[l]vage.

658: I forgot the logic of amnesia.

659: I forgot what was never called by a name.

664: I forgot the jagged edges of music still searching for archetype.

728: I forgot the ziggurat tattooed on an inner thigh, an area where inscription must have surfaced with anguish, then desperation, then a hymn long-forgotten as I'd forgotten how to attend anyone's church.

729: I forgot a body drowning in light as a hand wrote. I forgot eyes leaking flames.

820: I forgot a yellowed photograph slipping from brittle pages.

64: I forgot artists rise (or fall into) desecrated battlegrounds.

868: I forgot looking at glass and not seeing its transparency.

961: I forgot anthologies of glass.

933: I forgot the color of your eyes which is grey.

969: I forgot the texture of your cheeks which is stubble-rough, the secret of your cheeks which are dimples, the seduction of your cheeks which are slanted cheekbones, and the scent of your cheeks whenever it became me.

979: I forgot yet another cliché—how I came to consider anew the significance of a scarf

as it tears

as it ties

as it muffles

as it falls

as it knots

as it hides

as it binds

as its colors fade despite the absence of light deep within a locked closet.

983: I forgot that even the most unbearable parting never made me doubt that I was

285

happier because of our history. I never questioned my joy at the candle-lit room we created from a single chair. *The door always opened to the scent of magnolias crushed to release perfume.*

987: I forgot the Sphinx's unasked riddle:"Which is more powerful?A moon so bright it erases nightorA sun so bright it darkens vision?"

1,000: I forgot clarity. I forgot you became angry when I insisted on seeing as if I still wore a blindfold. I forgot I saw blue velvet fall and its flowing aftermath softened the concrete.

990: I forgot how you mastered by discerning unawakened longings. You saw Me. Including that I would control the *Aftermath*...

1,016: I forgot because I thought it best to forget everything rather than remember schemes informed by my desire rather than what actually transpired.

1,017: But I will never forget we walk on the same planet and breathe from the same atmosphere. I will never forget the same sun shines on us both. I created my own legacy: *No one is a stranger to me.*

1,034: I forgot the anguish of knowledge.

68: I forgot love stutters over a lifetime.

1,106: I forgot I admired encaustic for protecting forever the fragility of paper.

901: I forgot the poem whose page was a glass pane etched with words—that paper would be too soft a field for your hand leaving my waist.

1,167: I forgot my poetry is going to change the world. I forgot my words are healing. I forgot my words are holy. I forgot my words are going to lift you—all of you! —towards *Joy.*

Selected Notes, Sources,
&
Acknowledgements

Deep gratitude to those who've helped me create DoveLion: *Thomas Pollock; Leny Mendoza Strobel and the Center for Babaylan Studies community; reader-editors Reine Arcache Melvin, Addie Tsai, Nick Carbo, Brian Marley and Ken Edwards for their treasured input; Holly Crawford, R. Hazell and AC Books for asking, supporting, and publishing; Dr. Jeannie Celestial for a discussion on mother-child bonding; Lizae Reyes, Mila Anguluan, Matt Manalo, and The Society for Indigenous Wisdom and Ancestral Healing / Circle for Original Thinking for helping manifest* DoveLion *in the 2020 "Dancing With Uncertainty" conference; Campania Flemenca Alhama's "Viva Sevilla" for duende as editing music; and, always, the poets. This novel also stems from my love for the Philippines—my birth country that I refuse to define as Loss.*

TITLE

"DoveLion" refers to the fictional country in this novel and its name was inspired by José Garcia Villa's coining of "Doveglion", an abbreviated reference to Dove, Eagle, and Lion. Other than honoring the Philippines' most important 20th century English-language poet with this reference, the novel "DoveLion" has no relationship to José Garcia Villa.

4 AUGUST

Tasaday tribe in Wikipedia: https://en.wikipedia.org/wiki/Tasaday

The line "Love is always haggled" is from Eileen R. Tabios' poem "Corolla" in *Reproductions of the Empty Flagpole* by Eileen R. Tabios (Marsh Hawk Press, 2002).

16 MARCH

"Average age of cataract surgery is dropping," YourSightMatters.com: https://yoursightmatters.com/average-age-for-cataract-surgery-is-dropping/

29 NOVEMBER
"Boredom-Boredom" was quoted from Caterina Fake in a post at her blog Caterina.net

24 JANUARY
The statements regarding photoshop were informed by *Old in Art School* by Nell Painter (Counterpoint, Berkeley, 2018).

The paragraph on David Bowie was first published as a prose poem in *The Stars Look Very Different Today: a David Bowie Tribute,* Editor Richard Robert Hansen (Poems-for-all, San Diego, 2016).

9 APRIL
Information on "pepper torture" from "Worse than death: torture methods during martial law" by Don Kevin Hapal, *Rappler,* Feb. 23, 2016.

27 FEBRUARY
"Poetry must burn!" is a quote from poet Jean Vengua

3 OCTOBER
The description of "limestone hotel" was inspired by Chateaux Galatea, Saint Helena, CA.

1 DECEMBER
The author named the referenced German Shepherds after her real-life furry babies Achilles, Athena, Ajax, Neoptolemus, and Nova—*not vice versa.*

12 FEBRUARY
The referenced high heels were inspired by Christian Loboutin's iconic red-soled shoes.

7 NOVEMBER
Kazemir Malevich on Wikipedia: https://en.wikipedia.org/wiki/Kazimir_Malevich
"Five Ways to Look at Malevich's Black Square", *TATE*: https://www.are.na/block/3936316

21 DECEMBER
"Cloudygenous" and "E-magination" are terms invented by the author for *CounterDesecration: A Glossary for Writing Within the Anthropocene* (Wesleyan University Press, 2018), Linda Russo and Marthe Reed's project on working on "the collective glossary of place/ecopoetic terms, interested in particular in the intersections of place/landscape/ecosystem and the human/social/political, all the complex permutations of human history and human/other-than-human that suggests": http://jacket2.org/commentary/place-relation-ecopoetics-collective-glossary

28 AUGUST
The poem "Poetics (#1)" was first published in *The In(ter)vention of the Hay(na)ku: Selected Tercets* by Eileen R. Tabios (Marsh Hawk Press, 2019).

19 JUNE
A "bailaora" is a female flamenco dancer.

15 MARCH
According to "Roots of Filipino Humanism (1) 'Kapwa'" by Karina Lagdameo-Santillan, *pressenza*, 24 July 2018, the word "kapwa" seems to have originated from two words: *Ka*– a union that refers to any kind of relationship, a union, with everyone and everything; and *Puwang*– space.

Professor Virgilio Enriquez, founder of Sikolohiyang Pilipino, says, "Kapwa is a recognition of a shared identity, an inner self, shared with others. This Filipino linguistic unity of the self and the other is unique and unlike in most modern languages. Why? Because implied in such inclusiveness is the moral obligation to treat one another as equal fellow human beings."

3 MAY
Information on Phobos is from Space Facts: http://space-facts.com/mars/

18 MARCH
The quoted poet is Eileen R. Tabios who can't recall in which poem she'd written the referenced tercet.

Information on the Asian ostrich from Wikipedia: https://en.wikipedia.org/wiki/Asian_ostrich (In *DoveLion* the ostrich becomes transformed to a peacock because "color is a narrative.")

22 SEPTEMBER
Information on peacock eyes from "Mystery Solved: Why Peacocks Got Their Eyespots" by Carrie Arnold in *National Geographic* online, July 15, 2014: https://news.nationalgeographic.com/news/2014/07/peacocks-tails-eyespots-feathers/

13 JULY
The Montana Ray reference comes from Footnote 6 to *MIRRORING* by Montana Ray (Belladonna Chaplet #238, Brooklyn, 2018).

19 MARCH AND 10 NOVEMBER
INSURRECTO by Gina Apostol (SoHo Press, 2018).

4 FEBRUARY
The author long attributed the phrase "What fresh hell is this?" to William Shakespeare. But it's by Dorothy Parker.

18 SEPTEMBER
Madeleine Knobloch in Wikipedia: https://en.wikipedia.org/wiki/Young_Woman_Powdering_Herself_(Seurat)

4 NOVEMBER
Sampaguita is the Philippines' national flower.

30 APRIL

As regards flamenco dance, credit is given for lessons learned from "The A to Z's of Flamenco Dance" by Linda Machado for DANCEUS.org: https://www.danceus.org/flamenco/the-a-to-z-s-of-flamenco-dance-b-is-for-braceo/

14 JULY

The Franz Kline reference is after "Franz Kline Discussing Black and White (1960)" by the ASX Team, Dec. 8, 2015 excerpting an interview conducted by David Sylvester in 1960: https://americansuburbx.com/2015/12/franz-kline-discussing-black-and-white-1960.html

28 FEBRUARY

The poem "And what is seeing?" is crafted from the third paragraph of the author's prose poem "THE COLOR OF A SCRATCH IN METAL" from *Reproductions of the Empty Flagpole* by Eileen R. Tabios (Marsh Hawk Press, New York, 2002). The blurb by Alfred Yuson is one of the blurbs of the same book.

26 JANUARY

"Pagpag" is a Filipino word with several definitions; one definition is associated with food scavenged from garbage dumps in the Philippines.

"[T]he sweetness of damp cheeks" is from the poem "The Singer and Others: Flamenco Hay(na)ku" by Eileen R. Tabios

"HUNTER ORDERED" is a detail inspired by "AN ARROGANT WAY OF KILLING" by Evan Ratcliff, *The Mastermind*: https://magazine.atavist.com/an-arrogant-way-of-killing

17 OCTOBER

Information on Lakapati from "Lakapati, Transgender Tagalog Goddess of Fertility & Agriculture" by Stephanie Gancayco, '*hella pinay*, Nov. 20, 2016: https://www.hellapinay.com/blog/2016/11/20/lakanpati-tagalog-transgender-goddess-of-fertility-agriculture

14 FEBRUARY

While proofing the novel's manuscript, the first paragraph blossomed forth this chained, reverse hay(na)ku poem that would appear in the *Scents Anthology*, Editor Ayo Gutierrez (GMGA Publishing, 2020):

The Significance of Perfume

Jasmine
means you—
garden beyond window

Tobacco
means you—
cigar, brandy, library

Vinegar
means you—
a sweat-drenched run

As oenophiles attest
"scents become
Eternal

through the sharing
of powerful
memories"

Musk
means you—
entwined with me

12 APRIL
Quote by Eileen R. Tabios is from an essay in *THE AWAKENING* by Eileen R. Tabios (theenk books, New York, 2013).

5 FEBRUARY
A hay(na)ku is a 21st century poetic form invented by Eileen R. Tabios. It is a six-word tercet with the first line being one word, the second line being two words, and the third line being three words. For more information: **https://eileenrtabios.com/haynaku/**

17 SEPTEMBER
Lucas "Lucifer" Straight's described paintings are inspired by Randy Dudley's paintings of the polluted Gowanus canal.

3 NOVEMBER
Image refers to a photograph of the Ferdinand Marcos family on a balcony in Malacanang Palace during the Philippines' "People's Revolution" that overthrew the martial law dictator.

18 OCTOBER
Both Rapunzel poems are excerpted from poems in *Reproductions of the Empty Flagpole* by Eileen R. Tabios (Marsh Hawk Press, New York, 2002):

Rapunzel, Enrapt

She locks the entrance to the turret containing a thousand diaries whose papers are yellowed and leather covers cracked. Then she feeds the key to an alligator. She is outside where ants clamber up the velvet folds masking her thighs (she actually scents grass!). She understands gloves are old-fashioned but has resigned herself to certain constraints:

it takes time for the ink stains on her hands to fade. But she has crossed the moat. As she peers at the stolid, grey tower that she once draped with her hair, that a man once climbed, she shivers but smiles.

First, she must eliminate her guides. Her godfather—an emperor of two continents and the eagles overhead—has sent a troop of retired generals. She can feel their white beards swaying as they urge black stallions toward her. She can hear the horses gasp as effort glazes a wet sheen over their hides. Though the shimmer of air in the distance simply may be the temper of a summer day, she lifts her skirts and breaks forth into a run.

Once, a man buried his face into her shaking hands. She treasured the alien rush of warmth against her fingers as he spoke of sand, gritty but fine; of waves, liquid yet hard; of ships, finite spaces but treasured for what they may explore; of ocean breezes, invisible but salty on the tongue. "Like the potential for grief?" she asked. He raised his eyes in surprise and she captured his gaze. She pressed on, "I have read that grief is inevitable with joy." Still, she woke one day to a harsh rope dangling from an opened window, and emptiness was infinite by her side.

Now, she is taking the path opposite from the direction she saw the man choose when he departed. As his hands left the rope, he looked up and saw her lack of bitterness framed in the window. The forest respected her grief with a matching silence. But she had learned from the Egyptians how to measure intangible light, a lesson that revealed the earth to curve. Now, she runs and as she begins to gasp, she can feel the sand between her toes, the breezes tangle the long strands of her hair and the waves weight her skirts. And as she begins to feel his ship disrupting the horizon, a sheen breaks across her brow and she feels her lips part. Enrapt, she knows she soon will take off her gloves. Enrapt, she feels she is getting there

Against Disappearance

After she climbed down the tower, Rapunzel looked at the welts rising on her palms. She had not expected the burn inflicted by the braided rope. Still, she allowed her tears to water the red tracks that began her new journey. For she had learned that bliss is possible only to those who first experience pain. As the salt of her tears stoked the fire in her grasp, she pronounced to the doves she felt lurking among the high branches of surrounding trees: One must fly toward the space where the distance towards the horizon can never be measured.

Once, a man dodged the floating spotlights of her guards to climb towards the window of the turret where she spent her days in velvet gowns, living through words she read behind covers of cracked leather. She was surprised as she had not thrown down her hair which remained pinned under her inheritance of gold combs festooned with diamonds, rubies, emeralds and pearls. "Don't move," he ordered as he walked towards her. "I want to memorize the way you look, before your hair will fall from the pleasure I will teach you." And as the sun's departure stained the sky beyond her window, her hair fell. And her lips parted. And her gown slipped down her shoulders to reveal the silk and lace woven by those who once served her ancestors whose portraits adorned her walls. She looked at her father and nodded slightly to acknowledge the foretelling of a frown the artist had painted on his brow. But her hands rose to grasp the man tighter against her breasts as she whispered: Before the first one, how does one know sin?

The shadow of a dove in flight interrupted her reverie. Her tears ceased and she wiped her palms against the velvet covering her thighs. Then she lifted her skirts and danced down a gravel path whose unknown destiny she did not mind. She danced with a swath of silver butterflies who appeared from nowhere and lingered over her smile. Until an old male dwarf from another fairy tale popped his head from behind a boulder by the bend of the path and asked, "Who are you?" She proclaimed with glee and pride, "I am Rapunzel." To which the dwarf replied, "Nonsense: Rapunzel has long hair!" And she laughed and announced as she twirled in a circle so that her skirts flared high to reveal her bare legs, "I cut my hair, braided it into a rope, and used it to escape my turret!" Amazed, the dwarf said, "How did you think of that unusual idea?" Rapunzel stopped her dance, fixed a cold stare at the dwarf and hissed like Clytemnestra: When women control their destinies, they are only exercising a law of nature. How dare you be surprised!

23 JUNE
The poem "That Sudden Affinity" was first published under the title "Achilles" in *HIRAETH: Tercets From The Last Archipelago* by Eileen R. Tabios (The Knives Forks Spoons Press, U.K., 2018).

13 APRIL
All of the names were suggested in a Facebook posting by several of the author's friends who suggested names for the character. The choice of "Cristy Maruja" stemmed from the suggestion of "Maruja" by Reme Grefalda. Other suggestions were made by Ivy Alvarez, Leny Strobel, Jean Vengua, Amy Pabalan, Ryan Kitchell, Catherine Daly, and Meryl Messineo.

1 SEPTEMBER

Kali is Filipino martial art. The author briefly studied kali under Gura Michelle Bautista.

16 JULY

The June12.com rebel organization was inspired by The Philippine Revolution against colonizers: https://en.wikipedia.org/wiki/Philippine_Revolution. It is further informed by Philippine President Rodrigo Duterte's use of a netizen army to spread propaganda and disinformation, as well as the author's political science thesis written as a student at Barnard College.

9 AUGUST

"Damul" is the inverted reference to the "Lumad": https://en.wikipedia.org/wiki/Lumad

The name *Lumad* grew out of the political awakening among indigenous tribes during Ferdinand Marcos' regime.

The referenced poor grades was inspired by Imee Marcos' poor grades at Princeton University and University of the Philippines Law School, two schools on her resume but from where she failed to graduate.

The reference to Panamanian accounts is informed by offshore accounts held by Ferdinand Marcos' family members: https://newsinfo.inquirer.net/777754/imee-3-sons-on-panama-papers-list-jv-ejercito-too

The Disneyland reference is informed by Calauit Island, a game reserve featuring African mammals translocated there under the orders of Ferdinand Marcos: https://en.wikipedia.org/wiki/Calauit_Safari_Park

The poetry book title *HIRAETH: Future Lost Tercets* is informed by the title of *HIRAETH: Tercets From the Last Archipelago* by Eileen R. Tabios (The Knives, Forks and Spoons Press, 2018).

11 NOVEMBER

The reference to the David and Louise Turpin family is based on a true story as described by *HuffPost*: https://www.huffpost.com/entry/house-of-horrors-turpin-children-speak_n_5cba0bc8e4b032e7ceb808a8

25 SEPTEMBER

The adobo recipe is by Matt Manalo.

10 OCTOBER

The incident with Goya's "The Marquesa" is inspired by "The $10bn Question: What Happened to the Marcos Millions" by Nick Davies, *The Guardian*, May 7, 2016:

http://www.theguardian.com/world/2016/may/07/10bn-dollar-question-marcos-millions-nick-davies?CMP=share_btn_fb

The reference to the Panama Papers is after "Panama Papers Source Breaks Silence and Offers To Aid Authorities for Immunity" by Caroline Coopley; Editing by Louise Ireland, *The Huffington Post*, May 6, 2016: http://www.

huffingtonpost.com/entry/panama-papers-immunity_us_572d5d04e4b0bc
9cb0470457?ir=WorldPost&section=us_world

6 JANUARY

The "Yellow Revolution" is inspired by the Philippine People Power Revolution about which Wikipedia notes: "The People Power Revolution has inspired a call for a change of government through peaceful protests rather than bloodshed. Many similar revolutions have followed since then, taking the Philippine example of nonviolent regime change, such as that in East Germany and many other former Soviet Bloc countries. It also helped inspire the Arab Spring in 2011." —https://en.wikipedia.org/wiki/People_Power_Revolution

"Maharlika Palace" is informed by the Philippines' Malacanang Palace where the President and their family can reside.

30 MAY

Wikipedia on benign dictatorships: https://en.wikipedia.org/wiki/Benevolent_dictatorship

The reference to "University of San Toma" is informed by the history of the Philippines' University of Santo Tomas which was used as a World War II internment camp by the Japanese.

7 MAY

Adurag is the reverse spelling of, from Philippine myths, Garuda, a large birdlike creature, or humanoid bird with the muscular upper body of a man but the face and large wings of the great eagle who is believed to eat men: https://en.wikipedia.org/wiki/Philippine_mythical_creatures

Scholar Nerissa Balce's notes on "Race and Humor" was part of her presentation about the author's short story collection, *PAGPAG: The Dictator's Aftermath in the Diaspora* by Eileen R. Tabios (Paloma Press, 2020) during its July 2020 Book Launch; in gratitude, the author collaged Nerissa Balce's notes into this novel.

3 JUNE, 19 JANUARY, AND 28 MARCH

Pacifica's description as a paradise is partly inspired by the results of a Google search for "beautiful islands" that presented 2 links: https://www.islands.com/most-beautiful-islands-in-world#page-6
and https://theculturetrip.com/asia/articles/asia-s-15-most-beautiful-paradise-islands-to-visit-in-2015/

3 APRIL

"Creeley's Disease" is a term inspired by the author's read of—and aggravation over—the first sentence to Robert Creeley's *AUTOBIOGRAPHY* (Hanuman, Madras & New York, 1990): "I've spent all my life with a nagging sense I had somehow the responsibility of that curious fact, that is a substantial *life*, like a dog, but hardly as pleasant, to be dealt with no matter one could or couldn't, wanted to or not." This sentence so aggravated the author that she decided to create "Creeley's Disease" for the purpose of the novel—a neurogenerative illness that manifests itself in memory "scrunches" (vs memory "lapses") whereby those afflicted do not so much forget events but "scrunch" them together as if they all occurred simultaneously.

3 APRIL AND 13 JANUARY

The novel's "Baybay" is inspired by the Philippine "Babaylan," an indigenous spiritual/community leader. For education about the Babaylan, the author is grateful to Leny M. Strobel and the Center for Babaylan Studies.

26 SEPTEMBER

The character Peony is inspired by Imee Marcos, and the reference to England and Oxford is inspired by Ferdinand "Bong Bong" Marcos, Jr.'s experience of (attempted) studying in England.

1 NOVEMBER

"Lt. Expendable" is derived from what "Star Trek" fans call minor characters who usually get killed off.

12 NOVEMBER

Wikipedia on the Talosians of "Star Trek": https://en.wikipedia.org/wiki/The_Menagerie_(Star_Trek:_The_Original_Series)

1 JUNE

The paraphrased poem that ends the chapter is "Harlem" by Langston Hughes.

7 JULY

Remedios "Remy" Con's name was taken from one of Imelda Marcos' middle names: Imelda Remedios Visitacion Romualdez Marcos.

29 JULY

Wikipedia's list of revolutions and rebellions at https://en.wikipedia.org/wiki/List_of_revolutions_and_rebellions

"Top Ten Shortest Wars" by Jamie Frater, *Listverse*, Sept. 30, 2007 at http://listverse.com/2007/09/28/top-10-shortest-wars/

"A New Theory on Time Indicates Present and Future Exist Simultaneously", Physics- Astronomy2 Blog, Jan. 8, 2019, referencing *Objective Beginning* by Dr. Bradford Skow: https://physics-astronomyblog.blogspot.com/2019/01/a-new-theory-on-time-indicates-present.html

13 NOVEMBER AND APPENDIX I

The poem "The Return of DoveLion" was created through Eileen R. Tabios' MDR Poetry Generator (https://eileenrtabios.com/poetry/murder-death-resurrection/).

31 OCTOBER

The referenced "DoveLion human" is inspired by Filipino novelist N.V.M. Gonzalez's views of the "mythic man."

15 DECEMBER
Romanian orphanage information from http://www.worldaffairsjournal.org/article/orphaned-history-child-welfare-crisis-romania

2 APRIL
"The Wire Sculpture" is an edited version of the poem from *THE THORN ROSARY: Selected Prose Poems & New (1998-2010)* (Marsh Hawk Press, New York, 2010).

18 FEBRUARY
Beyond Life Sentences (Anvil, Philippines, 1998) is the author's first book.

2 JUNE
The line "see the thing as what it is" is from Eileen R. Tabios' poem "Faith in the Time of the Coronavirus." The poem and related discussion on (the untranslatability) of the concept are in *INCULPATORY EVIDENCE: The Covid-19 Poems* by Eileen R. Tabios (Laughing / Ouch / Cube Productions and i.e. press, 2020).

9 JANUARY
The line "Steel bends to form a heart" is the last line in the poem "I Forgot the Logic of Amnesia" in the author's *AMNESIA: Somebody's Memoir* (Black Radish Books, 2016).

8 FEBRUARY
The Lily Montvale necklace-related incident reflects a memory of a real-life incident from when the author was about 12 years old.

17 JUNE
The incident in Tokyo was inspired by a *NYTimes* article on private clubs (date forgotten but it was during the 1990s). The shibari research is from Wikipedia on "Bondage positions and methods" as well as the article "Intimate Knots: Exploring the art of shibari" by Daniel Crump for http://uniter.ca/view/intimate-knots, March 23, 2017.

7 OCTOBER
Depending on the source, estimates for the number of orphans worldwide range from 147 million to over 200 million.

7 DECEMBER
Information sourced from the "TOP 10 MOST BRUTAL WAYS TO DIE" site at https://listogre.com/2014/01/15/top-10-brutal-ways-die/

Information on the "Brazen Bull" is from Wikipedia: https://en.wikipedia.org/wiki/Brazen_bull#CITEREFDiehlDonnelly2008

Information on the Chinese bamboo torture from Wikipedia: https://en.wikipedia.org/wiki/Bamboo_torture

13 AUGUST

Information on crying is from http://psychcentral.com/blog/archives/2009/06/06/7-good-reasons-to-cry-your-eyes-out/

17 MAY

Information on various ways to describe a person without a country is from http://www.wordhippo.com/what-is/another-word-for/man_without_a_country.html

5 SEPTEMBER

Information on diamonds from http://www.lumeradiamonds.com/diamond-education/diamond-clarity

29 SEPTEMBER

The line "It need not take more than one person to bring the world to ruin" is from the author's poem "Mustering," which was written in response to—and inspired by—Eric Gamalinda's poem "Factory of Souls" which contains the line "It takes just two people to bring the world to ruin." The author's poem is published in *Reproductions of the Empty Flagpole* (Marsh Hawk Press, 2002) and Eric Gamalinda's poem in his book, *Zero Gravity* (Alice James Books 1999).

The bedtime parable is a childhood tale heard by the author from her Apong or grandmother.

8 DECEMBER

The rippled mirror hay(na)ku poem was published under the title "Ferdinand Edralin Marcos" in *The In(ter)vention of the Hay(na)ku: Selected Tercets* by Eileen R. Tabios (Marsh Hawk Press, New York, 2019). More information on the hay(na)ku is at https://eileenrtabios.com/haynaku/haynaku-variations/

29 OCTOBER

Wikipedia on memory: https://en.wikipedia.org/wiki/Long-term_memory

16 MAY

The beauty pageant reference is inspired by the real-life error made during the 2015 Miss Universe Pageant. Host Steve Harvey mistakenly announced the winner was Miss Colombia instead of Miss Philippines. The description that Miss Colombia agreed she should not have won is pure fiction.

The list of beauties comes partly from "The Most Beautiful Women of the Ancient World": https://www.thoughtco.com/most-beautiful-women-116952

21 FEBRUARY

"Gago is Filipino slang for "asshole."

26 JULY

"Biko" is a Filipino rice cake desert.

2 FEBRUARY

"Gago is Filipino slang for "asshole."

"Pulutan" is a Filipino snack.

The raped girl incident is informed by the article "Girl, 9, gangraped" which describes a girl raped by her uncle who then passed her to 5 other construction workers for more raping. The incident occurred in Barangay Talaga, Argao town in Philippines. The girl's parents did not plan to file charges but the police are allowed to file complaints and they did so. *Sunstar/Yahoo Philippines*, March 27, 2019: https://ph.news.yahoo.com/girl-9-gang-raped-143000125.html

About one in 10 children will be sexually abused before their 18th birthday, according to Darkness to Light: https://www.d2l.org/wp-content/uploads/2017/01/all_statistics_20150619.pdf

30 MARCH

The "apis" is "sipa" reversed. Sipa is a game played in the Philippines.

23 APRIL

"Ag mano po" is a reference to Filipino culture's blessings: http://www.becoming filipino.com/four-filipino-cultural-traits-that-inspire-my-life

28 OCTOBER

The incidents relating to Ludwig and "Little Brown Brother" are informed by the history of the Philippine American War.

7 SEPTEMBER

Information on the bombardier beetle fire is at https://www.thoughtco.com/the-science-behind-flying-and-fire-breathing-dragons-4163130

1 JULY

The poem "The Great Grief" was first published in *Unlikely Stories Mark V 20th Anniversary Edition*, July 2018, Editor Jonathan Penton.

The poetry form "flooid" is informed by the ambahan, the indigenous poetry of the Hanunuo Mangyans of the Philippines' Oriental Mindoro. The ambahan was written on bamboo in the Surat Mangyan, a centuries-old pre-Spanish script. Source: Mangyan Heritage Center: http://www.mangyan.org/content/ambahan

The referenced "aknat" is the word "tanka" in reverse as the sample poem is written as tanka.

"Gabby Slang," the artist's name is inspired by "Gabriela Silang," the first Filipino woman general who had fought against Spanish colonizers.

Selected Bibliography:

The quote "Who we are—the languages we speak, the traditions we practice, our broader cultures—inform our identities far more than DNA" is quoted from Krystal Tsosie, geneticist and member of the Navajo nation, for her article "Elizabeth Warren's DNA Is Not Her Identity" in *The Atlantic*, October 17, 2018.

"DAWAC/Action—A Babaylan Poetics" by Eileen Tabios in *BABAYLAN: Filipinos and The Call of The Indigenous*, edited by Leny Mendoza Strobel (Ateneo de Davao, 2010)

Native American identity is about belonging to a community. It is a specific political, legal and social formation akin to a form of citizenship that is particular to each tribe, nation, confederacy or otherwise sovereign and self-determining Indigenous government
https://www.huffingtonpost.com/entry/opinion-elizabeth-warren-native-ancestry_us_5bc5f8d9e4b055bc947a6e13

Syllabus: Elizabeth Warren, Cherokee Citizenship, and DNA Testing: http://www.criticalethnicstudiesjournal.org/blog/2018/12/19/syllabus-elizabeth-warren-cherokee-citizenship-and-dna-testing

The quotes "How do you carry the lessons you've been taught by our indigenous Kapwa? Know how the shadows of History can be uncovered, acknowledged, and healed. With this new awareness, you will learn to dis-identify with the Story of patriarchy, supremacy, and capitalism. You will write new stories. You will make different choices." And "Yes, it is heartbreaking to hold this awareness. But agony is the least of our concerns." are from https://www.lenystrobel.com/single-post/2018/12/31/Dear-Motherland

Research from Center for Babaylan Studies and "Babaylan Women as Guide to a Life of Justice and Peace" by Marianita Girlie C. Villariba http://www.isiswomen.org/downloads/wia/wia-2006-2/02wia06_06GirlieA.pdf

23 JULY
When the author first re-became a poet in her mid-thirties, she stumbled across a quote by Danish poet Paul Lafleur which she's since held close to her heart: "To be a poet is not to write poems but to find a different [better] way of life."

11 DECEMBER
Wikipedia on assymetric warfare: https://en.wikipedia.org/wiki/Asymmetric_warfare

26 OCTOBER
The referenced poetry dance performance is based on "Poems Form/From The Six Directions," a poetry performance project by Eileen R. Tabios covered in her book *I Take Thee, English, For My Beloved* (Marsh Hawk Press, New York, 2005). Critical reception to the project includes

"In POEMS FORM/FROM THE SIX DIRECTIONS, Eileen Tabios introduces her 'Marriage to "Mr/s Poetry' with the description of her performance/exhibition of 'Poem Tree' held in March, August and September 2002 at Sonoma State University; Berkeley; and San Francisco. Photos of Eileen Tabios' original marriage are mixed with the ones of the happenings. We see the poet and students, or friends, wearing Eileen's bridal dress. The supporting notion of the various actions, as Tabios states, is modeled after a rite in Filipino and Latino weddings wherein guests pin money on the bride's and groom's outfits. The ritual symbolizes how guests offer financial aid to the couple beginning a new life together. For 'Poem Tree,' poems are pinned onto the dress to symbolize how poetry, too, feeds the world."

—"Eileen Tabios and the upturning of codified needs" by Anny Ballardini, *Jacket 35*, 2008: http://jacket1.writing.upenn.edu/35/r-tabios-rb-ballardini.shtml

30 JUNE
Information on improbable events came from:

> —story of homeless man being reunited with mother after 65 years: https://sanfrancisco.cbslocal.com/2018/03/15/kindness-reunites-67-year-old-homeless-man-with-birth-mother/

> —Quora: 4 improbable events that keep happening: https://www.quora.com/What-are-examples-of-highly-improbable-events

> —the miraculous place: Beatrice, Nebraska: https://rationalwiki.org/wiki/Improbable_things_happen

25 DECEMBER
Wikipedia on *Das Leben der Anderen (The Lives of Others)* which is written and directed by Florian Henckel von Donnersmarck, produced by Max Wiedemann Quirin Berg, and starring Ulrich Mühe, Martina Gedeck, Sebastian Koch, and Ulrich Tukur, with music by Gabriel Yared and Stéphane Moucha. While the character Georg Dreyman is shown in the film to quote Lenin about Beethoven's Appasionata, the featured music was actually created for the movie by Gabriel Yared. Information at https://en.wikipedia.org/wiki/The_Lives_of_Others

Also referenced was Bertolt Brecht's "Memory of Marie A. (1920)" at https://cindydyer.wordpress.com/2012/11/26/memory-of-marie-a-by-bertolt-brecht/

2 OCTOBER
"Firebird" appeared in an earlier form in the author's *Reproductions of the Empty Flagpole* by Eileen R. Tabios (Marsh Hawk Press, 2002).

Information on the color green was aided by "The Meanings of Green": https://www.colormatters.com/the-meanings-of-colors/green

5 MARCH
Information about the name "Elena" is from http://www.behindthename.com/name/elena

24 JULY
Information about Czeslaw Milosz is from Introduction by Bogdana Carpenter and Madeline G. Levine in *To Begin Where I Am: Selected Essays by Czeslaw Milosz* (FSG, New York 2001).

APPENDIX I
"The Return of DoveLion" previously appeared in *Erotoplasty 7*, Editor Colin Lee Marshall.

Eileen R. Tabios has released over 60 collections of poetry, fiction, essays, and experimental biographies from publishers in 11 countries and cyberspace. *DoveLion: A Fairy Tale for Our Times* is her first long-form novel. Her 2020 books include a short story collection, *PAGPAG: The Dictator's Aftermath in the Diaspora*; a poetry collection, *The In(ter)vention of the Hay(na)ku: Selected Tercets 1996-2019*; and her third bilingual edition (English/Thai), *INCULPATORY EVIDENCE: Covid-19 Poems*. Her award-winning body of work includes invention of the hay(na)ku, a 21st century diasporic poetic form, and the MDR Poetry Generator that can create poems totaling theoretical infinity, as well as a first poetry book, *Beyond Life Sentences*, which received the Philippines' National Book Award for Poetry. Translated into 11 languages, she also has edited, co-edited or conceptualized 15 anthologies of poetry, fiction and essays. Her writing and editing works have received recognition through awards, grants and residencies.

More information is at http://eileenrtabios.com

Other Titles by Author

FICTION

Behind The Blue Canvas, 2004

SILK EGG: Collected Novels 2009-2009, 2011

PAGPAG: The Dictator's Aftermath in the Diaspora, 2020

DOVELION: A Fairy Tale For Our Times, 2021

Poetry

After The Egyptians Determined The Shape of the World Is A Circle, 1996

Beyond Life Sentences, 1998

The Empty Flagpole (CD with guest artist Mei-mei Berssenbrugge), 2000

Ecstatic Mutations (with short stories and essays), 2001

Reproductions of The Empty Flagpole, 2002

Enheduanna in the 21st Century, 2002

There, Where the Pages Would End, 2003

Menage a Trois With the 21st Century, 2004

Crucial Bliss Epilogues, 2004

The Estrus Gaze(s), 2005

Songs of the Colon, 2005

Post Bling Bling, 2005

I Take Thee, English, For My Beloved, 2005

The Secret Lives of Punctuations, Vol. I, 2006

Dredging for Atlantis, 2006

It's Curtains, 2006

SILENCES: The Autobiography of Loss, 2007

The Singer and Others: Flamenco Hay(na)ku, 2007

The Light Sang As It Left Your Eyes: Our Autobiography, 2007

Nota Bene Eiswein, 2009

Footnotes to Algebra: Uncollected Poems 1995-2009, 2009

On A Pyre: An Ars Poetica, 2010

Roman Holiday, 2010

Hay(na)ku for Haiti, 2010

THE THORN ROSARY: Selected Prose Poems and New 1998-2010, 2010

the relational elations   of ORPHANED ALGEBRA (with j/j hastain), 2012

5 Shades of Gray, 2012

THE AWAKENING: A Long Poem Triptych & A Poetics Fragment, 2013

147 Million Orphans (MMXI-MML), 2014

44 RESURRECTIONS, 2014

SUN STIGMATA (Sculpture Poems), 2014

I Forgot Light Burns, 2015

Duende in the Alleys, 2015

INVENT(ST)ORY: Selected Catalog Poems & New (1996-2015), 2015

The Connoisseur of Alleys, 2016

The Gilded Age of Kickstarters, 2016

Excavating the Filipino in Me, 2016

I Forgot Ars Poetica, 2016

AMNESIA: Somebody's Memoir, 2016

THE OPPOSITE OF CLAUSTROPHOBIA: Prime's Anti-Autobiography, 2017

Post-Ecstasy Mutations, 2017

On Green Lawn, The Scent of White, 2017

To Be An Empire Is To Burn, 2017

If They Hadn't Worn White Hoods... (with John Bloomberg-Rissman), 2017

What Shivering Monks Comprehend, 2017

YOUR FATHER IS BALD: Selected Hay(na)ku Poems, 2017
IMMIGRANT: Hay(na)ku & Other Poems In A New Land, 2017
Comprehending Mortality (with John Bloomberg-Rissman), 2017
Big City Cante Intermedio, 2017
WINTER ON WALL STREET: A Novella-in-Verse, 2017
Making National Poetry Month Great Again, 2017
MANHATTAN: An Archaeology, 2017
Love In A Time of Belligerence, 2017
MURDER DEATH RESURRECTION: A Poetry Generator, 2018
TANKA, Vol. I, 2018
HIRAETH: Tercets From The Last Archipelago, 2018
One, Two, Three: Selected Hay(na)ku Poems (Trans. Rebeka Lembo), 2018
THE GREAT AMERICAN NOVEL: Selected Visual Poetry 2001-2019, 2019
The In(ter)vention of the Hay(na)ku: Selected Tercets 1996-2019, 2019
Witness in the Convex Mirror, 2019
Evocare: Selected Tankas (with Ayo Gutierrez and Bianca Nagac), 2019
WE ARE IT, 2019
Inculpatory Evidence: The Covid-19 Poems, 2020
Double-Take (French translation by Fanny Garin), 2021
The Erotic Life of Art: a séance with William Carlos Williams (French translation by Samuel Rochery), 2021

PROSE COLLECTIONS
Black Lightning: Poetry-In-Progress (poetry essays/interviews), 1998
My Romance (art essays with poems), 2002
The Blind Chatelaine's Keys (biography with haybun), 2008
AGAINST MISANTHROPY: A Life in Poetry (2015-1995), 2015
#EileenWritesNovel, 2017